EllRay Jakes
the Recess King!

OTHER BOOKS ABOUT ELLRAY JAKES

* * *

EllRay Jakes Is Not a Chicken!

EllRay Jakes Is a Rock Star!

EllRay Jakes Walks the Plank!

EllRay Jakes the Dragon Slayer!

EllRay Jakes and the Beanstalk

EllRay Jakes Is Magic!

EllRay Jakes Rocks the Holidays!

EllRay Jakes the Recess King!

BY **Sally Warner**

ILLUSTRATED BY

Brian Biggs

VIKING

An Imprint of Penguin Group (USA)

VIKING

Published by the Penguin Group

Penguin Group (USA) LLC

375 Hudson Street

New York, New York 10014

USA ✱ Canada ✱ UK ✱ Ireland ✱ Australia ✱ New Zealand ✱ India ✱ South Africa ✱ China

penguin.com

A Penguin Random House Company

First published in the United States of America simultaneously by Viking and Puffin, imprints of Penguin Young Readers Group, 2015

LIBRARY OF CONGRESS CATALOGING-IN-PUBLICATION DATA

Warner, Sally, date– author.

EllRay Jakes the recess king! / by Sally Warner ; illustrated by Brian Biggs.

pages cm.—(EllRay Jakes)

Summary: Eight-year-old EllRay Jakes of Oak Glen Primary School is looking for a new best friend, and he decides that the best way to find one is to come up with a bunch of amazing things to do at recess—and see who shares in the fun.

ISBN 978-0-451-46911-3 (hardcover)

1. African American boys—Juvenile fiction. 2. Best friends—Juvenile fiction. 3. Friendship—Juvenile fiction. 4. African American families—Juvenile fiction. 5. Elementary schools—Juvenile fiction. 6. Oak Glen (Calif.)—Juvenile fiction. [1. African Americans—Fiction. 2. Best friends—Fiction. 3. Friendship—Fiction. 4. Family life—Fiction. 5. Schools—Fiction.] I. Biggs, Brian, illustrator. II. Title. III. Series: Warner, Sally, date– EllRay Jakes.

PZ7.W24644Eo 2015 813.54—dc23 [Fic] 2014043907

Manufactured in China

3 5 7 9 10 8 6 4

Designed by Nancy Brennan Set in ITC Century

To Todd Warner, best brother ever! —S.W.

•••

For Liam, Recess King of Penn Wynne —B.B.

CONTENTS

★ ★ ★

EllRay Jakes

the Recess King!

1

THE TERRIBLE TRUTH

"What's so great about going to the grand opening of the park tomorrow?" I ask my sister Alfie, as I make a snow angel on her fluffy bedroom rug. "So they fixed it up a little. It will still be the same old boring place."

My name is EllRay Jakes, and I am eight years old. I know this kind of stuff.

"Nuh-uh," four-year-old Alfie argues, scowling. "It said 'new' on the sign in the post office, didn't it? And signs don't lie. It's against the law. There's gonna be fwee hot dogs, Mom said, so we each get to ask a fwend."

"*Fwee*" means "free" in Alfie-speak. And "*fwend*" means "friend." Alfie's *r*'s sort of come and go.

I sigh. "A park's not new just because they plant better grass, and change the benches so people can't sleep on them, and paint over the graffiti. Dad said that's all they were going to do. And it's January, Alfie. It might be raining."

"But there's probably a better play area now," Alfie says, ignoring my weather forecast.

The old play area at Eustace B. Pennypacker Memorial Park only had one swing set, and one tetherball pole that has been missing its actual ball for almost a year, I remind myself. So it would be hard to make the play area any *worse.*

"Listen, Alfie," I say. "We already saw the so-called new park the other day, didn't we? When Mom got lost on the way to Trader Joe's? We drove right by it."

Our mom sometimes goes a different way to the store when traffic gets too crowded. She also likes to park our Toyota with plenty of space on each side, even though the car is older than I am.

Mom is a very careful driver.

I am going to have the coolest car *ever,* when I grow up! It will always be new, and it will have flames painted on the sides. Or at least skinny stripes.

"But when we saw the park, it didn't have a wibbon in fwont of it for our queen to cut with giant scissors, *EllWay*," Alfie says, as if I have just missed the most obvious point about Oak Glen's newest old park, which is opening tomorrow morning, like I said. Saturday.

"EllWay" is Alfie's version of "EllRay," which is a shorter—and less awful—version of "Lancelot Raymond," my full, official name.

My mom writes love stories for ladies, see, about dead or imaginary kings and queens. I guess she got a little carried away naming me when I was born. Moms sometimes do that, in my opinion. And my college professor dad was probably too busy studying weird rocks to put up an argument.

Later, as time went by, my too-fancy name was shortened first to L. Raymond, and then to L. Ray.

But now, everyone just calls me EllRay.

And I won't do much more translating for Alfie, I promise.

"This is California, Alfie," I remind her. "Oak Glen doesn't *have* a queen. That lady you're talking about is our new mayor. She just *acts* like a queen."

The new mayor shows up everywhere, wearing a fancy hat. It is the only ladies' hat in Oak Glen, I think. She also waves a lot.

I try not to sigh again as I click my robotic insect action figure—already cool enough!—into a deadly-looking tank. I start rolling it toward the lavender pony whose long blond tail Alfie is combing. I imagine destroying its golden corral.

C-R-R-R-U-N-C-H!

Nothing personal, lavender pony.

"That lady *is too* the queen," Alfie informs me. "Just because she doesn't wear her queen-hat all the time," she adds, shaking her own head so hard that her three soft, puffy braids swing back and forth. "You probably think she should wear it to bed, don't you?" she continues. "Or when she goes swimming? But real queens don't do that. I asked Mom once, and she said no. So, *hah*."

Alfie has recently discovered sarcasm, I am sorry to say.

"You're mixing stuff up," I tell her. "First, it's called a crown, not a 'queen-hat,'" I begin. "And second—"

But Alfie has moved on. "You don't *have* anyone to invite to the park," she interrupts. "Because you're running out of fwends."

I feel my cheeks get hot, because what Alfie just

said is basically the terrible truth. And I'm her big brother, and she needs to look up to me! "What? I am not running out of friends," I argue, but I don't sound very convincing.

"Well, I have Suzette, Arletty, and Mona to choose from," Alfie says, setting aside her star-spangled horse to argue with me. "And you just have Corey, only he's always busy swimming."

My best friend, Corey Robinson, is an eight-year-old swimming champion. He will probably be in the Olympics some day, everyone says.

I don't know what his plans are after that. Neither does he. His parents haven't told him yet.

"I have other friends, too," I tell Alfie. "What about Kevin?"

Kevin McKinley is the only other boy with brown skin in Ms. Sanchez's third grade class at Oak Glen Primary School, in Oak Glen, California. He has been one of my two best friends for a couple of years. But lately, he's been hanging out a lot with a couple of kids who live on his street, but who go to private school. I don't even know their names.

It's too risky for me to ask Kevin to come to the park tomorrow, even though he really, really likes hot dogs. He might say no! Or he could tell the other guys in our class that it's babyish for an eight-year-old to care about a new play area in some lame new-old park.

And then our friendship would really be over.

"I thought you said Kevin was sometimes *Jared's* fwend now," Alfie says.

Jared Matthews, my part-time enemy.

"I never told you that," I object. "Anyway, it changes around. And since when do you keep track of my life? Mind your own business, Alfie. You've got enough problems."

"You need a spare fwend," Alfie tells me, ignoring what I just said about problems. "You know," she says, grabbing another horse to brush. "The way Mom's car has a spare tire."

Both of us were in my mom's car last week when it got a flat tire on San Vicente Street, which is always super busy. Mom steered our wobbling car over to the side of the road. She told us to stay put while she called for help. But it was scary, waiting in the backseat as all that traffic whizzed by. I pretended it wasn't scary, though, because of Alfie.

I look out for her—in secret.

The spare tire that the auto club guy put on our car looked like it belonged to a clown car, it was so little. I was embarrassed for our poor Toyota.

I don't want a spare *friend* like that!

I'm already the smallest kid in my class, aren't I? I could use someone big.

"*You* know," Alfie continues. "A spare. For emergencies, like this one."

"For your information, *Alfie,* going to Pennypacker Park for a free hot dog isn't an emergency," I tell her, getting to my feet.

Alfie and her goofy opinions can just stay here playing with sparkly fake horses, I tell myself. I am trying to ignore the voice in my head that is saying she's a little bit right.

"You should hold an audition," Alfie announces before I can escape. "That's what we're doing at *my* school. It was all Miss Nancy's idea."

Alfie goes to Kreative Learning and Daycare, even though they spell "creative" wrong, which drives my dad bonkers. "You're auditioning friends at daycare?" I ask, tossing in a little sarcasm of my own.

"No," Alfie says, calm as anything. "We auditioned for our spring show last week. The best part of the show is called *Brown Bear, Brown Bear*. And I'm gonna be the *star*. Mom already started making my costume."

"You're the bear?" I ask, my forehead wrinkling. Because usually, Alfie is more of a kitty or a bunny or a sparkling pony kind of girl.

She might make an exception if she could be a panda, but Ms. Sanchez says pandas aren't really bears. Anyway, they're black and white, not brown.

“I’m the *goldfish*,” she says, sighing at having to explain something so simple. “I want to be the last animal everybody sees, so I’ll get all the clapping. I figured it out.”

“Good luck with that,” I call over my shoulder as I leave Alfie’s pink and purple palace. I mean room.

“At least I have *fwends*!” Alfie yells after me.

2

MY POSSIBILITIES

Okay, so I went to the grand re-opening of Eustace B. Pennypacker Memorial Park yesterday without bringing anyone with me. So what?

But it made me think about what Alfie said.

Maybe I *am* running out of fwends. I mean *friends*.

Everyone in my class seems to like me just fine, except for Jared Matthews, sometimes. But he takes turns being grouchy with everyone. And Stanley Washington is kind of like Jared's personal assistant, the way Fiona McNulty is Cynthia Harbison's personal assistant, so sometimes he stays away from me, too.

Cynthia says that movie stars have personal assistants, so why not her?

It's her latest thing.

Cynthia is basically the girl version of Jared in our class, only worse. She thinks faster than Jared, and she speaks up quicker.

I will take a new look at all the guys in my class before school starts tomorrow morning. It would be great to make at least one spare friend by this Friday, because that's when Alfie's show is going to be. My new friend and I can sit through that, then we will all go out for pizza or ice cream, so that will be fun. And then we can have a sleepover, which will be the most fun of all.

I already know Corey can't do it, because he has swim practice every Saturday morning. Early, like at six-thirty.

There are only ten boys in Ms. Sanchez's third grade class, and there are fifteen girls That means the girls are winning—in population, anyway. But it also means there are five other guys in my class—besides Corey, Kevin, Stanley, and Jared—for me to be friends with. Maybe.

The five extra boys are: Major Donaldson, Marco Adair, Nate Marshall, Jason Leffer, and Diego Romero.

Those are my possibilities.

Major mostly hangs out with Marco. In fact, Ms. Sanchez sometimes calls them "M and M" for short. When she calls on Marco in class, though, she usually calls him Mr. Adair, because when she accidentally calls out, "Marco," someone always says, "*Polo!*"

And everybody laughs.

Third-graders need easy stuff like that to laugh about, in my opinion. Our school days are long, and we get desperate for entertainment.

There are lots of reasons to like Marco Adair. He's always fair with the kickballs, and with choosing sides when we play games at recess. Also, he can make funny armpit noises better than any other boy in our class. Only on the playground, of course. Ms. Sanchez is not the type of lady who would think it's funny when you make your armpit go **FLIRRRRPPT.**

Major Donaldson is cool, too. In fact, my dad claims that Major has the best name in the world, because the word "major" means so many different things.

1. Major can mean *important*, like when someone says, "This is really major."
2. It also has something to do with music. I forget what.

3. And in college, Dad says that your major is the main thing you study. For example, my dad's major was geology. My mom's major was comparative literature, whatever that means. I don't know yet what my major in college will be. Maybe the History of Video Games?
4. But best of all, a major is a very important officer in the armed services, like the army or the marines.

My dad teases, threatening to salute whenever he sees Major Donaldson. That's the kind of sense of humor he has.

The only problem is, Marco and Major are so tight that it might be hard to squeeze my way into being their friend. There might not be enough room. They've known each other since kindergarten, and they're not sick of each other yet.

Nate Marshall is another friend possibility, though. He doesn't hang with anyone special. His red hair sticks up in front, like he's got a little rooster crest there. But on him it looks good—like an exclamation point.

The most unusual thing about Nate—that I

know of, anyway—is how much he knows about cars. Well, about vehicles in general. They are his obsession. What he *really* loves is to explain something like spark plugs, for example. He goes on and on until you can either prove you understand what he's saying, which I hate, or until the school buzzer sounds. Whatever comes first.

I'll keep Nate in reserve. He's not perfect, but I could probably fix that.

Jason Leffer might be a better friend possibility. His name should be Jason *Laugh-er,* because he turned into the class funny guy last fall. And he's not just funny with words, even though he does tell a pretty good knock-knock joke. But he also owns fake dog-doo and rubber barf, useful prank stuff like that. And he sneaked a whoopee cushion into school one day a couple of weeks ago.

In case you didn't know, a whoopee cushion is sort of a balloon pancake that you blow air into, and then it makes a really gross noise when your joke victim sits on it. Marco Adair the armpit noise king thinks it's hysterical, of course.

But even Jason doesn't dare try out the whoopee cushion on beautiful Ms. Sanchez.

Ms. Sanchez and whoopee cushions do not go together. Also, our class would never forgive Jason if she sat down at her desk one day in a pretty dress and made that noise.

Nobody wants her to get embarrassed so close to her getting married. The girls all say that her head is filled with wedding stuff—not to mention what the man who is going to be Ms. Sanchez's husband would say or do if someone insulted her.

His name is Mr. Timberlake, but he's not the *famous* Mr. Timberlake. Ms. Sanchez's Mr. Timberlake runs a sporting goods store full of bats, nets, balls, surfboards, and climbing gear. And he looks like he knows how to play every single sport, surf each giant wave, and climb every mountain or climbing wall better than anyone. So none of us guys wants to make him anything even *close* to mad.

The truth is, lots of kids—like me, for instance—secretly wish Ms. Sanchez would just stay the same as always, *forever*, without having a new husband hanging around at open houses and assemblies. She acts different when he's here.

And she's got enough to think about with us kids, hasn't she?

Jason is kind of a chunky guy, but it's mostly muscle, he says. And I believe him. He has buzz-cut hair, like the fur of this hedgehog I saw once in a nature book. And his ears stick out a little, but in a good way. You definitely know they're there.

I think I could turn Jason into a pretty cool friend, especially if I can get him to stop making jokes and pulling pranks all the time. Stuff like that is funny, and I love funny. But it can wear a person out after a while.

Also, I like the chance to be funny, too.

My last friend possibility is Diego Romero. My mom says that *his* name sounds like it belongs to a movie star. And I can tell that a couple of girls in our class kind of like him, even though Diego is a quiet guy. He likes to read. He even reads instructions! And sometimes he brings these really thick books to school to share with Ms. Sanchez.

But he's not a kiss-up, he's cool. And I think I could loosen him up.

Okay. Now that I think about it, maybe none of

these five guys is *perfect*, but like I said about Nate, I can fix that. All I have to do is to hang out with them more, get to know them better. Starting tomorrow morning.

And then I can choose which kid I want to be my spare friend.

Who will it be? Major, Marco, Nate, Jason, or Diego?

Maybe the winner can even become *my* personal assistant some day! I know Corey's way too busy winning swim meets and polishing his medals to take on that role, even if he would. But having a personal assistant does sound pretty cool.

Now, all I need is to figure out who the lucky kid will be.

It would be great to have a new friend by Friday, the day of Alfie's show. But my long-term goal is to have one by the end of this month.

January.

Then I'll have a happy new year for sure!

3

SECRET PLAN

"Hurry up, EllRay," Mom says as I shovel a last spoonful of cereal into my mouth. The spoon is heaped so high that the milk in it trickles down my wrist. It makes my sleeve feel wet and sticky.

What's the big deal about making me take a shower and then put on clean clothes every morning, when messy stuff like trickling cereal milk happens before I'm even out the door?

Give it up, Mom! It's hopeless.

"Don't forget your lunch," my mother reminds me.

Like I *would*. Food is just about my favorite thing. Also playing, and TV. "Where's Alfie?" I ask, trying to turn the mom-spotlight away from me for a second.

"She's upstairs, changing her barrettes," Mom says, shaking her head. My mom is tall, thin, and pretty, and her skin is the color of the best caramel you ever saw. She likes to wear headbands, but not the scary plastic kind with teeth that Cynthia Harbison wears to school. Cynthia's headbands look like they're mad at her head. "Alfie forgot that she already wore the barrettes she put on this morning," Mom tries to explain. "Just last Thursday. It was a narrow escape," she adds, laughing.

Alfie is turning into a fashion diva, Mom says. Whatever a diva is.

I think it means spoiled.

"She better not make me late for school," I say.

See, Dad has already left, because he has an hour-long drive to San Diego. Like I already said, he teaches geology at a college there. So Mom has to drive both Alfie and me to school every day. Alfie gets dropped off first each morning, and sometimes it takes her a long time to leave the car.

Here is an example of how hard it can be to get Alfie to leave Mom's Toyota. One morning when Alfie was about to get out of the car at school, she discovered that she had put on shoes from two different pairs of sneakers, one pink and one blue. That was a *major* meltdown. Alfie cried so hard that she yakked out the car window, and then she and Mom had to go home and lie down after they dropped me off at Oak Glen and Mom hosed off the car.

I'm glad I missed that part of the morning.

Another time, Mom caught Alfie trying to sneak a new doll into school. That's against the law at Kreative Learning and Daycare—which has a sign outside that my dad just loves, for some reason. The sign reads, *Featuring Spanish, Computer Skills, and Potty Training.* Dad sometimes makes a joke about how hard it would be to teach all three things at once.

I guess that's how teachers think. Even college teachers.

But like I said, Alfie sometimes refuses to leave Mom's car, which is why I'm worried about being late on this very important Monday.

Day one of my secret plan.

The day when I figure out which new friend to choose.

"EllWay, *c'mon*," Alfie is saying, hands on her hips as she stares at me from the kitchen doorway. "Wake up!"

“I’m awake,” I tell her. “Anyway, Mom and I were waiting for *you*, slow-poke.”

“Mom’s already in the car,” Alfie informs me. “And me and my cute barrettes don’t wanna be late.”

“Me neither,” I say, locking the kitchen door behind me on my way out.

Not today, of all days, I add to myself.

✲ 4 ✲

LIKE A SPY

Oak Glen Primary School goes from kindergarten through sixth grade, which puts our third grade class right in the middle, if you count kindergarten. And us third grade kids are in the middle sizewise, too, except for me. I am the shortest kid—boy or girl—in Ms. Sanchez's class, and I have been all semester. I keep hoping that someone even shorter will transfer in, like a leprechaun maybe, but no such luck.

Dad tells me I'll start growing taller pretty soon, but when?

If the weather is nice, which it almost always is in Oak Glen, we play outside near the picnic tables before school starts. Well, the boys play, and the girls in our class mostly just hang, talk or whisper, and make fun of us boys. My opinion is that the girls don't want to mess up their clothes first thing in the morning. Excuse me, their *outfits.*

They save their running around for later in the day.

I walk toward the picnic tables as if I am seeing the guys in my class for the first time. I feel like a spy.

"Hey, EllRay!" my friend Corey calls out, waving at me.

Corey has blond hair and freckles, and he usually smells like chlorine. He works out before school at a swimming pool in an Oak Glen gym, that's why. And then, after school, he works out at an aquatics center in a bigger town nearby.

"Aquatics" means doing stuff in the water.

An aquatics center has more than one pool, Corey says. Also, they're longer and more official looking. And nobody has fun there, the way Corey tells it.

But he's having fun now, at least. Corey is playing with a wooden paddleboard, his latest obsession. He must have sneaked it into school in his backpack. This doesn't break any *big* rule, except for the one that says you can't bring toys to school.

And Cynthia and Fiona say that the paddle part of the toy could be used as a weapon. They keep threatening to tell on him.

But Cynthia's toothy *headband* could be used as a weapon.

So could a book, if it was thick enough!

Corey says that paddleboarding is a sport—this kind of paddleboarding, with a red rubber ball attached to a small paddle by a piece of elastic string,

not the kind you do standing on a board in the ocean. And grownups are always trying to get us kids to do more sports, aren't they?

They have meetings about it all the time. With *cake.*

Also, Corey never plays with his paddleboard in class.

I'm not saying he's *right* to sneak it into school. I'm just reporting the facts.

Another fact is that until he gets caught and the paddleboard gets taken away from him, Corey is likely to keep bringing it to Oak Glen. "Watch this," he tells me, bouncing the ball off the board about ten times in a row.

BAM, BAM, BAM, BAM, BAM, BAM, BAM, BAM, BAM, BAM.

"Don't you dare hit me with that thing, Corey Robinson, or I'm telling," Cynthia calls out from one of the girls' picnic tables, right on schedule. She is about ten feet away from Corey, who, of course, ignores her.

I sneak a spy-like peek over at Marco and Major, who are playing on the beat-up grass. They are huddled over these little plastic knights Marco collects—and sneaks into school.

We don't mean to be bad. We are just trying to have some extra fun.

I think Marco would live in the olden days if he could, and Major would be right there with him!

Me, I'm more of a modern day kind of kid. I like cell phones and tablets, and the more apps stuffed into everything the better. Most of all, I like video games. My current favorite one is *Die, Creature, Die.* I got it for Christmas. It's handheld but still cool.

They didn't have *that* in the olden days, Marco.

I shift my sneaky spy gaze over to Nate Marshall. His red rooster crest looks extra perky today. He is explaining something to Kevin, who looks confused. Kevin is trying to sneak away. "See?" Nate is saying, keeping up with him, like they have magnets in their legs. "Don't you get it? The cylinder head *delivers* the spark."

"Sort of. I think I get it," Kevin says, looking around in a "*Save me!*" kind of way. I think Kevin is afraid there's going to be a quiz, and school hasn't even started yet!

Hmm, I think. Turning Nate into a spare friend might be too much work. Especially now, when I need fast results.

Meanwhile, Jason Leffer is laughing with Jared and Stanley on the other side of one of the boys' picnic tables. I think he's pretending he just pulled a giant booger out of his nose, only it's really a raisin from his lunch sack.

Excuse me for saying "booger." I am just reporting the facts.

"He's gonna eat it," Fiona shrieks from one of the girls' picnic tables.

They don't officially have "girls' tables" or "boys' tables" at Oak Glen Primary School, by the way. I think doing that is against the law. It just works out that way, about girls' tables and boys' tables, once you get past first or second grade.

I forget. That was a long time ago.

The point is, Jason is *fun.*

But Diego Romero can be fun, too, I remind myself. Right now, Diego is leaning against a tree, reading a car magazine. I don't know much about cars, but the magazine looks pretty cool. And once Diego is my friend, I can sort of scootch him over to stuff that doesn't involve reading. Things *I* like to do.

So, Diego and Jason it is, I decide. If I play this right, I'll have *two* spare friends!

A spare, and a spare-spare.

Alfie will be so impressed. She'll feel good about coming to Oak Glen Primary School next year.

"Hey," I say, scuffing my way over to Diego's tree. "Cars, huh?"

Brilliant, EllRay.

"Yeah," Diego says, marking his place with a finger and looking up at me with a friendly smile.

Hey. An accidental good start!

"What kind of car do you want to have when you turn sixteen?" Diego asks me, really curious.

Not my mom's old one, that's for sure, is all I can think. Because after all, turning sixteen is eight years away. And that's a whole other lifetime, since I'm only eight years old *now*.

But luckily, the warning buzzer sounds before I have to answer Diego. "Later, dude," I say, trying to match his earlier smile without being too weird. But Diego's not even looking at me. He's too busy getting his stuff together.

"Dude," Corey calls out, winding the elastic string loosely around his paddleboard handle and jamming it into his backpack. "Who you growlin' at?"

"Nobody," I say, trying to erase my goofy smile as we all head toward class.

Just a normal Monday morning, I tell myself. But things are looking up!

I've made my choice. My *choices*, I mean.

Now, all I need is to find a way to get Diego's and Jason's attention so they'll *want* to be my friends.

✲ 5 ✲

ELLRAY JAKES THE RECESS KING!

"You're awfully quiet over there, buddy," Dad says at dinner.

Turkey meatloaf, a huge blob of ketchup, carrot coins, and my mom's special potatoes.

"I'm good," I tell him.

"EllWay's just thinking," Alfie explains.

She's actually right. I have been trying to figure out the best way to make Jason and Diego want to be my friends. I mean, we're already *friends*, I guess, since we have been in the same class since September, and we have never had a fight.

But I want them to be *real* friends.

Friends I can hang with after school, on weekends, and even during the summer.

Friends like Corey is, when he's not busy swimming, or like Kevin is some of the time.

"Hold on a second, EllRay," Dad says, his always-solemn face creasing into an even more serious expression. "Is everything okay at school?"

His fork has stopped halfway to his mouth.

"Now, Warren," my mom says, probably hoping to calm him down.

Okay. Here's what is going on.

1. My mom and dad moved us to Oak Glen from San Diego when I was in kindergarten, even though the move meant that Dad would have a much longer drive to work. All the way down to San Diego—and back.
2. But almost the minute we got to Oak Glen, I think my dad was bothered that there weren't more brown faces around town.
3. What worried him even more was the idea that kids my class might pick on me because my skin *is* brown. And when Alfie came along, *whoa.*
4. So far, there hasn't been any trouble like that. There are plenty of *real* reasons for kids to get irked with me, and the other way around! Me with

them, I mean. And the same with Alfie, for that matter. *Normal* reasons.

5. But Dad's worries still stick in his head—like a splinter, I guess. You know how, when you have a splinter in your hand, and you can't get it out, the thought of it always fills your brain? Even though the splinter is only in one little part of your body?

    Like that.

    Like the way I feel about being short.

"I'm only asking, Louise," Dad tells my mom, putting down his fork. "It's a perfectly reasonable question."

Notice how my mom and dad get to have regular names, by the way? Louise and Warren? But Alfie and I have names we have to *explain.*

Like I said, parents should not do that to their kids. In my opinion.

"Don't worry, Dad. Everything is fine at school," I say. "I just feel kind of quiet tonight, but in a *good* way. Like Alfie said, I'm thinking."

"Anyway, *I'm* the chatterbox around here," Alfie says, sounding proud.

As if we needed telling!

"And you'll never guess where Suzette Monahan thinks baby kitties come from," my little sister adds. She leans forward, her brown eyes wide.

"Oh, heaven help us," Mom says. "Here we go."

And—I actually stop trying to figure out how to con Jason and Diego into being my friends for a minute. What Alfie says next will either be completely rando, like our teenage babysitter says, or it'll be really good.

Dad looks worried again. "I'm not sure that telling us where kittens come from is the best subject for the dinner table, Alfleta," he says.

Alfleta. *"Beautiful elf,"* in a language only my mom knows anymore.

See what I mean?

"Why?" Alfie asks, her golden face starting to crumple. "You don't like *flowers*? Because that's where Suzette found a whole *bunch* of kitties, she said. In their garden. And she'll sell us one for only a hundred dollars."

And Mom, Dad, and I all start to laugh—which, of course, only makes things worse with Alfie.

But that's okay, because she gets over things fast.

I guess she doesn't have any brain splinters yet.

Later, in bed, I stare at my ceiling in the dark. I am trying to figure out my friend problem in a logical way. That's what Dad is always telling me to do. "Be logical."

He's a scientist, remember.

Jason Leffer is already the funny kid in our class, I remind myself. So I can't win him over with pranks and jokes. Diego, either.

And I can't *bribe* them into being my friends. I don't have enough money! I only have enough saved up to bribe maybe half a person for five minutes, tops.

My dad says I'm one of life's big spenders, that's the thing.

Besides, Mom and Dad would never let me get away with something as bad as bribery.

But there's another thing I'm good at beside

spending money, and that's having fun. I can really get into it.

And when does a kid have the most fun at school?

During recess.

So if I can figure out a way to be the most fun kid in the world at recess, if I can turn into the kid with the best ideas of stuff to do, then Jason and Diego are sure to want to be my new spare friends!

I can fix what's wrong with them after that, I tell myself—like Jason cracking jokes all the time, and Diego thinking there's nothing better to do than read.

They'll *thank* me someday.

But first, I have to become EllRay Jakes, the recess king!

Genius.

6

COMPUTER TIME

"Can I use the computer after dinner?" I ask Dad. It is Tuesday, the day after I got my bright idea.

I don't tell my dad that I need to do some research. If I tell him that, he will peek over my shoulder and make suggestions the whole time. Dad *loves* research.

But this is my thing.

"I think you mean *may* you use the computer after dinner," Dad says. His look shows that he has covered this subject a number of times before.

Okay, about a zillion.

"Because yes, you *can* use the computer," he continues. "You are physically able to use it, of course. But *may* you use it? That involves getting permission, and permission is a whole different matter. Is your homework done?"

"Yes," I say, remembering at the last second not to say, *"Yup."*

Because then there would be a whole different lecture.

Dad says it's the little things in life that count. But he turns everything into something big.

"I finished my homework before dinner," I tell him. And even *I* sound amazed. On a normal night, I can gripe so long about my homework that it doesn't get done until minutes before bedtime.

Not tonight, though!

"That's my boy," Dad says, looking pleased. "And yes, you *may* have some computer time. I'll keep you company while your mom tackles Alfie's bath."

Our big computer is in the family room, and Alfie and I have to ask permission to use it. I guess the idea is that Mom and Dad want to keep track of what we're doing on the computer. That's probably not such a bad idea, or Alfie might start buying stuff online. Barbie mansions, buckets of candy, the cutest outfits in the world, you name it. At the very least, she would buy more plastic horses, a glittery stable, and a golden corral big enough to go around our entire house, if they make such a thing.

Luckily, she doesn't know how to buy things online. *Yet.*

Neither do I.

But my plan tonight is to research a bunch of amazing things to do at recess. Then I can look like I'm thinking up brilliant ideas—***WHAM!*** just like that!—while us guys are hanging out, doing the usual boring recess stuff. They'll be saying, *"Whaddya wanna do?"* And, *"I dunno. What do you want to do?"* over and over again.

It's kind of our thing.

And then I, EllRay Jakes the recess king, will come up with something great.

Who wouldn't want to be friends with a new-idea-guy like that? I mean, like me?

The new and *improved* me.

I drag the big chair in toward the desk and make a list of things to look up. You have to be careful on the Internet, or you can jump to some really weird stuff by accident. And then you will never be allowed to use the computer again until you are an old man—at least not at *my* house.

But here is my list of things to look up:

1. Playground games.
2. Third grade recess.
3. Ideas for recess games.

You have to give the computer lots of hints and choices to get your research started.

Mom and Dad would be okay with me looking up those three things.

As usual, *boom*, just like that, some of the sites try to sell me something: a pair of shiny high heeled

shoes, vitamins, life insurance. I don't even know what life insurance is, but it sounds like a tough guy high school threat, like, "You better do what I say—*or else*."

They don't know I'm just a kid with no money.

Better luck next time, ads.

But there are some sites with pretty good ideas, I see, scrolling down. A few of them even have videos that some faraway primary schools made. They show sample kids playing sample games. The kids look a little embarrassed, knowing they're being filmed, but the games aren't bad.

I pull my notebook closer so I can write stuff down. But first, in my brain, I cross off every online idea that starts with *equipment*, even simple equipment such as tarps, tires, or those foam noodles kids play with in swimming pools. We're not supposed to bring stuff like that to school. It might mess up our playground's special design, I guess.

That design is basically an empty square, except for the grassy hill where our picnic tables sit. There is a paved area with a couple of overhead ladders, some creaky swings, and a slide. A first grader hurled all over the top step of the slide ladder last week, so now no one wants to use it.

It's been scrubbed clean, but no takers.

Oh, and there's a locked storage shed in the corner of our playground. It's full of deflated kickballs and grimy hula hoops, even though it's only January. There are five months to go before school is over for the year.

Too bad for us, I guess.

I cross off all the girl activities, too.

I decide to write down ten things in my notebook, then choose my cool recess ideas from those. What I really want is to find special activities that Jason Leffer and Diego Romero will want to do!

Funny stuff for Jason, and I'm-not-sure-what-kind-of-stuff for Diego.

Nothing to do with reading during recess, that's for sure.

After I rope Jason and Diego in with how much fun I am, I can teach them the kinds of things *I* like to do, like playing Sky High Foursquare or Shadow Tag. Running-around stuff like that.

Then I'll have a friend, *Corey*, a half-friend, *Kevin*, a spare friend, *Jason*, and a spare-spare friend, *Diego*.

I will be rich. Rich in friends!

"You about done here, buddy?" Dad asks over my shoulder. "Did you find what you were looking for? Because you need some time for your eyes to unwind after using the computer, you know. And your mom wants to read to you."

I nod, trying not to think of my eyes unwinding, which is just gross. Dad says stuff in a complicated way sometimes, probably because he is so smart. But I kind of know what he means. A person's eyes do get jumpy, staring at the computer screen. But computers are cool! You can look up anything.

1. I can look up my own *dad* on the Internet.
2. I can spy on any place in the world in one second flat.
3. I can even scare myself, looking at pictures of leopard sharks or hungry polar bears who might be looking for an EllRay sandwich.

Mom reading to me will be the perfect medicine for my jumpy eyes, even though the book she's reading me is very exciting. It is *The Sword in the Stone*, by T. H. White. I guess the first part of his name is a secret. That's why he uses his initials.

The book is a lot different from the old cartoon movie version Alfie has. In the book, the wizard Merlyn turns Wart—who grows up to become King Arthur, Mom says—into lots of different animals, and Wart learns something important from each one. For example, in the chapter we are reading now, Merlyn turns Wart into a goose. Wart learns that geese don't fight each other. They stick together, fly together, and protect each other. They only fight when they are attacked by outsiders.

Unlike some of the other animals, like ants—who *love* to fight.

"Then shut her down and go brush your teeth," Dad says, knuckle-rubbing my hair—which only he is allowed to do. It's his version of a hug.

"Her." Our family room computer is a girl, I guess. That's strange. Well, girls *are* pretty smart.

"Okay, Dad," I say, ducking my head and grabbing my notebook. "Good night."

"Night, son," my dad says, and he gives my chicken-bone shoulder a dadly squeeze.

He's pretty cool, my dad!

✲ 7 ✲

A VERY GOOD IDEA

"I forgot to ask you something," I say to Mom the next morning, right before we leave for school.

I timed it this way.

"What is it?" Mom asks, sounding busy as she finishes up my lunch—which I plan to eat before the first buzzer rings.

"I need to bring something to school," I tell her. "From the pointy closet. Can I go get it?"

We have this weird closet under the stairs. You can't hang coats in it because the ceiling slopes, so Mom decided it was the perfect place to keep the extra stuff we get at that huge store up the freeway. The store where you have to buy twenty boxes of tissues at a time, or huge jars of pickles. *That* place.

"What do you need?" Mom asks, washing her hands at the sink and then looking around for Alfie.

"TP," I whisper.

"Excuse me? What did you say?" my mom asks, turning to face me.

Great. I have her full attention, and I was hoping to slip this one past her.

"TP," I repeat, shrugging. "That's short for toilet paper, Mom."

"I know what it's short for," Mom says, her eyes wide. "Are you telling me that you're supposed to bring your own toilet paper to school these days? Things are *that bad*?"

"We don't *have* to bring it," I say, sliding my eyes away from hers as I cross my fingers behind my back.

No, I haven't told a lie yet. But I'm getting kind of close.

It's true that I don't *like* the TP at Oak Glen Primary School. It isn't like regular TP at all. It's not even rolled up. School TP is more like little squares of tissue paper stuffed into a metal box. But it's okay. At least it's paper. It's not like we have to use leaves or something.

"Hmm," Mom says, thinking.

The truth is, I need that roll of TP—or I *want*

it—for my plan to coax Jason Leffer into being my spare friend. It'll be a start, anyway.

"We're late," Alfie shouts, skipping into the kitchen in a pink and purple blur. "And I get to be the magic kitty this morning! So let's *go*!"

Mom is still staring at me. It's like she's counting up all the things that are wrong with Oak Glen Primary School.

"Listen, Mom," I say. "Never mind. I—"

"EllRay, for heaven's sake. Go ahead and take a roll of toilet paper," she says, shaking her head as she gathers up our things. "Of *course* you can bring your own TP to school if you need to. Grab a roll from the open package, and stash it in your backpack, if there's room."

"*What*?" Alfie asks, as if she can't believe what she just heard.

"It's a long story," I tell her.

"It better be a quick one, EllWay," she says, looking half curious, half grossed-out, and half crazy-impatient to leave.

Wait. That's one too many halves.

But in less than ten seconds, I zip into the hall, open the closet door, grab a roll of TP from the tower of supplies jammed inside, and cram the roll into my backpack.

Man, I hope it doesn't fall out at an embarrassing time.

1. That roll of TP could tumble out of my backpack on the front steps of the school, where Principal James greets each of us by name in the morning. It could bounce down the cement steps, *bump, bump, bump*. I would never live it down.
2. Or the roll of TP might fall out of my backpack as I walk down the hall toward class. I would leave a long trail of paper behind me.

   Not. Gonna. Happen.
3. Or the roll of TP could topple out of my backpack and onto the floor in our cubby closet in front of *all the girls*, when I'm putting my stuff away. "Lose something?" Cynthia would ask, waving the roll of TP in the air for all to see.

There are a lot of disaster possibilities when you bring a roll of toilet paper to school.

This better be worth it.

"Paper and pencils out, girls and boys, boys and girls," Ms. Sanchez tells us right after she takes attendance. She likes to treat us equally. "We're having a quiz on the spelling words from the last two weeks," she says. "Surprise!"

Ms. Sanchez is usually a very nice lady. But saying *"Surprise!"* in such a situation is just mean, in my opinion. She always tells us that she wants us to know how to spell words *forever,* though, and not just for the week of the quiz. Ms. Sanchez says she does not want our motto to be, *"In one ear and out the other."*

I think that means she wants the words to stay in our brains for a long time. Long enough for us to be able to use them again in an emergency, for example. Although in my opinion, *short* words are probably best when it comes to emergencies.

Words like, *"Fire!"* and *"Help!"* and *"Giant snakes!"*

Our low chorus of grumbles is muffled by the **CLANK** of our three-ring binders and the

R-R-R-RIP! of notebook paper being wrestled from them.

If we could make any more noise, we would.

"*Stairs*," Ms. Sanchez begins. "As in the stairs that you climb. And use each of your words in a sentence, please."

I'm a pretty good speller most of the time. "S-T-A-I-R-S," I print. "*We walk down the stairs to the playground.*"

"*Sometimes*," Ms. Sanchez says, moving on to the second word.

"S-O-M-T-I-M-E-S," I write, smiling as I think about the recess to come. Awesome! "*Somtimes I get a very good idea.*"

I'm not sure yet how to spell "excellent," or I'd say "*an excellent idea.*"

"*Prepared*," Ms. Sanchez says, perching on the edge of her desk and admiring the toe of one of her shoes. There's a bow on it.

"P-R-E-P-A-R-E-D," I print, my pointer finger already creased from the pencil. "*I am prepared to make a new friend.*"

And on and on our teacher goes.

This is going to be the longest morning ever. E-V-E-R.

But it'll be worth the wait, I tell myself, half hiding a secret smile.

Recess is gonna be *so much fun.*

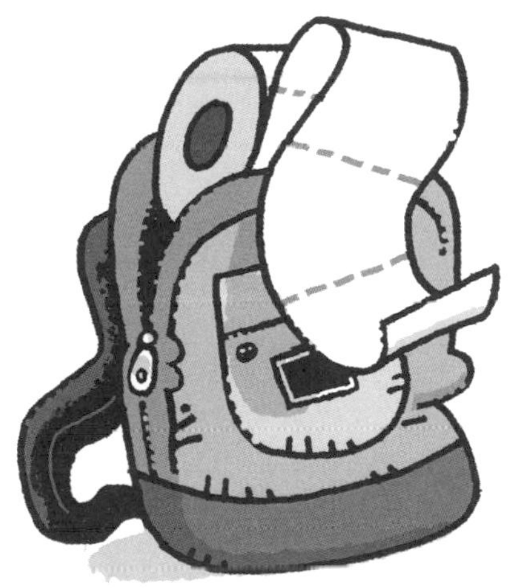

8

THE CURSE OF THE MUMMY ZOMBIE

"You look weird," Emma McGraw says as we push our way out the classroom door and into the hall, because—it's finally recess! "Do you have a tummy ache?" she asks.

All the other guys are already out on the playground. I'm losing recess time.

"I'm fine," I tell her. I am just trying to hide the roll of toilet paper under my jacket. "And P.S., Emma," I say. "You shouldn't tell people they look weird."

"But you do look weird," Annie Pat Masterson says. She is defending Emma, her best friend. "No offense," she adds.

"I don't think you can say '*you look weird*' and '*no offense*' at the same time," Kry Rodriguez says as we make our way down the crowded hall.

Me and *three girls.*

Emma, Annie Pat, and Kry are the best girls in our class, though. They don't whisper or giggle behind their hands when a boy messes up, or act like they're so great, the way Cynthia and Fiona sometimes do.

But this was not the way I wanted this special morning recess to start.

"Bye-ya," I tell Emma, Annie Pat, and Kry, and *zoom!* off I go, heading for the door like a football player racing toward the end zone.

Okay, like a *small* football player—holding a roll of TP instead of a ball.

"No running in the halls," I hear a grownup yell behind me, but I'm already gone.

Jason Leffer, here I come!

"Look who's finally here," Stanley calls as I come trotting up, still hiding the TP under my jacket.

"C'mon, EllRay. We're about to play Bubblegum

Foursquare," my sometimes-friend Kevin says. He bounces the dark red ball a couple of times to tempt me.

Bubblegum Foursquare is really fun. In the Oak Glen Primary School version, the fourth person to hit the ball has to stay frozen to that spot for the rest of the game—like they're stuck there with gum.

But I have other plans. "Later, dog," I say, looking for Jason.

He's over at the boys' picnic table with Corey, Diego, and Major. They're stuffing their faces, of course. "Hey," I say, walking over to the table. "Have you guys ever played Mummy Zombie?"

"Never heard of it," Corey says through his turkey-cheese roll-up.

Corey's big into protein. Or his mom is, anyway.

"And I've never *read* of it," Diego says.

"Then it doesn't exist," Jason announces, laughing. "EllRay's just making stuff up—probably because he already ate all his food."

"I'll share," Corey offers, holding out his drooping snack.

"No, thanks. I'm good," I say, looking around for the playground monitor. It's Mr. Havens today, but he's way across the playground. He's huge and he teaches second grade. I guess he's subbing for the real monitor.

I take out the roll of TP from under my jacket. "Ta-da!" I say, holding it up.

"Dude," Jason says, slapping his forehead like he cannot believe his eyes. "You can't use that stuff out here. You gotta go *inside*, to the room that says *Boys* on the door. Right, guys?" he asks, already cracking up at his own joke.

"No. Listen, Jase," I say, pulling the end of the paper free. "I saw this on the Internet. The 'mummy' part, anyway. I made up the rest. But see, I'm gonna wrap this TP all around you, and turn you into a mummy *zombie*, okay? And then whoever you tag *also* has to be a zombie. Except only you get to be the *king* mummy zombie," I add, trying to make it sound extra special.

Jason's eyes light up, and his buzz-cut hair seems to sent out sparks. "Do it," he says, holding out his arms. "Wrap me up quick, dude. I'm in!"

“I need some help,” I say to the guys sitting at the picnic table. Corey, Diego, and Major have stopped chewing, I see.

This is perfect! I have made Jason Leffer the star of morning recess, which is probably a dream come true for him.

Of course he will want to be my new spare friend!

“C’mon, you guys,” I say. And in two seconds, Corey, Diego, and Major are helping me wrap the toilet paper all over Jason: around his middle a few times, then up around one arm, then across to the other arm. And then we start in on his fuzzy mummy zombie head.

"RAW-R-R-R-R!" Jason bellows, getting into it.

By now, of course, we have a pretty big audience.

“The buzzer’s gonna sound,” Corey warns, and Jason takes off into the crowd.

“RAW–R–R–R–R!” he howls again, staggering stiff-legged toward the kids that surround us. He reaches out his arms. Flaps of TP trail behind him like—well, like flaps of TP. A couple of pieces of toilet paper float free.

"It's the curse of the mummy zombie," Major yells, explaining it to the running kids. "And if he tags you, you have to be a zombie too! Like, *forever*," he adds, waving his own arms in the air.

Hey. I didn't say *forever*. My own game is getting away from me!

But, **"EEE-E-E-E-E!"** everyone shouts, scattering wide. The girls are laughing and screaming at the same time.

"What's a zombie?" a little boy asks. He's a first-grader, I think. What's he doing over here with us big kids? Is hc lost or something?

"Zombie—gonna—get—you," Jason yells, heading first for the bunch of third grade girls, and then lurching back toward the little boy. "Zombie gonna *eat* you."

"WAH-H-H-H-H," the kid cries. His fists are up against his mouth. He is frozen where he stands.

This kid will be really good at Bubblegum Four-square some day, I can't help but think. Only that's not what we're playing right now.

This is out of control.

And not in a good way.

"Don't eat me," the little guy begs, trying to hide his head with the front of his red zippered sweat-shirt. He crumples onto the grass, surrendering.

"It's only pretend, kid," I yell as a couple more toilet paper squares flutter to the ground.

TWE-E-E-E-E-T!

A whistle blows about two inches from my ear.

It's Mr. Havens, the gigantic playground monitor. And boy, does he look mad!

"Exactly *what* is supposed to be happening here?" he shouts, his big hands on his hips.

And nobody moves, not even the little boy on the grass.

It's like Bubblegum *Recess*, we're all holding so still.

9

EPIC FAIL

"This is all your fault, Mr. Mummy," Cynthia whispers to Jason—the mummy zombie king—as we file back into Ms. Sanchez's classroom. It's like we are cartoon bad guys marching off to jail in black-and-white striped uniforms. Ms. Sanchez is still in the hall talking to Mr. Havens.

I guess this was not his lucky day to substitute.

Join the crowd, Mr. Havens.

Jason shoots me a dirty look, but he doesn't say anything. There are a couple of squares of TP still hanging from the back pocket of his jeans, but I pretend I don't see them.

"Yeah, *Mr. Mummy*," Fiona echoes, glaring at Jason. "You made that little boy cry."

"Everyone was having fun until that happened," loyal Corey points out, giving me a secret nudge of support.

"I didn't see how it started," Annie Pat complains. "Where did all that toilet paper come from?"

"It was probably Jared's bright idea," Cynthia announces, scowling.

All the boys in our class, even Jared, make a point of not looking at Cynthia—or at me. But they *know* where that roll of toilet paper came from.

I guess us guys are gonna stick together on this one. We're like the loyal geese in *The Sword in the Stone.* For now, anyway.

In terms of making a new spare friend, though, this has to go down as an epic fail. Jason Leffer looks like he'll never laugh again.

Good one, EllRay. So much for inviting Jason over Friday—to see Alfie's goofy play, and then maybc have pizza or ice cream, and some sleepover fun.

Ms. Sanchez comes gliding back into the classroom like the ice queen in one of Alfie's cartoon movies. "Well," she begins, sitting down. "Imagine my surprise." She lays her hands flat on top of the desk, which is kind of scary for some reason.

"Us *girls* didn't do anything," Cynthia says, talking and raising her hand at the same time.

“Quiet, please, Miss Harbison,” Ms. Sanchez says, not even looking at Cynthia.

Uh-oh. She calls us “Miss” and Mister” when she’s really angry.

“We have some things to sort out,” Ms. Sanchez says in a solemn voice. “Now, we *were* going to do some math word problems before lunch,” she continues.

Math word problems are usually pretty fun, unless your name is Corey Robinson. Corey can compete in a swim race in front of one-hundred people, and win, but math makes him panic.

Here is an example of a math word problem, in case you didn't know:

There are twenty-five (25) students in Ms. Sanchez's third grade class. Ten (10) of them are boys. One (1) boy hates math word problems. How many boys in Ms. Sanchez's class don't hate math word problems?

"And then," Ms. Sanchez continues, "as a reward for working so hard on your math, I was going to read aloud to you. It was a really funny book, too. But I guess we won't have time for that, now," she says, shaking her head.

Corey's hand inches up. "What do we have to do instead?" he asks in a nervous voice after Ms. Sanchez calls on him.

He's probably worried it'll be something even *worse* than math word problems.

Like taking out our own tonsils, maybe.

"I'm so glad you asked, Mr. Robinson," Ms. Sanchez says. "First, you will all write notes of apology to Iggy Brown."

"Who's Iggy Brown?" Emma asks, not even raising her hand first. She sounds one-hundred percent (100%) confused.

"Iggy Brown is the little first-grade boy who got knocked down by a bunch of stampeding third-graders at morning recess," Ms. Sanchez says, her voice cool.

"Nobody knocked him down," Jason mumbles. "He *collapsed*."

"Did you say something, Mr. Leffer?" Ms. Sanchez asks.

"Nuh-uh," he says, shaking his head.

"Good," Ms. Sanchez says. "Because poor little Iggy was really scared. His mama is having to leave work to bring him a change of clothes, so he can finish out the day."

"It wasn't *that* dirty on the grass," Marco says, his voice low—but not low enough.

"Do you have something to contribute, Mr. Adair?" Ms. Sanchez asks.

"Nope," Marco says, sounding hopeless.

"Me neither," Major chimes in.

He's the other M in "M and M," remember?

"Iggy wet his pants because of the mummy," Fiona loud-whispers. "I saw. It was sad. Poor little guy."

"Poor little guy," the other girls echo.

And I kind of agree with them. Because what if it had been my little sister Alfie, and not Iggy, who wandered over to the wrong area of the playground? She gets lost all the time! And what if *she* had been the one to wet her pants at school?

The world would come to an end. Her world, anyway. For a while.

I feel really terrible now.

I never meant for this to happen. But it happened anyway!

"It's okay," Marco Adair whispers to me. "You didn't know."

"Ms. Sanchez, Ms. Sanchez," Cynthia says, waving her hand in the air as if she has something really urgent to say.

Ms. Sanchez sighs. "Yes, Miss Harbison, Miss Harbison?"

"Iggy probably can't even read," Cynthia says, like she just won an argument. "Anyway, he's the one who strayed into our herd."

She said "our herd!" Maybe while I've been reading about Merlyn and the geese, as well as all the other cool animals in *The Sword in the Stone*, Cynthia's been reading some other animal book. Probably about magic ponies or something.

"And *us girls* didn't do anything wrong," Cynthia finishes, folding her arms across her chest. "So I think the boys should write the I'm-sorry-letters, and us girls can hear the funny story."

"It's 'we girls,' not 'us girls,'" Ms. Sanchez informs her. "You would say, 'We can hear,' not 'Us can hear,' wouldn't you? That's the test. But sorry, ladies. It's not going to work that way. This class is a unit—or 'a herd,' if you prefer. It's not two teams, the boys against the girls. So get out your best pens, if you please, and I'll pass out some nice paper for you to write on. Iggy's parents can read him your notes, if he can't read them himself. I'll write a few vocabulary words on the board to help get you started," she adds.

My dad would call that "throwing us a bone."

"And then lunch?" Jared Matthews asks, sounding hopeful.

"Oh. About lunch," Ms. Sanchez says, as if Jared just reminded her of something important. "You are all marching out onto that playground as soon as the lunch buzzer sounds, and you're picking up *every scrap of toilet paper you can find.* And any other litter, as well. After that, you can wash your hands thoroughly, and *then* eat your lunch."

"But the best food will be gone in the cafeteria," Kevin cries.

"That's true," Ms. Sanchez says in a thoughtful way, as she examines her shiny fingernails. "I'm sure there will be *something* left, though. No one will starve."

And she's usually so nice.

This is all my fault—no matter *what* Marco says.

And my stomach is already growling!

"*Iggy*," Ms. Sanchez writes on the white board. "*Apologize.*" "*Sincerely.*"

The entire third grade flock, or herd, sighs as if it were one giant creature.

And we start to write our notes to poor wet Iggy.

10

UH-OH

I jump into the back seat of Mom's car about three minutes after school lets out. There is a long line of cars waiting at the curb. They all have their lights on and wipers going, even though it's still daytime. It has just started to rain.

I am *so* glad Mom said she would pick me up today. I didn't want the guys in my class griping again about what happened this morning.

I'm gonna end up with *no* friends, at this rate.

"Don't get me wet, EllWay, or you'll be sowwy," Alfie warns.

That's *"you'll be sorry"* in Alfie-speak.

"What's *your* problem?" I ask, wrestling with my seat belt. "What's her problem?" I ask Mom when Alfie doesn't answer me.

My sister looks like a grouchy cartoon character with a little black storm cloud over her head—

which matches today perfectly, now that I think about it. Alfie's arms are folded across her chest. She is slumped in her car seat like a rag doll. She kicked off one of her sneakers, too.

Uh-oh. That's never a good sign. I hope it didn't go out the car window.

"Talk to your brother, Alfie," Mom says, signaling to pull into the traffic. "I'm too busy trying to drive in this crazy rain to explain what happened."

"I wanna go home," Alfie says, trying to kick the back of Mom's seat, which luckily is a good eight inches from Alfie's toes. "No chores! No chores, Mom," she says, wriggling in her car seat. She aims another kick Mom's way.

"Don't do that," I tell Alfie. "It's dangerous. And you're acting like a baby."

That's the worst insult you can give her.

"You can't tell me what to do, EllWay," Alfie says. "You're not the boss of me."

"I don't even want to be the boss of you," I inform her. "Where are we going?" I ask Mom. I'm hoping for a surprise trip to a drive-through, but that hardly ever happens.

Mom and Dad want us to have all kinds of experiences. Even fast food ones.

Only not very often.

"We're headed back to the arts and crafts store, and then I need to swing by the library," Mom says, not even looking at me in the rear view mirror. That's how nervous she is about driving in the rain—or how angry she is at having to return to that store. It drives Mom nuts how messy the shelves are. She's a very neat lady.

She could organize the world if she ever got the chance.

"But I thought you got everything you needed for Alfie's goldfish costume," I remind her. "You already started making it, didn't you?"

"Miss Nancy decided Alfie would do better in another role," Mom tells me, her voice sounding a little tight. "Our Miss Alfie was saying everyone's lines for them, it seems. And she had some trouble settling down."

"Yeah. Miss Nancy cheated the rehearsal," Alfie says, pouncing on Mom's words.

"Cheated *at* the rehearsal," I correct her. "Because you can't cheat a rehearsal, Alfie. That doesn't make any sense."

"EllRay," Mom says to me from the front seat. "You're not helping."

"Did that stuff really happen?" I ask Alfie. "You saying other kids' lines?"

I'm pretty sure she's ready to talk now. Getting her to stop up will be the hard part.

"Well, I knowed 'em all, and the other kids didn't," my sister says. "Not fast enough, anyway. So Miss Nancy said I have to be the *red bird*," Alfie tells me, almost spitting out the last two words. "Just because I was saying all the lines, and maybe bothering my neighbor. It's so she can keep an eye on me, Miss Nancy says. But I don't *wanna* be the red bird. The red bird comes first, and then she just stands there like—like a *baby*. I wanna be the goldfish and come last."

"I think you 'just standing there' is the idea, Alfie," Mom says. "And it's not up to you. It's up to Miss Nancy," she adds—from the safety of the front seat, remember.

Thanks, Mom.

"There are nine characters," Mom continues. "Not counting the teacher and the children in the story. So you're lucky you're in the skit at all, especially after disrupting the rehearsal the way you did."

"What's a skit?" Alfie asks, starting to get mad all over again.

"It's, like, a little play," I tell her. "A short one."

"But this is gonna be a *big* play," Alfie argues as Mom pulls into the arts and crafts store's shiny black parking lot. "And I'm *not gonna be the red bird*. I'm telling you that much wight now."

Right now.

"Then close your eyes when we get to the red tissue paper aisle, young lady," Mom tells her, handing me a ladybug umbrella. Like that's gonna happen. "Because I don't want any unpleasant scenes in the store."

"Then I'll make a *pleasant* scene," I hear Alfie mutter once Mom is out of the car.

Uh-oh, part two.

Dad gets home late from work a couple of Wednesday nights each month because of some meeting they have in the geology department of his college. Tonight he has gotten home even later than usual, because rain messed up the traffic.

It's almost my bedtime, and I've been looking at this really cool book Mom let me check out of the library this afternoon. The book is the equipment for my Diego Romero Spare Friend Plan that I'm gonna try to pull off tomorrow at school.

If anyone is still speaking to me, that is.

Dad has just finished eating the dinner Mom heated up for him. But instead of watching the news, he wants to talk to me. I guess I'm the news, tonight.

Uh-oh, part three.

"Come on down to my office, son," he has just called up the stairs.

About ten maybe-bad things I've done leap into my brain—and also one or two for-sure-bad things. I did them by accident, but what difference does that make to Dad? They still happened.

"Ooh, busted," Alfie says from her darkened room, as I walk past her partly open door.

"You're supposed to be asleep," I inform her.

"I'm too angwy to sleep," she says.

Angry.

"You think you have problems *now*," I say over my shoulder, because—I'd give anything to have a *Brown Bear, Brown Bear* kind of problem.

Being a red bird instead of a goldfish? Big deal!

Wait until she learns about the *real* world.

"Take a seat, EllRay," Dad says from behind his desk, which has several large sparkling rocks sitting on it. It's like he's a king sitting on his throne, surrounded by a wall of crystals.

Wait. Those rocks aren't *that* big.

I know I'm in some kind of trouble, though. Mom probably heard about all the stuff that happened today at school but decided to let Dad handle it when he got home.

That must be it.

Things will go better for me if I take the first step, I decide. "Look," I say to my dad, gripping the arms of my chair like that's going to save me. "Is this about the punishment we got at lunch for making that big mess in the playground during recess? Is that why you wanted to see me? Because we picked it all up. Every scrap of paper."

Dad looks at me, his head tilted a little.

"No, wait," I say quickly. "Is this about Iggy getting so scared that he wet his pants? Because we apologized for that. We wrote him twenty-five fancy I'm-sorry letters, with correct spelling and everything. Even though he probably can't even read. Well, twenty-four letters," I correct myself. "Because one of the girls was absent today. I forget her name."

Now, Dad's looking a little confused. Like—*Iggy? Iggy who?*

So that's not it. "Is this about the Curse of the Mummy Zombie thing?" I babble on, as if my mouth is not connected to my brain in any way. "Because I didn't make up the 'curse' part, Dad. That was Major's idea. And it wasn't 'curse' like a swear. I *did* make up the mummy zombie thing, but I had a really good reason. I had *good intentions*," I add, remembering an expression Dad sometimes uses.

Parents like it when you quote what they say, even though they've already heard it before. Obviously.

By this point, the expression on Dad's face is

impossible to read. It almost looks like—like he's about to laugh? But that can't be right.

"Wait. Is this about the toilet paper I took to school?" I ask, using up my last idea. "Because I can pay for it out of my allowance!"

"The *toilet paper*?" Dad echoes. "You'd better just stop talking, son. I only wanted us to catch up a little. We haven't had any time alone together in days. But obviously, there's been a lot going on." And he leans back in his chair, inspecting me like I'm some surprising new specimen.

What have I done?

"We don't really need to talk," I jibber-jabber, wishing I could delete the past few minutes from my dad's memory bank. Wipe it clean. "Everything's good. Really! At school, I mean. *And* at home. It's good everywhere, in fact. Good, good, good!"

"Oh, it is, is it?" Dad says, like it's not really a question. "Well, why don't you tell me about the Curse of the Mummy Zombie anyway, son? I could use a good laugh about now. And we can move on to the story about the punishment at school, and then you can tell me about little Izzy's wet pants."

"Iggy," I mumble.

"Excuse me?" Dad asks.

"It was *Iggy* who wet his pants," I say, staring at my bare feet. They look so happy, so innocent! It's as if they're not attached to the rest of miserable me. "He's in the first grade, Dad."

I'm gonna be here *forever.*

And Dad's never going to understand about me needing a new spare friend by Friday, which is sure to come up.

Man, I hope I don't start crying.

But there is no other way out of this tangled-up crystal maze, so I start talking.

11

BABY TALK THURSDAY

"How come the wind always blows after it rains?" I ask my mom. We have just dropped off Alfie at Kreative Learning and Daycare.

It is Thursday, the day after my toilet paper disaster, and the day before Alfie's big show. Wow, I'm glad I'm not Miss Nancy today. Wait—I'm *always* glad I'm not Miss Nancy! But especially today, when she's facing one of the few rehearsals left before tomorrow's *Brown Bear, Brown Bear* disaster.

Alfie is still saying "No way!" to the whole red bird thing.

"Good question about the wind, honey," Mom says, glancing out the car window at the bending trees and skittering leaves. "You know, I always picture a rainstorm as a beautiful lady sweeping through her castle," she says. "Maybe the swish of her skirts creates a breeze as it follows her out the door."

Yeah, right, I think, trying not to make a face. I'll keep that theory to myself, if anyone asks at school. Especially during science this morning.

But that fancy explanation is pure Mom.

I hug my backpack to my chest. Inside is the big library book, wrapped every which way in aluminum foil in case it starts raining again.

I am taking no chances today.

Okay, yes, I am basically sneaking it into school. And that is against the law at our house.

1. Library books are expensive, Mom says. And the librarians work hard ordering them, and getting them ready to be checked out.
2. It is a privilege to borrow library books.
3. That's why you have to pay a fine if you bring them back late.
4. And if you damage or lose a library book, you have to pay for it. It will cost more than if you just went to the store and bought a new one, too, because of all that librarian work.

Am I *asking* for trouble?

No, I am not. I do have a plan, though. I have given up trying to convince Jason Leffer what a great-idea guy I am. Instead, I am now trying for Diego Romero, the kid who likes books. Books about cars.

He can be my new spare friend.

This library book is perfect for Diego! It's all *about* cars. It has a gold race car on the front, and lots of really cool pictures inside. But it has writing, too. Diego likes writing. We can look at the book during together recess and lunch. I'll just kind of surprise him with it.

And then later, after I invite Diego to Alfie's show tomorrow night, I can teach him some of the fun stuff *I* like to do—like play *Die, Creature, Die.* He will then be the *new-and-improved* Diego Romero.

Once we're friends, I won't be stranded every time Corey goes to swim practice, or Kevin decides to mooch around with his neighbors instead of with me.

"EllRay?" Mom says, giving me a funny look in the rearview mirror.

"Hmm?" I say, still thinking about hanging with Diego at recess, and about him unwrapping the book. I can't wait to see the look on his face!

"We're here," she tells me. "At school," she adds, as if I might need more of a clue.

"Okay. Good," I say, escaping from my seatbelt. I open the car door, get out, and lug my too-heavy backpack after me. *Ugh.* "See ya," I shout through the car window, waving bye to my mom.

Out on the playground, the girls in my class are acting extra goofy today—as if the beautiful rain lady sweeping her skirts through the castle got *them* all worked up, too. The boys are kind of standing back and watching the girls, for once.

Girls-acting-goofy just happens sometimes—for no known reason. They are like stampeding cattle in a cowboy movie, only smaller. Fads happen a lot with girls, too. In fact, the girls in my class run through fads so fast that by the time you realize one is happening, it's old news—and another fad has taken its place.

Pink Day? They had that before Christmas. No announcements or anything.

Skipping Day? Been there, saw that. The girls even tried skipping in class, until Ms. Sanchez said no. She said a few other things, too.

Don't-Say-"Boy"-Day? The girls had that one, only nobody noticed until it was almost over. They mostly ignore us boys *every* day, it seems to me.

So what fad is it going to be today?

"Goin' onna fwing, EllWay," Cynthia says, running toward the swing. There's a pink sweater wrapped around her head.

"Yeah," Heather says, racing after her. "Goo-goo, gah-gah! Toopid *boy,*" she adds, pointing at me.

At me! What did *I* do?

Today, I mean.

Next to the girls' picnic table, three of them are clustered together, cooing at one another. "You so cute!"

"No, *you* so cute."

"Widdle babies," Fiona chimes in, hugging the other two.

The boys are watching this with nauseated expressions on their faces. I join them. "Hey. What's

up with them?" I ask, clunking my backpack onto the table.

I'll see if anyone is still talking to me after what happened yesterday.

"Kry says it's Baby Talk Thursday," Kevin reports, frowning. "Only I don't think *she's* doing it much. And Emma and Annie Pat can't decide if they even want to."

I laugh. "I thought it was Wear Your Sweater on Your Head Day," I say, trying out a joke.

"That's supposed to be a baby hat Cynthia has on," Kevin says, serious as anything. It's as if he is interpreting the girls to us—like some kind of goofy puzzle-solving scientist.

Kevin is not taking his worried eyes off those girls, in fact.

But me? I'm *relieved* it's Baby Talk Thursday! After all, just about every day has to be something if you're in the third grade at Oak Glen Primary School.

Hurt Feelings Day.

Scared About That Test Day.

Emma's Birthday Day.

So if this wasn't Baby Talk Thursday, it might be Thanks a Lot, EllRay! Day. And everyone would still be mad at me.

But because of the girls, we have officially "moved on," as Ms. Sanchez would say.

"Aren't you gonna eat anything?" my friend Corey Robinson asks, eyeing my backpack. Corey is always hungry, because of the swimming.

"I guess not until later," I say. I don't want anyone seeing the library book yet—or even spotting the aluminum foil it is wrapped in. Aluminum foil inside a kid's backpack usually means something yummy is inside the foil.

Like leftover birthday cake!

My mouth starts watering for a turquoise-blue frosting rose.

"Shove over. I want a front row seat for this," Marco says to me, but in a friendly way. I make room for him on the bench.

Two girls skip by, arm-in-arm. "We fwying, Marco!" one of them calls over her shoulder—as if she's showing off just for him.

"They're frying?" Marco asks, leaning forward like he just missed something.

"I think she said they're *flying*," Major tells him. "But I don't know for sure."

"How long are they gonna keep this up?" Diego wonders aloud.

"Probably all day, knowing them," I say. I try not to sound too overjoyed.

But if the girls *do* act like babies for the entire

day, then I'm out of trouble for sure! Because their being babies will soak up all the attention around here. And that's a fact.

It's kind of hard to know how to act around all this baby stuff, though. That's the only bad thing about today so far.

Are we boys supposed to ignore it?

Or go along with it?

Or argue with it?

Or wrap sweatshirts around our own heads and start making fun of it?

"Let's see what Ms. Sanchez has to say," I tell the other guys at the table. "I have the feeling babies aren't really her thing."

"Not yet, anyway," Corey says. "At least not crawling around her classroom, if that's what they've got planned."

"Yeah," I agree as the buzzer sounds. And we start for class, dodging a couple of skipping, babbling girl-babies.

Geez, what a break.

Maybe this is my lucky day!

✲ 12 ✲

HIGH PRESSURE SYSTEM

"Settle down, everyone," Ms. Sanchez says after she has taken attendance and put on her science apron. It's the sight of that apron that got us excited, because she usually plans really fun experiments for us to do. And the ones that don't work out the exact way she planned can be even better. Messier, but better.

Which is why she wears the apron.

"Now, you may have noticed how windy it is outside," Ms. Sanchez begins, perching on the front of her desk, as usual.

"Goo-goo, gah-gah," Heather murmurs, swapping baby glances with Cynthia.

"Shh," Annie Pat whispers, scowling. She and Emma want to be scientists when they grow up, and they probably think Heather and Cynthia are trying to mess with the lesson. Which they are.

"Shh, yourself," Cynthia whispers back, shrugging to show how bored she is with Annie Pat—and with science, for that matter.

"So," Ms. Sanchez continues, "does anyone know *why* it's windy outside?"

Wow, I think, and my eyes are big with surprise. That is just what I was asking my mom!

Stanley Washington's hand shoots up.

"Yes, Stanley?" Ms. Sanchez says.

"It's windy because the weather-guesser on TV *said* it would be windy," he says.

"I think they prefer to be called *meteorologists*, not *weather-guessers*," Ms. Sanchez says, laughing. "And before anyone asks, the term 'meteorology' comes from an ancient Greek word that refers to any event taking place in the sky. That's how meteors got their name, I suppose, since they are one thing that can happen in the sky. But what *weather-related events* take place in our earth's atmosphere?"

Emma raises her hand. "Rain?" she says after Ms. Sanchez calls on her.

Emma can make things sound like questions even when they aren't.

“That’s right,” Ms. Sanchez says. “And snow, and—”

“And UFOs,” Jared Matthews says, excited enough to interrupt.

“Like, with space aliens inside?” Heather asks, forgetting for a second to be a baby.

“Raise your hands, please,” Ms. Sanchez reminds them. “And let’s leave UFOs and space aliens for another lesson. Probably not science,” she adds, laughing again. “We’ve got our hands full today with the weather. We were talking about— ”

“*The wind,*” a few kids say together, finishing her sentence the way she sometimes wants us to. We can always tell when.

“Right,” Ms. Sanchez says. “And it’s windy today because the air pressure is trying to adjust itself after the rain. It likes to be nice and balanced. So the air pressure is trying to move from the *high pressure system* of the cold, heavy rainstorm we had last night to a lighter and and more normal *low pressure system* today. And that’s what is making the wind blow.”

Annie Pat raises her hand. “But you can’t really see air pressure, right?” she asks after Ms. Sanchez calls on her. “Except when the wind blows?”

“That’s right, Annie Pat,” Ms. Sanchez says, smiling at her. “But you are seeing the *effects* of air pressure when the wind blows, not seeing the air pressure itself. Sometimes you can feel air pressure, though. Did any of you ever get to fly in an airplane when you were a baby?”

Lots of hands shoot up into the air. Even mine, because we flew to see my grandparents once. I don’t remember it, but I’ve seen the pictures.

There still used to be paper photographs when I was a baby. Pictures weren’t just on people’s phones or cameras, like now.

“And did one or two of you get an earache in the plane?” Ms. Sanchez asks.

Corey raises his hand. “My mom said I did, once,” he reports, sounding proud. “She said I screamed and screamed when we were landing, and people gave her dirty looks. So she gave me a bottle.”

“Ooo,” a couple of the girls say. One of them pats Corey’s back, as if his plane just now landed, and he might still need comforting.

Next, they’ll probably want him to join their goo-goo, gah-gah baby club.

Good luck with *that.*

"Your poor little ears hurt because of the air pressure change in the plane's cabin," Ms. Sanchez tells Corey. "It's something babies grow out of, thank goodness. But that's what we'll be talking about this morning, people: air pressure. And we have three air pressure experiments to get through. So come on up here, Cynthia," she says. "And Corey, too. And—how about EllRay? We need three students with good sets of lungs to blow up a few balloons."

"Don't wanna," Cynthia says, turning into a baby again. She sinks down in her chair like she's melting. **"WAH-H-H,"** she fake-cries, peeking around to see how we're taking it.

"I didn't ask if you wanted to, Miss Harbison," Ms. Sanchez says. She still sounds pretty cheerful, in spite of everything. "And remember," our teacher adds. "This is a science class, not a drama class."

She says that when someone—usually one of the girls—starts acting up.

Wait until Alfie is in her class!

"But I'm feepy," Cynthia says in baby talk, cradling her arms on her desk and putting her head down for a pretend nap.

"Poor widdle baby," Heather says, petting her arm. "So *cute.*"

"Not cute at all," Ms. Sanchez says, snapping out the words. "And *right—now,*" she adds, clicking both fingers as she speaks. "Also, no more baby talk, if you please, ladies—or I'll send out for a few jars of strained lima beans, and we'll see how you like *that.* Hurry," she adds, her usually warm voice turning cool. "Tick-tock."

Uh-oh. There's a high pressure system building up.

Cynthia hurries.

And we begin our three air pressure experiments.

"I liked the trick where Jared and Emma jammed their straw into the potato," Stanley says as we paw through our cubbies, getting out snacks for morning recess.

"We did it using air pressure," Annie Pat points out, shrugging her arms into her jacket. "And it was an experiment, not a trick."

"If you say so," Stanley says, laughing.

"I *do* say so," Annie Pat tells him.

"I liked the trick where Ms. Sanchez made the hard-boiled egg squeeze into the bottle," Jared says. "Like magic. ***POP!***"

"Using air pressure," Annie Pat says again.

Give it up, I think, hiding a smile. I zip up my dark blue San Diego Padres sweatshirt and give my backpack—and the hidden library book inside—a friendly pat. Ms. Sanchez says that the meteorological event happening outside now is that it's drizzling. I can't risk getting drizzle all over the book.

I'll wait until lunch to bring it outside, but it has to happen today.

Because I am running out of time.

Drizzly mornings are perfect for kickball and foursquare, though—and also for yelling and running around. My legs are itching to run, in fact.

"Did you eat your snack yet?" Marco asks, jamming a few little plastic bags into his sweatshirt pouch.

"Most of it," I admit.

"EllRay likes to chow down before school even starts," Corey tells Marco, laughing. "You know. Get it over with so he can play more. He even eats what he's gonna have for lunch, sometimes."

"Hey. I eat half *my* lunch before school," Major says to me, amazed at the coincidence.

"Huh," I say, grinning at him. "I should try that, so I don't starve by the time school is out. Anyway, Corey should talk," I tell Major and Marco, giving Corey a shove. "He's *always* eating. His mom packs him twice as much food as normal, that's the thing. And it's all healthy."

"It's true," Corey tells Marco and Major, a smile spreading across his friendly, freckled face. "I love to eat. And my mom says if you eat healthy, you can eat more."

I look around to see where Diego is, but he's probably already outside, playing.

Your life is about to change for the better, Diego Romero. So get ready!

"I'll share," Marco tells me, keeping his voice low.

"Huh?"

"I'll share my snack with you if you're hungry," he says, repeating the offer. "I've got string cheese in one bag, and some mini muffins in the other bag. My mom made ’em. And I brought some of my knights to play with, too.”

“I like all that stuff,” I admit as we churn out the door.

Okay. My stomach is officially gurgling now.

“You even like the knights?” Marco shouts over the noise in the hall. “I’ve got a couple of dragons, too!”

“He does have dragons,” Major says. “He’ll even share.”

“I *guess* I like them,” I say as we run outside. I scan the playground first for my future friend Diego, who is nowhere to be seen. Then I look for Mr. Havens. He is handing out kickballs slowly, like he’s a Santa Claus who is running out of presents.

Are any kickballs going to be left?

And if there are, will Mr. Havens give me one—after what happened yesterday?

I don’t think so.

“I’ll take a muffin, I guess,” I tell Marco, shrugging. “If you really mean it.”

“Why wouldn’t I mean it?” Marco asks, pulling a plastic bag from his sweatshirt pouch. He hands me not one but *two* little muffins. Yum! I peel the paper off one and cram it into my mouth.

"C'mon, you guys," Corey yells. "It looks like there's only one kickball left—and we gotta score it!"

"Race ya," Major shouts.

"Yeah. Race ya," Marco says.

"Mmph," I say, sputtering muffin crumbs.

And all four of us take off running across the wet playground, our sneakers flashing.

❋ 13 ❋

KEEP-AWAY

"The sun is shining," Kry says at lunchtime, as if we can't see out the window ourselves.

But we don't mind it when she tells us obvious stuff. Everyone likes Kry.

I turn my back to the other kids in the cubby area. I wiggle the foil-wrapped library book out of my backpack. The book is bigger than I remember. But it's flat—compared to yesterday's lumpy roll of toilet paper, anyway.

I slide the wrapped-up library book under my sweatshirt.

There. Do I look perfectly normal?

No, I do not. In fact, I look like I am wearing a bulletproof vest under my sweatshirt, like some guy on a TV show. Or maybe I look like I'm wearing a thin suit of armor. Marco will think I'm a secret knight—but a lot bigger than the plastic ones he sneaks to school.

It's cool being bigger than *something.*

But Diego is gonna think this book is great, so it's all worth it.

I'm just one small step away from having my plan come true. I *am* going to be the recess king! I will invite Diego to come to Alfie's show tomorrow night. Then we'll all go out for pizza—or ice cream. Whichever he likes best.

Especially if it's what Alfie likes best, too.

We'll be friends *for sure.* And then no matter how busy Corey is with swim practice, or how much fun Kevin is having with the neighbor kids, I'll always have a cool spare friend to hang with.

I can work on digging up a spare-spare friend after that, once I rest up from finding this one.

I don't want to brag, but I think I am turning into a good idea guy.

Outside, puffy white clouds are bouncing around the cold blue sky the same way that we kids are bouncing around the playground. "Hey EllRay. Over here," Kevin says from one of the boys' picnic tables. And so I hold the library book in place and trot over, covering my chest the best I can with my lunch bag.

Most of the guys are already at the table. The ones who aren't eating in the cafeteria, anyway. But my theory is that you miss out on too much playground time when you eat in the cafeteria. It just doesn't make sense.

This is Oak Glen, California, after all. Not the North Pole.

Even Jason is sitting at the picnic table, but he's been pretty much ignoring me since yesterday. Oh, well.

"EllRay's running funny," Jared calls out, laughing in his *haw-haw* way.

"Like a girl," Stanley adds. But *he wishes* he could run like Kry Rodriguez does.

Well, he doesn't really wish that. But he is not as good a runner as Kry.

I'm just saying.

"I'm trying to stay warm," I pretend-explain, still hugging my sweatshirt—and the book—to my chest. I squeeze in between Diego and Kevin. Diego is sitting at the end of the bench, which is perfect. I try to paw through my lunch bag with my right hand, while still holding the foil-wrapped library book to my chest with my left hand.

It's at a time like this when a person could use three hands, in my opinion.

All that's left of my lunch is a banana, some cheese squares, and three oatmeal cookies that are so small an elf could munch them down without any problem. That's Mom's latest thing, making food small, especially treats. So an actual person has to eat a ton of them for it to come out right.

Dang, I'm hungry.

But I am also excited, because of my excellent plan.

I slide a miniature oatmeal cookie into my mouth, and the book under my sweatshirt slips a little.

"Watcha got there?" Jared asks, spying a triangle corner of the foil-wrapped book. "Treats?"

Jared is always hungry. Well, most of us guys are. We're like sharks, who are "eating machines," Annie Pat tells us. She wants to be a fish scientist when she grows up, so she knows stuff like that.

As I said before, the best things to eat at Oak Glen Primary School—like leftover birthday cake—usually come wrapped in aluminum foil. So Jared thinks he's really onto something.

"It *is* treats," he tells the whole table of boys. "And EllRay's hogging."

"I am not hogging," I say, my heart starting to thud.

This is not going the way I thought it would, that's for sure. Oh, it's not going *terrible*, because what do I care if the guys in my class discover I checked out a library book about cars? It's not like I sneaked in a Barbie encyclopedia or something.

Which Alfie would just love, by the way.

This was going to be a private thing between Diego and me, but I decide to get it over with. "Look. I'll show you," I tell everyone at the table. I pull out the foil-wrapped book from under my sweatshirt. I start to unwrap a corner while I hold the book up for everyone to see. I sneak a look at Diego. "It's this really cool—"

"Gingerbread!" Jared says, reaching across the table like lightning, and grabbing the foil-wrapped package from my hands. "A whole slab of it! And EllRay wasn't even gonna share!"

Jared untangles himself from the picnic table bench and takes off with his prize, *my book*, shouting, "Gingerbread!" He is holding the library book over his head like a trophy as he runs. Stanley, Jason, and Kevin take off after him, laughing.

Gingerbread? He *saw* part of the cover! And that book's as hard as a rock.

Well, as hard as a book, anyway.

A *library* book.

Taken out in *my name.*

Dollar signs, and scoldings from my parents—*and the librarian*—pop into my head like cartoon thought-balloons. And before I know it, I'm chasing my book's kidnappers, even though chasing Jared is probably exactly what he wants me to do.

But I can't help it.

I don't even look to see if anyone's following me.

"HAW, HAW, HAW," Jared donkey-laughs again, seeing me come after him. He starts shedding pieces of aluminum foil as he runs. He doesn't even care about the litter lecture we're sure to get from Mr. Havens, who is still the substitute recess monitor. I think maybe the regular guy ran away from school.

Where is Mr. Havens, by the way?

"Hey," Jared is shouting now, shaking the library book in his big pink hand as he runs. "What it this, anyway? A *book*?"

He sounds angry, like I really put one over on him.

"Yeah, it's a book, *Einstein*," I yell, pounding after him. "A library book. You can't eat it. So give it here!"

Jared stops for a minute, waggling the book as he holds it out toward me. "Come and get it," he says, in a mocking voice.

And then he hurls it through the air to Stanley, his personal assistant.

"Keep-away!" Jared cries.

"Keep-away," Stanley echoes.

Okay, I think, crouching low like a ninja as I plan my attack. Keep-away is something that is supposed to be a game. Except really, it's usually just big kids being mean to smaller kids.

And unfortunately, today, I happen to be the smaller kid involved.

A really fair "game," right?

Where's Merlyn when you need him? He could turn Jared into a bug!

The script for keep-away never changes. There are only three sure-fire lines.

1. There's "*Keep-away!*" and
2. "*Give it here,*" and
3. "Come and get it!"

That's about it.

Stanley tosses my library book to Jason, and its pages flutter as it flies through the air. "Come and get it," Jason shouts, barely holding onto the book—even though the grassy hill is muddy from the rain.

As if he can read my mind, Jason opens up the book and puts it on his head like a funny hat. "*La-la-la-la-la,*" he chants, prancing around. "Look at me! I'm so *beautiful*. Hope I don't drop this thing. And thanks for gettin' me in trouble yesterday, dude," he adds, being Jason again.

Jason Leffer, who was going to be my new spare friend.

"I didn't mean to," I say, barely aware of the kids moving up behind me. "How did I know that little guy was gonna spring a leak and bring us all down? Come on, Jason. Give it here," I say, holding out my puny Tyrannosaurus-rex hands.

"Keep-away," Jason jeers, tossing the book back to Jared.

It cartwheels through the air in slow motion.

And that's when the kids behind me spring into action. "Get it," Corey shouts, making a side run around Stanley and heading toward Jared. Jared is not a very fast thinker in situations like this.

He's big, but he is "definitely not quarterback material," as my dad would probably put it. We watch a lot of football together.

And out from behind my other side sprint Nate, Major, Marco, Kevin, and Diego. That's a total of six kids on my side. *Six whole kids.*

Seven, counting me. Seven against three!

I had no idea I had so many friends.

There's no time to feel happy about it, though. "Come and get it," Jared shouts for the second time.

But he is now keeping a wary eye on the line of fierce-faced kids heading his way.

Stanley looks like he has changed his mind about the whole keep-away thing, but Jason's still in. *Wow*, he must really be mad at me. "Throw it here," Jason yells to Jared. He claps his hands a couple of times, to warm them up for the big catch, I guess.

So much for pizza and ice cream, dog. And for me teaching you the secrets to *Die, Creature, Die*.

"Don't come any closer," Jared warns my friends, but they creep toward him anyway, like silent warriors. I'm heading his way, too.

We approach our enemy. Like I said, my loyal army consists of:

1. Corey Robinson.
2. Kevin McKinley.
3. Nate Marshall.
4. Major Donaldson.
5. Marco Adair.
6. Diego Romero, my maybe new spare friend.
7. And me, EllRay Jakes.

"Stop right there, or I'm gonna throw this dumb book on the ground," Jared shouts. His eyes look a little wild.

"You can't," Diego says. "That's a library book! It's against the law!"

Like, *"That's that, dude."*

Only that *isn't* that. Not with Jared Matthews, it isn't.

"Oh, yeah?" Jared says. "Well, it's not against *my* law. Watch this, stupid-heads," he says.

And he opens up the book as wide as it will go, hurls it onto the playground, and grinds it into the grass and mud with one gigantic sneaker. "*Take that*," he yells at the book. At the book! How messed-up can you get? "Now, what are you gonna do about it?" he yells at us.

And he beckons us toward him with both hands. Like, *"Bring it."*

And so, even though this was not what we planned, and even though I, for one, do not have a whole lot to bring, we do.

We bring it, I mean.

14

"FIGHT! FIGHT!"

Seven of us is more than three of them. Jared, Jason, and Stanley. So my side is lucky—in numbers, anyway. But the three other guys are larger than us in size and fury. Jared is just plain big and angry, even though I'm thc one who should be mad. Stanley is tall. And, as I mentioned once before, Jason is kind of on the chunky side, even if it is pure muscle, like he says.

Plus, Jason's probably got the whole pay-back thing revving him up, because of our toilet paper adventure yesterday.

All ten of us start to circle, not taking our eyes off one another. And as we pace, the circle gets smaller.

It's getting pretty intense around here.

Jared Matthews is giving me the stink-eye.

Armpit Noise King Marco is scowling at stringbean Stanley and his very plaid shirt.

Stanley is darting his meanest look from Marco to Major, then back to Marco again. He probably can't remember which one's which.

Buzz-cut Jason is staring hard at Corey Robinson. Corey is pale but determined-looking under the three hundred freckles on his face. It sometimes seems like Corey is made out of pipe cleaners, but the whole class knows how strong he is from all that swimming.

It looks like Diego Romero is "reading Jared like a book," as my Dad sometimes says. I think that means Diego knows what's up with Jared and his hot-headed ways.

And Nate's red rooster crest of hair is almost standing at attention as he shifts his furious glare from Jared to Jason to Stanley. Nate's hands are even clenched like rooster claws. He is ready to pounce.

Yoo-hoo! Mr. Havens! Where are you? Getting a nice energy drink?

Our circle keeps getting smaller, like it's a spring winding tighter and tighter. It's about to go **BOING**. Pretty soon there will be no place left to go, and nothing else to do but fight—which means we'll be busted big-time.

Listen. *Running in the halls* is against the rules at Oak Glen Primary School.

Not rinsing out your milk carton before recycling it is against the rules.

You can probably guess how they feel about playground brawls around here!

I'll admit it. Part of me wouldn't *mind* fighting, not after what Jared did to my very expensive library book, which, P.S., I will now have to pay for. It wasn't the book's fault that it wasn't a sweet and crumbly slab of gingerbread, was it?

But I don't like the getting-in-trouble part that comes *after* a fight.

Not to mention what will happen to me at home. Because basically, you can at least double any scolding I get at school, and you'll be close to what happens when my mom and dad get hold of any bad news about me.

Also, fighting won't help my wrecked library book any, will it?

I think about mom and dad. I also think about how boring it is, circling around and around like the ants in *The Sword in the Stone*, who are always getting ready for war—even though they don't know why. I try to plot how to get out of this goofy situation without looking like a chicken or a fool. But just when my brain starts to ***TICK, TICK, TICK,*** trying to come up with an idea, the dreaded words come floating across the playground. "Fight! Fight!"

The older boys have spotted us. And almost *all* the lunch kids on the playground race toward us. Nobody wants to miss a moment of this stupendous, ten-person battle, even though we are only third-graders.

If it actually happens, our fight will make Oak Glen Primary School history.

And not in a good way.

"Fight! Fight!"

Okay, here is the embarrassing truth about the whole **"FIGHT! FIGHT!"** thing.

1. If the kids who are mad are still throwing stink-eyes and making threats after five minutes, not pounding on each other, they are about ready for the whole thing to be finished, in my opinion. Not

because they're scared, but because they're over it. Face it. Other stuff is more fun. And how long can a person stay mad?

2. But then *other* kids see what's happening, and they gather. They say things like, *"Go ahead! Hit 'im!"* Because what do *those kids* care if the fighting kids get in trouble? It's just more entertainment for them!

3. That's when it's hard for fighting kids to back down, though. Even if they really *are* over the whole thing.

   Like I am here, now.

   That's when it takes guts to stop.

4. So, what's a kid supposed to do? Especially when there are no grown-ups around?

Hope that energy drink is extra good today, Mr. Havens!

And—***FWUMP.***

I'm flat on the ground.

Then, **BAM, BAM, BAM**. Other guys pile on top of me. It's like we are making a sky-high, noisy, third-grade kid sandwich.

OOF!

I can hear the older kids hooting and jeering at us.

A few of us third-graders *are* trying to fight a little, or we're pretending to. It's like we have to put on enough of a show to satisfy the older kids—even though we're so mooshed together we can barely move. I have hold of one of Jason's sticking-out ears. Corey is growling. And some other kid—

probably Jared—is twisting my sweatshirt so tight that it's like he's trying to wring me out.

And then, **FWOOSH**.

Jared seems to fly off me, leaving my sweatshirt wrinkled, but in one piece.

Corey disappears from the pile, too.

Jason, Stanley, and Kevin have been lifted off as well, and now it's easier to breathe. What is happening?

Even though I am still on the ground, I peek around for a clue.

And I see several pairs of grown-up feet.

Mr. Havens is here, hoisting kids off the pile left and right, and so is Principal James. And even Miss Myrna, the little old lady who helps out in the auditorium.

How embarrassing.

All the big kids have disappeared, of course. They seem to have melted into the playground.

And all that's left is goofy, guilty *us*.

"Okay," Principal James says. "Break it up. Break it up."

I feel like explaining to him that there isn't really anything to break up. This whole thing was just a keep-away game gone wrong! And then, when we were facing off, we kind of got forced into a fake fight by the big kids.

"I turn my back for *one minute*," Mr. Havens says, holding tight onto Marco's shoulder, as if he might run away at any second.

And go where, Mr. Havens?

I get to my feet one sore inch at a time.

"It's not your fault, Mr. Havens," Miss Myrna is saying, trying to make the second grade teacher feel better, I guess. "You were taking care of Little Miss Nosebleed, over by the swings."

Wait. They have *nicknames* for us? That's messed-up!

I wonder what *my* nickname is?

B-Z-Z-Z-Z-Z! The buzzer sounds.

"In my office, each and every one of you boys," Principal James says in a voice that tells us we'd better not argue. Like we *would*! "Miss Myrna," he adds. "Please go tell Ms. Sanchez that she'll be missing a few students for a while. I'm sure she'll be interested to hear how they spent their lunch break. Now, march," he tells us, like we're soldiers. Or prisoners, maybe. That's more like it.

"Can I get my library book?" I find the courage to ask, trying to keep my voice steady, in spite of all the trouble I'm in. "It, um, fell. It's on the ground over there," I add, pointing.

"And that, Mr. Jakes, is why we don't eat lunch with library books," Principal James says, his beard bristling. "Grab it fast, and then follow me."

So I do, and I do.

We *all* do.

We follow Principal Harry—*Hairy*—James, I mean.

Left, right. Left, right. Left, right.

Off to meet our doom.

15

BIRDS OF A FEATHER

"We covered for you yesterday, dog. So you better not tell," Jared says to me under his breath. We are making our way toward the school building, following Principal James like—well, like a bunch of bad geese who have been placed under arrest. You know, geese. Like in *The Sword in the Stone.*

"Yeah," Stanley and Jason chime in.

"Dudes. You don't have to threaten me," I say, shaking my head. "If I was going tattle on you guys, wouldn't I have already done it? Principal James asked what happened. And I didn't blab."

Jared looks like he can't remember back that far. It's been three whole minutes, after all. But hey, he's still one of the flock. Or "herd," as Cynthia would say.

"Yeah," Marco says, backing me up. "EllRay

would have already blabbed. And he *didn't*."

Corey, Kevin, and Major nod, backing him up.

Diego and Nate just keep plodding along.

"I told Principal James the book fell on the ground, remember?" I tell Jared, Stanley, and Jason, and whoever else is listening. "*I'm* the one who got yelled at for bringing a library book to lunch. *I'm* the one who's gonna have to pay it off for the next ten years. Not to mention what happens when my mom and dad find out," I add, shuddering.

"What *about* your mom and dad?" Stanley asks as we start down the hall.

"You think they're not gonna get mad at me about this?" I ask. "Have you *met* them?"

"They're kinda strict," Corey says, cluing Stanley in.

He should talk! Corey's mom runs his whole life, practically. But this is no time to pick a fight with my one-and-only friend. That would *really* mess things up.

All I wanted in the first place was *more* friends. And I wanted them bad!

I *need* more friends, so I will always have someone to hang with after school and on weekends. Someone to play video games with. Stuff is just more fun that way.

Also, this may sound weird, but I want Alfie to think I'm at least a little bit popular. I'm her *big brother.* And she'll be in kindergarten here soon. I don't want her to think Oak Glen Primary School is a tough place for us Jakes kids to make friends.

Like I said before, I look out for my little sister.

Jason doesn't seem at all interested in being my friend, though. Not after yesterday. And Diego is off in his own daydreamy world again. He never even noticed the book!

That leaves me with no one but almost-always-too-busy Corey, who I've kind of been ignoring lately. I admit it.

"Into the office," the head secretary says, shooing us with her hands.

"All ten of us?" I ask, surprised. Because usually, from what I hear, Principal James likes to talk to kids one at a time when there's trouble. It's probably so they can't all grab onto some fake story like it's a life-raft that might save them all.

"That's right," the secretary says. "Each and every one of you."

And so in we go, in clumps:

1. Jared Matthews, Stanley Washington, Kevin McKinley, and Jason Leffer.
2. Diego Romero and Nate Marshall.
3. Major Donaldson and Marco Adair.
4. And Corey and me. Or I.

There are two visitors' chairs in Principal James's office, but none of us kids sits down. Nobody wants to look that permanent, in my opinion.

"Eyes front, gentlemen," Principal James says from behind the desk. He raps his stapler on it to get our attention—which he already has, believe me.

I think he's being sarcastic, calling us "gentlemen," by the way. But it's hard to tell, with that beard on his face.

"Now, we have a problem," he begins—and I wait for him to ask who did what.

Grownups don't usually care about the "why" or "when" parts all that much.

But I don't think anyone's gonna blab.

"Birds of a feather flock together." My mom told me that once. It's an old saying from at least five hundred years ago, in England, she said. She was explaining the geese in *The Sword in the Stone* to me at the time. But I think the guys in my class are going to flock together today, too.

Especially since that's what we did yesterday.

"EllRay?" Principal James begins. "You were at the bottom of the pile, and your book got ruined. So I guess you are the injured party here. Do you have something to say?"

"I'm not injured," I tell him really fast. "I was just smooshed, that's all. Everyone was. We were only playing, see."

"I meant that your *book* was damaged," Principal James says, his glasses glittering. "Your library book—which is city property, by the way."

"Oh," I say, holding what's left of the book against my muddy sweatshirt. I am trying to think fast. "It was just an accident, like I said. The book fell," I try to explain.

"It looks like a steamroller ran over it," the principal says. "Nothing to report?"

"Nope," I say, shaking my head again.

If this was a bullying thing, I would speak right up. Maybe not here, in front of everyone. But if some kid was getting pushed around, I'd speak up for sure. You just *need* to.

Everyone knows that, nowadays.

But today, at lunch, that was just us guys "getting carried away."

That's how my mom sometimes puts it when Alfie and I are throwing pillows at each other, and we break a lamp or something. "It was on accident," Alfie always says, making everything worse—because you're supposed to say *"by accident."*

At my house, you can sometimes do stuff wrong, as long as you say it right.

"Then we'll move on to *my* problem," Principal James tells us through his beard, yanking my thoughts back to what's happening now. "Want to know what my problem is?"

"Yeah." "Sure." "I guess," a few of us mutter. The rest of us just nod or stare down at our muddy sneakers.

But Principal James isn't really waiting for our answer. "*My* problem is that I want our playground to be a nice, safe place for everyone to be," he tells us. "Both at recess, and during lunch. Right?"

"Right," one or two kids squawk. It's like they've been hypnotized into saying the correct thing.

But Principal James is not even listening. "So," he continues. "When the playground is *not* a nice, safe place for everyone, what are my options?"

For one crazy second I'm afraid Corey is going to raise his hand and ask what the word "options" means, but he doesn't. I think he may be paralyzed by fear. He has never been in this much trouble before.

You can see every freckle on his face, he is so pale.

"I *suppose* I could cancel third grade recess altogether, *forever*," Principal James says. He taps his hairy chin as he pretends to come up with this great choice. Or *option.*

Kevin squeaks, I guess at the thought of going an entire morning or afternoon without recess. Recess is his favorite part of the day! Jared nudges him to shut up.

We're not allowed to *say* "shut up" at Oak Glen, but we can nudge it.

"And for lunch," Principal James continues, "maybe I should assign each of you boys a seat in the cafeteria. You can sit boy, girl, boy, girl. And after eating, you can march straight back to class and practice your vocabulary words, instead of playing outside. How does that sound? Is *that* the solution to my problem?"

Don't answer him, I brain-wave to Cody. *It's not a real question, dog.*

Luckily, Cody is still frozen where he stands.

"For reals?" Stanley finally asks, as if all hope is lost.

"Not necessarily," Principal James says. "But I think you can see where I'm going with this," he adds. He leans forward.

Not really, I think as Major and Marco take a small step back. Because—is this what Principal James is really gonna do, or not?

"Do I have to spell it out?" our principal asks.

Spell it out. Spell it out. Spell it out, I think, now trying to brain-wave Principal James, of all people.

"Okay, here's the deal," the principal says. He

holds out his big skinny hands palms up, like he's giving us a present. "We can let what happened today slide, if—and only if—you vow never to let it happen again. No more destruction of private property on my playground. No more pile-ups. And no more fights, or I *will* crack down. And I know you know I mean it. Do you understand me? Do you *vow*?"

Jason puts his hand on his chest like he's saying the Pledge of Allegiance. "I vow," he announces in a shaky voice.

And he's not even joking, for once.

"*Dude*," Jared says, now giving *him* an elbow in the ribs.

"You have an objection, Mr. Matthews?" Principal James asks Jared.

"Nuh-uh," Jared mumbles.

"Excuse me?" the principal asks, cupping a hand to his ear.

"No objection, sir," Jared says, louder this time.

"So, vow," Principal James says.

"*We vow*," we all say in union.

"Excellent," Principal James says, getting to his

feet. "Now, you can all walk *quietly* back to class," he tells us. "Miss Myrna will accompany you. And each of you will thank her when you get there."

Nobody argues.

"Parents *may* be notified about this," the principal continues. "And you boys will miss afternoon recess today. You need to make up this morning's work. But, good news! I'll come supervise, so Ms. Sanchez can still have her break. There's no reason she should have to suffer for your bad choices."

Wait. He *might* tell our parents? That's worse than saying he *will* tell them! It means we will have to tell them first, just in case. And maybe for *no reason*.

And he's going to supervise us *in class* all during recess?

I thought we were home free—with just a scolding!

"Any problems with that? Any dissent? Any *discussion*?" Principal James asks, hand cupped to his ear again.

"Naw. We're good," Nate says, speaking for all of us.

"Excellent," Principal James says, smiling. "Until we meet again, gentlemen."

We just stand there and stare at him.

"I think that means we can leave," I finally tell everyone.

And so down the hall we go. Quietly, just like Miss Myrna tells us to do.

Man, what a terrible Thursday.

16

NERVOUS

"Pile in, honey," Mom says later that afternoon, through the partly open passenger side car window.

It has started raining again, so I am glad to do it. But when I open the rear door, I am surprised to see a wall of plastic-wrapped toilet paper between my seat and Alfie's. "I'm over here, EllWay," she calls out. "Don't wowwy."

Which means "*worry.*" Too bad Cynthia, Heather, and Fiona missed out on that one today, on Baby Talk Thursday.

Another two huge packages of TP are on the car floor in front of Alfie. They are basically blocking her in. Sweet!

"We don't even need seat-belts anymore," Alfie tells me.

"Yes, you do," Mom says from the front seat. "Buckle up," she reminds me.

"I'm buckled," I say. "You went shopping."

Now *I'm* Einstein.

"Sure did," Mom says, signaling to pull away from the curb.

"Did you get any fun stuff?" I ask. "Is it in the trunk?"

"Nuh-uh," Alfie calls out, answering the question. "This is it. And it's a present for your school!"

"Alfie," Mom pretend-scolds. "It was supposed to be a surprise. I got a few families to make donations," she explains to me.

Oh, geez.

"I'm not even *going* to kindergarten if they don't have toilet paper when I get there," Alfie announces from behind her cushiony wall. "And nobody can make me," she adds. Just for good measure, I guess.

She's pretty brave when she's inside a TP fortress.

I shrink back into my seat. "How many other families did you call?" I ask my mom.

"Oh, three or four," Mom says, her signal ***TICK-TICK-TICKING*** as she changes lanes. "But I left messages on a couple of other answering machines. One of the families has a big van, so they'll be picking up all the packages over the weekend. We'll surprise Principal James with it on Monday morning."

You sure will, I think, imagining the scene. Pretty soon, I'll be able to find my way to his office with a blindfold on. "*Mom,*" I say, trying to sound normal. "Why?"

"How can you even ask?" Mom says, flashing me a smile in the rearview mirror. "I'm not going to let you children get tummyaches and what-not because you don't want to use the bathrooms at school."

"I never said kids were getting tummyaches," I remind her. "And those aren't even gonna fit," I mumble, looking at the plump rolls of paper. I picture the silver metal boxes that hold the waxy squares of TP we use at school.

"We'll solve each problem as it arises," Mom promises me. "Parent power, EllRay. We are here for your school! Never fear."

I chew my lower lip. One or two problems are going to come up a little sooner than she is expecting, I think. Like the truth about Oak Glen Primary School's so-called toilet paper shortage, for one.

And what happened to my expensive library book today, for two.

But I'll just let it all unroll naturally—like a really long piece of soft white paper.

What choice do I have?

"Um, listen. There's something I have to say," I tell Mom and Dad after dinner. The three of us are still sitting at the table. Alfie asked to be excused so she could squeeze in some horsie time before her bath.

"I thought there might be," Mom says. "The state you came home in."

"What? *California*?" I ask, frowning, because—what state did she *expect* me to come home in?

Dad clears his throat a couple of times.

"No. Covered in mud," Mom explains. "And looking like you lost your best friend in the world. Rough day, honey?"

If she gets any nicer, I'm gonna start crying.

Wait until she hears what *really* happened—apart from the whole mummy zombie thing, which they already know about.

1. First, there's the TP-shortage-at-school misunderstanding. Okay, fib. Okay, lie.
2. And then there's me sneaking that library book into school.
3. This is followed by the book getting ruined. Oh, and by ten of us boys getting called into Principal James's office for supposedly fighting during lunch.

Not to mention the complete failure of my spare friend goal—and what a bad example I'm setting for Alfie. You know, about making friends in primary school.

Mom's not gonna be so nice to me *then.*

"A rough *two* days," I say. I brush a few crumbs from the table into my hand. I look around, not knowing what to do with them. So I eat them.

"Want to talk about it here? Now?" Dad asks. "Or should the three of us meet in the family room in half an hour, after Alfie gets tucked into bed?"

In *half an hour*? What planet is my dad living on? Getting Alfie into bed takes forever. She is the world's slowest bath-taker, for one thing. First, you have to talk her *into* the tub. And then she won't get *out,* she's having so much fun. Also, Alfie has a ton of nighty-night routines that have to go just right, or she'll say she can't sleep.

Or let anyone else sleep, either.

But even though I'm the one who told Mom and Dad we should talk, I'm nervous about it. So I don't mind the delay.

"We can wait," I tell my dad.

"EllRay," Mom says, leaning forward as if she just got the best idea in the world. "You go talk to your little sister, okay? Just kind of ease her toward the idea of bath-time. Get her calmed down. She's all excited about the show tomorrow at Kreative Learning and Daycare."

"Listen. We all are," Dad says, and Mom starts to giggle.

"Warren," she says, giving him a look.

"I am *not* giving her a bath, even if it's an emergency," I inform my mom. "*Or* staying in the bathroom with her when she's in the tub, either. So please don't ask me to."

"Not a problem, buddy," Dad says, laughing.

"That's right, honey-bun," Mom agrees. "I'm just asking you to talk to Alfie in her room. Ask her how the *Brown Bear, Brown Bear* rehearsal went today. That sort of thing."

"I guess I could talk to her," I tell them.

Maybe I can really drag it out, I think, already plotting. *I know.* I'll ask Alfie what it's like being the red bird in the skit. I mean in the *play.*

That ought to chew up an hour or two.

With any luck, Mom and Dad will be too tired to meet later in the family room. And they will never find out what's been happening at school.

But at least I can say I tried to tell them.

17

MR. BRIGHT IDEA

"Knock, knock," I say at Alfie's bedroom door.

"Come in," Alfie says. "*I see a lellow duck looking at me*," she announces in a loud and gloomy voice as I enter her room. "That's my whole speech for tomowwow. *Supposedly,*" she adds. "And then I have to just stand there quietly and pwetend I'm listening to everyone else," she finishes, shaking her head in disgust.

Yeah. *That's* gonna happen. And she's mixing up her Ls and Ys again, like she did a couple of years ago. Is it going to be Baby Talk Friday at Kreative Learning and Daycare tomorrow night?

Alfie is wearing striped leggings, a tutu, and a shrunken T-shirt. In other words, she is not ready to take a bath. Instead, she is putting two of her plastic horses to bed—but on their sides, under a tiny quilt. "Want to practice your speech again?" I ask. "You were perfect, Alfie," I tell her. "Only it's '*yellow*,' not '*lellow*.' Remember how you learned to say it? '*Yes, yes,* yellow.'"

"*Yes, yes,* lellow," Alfie repeats, as if she's cooperating with me. "There. Are you happy now, Ell-Way?"

"Sure," I say, sitting down next to her on the fluffy rug.

I'm happy except for the part where I have to tell Mom and Dad what's been going on at school, that is. Let Alfie say her line however she wants—as long as she doesn't wreck the skit. Or embarrass Mom and Dad. "Hey, Alf," I say. "You know what would be fun?" Mr. Bright Idea, here.

"What?"

"A bath," I say. "A *bubble* bath. With lots of toys."

"Go ahead and take one, then," Alfie says, shrugging. "Only don't play with my seahorse."

"I meant *you*," I tell her. **YEESH!**

"I'm busy," Alfie says, and she tugs up the horses' quilt under their chins—if horses even have chins. "Is a fwend coming with you to my *Brown Bear* show?" she asks, looking up. "Like maybe Corey?"

Alfie *loves* Corey. He told her once that her shoes were pretty, and that was it for her.

"He can't come," I say. "He has to get up early the next day, when it's still dark out, because of swimming. So he has to go to bed right after dinner, almost."

"Aw," she says, drooping. "Who wants to swim in the wain?"

That's *"In the rain."*

"I think there's a big roof over the aquatics center," I say. "But I have lots of other friends who might come," I fib. "I was gonna ask Jason Leffer, but—but that didn't work out," I fumble. "He was busy."

Okay, it's a lie, but just a little one. Jason *has* been busy, *trying to avoid me*, ever since the toilet paper thing.

"Huh," Alfie says. "*I see a lellow duck looking at me.*"

"Then I thought maybe Diego Romero could come," I say, ignoring the news about the nosy yellow duck. "Only he's already doing something."

Reading, probably. And staying away from kids who wreck library books.

Some recess king *I* turned out to be!

"Huh," Alfie says again. "I don't even know him. But sometimes Suzette and Mona and Arletty are too busy for me, too." She droops even more.

Those are her three best friends at Kreative Learning and Daycare.

"But only *sometimes*," I point out. "Because you play with them a lot. Mostly one at a time."

"I play with Arletty, anyway," Alfie agrees. "She gets to be the green fwog in our play. That big *lucky*."

"That's cool," I say. I'm wondering when I can give up and leave.

Bath or no bath—*I* don't care!

And maybe Mom and Dad have forgotten all about the whole "There's-something-I-have-to-tell-you" thing. Which was my own bright idea, of course.

Another good one, EllRay.

"Alfie-kins," Mom says, popping her head into the room. "Bath's all ready, sweetheart. Come with me."

"But I'm putting my horsies to bed," Alfie says.

I can tell she's not really into the argument, though—and that bath-time will happen in a couple of minutes, tops.

Mom gives me a wink and a thumbs-up as I slip out the door.

18

BRAIN SPLINTER

"So, EllRay," Dad says in the family room, his feet propped up in front of him on the long part of the sofa. We are waiting for Mom, who is now trying to get Alfie *out* of the tub, just like I said would happen. "What's up at school? Still leading a rich, full life?"

"I wouldn't say 'rich,'" I begin, thinking of my allowance.

But now's not the time to complain about that, the last logical speck of my brain informs me. Not when there are so many bad things I have to tell him.

In fact, I have *way too much* to tell my mom and dad. The fake TP shortage. The wrecked library book. Us boys fighting during lunch. Well, Mom and Dad might already know about that, thanks to Principal James and his horrible "parents may be notified" threat. In my opinion, that's about ten times worse than yelling, *"I'm gonna tell!"*

I don't think Principal James called, though. That's one good thing. Because if he *had* called, Dad would not be asking, "What's up at school?" He'd be saying, "*What in the world is going on over at Oak Glen Primary School*?" in a very loud voice.

"EllRay?" Dad asks again. "School?"

Okay. Go.

"There have been some problems," I begin, fidgeting in my seat. "Well, *a* problem," I correct myself, thinking of my quest to make at least one new, spare friend by the end of January. I should start with that.

But—instant complication! Because I don't want Dad thinking I'm not popular.

See, that's the whole "brain splinter" thing I was talking about earlier. Like, *my* brain splinter is that I'm the shortest kid in the third grade. And no matter how tall I'm gonna grow later, which Mom and Dad keep promising I will, that doesn't change my shortness now.

1. I can do great on my vocabulary words for the week, but I'm still short.
2. Everyone can laugh at a joke I tell, but I'm still short.
3. I can beat my personal best at *Die, Creature, Die* but I'm still short.

It's always there, like a splinter in my brain.

And, as I said before, my *dad's* brain splinter is that there aren't more brown faces—*families*—around Oak Glen. And he's the one who really wanted us to move here.

So I think one small part of his gigantic brain is always secretly afraid that kids might pick on Alfie and me because our skin is brown.

Well, not afraid. Not Dad. More like *alert.*

But *also* like I said before, and as I have recently proven, there are other reasons for kids to get irked at me.

And Alfie's no picnic either. No offense.

"Finally," Mom says, gliding into the family room. Her clothes are still wet from Alfie's bath. She flings herself onto the other end of the sofa and sighs. "Honestly," she says. "I don't know whether it'll be better or worse when she turns five."

"Probably better," I say, looking on the bright side. I'm about to remind her that *I* turned out pretty well, didn't I? But then I remember why we're all sitting here. "Or maybe not," I say. I grab for a small round pillow and clutch it to my chest like it's a life preserver.

My mom puts little pillows all over the place.

Before even starting to talk again, I decide to skip the making-a-new-friend part of my story. It's too complicated and personal to explain.

I clear my throat. "So, there are three things I want to talk about."

Mom beams a smile in my direction. "Oh, I just love how you're so organized sometimes, EllRay," she says. "You and your lists."

Typical Mom.

"What three things?" my father asks. He is holding very still, probably so that his brain splinter won't start poking him. See, he's already imagining the worst!

Typical Dad.

"Okay," I say. But I feel like I'm sinking to the bottom of a very deep pool, life preserver or no life preserver. "I'll just start. First, there is no toilet paper shortage at Oak Glen Primary School. I never said there *was* one, not really. I just wanted to bring a roll of TP to school for—well, for kind of a joke."

Mom's golden-brown eyes are wide as she takes this in. She is probably picturing the hundreds of rolls of toilet paper she has gotten the other parents to buy. She must also be imagining the embarrassing phone calls she will have to make. "But—but—but—" she sputters.

"You certainly let your mother *think* there was a

shortage," Dad rumbles. Then he turns to my mom. "Obviously, that roll of toilet paper he brought to school was what led to the whole Curse of the Mummy Zombie thing, Louise. But let's let him continue. Go on, son," he says, turning back to me.

Dad just called me "son." I *am* his son, of course, but still, it's not a good sign.

"There's also that library book you let me check out," I say, turning to face Mom. Mom the Merciful, I hope. "I decided to bring it to school," I tell her. "Okay, *sneak* it to school. But I had a really good reason," I add. "And I wrapped the book in aluminum foil so it couldn't even *think* about getting wet. I was taking *really good care of it.*"

"Even though it's against our family rules to bring a library book to school?" Mom asks. "Why, EllRay?"

"Well, I brought it to—to show someone," I say. "Only Ja—I mean, only *this other kid* thought it was gingerbread."

YEESH, I think, starting to sweat a little. I almost gave away Jared's name, after they all stuck up for me yesterday! That's not "flocking together."

And there's no point in getting anyone *else* in trouble around here, is there?

"Gingerbread," Dad repeats, giving me a look.

"I'm not even kidding, Dad," I say. "Gingerbread. And then this strange kid came out of nowhere and grabbed the book from me. And all of a sudden, the whole thing turned into a game of keep-away."

Jared *is* strange. Sometimes, anyway. So that's not a lie.

"Keep-away," Dad says.

I nod. "Only, when the guy found out the book *wasn't* gingerbread, it fell on the ground," I try to explain. "By accident. I don't know, it happened really fast. But I'll pay the library back," I say. "Every penny."

By now, Mom and Dad are just staring at me. "Is that it?" Dad finally asks.

"Only one more thing," I tell him. I mean them. "There was kind of a fake fight after the book accidentally fell in the mud."

"How do you have a fake fight?" Mom asks. She looks confused.

"A bunch of us *were* mad at each other," I admit.

I am trying to be as honest as I can. Well, almost. "And we were kind of *pretending* we were gonna fight. But then some big kids saw us, and started yelling, 'Fight, fight!' So we really had to. Fight, I mean."

"Who's 'we'?" Dad asks.

"Oh, most of us boys," I say, not wanting to be a tattle-tale. "But a lot of them were on my side. Corey, Kevin, and Nate. Major and Marco."

"Marco Adair?" my mom asks. "I met his mother at Visitor's Day. What a lovely woman."

"Yeah, Marco's really nice, too," I agree. "He's been sticking up for me a lot, lately, come to think of it."

"But you guys didn't have to fight," Dad informs me. "This was all about the library book, and nothing more? Because somehow, I'm not buying it."

Brain splinter.

And "I'm not buying it" means he thinks I'm lying. Or at least leaving something out, which I am. But it's not what he thinks.

"I guess the fight was also because the book wasn't gingerbread," I say, trying to remember. "It's kind of hard to explain."

"Apparently so," Dad says. "So is *that* it?"

"That's it," I say.

That's it until tomorrow, anyway. Until my next goof-up.

Dad runs his hands back through what is left of his hair. "I'd like to hear the part of the story you're leaving out, son," he says after one long, quiet minute.

"But I'm not—"

"Because *why* would you suddenly change from good old reliable EllRay Jakes into this—this absolute *gold mine* of bad ideas?" he asks. "In just the last two or three days? Swiping household supplies," he begins, like he's reading from a list. "Making a mess on the playground. Disobeying family rules about library books. Ruining public property. And getting goaded into a lunch-time brawl by a bunch of yahoos."

"I didn't *swipe* the toilet paper," I remind him. "I asked Mom, and she said yes."

"EllRay," Dad says. "What is going on?"

I think my mom is holding her breath. I can't even look at her.

"I—I only wanted to make another friend," I

manage to say, finally spitting out the truth. "A spare," I mumble. "So I came up with my recess king plan."

"Your recess king plan," Dad says. He is turning into an echo chamber tonight.

"But honey," Mom says to me. "You already have *lots* of friends."

"No offense, but you only think that because you're my mom," I inform her. "I have exactly one-and-a-half good, solid friends," I say. "Corey, and half of Kevin. Except Corey's busy with swimming most of the time. And me not having enough friends isn't setting a very good example for Alfie, is it?" I ask, the words spilling out of me now.

"What does *Alfie* have to do with any of this?" Dad asks, frowning big-time.

"She wanted me to bring a friend to her show tomorrow night," I try to explain. "And I couldn't think of anyone."

"Oh," Mom says. She—frowns, thinking.

"Other kids have *lots* of friends, Mom," I interrupt. "Tons of them. And no," I say, turning to face my dad. "*This is not because I have brown skin.*

Or because I'm short," I add, surprising myself. "I guess it's because I'm *me*."

Wow. Does that make things worse, or what?

"I don't understand where this is coming from," Mom says. "You get along with everyone, EllRay. Most of the time, at least. And everyone gets along with you. Believe me, I would have heard about it, otherwise."

"And no," Dad chimes in. "Other kids do *not* all have 'tons of friends,' as you put it. In fact, I think just about every kid in the world thinks other kids are swimming in friends." He shrugs. "And as I just told you, the answer is no, they aren't."

Huh, I think, wondering if what he just said could possibly be true. "I don't want to *swim* in friends," I tell him. "I just want a couple of spares, that's all."

"To set a good example for Alfie," Dad says, repeating my earlier words.

Does he think I'm lying?

"Look. Everyone's tired," Dad says. "We can sort out all these incidents over the weekend, after things have calmed down around here."

"Can't I just find out my punishment now?" I ask. "And get that part over with? Or I won't be able to sleep."

"Tell you what," Dad says. He gets to his feet in a that's-that kind of way. "You start thinking about how you're going to earn the money to pay for, say, half the cost of that library book. That ought to keep you busy for a while. And no more wacky recess king schemes, okay?"

I nod, hiding a sigh.

"EllRay, listen," Mom says. "I've got an idea. What about asking that boy Marco to come over tomorrow night. He sounds like someone you'd have fun with.

And she's right. I think I *would* have fun with Marco. He's been really nice to me lately.

1. Marco tried to tell Ms. Sanchez that the grass wasn't all that dirty when little Iggy collapsed on the ground during the zombie fiasco.
2. He shared his mini muffins with me at recess—and his dragons, too.
3. He even stood up for me in Principal James's office.

Why didn't I think of Marco before now? Just because he's friends with Major doesn't mean he can't be friends with me, too!

"You could call him, EllRay," Mom says. "I have their number in the other room. Call him now and invite him to spend the night tomorrow. We'll have a ball, I promise. I can talk to Mrs. Adair after you talk to him and we can work out the details."

"Just don't tell him he's Marco-Adair-the-Spare," Dad advises. "You should keep that little nugget to yourself."

Which I will.

"Okay," I say, bouncing to my feet like an EllRay cloud that just got lifted up by a gust of wind.

Because—*dude.*

Marco might be coming over!

19

BRAND-NEW EYES

"Hey, Alfie," I say in the back seat of the car the next morning on the way to school. "I'm bringing a friend to your show tonight."

"Shh. I'm busy pwacticing inside my bwain," Alfie says, scowling.

That's "*practicing inside my brain.*" Rehearsing her one line.

"Don't you want to know who I'm bringing?" I ask. "I'll tell you his nickname," I whisper, "It's 'the armpit noise king.'" And I make the noise with my tongue and lips as quietly as I can.

"Eww," Alfie says, but she's smiling big.

And I thought liking stuff like that was just a guy thing! I guess four-year-olds get it, too. "And you're bwinging Corey?" Alfie asks.

"I already told you, he can't come," I say. "This is a new friend."

I like the sound of those words. *"A new friend."* Just like I planned.

Okay, maybe not *exactly* as I planned—or even close, really. Because as of today, Friday, both Jason Leffer and Diego Romero are farther away from wanting to hang with me than ever before.

But that might change some day. You never know!

And Marco counts, doesn't he?

Just because I didn't plan it this way doesn't mean it's not cool!

"I see a lellow duck looking at me," Alfie says.

"That's 'yellow,'" I say. "Remember? *'Yes, yes,* yellow.'"

"EllRay," Mom warns from the front seat as she nears Kreative Learning and Daycare. "Okay, Miss Alfie," she says a minute later, sounding cheerful and matter-of-fact as can be. "Out you hop."

"That's *Arletty* who gets to hop," Alfie grumbles as I help her with the seatbelt. "Because she's the frog. That lucky."

"Now, I'm picking you up at two-thirty, remember," Mom tells Alfie, quickly changing the subject. She's had a lot of practice doing that. "We'll dash home for a fabulous snack," Mom continues. "And then you can take a rest before the big show."

"Where's her costume?" I ask, looking around the back seat.

"I turned it in yesterday afternoon," Mom half whispers, getting out of the car. "Miss Nancy is really on top of things this year," she adds as she opens Alfie's door.

"But she's not the boss of me," Alfie says, scrambling out of her car seat.

"Actually, she is," I point out. "At school, anyway."

Alfie had better not make that mistake at Oak Glen Primary School next year!

"Alfie knows that," Mom tells me, laughing as she straightens my sister's little pink jacket. She tweaks Alfie's braids. "She's only teasing, EllRay."

But I'm not so sure.

Tonight might be more entertaining than Mom and Dad are thinking it will be.

It's like I am looking around Oak Glen Primary School with brand-new eyes as I walk onto the sunny playground this morning.

Maybe it's because I don't know what's going to happen today!

I have no secret goal. I am not trying to move other kids around like checkers, making them want to be friends with me. There's just—*right now.*

It's a very relaxing feeling.

I already learned this week that *bad* things can happen even if you think you have made a really good plan. ***SURPRISE!***

But now, I know that *good* things can also happen without me having to come up with some goofy scheme—like my brilliant recess king idea.

Marco Adair wants to be friends with me. I didn't even have to trick him into it!

"Hi, EllRay," Corey shouts from way over by the playground shed. It looks like he has been showing off his mad paddleboard skills to Major. Luckily, Mr. Hale is busy at the swings, where someone—Little Miss Nosebleed again?—is having an emergency.

"Hi," I yell. I toss my backpack onto one of the boys' picnic tables. **THUNK!**

I look around with my new eyes. Diego and Nate are huddled together at the end of another picnic table. They are probably talking about cars.

Well, why not? They both like 'em.

I'm not even jealous.

Well, not *very*.

Behind the picnic tables, Jared, Kevin, and Stanley are hanging from the chain-link fence like bats, only not upside-down. Jared is higher than the other two, of course. But so what? Jared likes to be the boss, and I guess Kevin and Stanley don't mind being bossed. Every so often, anyway.

Me, not so much.

But it's like that with us guys. We're different from the girls in my class. They can take sides, hold grudges, and have invisible wars for days, and not even Ms. Sanchez knows what's going on.

With us boys, though, our friendships shape-shift and change the way my robotic insect action figure turns into a tank, then back into an attack bug again. And we're all pretty cool together, no matter how the shape-shifting comes out.

It's such a *relief,* being a boy and not a girl!

From now on, I'll have a new friend to do stuff with when Corey and Kevin are busy. And Major can hang, too, if he wants. And Corey, and Kevin. I like them all.

"Win-win," as my dad would say.

"Hey, EllRay," Marco calls out as he bounces onto the playground and heads toward me. "I brought some stuff to show you," he hollers. He looks around like a not-very-good secret agent.

But Mr. Havens is still busy over at the swings.

"Watcha got?" I ask, going over to meet him halfway.

And it's really okay if it's the plastic knights again, I remind myself. I can always teach him how to play *Die, Creature, Die* some other time.

Like—tonight!

20

WHAT DO YOU SEE?

The big room at Kreative Learning and Daycare is kind of rowdy during the pause before the last part of the show, Alfie's skit. We have already made it through the two-year-olds' songs, "The Itsy-Bitsy Spider," "Heads, Shoulders, Knees and Toes," and "If You're Happy and You Know It." Those three songs took a surprisingly long time.

In fact, it already feels like tomorrow.

Then we watched the three-year-olds' performance of "The Gingerbread Man," read aloud by Miss Nancy herself.

Gingerbread? It's following me around!

I half expected Jared to come bursting through the door, demanding his share.

And now it's almost Alfie's turn. Dad is checking something on his cell, but Mom looks nervous as the voices around us grow louder.

I give Marco a look. "Dude," I tell him. "Noisy, huh? And wait until you meet Alfie after the show. She's like the *princess* of noisy. She's gonna be the red bird in this skit," I explain in advance.

"The red bird," Marco says, like he's memorizing it.

"She wanted to be the goldfish, but it didn't work out," I explain.

"Huh," Marco says. He looks confused.

I think maybe he's an only child.

"Let's get this show on the road," a dad behind me says, and his wife shushes him.

"*Hello, everyone,*" Miss Nancy calls out again from the stage, which is really just the back part of the room marked off by blue tape. She claps her hands a few times to get our attention, and every one in the audience settles down.

"Oh, here we go," Mom whispers. Dad puts away his cell.

Miss Nancy clears her throat, and the microphone squeals. "Next, we have our four-year-olds' spirited version of that beloved children's book, *Brown Bear, Brown Bear, What Do You See?* The book was written by Bill Martin Junior, and illustrated by Eric Carle," she says. "And here's our cast!"

The four-year-olds march out dressed in their costumes. My dad nods his approval of Alfie's fluttering red feathers and yellow beak-nose. He gives Mom a thumbs-up. Everyone cheers and claps.

I clap too, because this might be as good as it gets.

I know this book very well. It goes through a whole bunch of animals seeing each other. Nine of them, Mom said. It ends with the last one—the goldfish Alfie wanted to be—seeing the teacher, who then sees all the kids.

In this skit, Mom told me that Miss Nancy is going to read the first line of the verse for each animal, asking, "What do you see?" Then the kids are supposed to say they see the next animal, and so on. It's better than I'm making it sound.

Miss Nancy clears her throat, then she asks the kid playing the brown bear what he sees. And unfortunately, when the bear steps up to the microphone, he says he sees the red bird. Alfie.

Then Miss Nancy asks the red bird what *she* sees.

And Alfie just stands there, staring out at the audience. Her eyes are huge.

It's as if my little sister didn't realize anyone would be watching the skit—even though she said she wanted to be the goldfish so she'd get all the clapping!

It feels like everyone in the audience is holding their breath.

Marco nudges me. "Dude," he whispers. "Is Fluffy supposed to be doing that?"

"It's Alfie, not Fluffy. And *nuh-uh*," I whisper back.

On the stage, Miss Nancy is nodding her head at Alfie, encouraging her to say her one line so the show can go on. So everyone can go home tonight. I can tell the teacher is about to repeat the opening question—which will not help Alfie one little bit.

I know my sister, see.

This is going to end in tears, or with a public meltdown. Either way, the next couple of weeks are going to be a disaster around our house.

Alfie might be small, but her temper is large.

The audience is murmuring now, but anything anyone does will only make things worse.

Almost anything.

"Do it," I tell Marco, giving him a look.

"Do what?"

"Your armpit thing. And *quick*," I whisper.

"You mean it?" Marco asks. He looks like he's about to faint.

"Hurry," I say, nodding. "Don't even think about it. Just do it."

Luckily, Marco already took off his jacket. And he is wearing a short-sleeved T-shirt.

He wipes his hands on his pants. Then he makes a cup shape with one hand and slides it under the

Yay, Alfie!

She steps back and bows.

And everyone claps and cheers again, this time just for her!

The show can't continue until things calm down.

Mom and Dad still look like they're in shock, after that astounding **FLIRRRRPPT**. But basically, if Alfie's happy, they're happy.

And Alfie is definitely happy.

"Thumbs up, dog," I say, giving my talented new friend Marco a nudge in the ribs—and a great big smile. "I owe you one."

"Nah. We're good," Marco says, grinning back at me.

And I realize that the remainder of the skit, and tonight—and the whole rest of the semester, for that matter—are gonna go great.

I just know it!

opposite shirt sleeve. He puts it really tight over his armpit, with no air holes allowed, he told me once. He bends that arm, lifting it up like a chicken wing. And then really fast, he lowers his elbow, flattening the cupped hand.

FLIRRRRPPT!

The armpit noise echoes throughout the room. It's like it's bouncing off the walls and onto the stage! Alfie jumps as if she just got a shock—and then she starts to laugh.

She knows it was Marco! *She's looking right at us!*

Corey had better watch his back, because I think Marco's her hero, now.

And I'm not jealous, even one little bit.

"That boy's full of surprises," Dad murmurs to Mom, who has both hands over her face.

"He's full of *something*," she mumbles through her fingers.

Alfie strides up to the microphone, flaps her fluffy red wings, and says her line nice and loud. "*I see a yellow duck looking at me!*"

No baby talk "lellow." No whispering into the microphone. It was *perfect*.

JOYCE'S *DUBLINERS*

To James Peter Beck

Warren Beck

JOYCE'S *DUBLINERS*

SUBSTANCE, VISION, AND ART

DUKE UNIVERSITY PRESS DURHAM N.C. 1969

L.C.C. card no. 78–86477

S.B.N. 8223–0212–8

PRINTED IN THE U.S.A. BY KINGSPORT PRESS, INC.

Acknowledgment

I acknowledge with gratitude the assistance of the American Council of Learned Societies, by the grant of a Fellowship in 1963, for furtherance of my studies on Joyce through a sojourn in Dublin. I am grateful also to the Corporation of Yaddo, and to Mrs. Elizabeth Ames as Director of Yaddo, for providing me, at different periods, with a quiet and congenial place for carrying on the writing of this book.

I acknowledge permission granted by the Viking Press, holders of the copyright, for use of quotations from Joyce's *Dubliners,* and permission granted by the Oxford Press for use of quotations from Professor Richard Ellmann's indispensable *James Joyce.* Having availed myself of the reciprocal agreement among members of the American Association of University Presses on permission to quote, I add a personal word of appreciation for this helpful privilege. And I thank the authors and publishers of other works, from which my citations are so brief as not to require formal permission, but which have been very useful, considering the range of current comment on Joyce.

I am especially obligated to Mr. James P. Beck for comments and discussion which considerably enlarged my view of one major aspect of *Dubliners* and regulated my evaluation of several of the most important stories.

Finally, I thank Mr. Ashbel G. Brice, Director of the Duke University Press, for wise counsel, given without stint and with unvarying patience, and so genially as to make correspondence a pleasure.

Warren Beck

Contents

INTRODUCTION

I

Joyce's drastic extensions of the fictional mode and his progressively original achievements therein have drawn attention away from his still considerable accomplishment in the short story. *Dubliners,* exasperatingly obstructed from publication for almost a decade, then scantily noticed, and soon eclipsed by the emerging *Portrait,* was peculiarly handicapped. It is not surprising if a writer's most impressive and culminating works fix a dominant image of him; but this need not minimize an earlier or more conventional practice. Joyce's is an extreme case, however, of movement beyond original grounds, not just as man and writer, but in reputation. Strong drifts of relative interest in Joyce's various works have followed the extraordinary turns they took; to some minds the "fame" which came to Joyce twixt Molly Bloom's sleep and Finnegan's wake has relegated *Dubliners* almost to the status of juvenilia.

That partial judgment is compounded when the stories are glanced at merely to discover fumblings toward the later work or glosses upon it. Such tendency to read Joyce backwards seems allowed by Marvin Magalaner, who in his elaborate interpretation of Maria in "Clay" as symbol of the Virgin Mary puts it that "Knowing his [Joyce's] love of multi-leveled symbolism in *Ulysses* and *Finnegans Wake,* one might well expect to find similar levels in his earlier books."[1] What critics feel they might well expect to find they often do, and such practice may make for incidental derogation, nor has *Dubliners* escaped it. A hyper-specialized approach was attempted in that strenuous combing of *Dubliners,* Richard Levin's and Charles Shattuck's "First Flight to Ithaca,"[2] which looked backward from *Ulysses* to treat the short stories entirely in terms of Odyssean analogy. Herein, wrote Anthony Ostroff, are "some of the most fascinatingly arbitrary constructions to be found in published criticism."[3] Magalaner too, citing an example, deprecates the procedure as "rather far-fetched," and then refutes from its source these critics' argument that Joyce's correspondence with his publishers shows him "operating under some structural compulsion."[4] As Magalaner notes, this reading-in of Homeric analogies in *Dubliners* nevertheless "has been much pursued." For too long it was widely regarded as a summary evaluation of the matter, and though it lost repute, influence from its methodology has lingered, secondarily encouraging some to rest the case for *Dubliners* on the isolating of symbols. Whatever substance there may be in "First Flight to Ithaca," its approach was presumptuous and its emphasis a distortion. It temporarily hindered attention to the stories *per se* and with closer regard to Joyce and Dublin than to either the *Odyssey* or *Ulysses,* and it stimulated a continuing tendency to use Joyce as launching pad for criticism's newer technologies, which may not only fragment but disrupt and distort.

Fortunately the stories have had increasing recognition as central and germinal work in the genre, deserving more than tangential or minimizing treatment. As to analogies, W. Y. Tindall has reminded his fellow-searchers that *Ulysses* is made mythical not by mere parallels to the *Odyssey* but by being "a narrative which, while uniting Joyce with tradition, projects his central concerns,"[5] and this principle may be applied to *Dubliners* as well, with or without claiming for it either analogues or archetypal significations. Indeed, a viewing of *Dubliners* which stands clear of any overcast from the later works may find that these stories express "concerns" quite as "central" to Joyce as anything he set forth, and that their "projection," while technically more conventional than his later fiction, was at the time and in its vein a major accomplishment, and so remains.

Dubliners points to what is discoverable in the later works, submerged and modified or even reversed, but still an index to a writer's further thrust. It shows that Joyce the great experimenter was, to begin with, a formed craftsman, purposing to mediate a humane communication. What he declared to Grant Richards in 1906—"I have written my book with considerable care ... and in accordance with what I understand to be the classical tradition of my art"[6]—is a claim borne out by the stories. Begun in Ireland and completed soon after Joyce's settling on the Continent, *Dubliners* also has prime significance by its closeness to his early local experiences and observations. While adhering to highly selective narration, it embodies freshest and most insistent recollection, evaluated and given telling containment. Thereby the stories show something of Joyce that *A Portrait* does not, and the collection extends its concern to a wider range in Dublin life. Joyce's letters from that period affirm his serious purpose to reveal and illuminate, especially for his own people, the life they endured together. If thereafter despair at not being heard might have made for some arbitrariness and even separatism in his experiments, and bent his enforced stoicism toward a more intricate and arcane comedy of devices, the stories themselves bespeak the wholly involved artist, in his poised ambivalence of rebellion and attachment.

This veiled disclosure of Joyce in his first stages of maturity and artistic endeavor is an aspect meriting special notice. Readings could look beyond Dublin mores, personages, and place names, and beyond the outward facts of biography as well, to glimpse a silhouette of personality and discover those charges of circumstance upon temperament which were transformed into the illuminating play of aroused imagination over detachedly considered realities. Such a critical approach need not be retrogressive or superficial; one current use is in the estimating of correspondences between Stephen of *A Portrait* and young James Joyce of Dublin as measure of the emergent artist, to supplement both biography and the identification of tendencies in the later works, and even to define a Joycean aesthetic. It is as much to the point to note how events in *Dubliners* describe those cultural nets which Joyce like Stephen encountered, defied, and evaded. Beyond such documentary matter, however, and looming more largely, is the tincturing of *Dubliners* with the intense, complex mood of Joyce's defiance and evasion, for from this mood—unpostulated, partially repressed, but pervasive —the stories' deepest resonances arise.

In July of 1905, while in that spurt which produced the greater part of the collection, Joyce wrote his brother Stanislaus from Trieste of "pros and cons I must for the nonce lock up in my bosom." Awareness of these ineradicable contraries had recurred when he admitted that the city's papers would "object" to his work "as to a caricature of Dublin life." Examining his attitude, he confesses that "At times the spirit directing my pen seems to me so plainly mischievous that I am almost prepared to let the Dublin critics have their way."[7] Only "almost," however, did he make such concession, and only in an artist's anxious pauses. The stories assimilate his "pros and cons," not by canceling out satire with misgiving but by making rigorous judgment and empathic intuition the poles of an experienced tension which gives *Dubliners* its haunting pensiveness.

Joyce's announced motives, however, were simpler and more objective than any such complementary resolution of a deep-felt ambivalence. In a positive letter to Grant Richards rebutting censorious objections to "Two Gallants" and to passages in "Counterparts," Joyce not only stated his "intention" had been "to write a chapter in the moral history" of his country, but declared a "conviction that he is a very bold man who dares to alter in the presentment, still more to deform, whatever he has seen and heard."[8] *Dubliners* is a simple honoring of this creed of faithful realism. Yet there was, of necessity, more to it than that. Since an artist's regard is what gives any imaginative work not just embodiment but idiosyncratic vitality, the dynamism of all Joyce's fictions is to be traced to temperament. Even his increasing experimentation illustrates an evolving personality, at once boldly originative and reciprocally limited by its predilections.

The whole of that progress remains to be critically traced, though Professor Ellmann's admirable biography has now provided wider bases. Certainly in any enlarged and deepened portrait of the artist as such, the evaluation of *Dubliners* will be as important a factor as any, if due regard is given its veiled subjectivity, and the pros and cons therein.

In 1922, during early flurries over the completed *Ulysses,* George Moore spoke to Barrett Clark of "this Irishman Joyce" as "a sort of Zola gone to seed,"[9] but when *Dubliners* was being launched, Joyce had rightly declared that to label his work product of an "Irish Zola" would not be a high "display of the critical intellect."[10] The artist who was to extend implicative analogy with such effect was from the start more than mere naturalist. Joyce had "seen and heard" acutely because he was deeply pondering, desirous of independent understanding, prompted by unappeasable restiveness. While scrupulously objectified, *Dubliners* is far from impersonal. In his very aloofness Joyce was most involved, and *Dubliners* echoed his knowing, reflective, and privately dimensioned melancholy. A complex of intense reaction, though always fictionally projected, seems basic to every story. Beneath the cold distaste, unsparing in its satire of a culture and a local society, are tokens of hidden grief and recurrent secret conflict. Ellmann has pointed to Joyce's "ambiguity of motive"[11] in the period in 1905 when he was at work on several of the *Dubliners* stories. It was the diminished harmonies of a mingled rebellion and nostalgia which made *Dubliners* much more than a compendium of sociological dissections and ideological remonstrances. A full sensing of the stories' implications can round out knowledge of a young artist and man whose successive withdrawals should not obscure either his essential humanity and concerned involvement or the consequent scope of even his simplest stories.

By that light any such partial treatment as in "First Flight to Ithaca" is the more inadequate. Through fascination with methodology it grew not only "far-fetched" but misrepresentative. Having admitted that in *Dubliners* Joyce maintains Homeric parallels with something less than "slavish care,"[12] its authors might have been admonished to that extent, but were not. They strove too much in saying, of "After The Race," that "the yacht reflects the Phaeacians' interest in ships,"[13] or in equating with Nestor the pervert in "An Encounter."[14] Despite these critics' admission that "it is difficult to assign specific analogue" to "Grace," they attempted it, declaring that Kernan's "bitten tongue and hazy memory . . . recall Odysseus' being left alone on the shore and his need to fabricate talk about his past."[15] In fact the sordidly disheveled Kernan, a tea-taster by trade but now incapacitated with a bloody tongue, is falling-down drunk, and with neither memory of any Troy nor a present purpose (save to have another little drink) to sustain him in his moral disaster incomparable to a seafarer's misfortune. Here as elsewhere the Levin-Shattuck procedure seems to go unaware of the principle that all analogical usage (such as in anything from subtlest irony to burlesque) depends upon the firmness of some certain crucial point of correspondence. Thus supererogation becomes irrelevance in "First Flight to Ithaca," as when it is stated that in "Clay" Odysseus "is figured in a woman," from which it was only one very long step to the notion that Maria's song is made to "express very prettily the mood and situation of Odysseus at the end of his visit with the dead,"[16] whereas what it most acutely suggests is that Maria has had no experience of such delights as she sings about, and perhaps inhibits herself from recalling the next stanza, which projects love's happy consummation. A passage so fraught with the psychology and pathos of self-deception deserved consideration quite other than Levin's and Shattuck's relentless mauling. No wonder, though, if at their rate when they came to "The Dead," it was asserted that "the analogizing process operates here as cogently by antithesis as by duplication, for the hero is notably unheroic."[17] Pointed antithesis, like analogy, can be thematic, but not as thus claimed for a Gabriel-Ulysses, and to rest on a classifying of Gabriel Conroy as "unheroic" is to miss half the substance and the whole point of that powerful story.

In *Dubliners* the stimulations to insights, far from depending on analogy, take the serious vein of an implicatively presentational narrative art, such as has been refined in modern times to become the middle way of much significant thematic-organic fiction. Obscuring this primary aesthetic aspect, and ungratefully suggesting that without something like their strained exegesis *Dubliners* would seem only "a pleasant readable minor effusion, a collection of discrete sketches,"[18] the Richard Levin and Charles Shattuck operation lapsed into presuppositional criticism's frequent offense, actually violating some of the stories as entities. By stating that in "A Little Cloud" the wife (certainly a key figure) "has no Homeric counterpart,"[19] these critics tacitly admitted the story is unamenable to the method they nevertheless pursued. Wandering in their formalized conjectures beyond the matter of *Dubliners,* they put it that in "The Sisters" the boy "does little but brood over the lost father" and that "the main theme" is "the boy's father-hunger and his Telemachan hope that the father is not dead,"[20] but this overlooks the boy's awkward sense of relief in escape to "the sunny side of the street" and his emotional-intellectual withdrawal which allows a finally detached view of the sisters.

Is it not time the long-lingering influence of such analogical-archetypal vaporings as the Levin-Shattuck piece and any later mutations of its methodology be aired out of the cubicles of Joyce criticism? Whatever is done with *Ulysses* (and who would ever be done with that multitudinous revel and dark enigma?) in all the short stories it was Dublin not Ithaca Joyce had his eye on. These Dubliners were seen *au naturel* by a young Dubliner and expatriate whose fidelities then comprised the view and the viewer, answering both to external realities and to the urgings of passions and vexations, in a precocious maturing and self-assertion.

From any artist of the first order each creation has its uniqueness arising from existential particularity, an immediacy within time and circumstances—historical, social, and personal. Among Joyce's four fictional works the variety is not only obvious but immense. Incisive judgment of each therefore depends less on correlation with the others than on differentiation, a turn from broadly inclusive generalization to definition of essence, and for each work as close an approach as may be to the quiddity integrated through mode and mood, the virtue of an artist's regard as proceeding from substance, structure, and tone. Appreciation of *Dubliners,* as of other excellent achievements, depends upon its being seen plain as it was evoked from the man whom the artist then showed himself to be, by what he made of what were then his experiences, concerns, and intimations.

2

During lengthy but fruitless early correspondence with Grant Richards about publishing *Dubliners,* Joyce declared his "intention . . . to write a chapter of the moral history" of his country, with Dublin as the scene "because that city seemed . . . the centre of paralysis."[21] Earlier, giving Richards his opinion that no writer before him had "presented Dublin to the world," he described as floating over his presentation "a special odour of corruption."[22] Therein he felt himself to be treating certain qualities inherent in his subject, as is shown in another letter—"it is not my fault that the odour of ashpits and old weeds and offal hangs around my stories"—and he believed he would be giving "the Irish people . . . one good look at themselves in my nicely polished looking glass."[23]

But in seeking to serve his people's conscience Joyce was also listening to his own, which enjoined a practice comprehending the whole matter. ("I have written my book with considerable care—in accordance with what I understand to be the classical tradition of my art.")[24] Edmund Wilson found Joyce "working in the tradition, not of English, but of French fiction," and declared "*Dubliners* was French in its objectivity, its sobriety and its irony, at the same time that its paragraphs ran with a music and a grace quite distinct from the taut metallic quality of Maupassant and Flaubert."[25] Stuart Gilbert put it that in *Dub-*

liners Joyce did not go beyond a fictional practice most directly derived from Flaubert,[26] whom Joyce had read sedulously. However, Joyce's sense of working in a still vital fictional form allowed him, in his "considerable care," to modify tradition by individual talent. Thus too in the stories' episodic framings he could reapply the perennial romantic concept of a transforming vision expressed, as Richard Sullivan has described it, "with nerves tuned to the tone of every syllable."[27]

Marvin Magalaner considers a possible influence from Chekov,[28] but Gorman had noted Joyce's saying that when he wrote the stories he had not yet read Chekov;[29] and writing his brother Stanislaus on August 18, 1905, when deeply engaged with *Dubliners,* Joyce discussed what was meant by the "Russian" mode and cited Turgenev, disparagingly, and Gorky and Tolstoy, admiringly, but made no mention of Chekov.[30] Yeats, writing Gosse in Joyce's behalf in 1915, mentioned *Dubliners* as a "remarkable book . . . satiric stories of great subtlety," but only generally called them "a little like Russian work."[31] Joyce's apparent lack of indebtedness to a particular influence does not prove him unaware of the main weight and wealth of tradition; neither does it indicate the onset of a conviction (such as Eliot advanced concerning Joyce and *Ulysses*)[32] that a *genre* was burned out and must be not just reconstituted from its ashes but metamorphized. In these short stories what is more important than specific influence, whether Russian or French, is Joyce's originality within a then fairly fixed mode, showing how sensitive the young writer was to the undefined currents of his time, and how purposefully experimental.

If more general influences are sought, then in line with Joyce's interests two certainly can be noted—from Ibsen, in the acute sense of psychological situation, and from a Thomistic-based aesthetic of epiphanies, which favored an open form with less emphasis on finality and more on implication than in tales calculatingly plotted. In nothing do the *Dubliners* pieces suggest Chekov more than in those endings—(". . . he had to ask his wife to tell him where the corkscrew was." "Mr. Crofton said that it was a very fine piece of writing.")—which are dramatically inconclusive and seemingly trivial yet are resonant to any inclined ear. Joyce's resemblance to Chekov as a writer of stories may have no closer connection than that each, in his own situation and way, grew especially aware of responsive consciousness as a continuum not to be structured into beginnings, middles, and endings. Herein Joyce's narrative techniques in *Dubliners* precede by decades the so-called "experimental" work of English and American writers, more or less derivative from Chekov, who have markedly advanced the short story. In this aspect *Dubliners* has remained "modern," and with distinction, through more than half a century.

It is most important, however, to see *Dubliners* not just as of a mode notable in literary history, but as outcome of a private necessity that fathered the subleties dramatized in the fifteen stories. Joyce as Dubliner had so mixed a heritage, both social and personal, and it pressed so hard upon one of his nature, that he was moved to withdraw. What he withdrew to, artistically, was a meticulous craft, practiced in the light of a considerable learning, with resolute transmuting of lingering personal feeling, however severe. That process, which was to carry Joyce so far, was firmly and brilliantly initiated in *Dubliners,* with its adaptation of narrative modes to socio-psychological subjects, in an aesthetic distancing enforced by intimate and even pained involvement. His stories, unostentatious but fully achieved, illustrate an artist's serious affiliation at a most responsible level. With transient but humanely significant experience identified, events are formalized and characters are accorded portraiture in a consummate work, by the decorum that preserves essence and uniqueness and yet allows largest concurrence. A writer of Joyce's grasp and power, crucially environed and acute in reaction, finds need for artistic as well as intellectual objectification in ratio to his concern. Supplying that, he allows his reader true access in a similar equilibrium of empathy and perspective. The result is the poise, the fair attitude of the *Dubliners* stories, and their pure sonority.

Some of the sustained excellences which made them really *le plus en avant* were defined by Ezra Pound in his early (July 15, 1914) review of *Dubliners* in *The Egoist.* He began by commending the book as a rare achievement in its "prose free from sloppiness . . . a clear, hard prose." Joyce, moreover, is termed "a realist," who "gives the thing as it is." He "is quite capable of dealing with things about him, and dealing directly, yet these details do not engross him, he is capable of getting at the universal element beneath them." Concerning the narrative technique, Pound said Joyce "presents his people swiftly and vividly, he does not sentimentalize over them, he does not weave convolutions." He is found free of the "tiresome" fashion of casting his material "into the conventional form of a 'story' " under which since Maupassant there have been "so many people trying to write 'stories' and so few people presenting life." Pound's early unreserved commendation of *Dubliners* had noted that Joyce "does not descend to farce" nor "rely upon Dickensian caricature," and "is not presenting a macabre subjectivity" but deals in "classic" fashion with ordinary people, as in "a committee room . . . a boarding house." And in relating Joyce to contemporary tendencies Pound declared "he excels most of the impressionist writers because of his more rigorous selection."[33]

But selection, the crux and proof of intention together with firm but unobtrusive ordering of what is selected, depends upon innate conceptual bent and power; and that, in turn, must draw on heritage, with its impact on temperament. Poor Ireland, where two nations and their many divisions adventitiously jostled, and the Roman Catholic Church there, and "dear dirty Dublin"[34] and various Dubliners beset or disorderly, and young James Joyce's family, friends and relations, and education—such as it all was, it did not do altogether badly by the artist. His youth was an exacerbation, his legacy an unamenable ambivalence between natural piety and skeptical dissent, and his responses were correspondingly extreme, but it was a richly, intricately textured existence, engaging him deeply, however deplorable he found much of its substance and tendency. Through sheer weight and insistence his surroundings had exacted, besides grief and defiance, an evaluation refined through artistic setting-forth, permitting the artist's veiled extension of fraternity.

Like many writers, Joyce began autobiographically, and in this vein he was to persist even in the later works, through semblables and partial alter egos; but he paused between *Stephen Hero* and the finally evolved *Portrait* to create short stories in a more objective and broadly critical mode, yet compassionately. Seldom has so youthful a writer, and one so distraught, taken more masterful grasp upon immediate material and given it such balanced consideration as did Joyce in *Dubliners*. Stanislaus Joyce reported that his brother's commitment to an observant realism rather than to the "adventurous" or "romantic" was shown from the first, in the "short stories he wrote at school," which "were already in the style of *Dubliners*." Stanislaus recalled one, titled "Silhouettes," in first person, of a boy's witnessing shadows on a window blind, "a man, staggering and threatening with upraised fist, and the smaller sharp-faced figure of a nagging woman."[35] Here was prefigured the embryonic fictionist's already alerted sense of a local sordidness and strife; moreover, the sketch as remembered by Stanislaus in some detail seems to have been episodic, open-structured, a close glimpse of situation, without stereotyped finality, yet with an intrinsic pathos, evincing concern.

The short story's history as a significant form in English in the twentieth century, particularly as to originations dynamic enough to maintain some continuity through decades, thus begins with Joyce, and not just by date of composition. While his stories, with their fine control, deserve the comparison Philip Toynbee makes to "the lovely classical drawings of the young Picasso"—this on the premise that each "great innovator had to prove to himself that he could excel in the idiom of the past before he could begin to transcend it"[36]—at the same time *Dubliners* is purposefully original, to serve the artist's rapidly clarifying personal need through an aesthetic transmutation, and this is at the heart of the stories' merit, along with their accessibility in terms of the tradition. The rounded richness of *Dubliners* comprises totalities, in each story, of alert observation and private vision, shaped into uniquely communicative form.

For all their containment by the city itself and by Joyce's view of a confining Irish "paralysis," the stories remarkably differ from each other as to theme, scene, and characters. Not being concerned in *Dubliners* with conventional plot or a devised substitute, Joyce had his concept of epiphanies to provide subjective progression and outcome, his sense of the fluidity of consciousness to furnish narrative momentum despite the characters' arrest by externals, and his understanding of Dubliners' ways to authenticate the casually eddying action. Since *Dubliners,* lying beyond sociological realism as well as formal analogy, implicated the moods of a personal separation, this required a correlative aesthetic withdrawal, of varying degree in the different stories, to the strategic vantage ground of fictional narration. Criticism of *Dubliners* should begin by recognizing its relative and uniquely shaded objectivity in the Joyce corpus, from the rest of which the stories can be thus differentiated without severing their deep subjective roots. Richard Ellmann, sketching the family tree, has identified originals of many *Dubliners* characters in Joyce's uncles, aunts, cousins, and others intimately known and probably observed from his boyhood on.[37] As for the likes of Stephen, and so of young James Joyce, "there is no doubt," wrote Frank Budgen, "that he is the unnamed narrator of the first three stories in Dubliners."[38] In addition, Budgen considered the "bold, sensitive, tenacious, clear-seeing boy" of *A Portrait,* protecting his identity from "extinction" by "defense and attack" and by "silence, exile and cunning," to be "the essential artist"[39] as Budgen knew him. Here, however, a useful distinction can be made. The first three stories, by narrative limitation, invention, and molding, are further removed from factual grounds than is *A Portrait.* So far as evidence of sources goes, all fifteen stories seem resolutely fictionalized, lifted out of immediate objective-subjective awareness into aesthetic entity and autonomy. Thus by contrast *Dubliners* illuminates *A Portrait,* with its more direct and constant autobiographical quality, and that of the "Telemachia" as well.

Compared to the many identifications between Stephen and Joyce, any equally obvious connections with the boy in *Dubliners* are few, and these scarcely central to the fiction. Stanislaus Joyce terms "a mistake" the assumption by Padraic Colum that "The Sisters" and "Araby" are "evidently recollections of childhood."[40] Stanislaus tells that while the Joyces were living on North Richmond Street the two brothers (in the story only classmates) did go truant and crossed paths with a pervert, as told in "An Encounter," but neither boy had any "notion" of what the fellow was, though "something funny in his speech and behavior" made them think "he might be an escaped madman";[41] however, the story's central and subjective point is the narrator's shadowy intimation of evil and his delayed flight toward a wholesome realization. And whereas in *A Portrait* Stephen-Joyce's father and mother are really and very much in the picture, the boy in "The Sisters" and "Araby" lives, fictionally, with an uncle and aunt, an index of Joyce's determined control of both composition and tone. The twelve third-person stories dealing with Dublin adults show traces of actual experience, but these are transmuted, in a sea-change at some depth. As to this practice, its complication of Joyce's private need and artistic aims is a question criticism may approach, if with discretion, and in this too *Dubliners* would be useful for comparative reference concerning trend in Joyce's works.

3

Beneath all autobiographical link and beneath Joyce's clinical scrutiny of other Dubliners there moves within the stories a real if mysterious contemporary presence. This adduces another kind of portrait of the young Irish artist, of unique aspect, in the background to *Dubliners*. Here is a defining contrast to what Joyce later was to be and do, in his progressive self-expression as artist and man. He pervades the stories in his primary ambivalence as the intuitive and empathetic though already alienated writer who could have said that there, but for his withdrawal and flight, were frustrations and a confinement which might have been his own. This concept has been stated by distinguished authorities; Professor Harry Levin put it that "Gabriel Conroy is what Joyce might have become, had he remained in Ireland,"[42] and Professor William York Tindall went on to say "Not only a picture of what he had escaped, the book [*Dubliners*] is a picture of what, had he remained, he might have become."[43] However, this scarcely authorizes expansion by others into an all-inclusive truism about *Dubliners,* a before-and-after which adumbrates an utterly somber prelude to a complete personal deliverance. What the artist created was a series of fables distilling a mood in which nostalgia and even some remorse were complementary to his resolute dissociation from such aspects of Dublin as he still chose to make the main substance of his work, then and always.

That this complementary element remained muted in *Dubliners* not only allowed the stories' fine objectification, it enhances their humane perspective. Rightly read, *Dubliners* suffices to put aside the persistent false stereotype: Joyce the wholly defiant rebel, whose self-assurance was absolute, whose uprooting produced no wilting, and whose personal severance from everything native to him was as simple as boarding ship, for easy transit from period one to period two in a writer's life. How such oversimplification can enervate criticism may be seen in David Daiches' discussion of *Dubliners,* especially his introduction of the subject. "James Joyce left his native Dublin at the age of twenty-two, and lived ever after in self-imposed exile on the Continent,"[44] he begins, and that "ever after" makes a fairy tale of a quite different story. Joyce not only returned several times, and for rather extended stays, but more than once he considered settling in Ireland, and on one trip back he had in mind applying for an academic post in Dublin.[45] Daiches further tidies up the history, injecting parenthetically that "*Dubliners* was written while Joyce was still in Dublin,"[46] which is true of only a few of the stories, and some of these earliest ones were then rewritten in Trieste. In Daiches' simplified view all of *Dubliners* becomes a matter of "thumbnail sketches of characteristic situations of the life of which he is still a part,"[47] a misrepresentation whether still being a part has to do merely with residence, or, as the context suggests, with direct personal connection. Daiches is intent on stipulating that "Joyce's literary career was a progressive attempt to insulate himself against the life which is his subject as an artist,"[48] and though something of this sort is a widely pondered concept, Daiches' formulation of it may mislead, since it blurs a distinction. The man Joyce did increasingly seek an "insulation," for private reasons; biography documents this and it is left to criticism to estimate the direction and degree of its influence on Joyce's art. While a man may finally island himself, no genuine artist seeks insulation but only detachment, and not in a walling-off from his experienced subject but for perspective on it, to see it steadily and dominate it for his own ongoing purposes, whatever their tangent and momentum. Where Joyce was carried and how it so happened is still being variously appraised. What seems presently most desirable in evaluating *Dubliners* is direct aesthetic engagement embracing this primary work entire and *sui generis,* uncolored by cross-lights from the differing creations that followed. Then there might be seen the special value of *Dubliners* in a relative assessing of Joyce's total accomplishment. Admittedly, however, a more enlivened view of *Dubliners* is the harder to come by not only since the incursion of fashionable ploys in Joycean criticism but because of the rightfully dominant place given *Ulysses* in twentieth-century fiction by learned and sober judges, and because of the isolation of *Dubliners* as the whole of Joyce's endeavors in the short story.

Frank O'Connor put it of *Dubliners* that Joyce "gave up writing stories after its publication"; actually, by the time *Dubliners* was issued, following long delays and many rebuffs, Joyce had written no more short stories for almost a decade. "Why did he give it up?" O'Connor continued pointedly, adding "it is typical of the muddle of Joycean criticism in our time that nobody seems to see the importance of this question, much less tries to answer it."[49] Surely the question has been at least tentatively dealt with, in a prevalent assumption that Joyce as theoretician and experimentalist determinedly went on, beyond the more conventional confines of *Dubliners* and even *A Portrait*, to find scope in later books for a new and unique creativity. O'Connor wondered, however, whether Joyce came to feel he "was not a storyteller," yet this notion not only overlooked the superlative brilliance of sustained episodes in *A Portrait* and *Ulysses* but would run contrary to evidence that Joyce had enduring confidence in what was achieved in *Dubliners*. Or, O'Connor continued to speculate, did Joyce feel "he had done all he could with the form?"[50] This can scarcely be true, since Joyce had projected a second volume, to be called *Provincials*, with some of its stories already conceived under certain titles.[51] O'Connor's answer to his question was that Joyce, as is "quite clear" from "The Dead," had "begun to lose sight of the submerged population that was his original subject,"[52] but this neglects their reappearance in numbers and variety even if sometimes only adjunctively in *Ulysses*—and might prompt the rejoinder that a character more "submerged" than Bloom could scarcely be brought to the surface, much less floated there. O'Connor's judgment in the matter is to be gauged by his summary derogation of "the short-storyteller [*sic*] who must make tragedy out of a plate of peas and a bottle of ginger beer or the loss of a parcel of fruitcake intended for a Halloween party."[53] Though "Two Gallants" and "Clay" have degrees of pathos, neither is advanced as tragedy; and who should have known better than the gifted Frank O'Connor that details in accomplished short stories are not isolable from their context, especially a character's sense of them, with their cumulative effect.

The question of Joyce's turn from the short story form has been approached in another way by Padraic Colum. Speaking of the publisher George Roberts' delayings with *Dubliners* (a maddening climax to long years of similar frustrations) Colum speculates: "Suppose it had been otherwise." Suppose, he continues, the work had gone forward and *Dubliners* had appeared, in Dublin. Joyce would have had "a different impression . . . of his native city," he "would have been happier . . . his mind would have been free of the suspicion of persecution he was prone to." A new look at Dublin by a markedly "happier" man freed from the chronic suspicions which were complement to his vanity—all this scarcely fits with the melancholy shape evolved by Joyce's biographers. Moreover, to suppose publication in Dublin would have changed Joyce's "impression" of the city is to suggest a venality incredible in this artist. Colum, however, does move toward a central question: given a less exacerbated Joyce, "would there then have been a literature of exile?"[54] Others have speculated about the event. "Joyce in exile had gone deeply, too deeply into himself," wrote Morley Callaghan, "but what if he had stayed in Dublin?"[55] To this perhaps greatest what-if in twentieth-century literary history there remains predominantly Harry Levin's answer, that Joyce would have been Gabriel Conroy. In any projection from this, however, it might be recognized that Gabriel Conroy, as the fugitive but incurably ambivalent Joyce conceived him, did, so to speak, live and deeply realize in Dublin the mounting, far-reaching experiences that round out "The Dead," a high particular attainment. Beyond that, in another dimension, Joyce not only settled himself in exile, but his successive works were a continuation of flight.

Less drastic speculation is that had the publication of *Dubliners* not been so long and discouragingly delayed there would have been at least another volume in the same mode. Joyce later said he was "too cold"[56] to write those proposed *Provincials* stories. He had not been too cold to write "Araby," "Clay," and "A Little Cloud," as well as "The Dead." What a subsequent coldness progressively consisted of is an enigma in psychography, vexatious to criticism, but not negligible. The frustration over *Dubliners* had been prolonged, embittering, perhaps traumatic; in that period even work on *A Portrait* was retarded and halted, and the intent almost repudiated. Then *Dubliners*, when it finally appeared, in 1914, was not much noticed. *A Portrait* furnished Joyce a reputation among the knowing, and gathered to him that certain faithful following he needed, and then came the turn to *Ulysses,* one of modern literature's major projections, however it is evaluated. Despite all the attention given Joyce, there has not been much approach to a consensus of relative estimations, and although *Ulysses* is usually given highest place, that has been for reasons almost as numerous as its advocates. In the cross-currents of professional concern *Dubliners* as a body of pieces with distinctive traits and cumulative weight is esteemed but still neglected as a primary point of reference concerning tendencies in Joyce's work. Since from youth on Joyce increasingly severed himself from pieties demanded by home, church, and nation, but suffered a consequent remorse and was fated to incurable unrest, the successive guises under which continuing stress penetrated his works raises a central issue. A return to *Dubliners* in this regard will scarcely derogate the stories, but rather through further penetration of substance may sharpen awareness of their art. To begin with, the "objectivity" of the stories (like the schemata of *Ulysses*) may be recognized for what it is, a literary means, its end the aesthetic transmuting of a private concern. In Joyce's artistic covering over of the mingled personal springs which supplied *Dubliners* he (like many another troubled man) may be found revealing himself by dissimulation, but certainly he lends out a perspective gained by resolute detachment. His art's candid yet reserved gesture suffices to confirm the stories' human significance as well as their superlative strategy in the expression of a transmuted ambivalence. In this aspect not the least of Joyce's successes, *Dubliners* is also a compass point.

Seen in essence, the book is what a still very young artist remarkably achieved through the personal withdrawal recorded in *A Portrait.* In stories so nearly perfected, conceptually and artistically, there should have been found from the first the mark of subtle genius and forceful idiosyncrasy, and plain promise of things to come. Perhaps it would have been noted, and Joyce thereby moved and aided to consolidate his stand on those grounds, had not publication of *Dubliners* been so long delayed, and into the bad times of war. Not that the postponement, even had it been longer than a decade, could have outmoded such advanced work, nor diminished its human plenitude or made its psychological significations inconsequential. Beneath their picturing a partial paralysis, found typical of Dublin, the stories communicate private ordeals, simply but with painful intensity, and also in life's common terms. *Dubliners* claims too that special charm of the first accomplished work of certain great artists which (contrary to much practice and more frequent cliché) is not primarily autobiographical or insistently subjective, but shows a willing suspension of personal claim, in a diffused relation of private issue to more general matters. It is a hardly achieved negative capability making for reflective yet feeling regard. Here the "nicely polished looking-glass" of *Dubliners* which Joyce felt could have contributed to "civilization in Ireland" by giving its people "one good look at themselves"[57] is clear of distortions—no "cracked lookingglass," as Stephen alleged of a servile Irish art,[58] and free of that methodic grotesquerie Joyce later adopted for other than realistic effect, and possibly for a further distillation of private unrest. In *Dubliners* the native who refused to serve, withdrew, and finally departed still remembers with deepest intuition some of those yet held in the nets.

4

Objectively naturalistic in its bases, *Dubliners* nevertheless supports primarily psychological structures, and concepts subjectively tinged. The book's generic title situates a variety of characters, and though with nothing of the sweep or plenteous detail of *Ulysses,* still with quite as acute an evaluation of their separate natures and needs. "In their own way," wrote Harry Levin, "the tangential sketches of *Dubliners* came as close to Joyce's theme—the estrangement of the artist from the city—as does the systematic cross-section of *Ulysses.*" Levin tellingly adds that the stories "look more sympathetically into the estranged lives of others" and "discriminate subtly between original sin and needless cruelty."[59] This has been pointedly considered by Anthony Ostroff, in "The Moral Vision in *Dubliners.*" He cites the fates of certain characters as not just "brought about by an environment of particular corruption," not just as "the failure of a whole culture," but as "individual failures."[60] These he sees as "both pathetic and monstrous,"[61] in their avoidance of moral challenge and responsibility. Such evasions, often related to the character's ambivalence, may compound it into further warping of personality. However, not all the tales are of a continued shunning, and in some there occurs a responsive advance. What is most inclusively significant is that the stories are more subjective than sociological, with conduct viewed in its essence, through consciousness itself. Strict judgment of behavior need not exclude its pathos, however; Joyce's scrutiny, sometimes critical, as of Farrington, was sometimes quietly compassionate, as with Eveline, and it could be both, as with Little Chandler and Gabriel. The *Dubliners* stories are furthest from formula in their transcending of any patterned response to a subject-matter conceived of in the lump. They bespeak their author's concern for each character uniquely as well as of a kind, and they contain a residue of empathy as between one grieved, rebellious Dubliner self-exiled and others forever immured. *Dubliners* might be considered the work which most nearly fulfils the intention proclaimed at the close of *A Portrait;* writing those diary pages, Joyce may well have been conscious of delegating to Stephen an enterprise he himself had already implemented, lacking only its acceptance as yet by others, but itself an accomplished serving of vocation.

Most notably *Dubliners* exemplifies Joyce's specific aesthetic theory of epiphany. It is by embodying such presentment psychologically in a sustained action that the stories can comprise cool assessment and humane intuition. Open-structured though they are, they are not just "happenings," and the vision allowed protagonists in some stories, and always open to readers, is of values. What occurs to the characters signifies, "means intensely," whatever the fatuousness of their errors, the pathos of their falling into evil, or their grotesque falling short of a possible good. Joyce's view of them, austerely unsentimental, is also alive with natural feeling in a way not so directly accorded most of the *Ulysses* folk or any figures in *Finnegans Wake*. In spite of Joyce's disdain there emerges in *Dubliners* something of involvement, a felt concern, linking the stories in tone with the young Stephen's deepest intimations. Joyce's term "epiphany" thereby appears as more than an affectation, and though Stephen's pronouncements on it were heavy with scholastic terminology, the august myth of a manifestation to men of kindly bent figures the young artist's care for the conscience of his race, and for his people singly, something to be made plain again and again in *Dubliners*.

Stephen Hero defined the matter as recognition of a "whatness," which "leaps to us from the vestment of its appearance," whereupon "The object achieves its epiphany."[62] Here too is Joyce's sense of tradition and learning as grounds for creative projection. The term involving historic Christian belief is taken as a new name for a constant in art, an intimation arising out of a pointed aesthetic arrangement, the object made radiantly evocative, and in an awareness of ambience. Similarly young Joyce used another term borrowed from the Church when, having published "The Sisters," he wrote Curran of the stories to come as *epicliti,*[63] derived from *epiclesis,* a part of liturgical invocation of the Holy Spirit. Evidently the spoiled priest saw himself still as ritualistic celebrant of mysteries. To his brother Stanislaus, in their Dublin days, he had spoken of an art transmuting the "bread of ordinary life into something that has a permanent artistic life of its own," for "mental, moral, and spiritual uplift."[64] And the letter to Curran connects artistic transmutation with evaluation; the "*epicliti*" to be called *Dubliners* are to disclose "the soul of that hemiplegia or paralysis which many consider a city."

Robert Scholes considers that in Joycean criticism too much has been made of "epiphany." Calling "epiphany-hunting" a "harmless pastime" comparable to "archetype-hunting, Scrabble, and other intellectual recreations," he suggests the term be limited to "those little bits of prose which Joyce himself gave the name to."[65] It might be noted, though, that those experimental passages are of two distinct kinds, and this may aid discernment of Joyce's larger and more significant fictional variations of the device. One sort of "epiphany" in the collection edited by O. A. Silverman[66] and the additions Scholes and Kain made to it[67] is merely of data glimpsed, a catching sight of what could be sketched factually into a naturalistic writer's notebook; another kind of epiphany represents more subjectively an access of vision —such as the one Joyce saw fit to include as the second-from-last diary entry at the conclusion of *A Portrait*. Though also imagistic, this second sort of epiphany extends to an insight. Quite relevantly S. L. Goldberg has put it of Joyce's "fundamental concept—the epiphany" that in this "conjunction of subject and object" the mind by apprehending "partly realizes itself."[68]

In this sense the quiddity or whatness which young Joyce sought out is utterly different from the inert matter of that exaggerated existentialism which proposes neither significance nor absurdity in phenomena but merely registers them. Such is a neorealistic focus on *chosisme*, a mere thingishness; such the spate of that avant-garde fiction which centers on no reality but sets up fabricated personae, whose spastic behavior dramatizes nothing but their inventor's peevish alienation. On the contrary Joyce was and knew himself the "sympathetic" alien, his stories show a Dublin recognizably peopled, and therein was found fit subject for critical and compassionate regard. Even those characters in *Dubliners* most shackled by environment and consequently most habit-ridden can act with intention, and consciousness in them is more than some ultra-modern fiction's sort of geiger-counter chatter in proximity to detail yet with no conceptual positioning of occurrence. Moreover, those *Dubliners* characters who do experience an epiphany take on large dimensions, even in the most tenuous of the narratives, by representative human function. They show how for the humble and bewildered, too, an awareness can dawn in the mind's magical way, by catalysis of influences, structuring vision. This represents "experience itself," not atomized and dissociated but, as Pater meant in his often reductively misread passage, "the focus where the greatest number of vital forces unite in their purest energy." Such, when it is also a further discovery, is an epiphany. These as represented by Joyce in *Dubliners* transcend for their moments that scholastically defined separation of existence and essence as the condition of finitude; *integritas* and *consonantia* pass beyond logic and rhetoric when *claritas* is reached, in the permeating radiance of consummate vision. As Joyce saw, here is the crucial step beyond formal intellection into the imaginativeness of art, creative of a higher order, in a personal evaluation. Speaking of the transformation of *Stephen Hero* into *A Portrait,* Padraic Colum put it that "The dialectician had become the revealer of the epiphany."[69] Joyce's school for that growth and the first fruits of it was the writing of *Dubliners,* and this was to remain a unique achievement.

The psychological and particularly the epiphanal element in *Dubliners* has been tributary to the modern short story's most significant advance, toward that open structure which renounces tidy denouement purchased by oversimplification. The concern of the Joycean, as of the Chekovian story, was not to plot a finality but to disclose those crests of consciousness within the flow of circumstance when there comes some heightening of awareness, momently consolidating. Moreover, as there are in Joyce's early experimental fragments two kinds of epiphany, the naturalistic-objective and the subjective-psychological, so too with *Dubliners.* In some stories the habit-ridden characters may exemplify chiefly their own unresponsiveness, and since for them self-knowledge is largely paralyzed, any epiphany must accrete in the reader's recognitions. In other stories characters themselves experience a crisis of emotion under stress of a further realization, which they demonstrate. Toward characters of the first kind Joyce's attitude is classically ironic, and this the reader can share, along with Joyce's degree of allowance for even the most impercipient Dubliner. Stories of the second kind, running deeper, more fully exercise the reader's empathy, in the wake of a character's expanding acknowledgments, and of course under the concerned author's providence. This subjective-representative tension, manifest in the action, echoed in the reader's consciousness, and sensed as proceeding from the artist, can give a fiction scope, veracity, and persuasiveness. Correspondingly Joyce with his doctrine of epiphanies (however trammeled in scholastic terminology) was being about his business and moving to the heart of the matter, where he arrived, early but truly, in *Dubliners*.

In the most impressive of the stories—those where the effect occurs not only as the reader's perception of the author's view and mood but through the conveyance of a character's responses, and where issue is fundamental—there may be one of two extremes or some mediation between them in the emergence of the epiphany. The character's awareness may slowly "gather to a greatness" or may "shine out like shook foil." In either kind of epiphany there has been, of course, an advance in the character's experience, like a further concentration until a crystal takes form, whether gradually or rapidly. From one story to another the difference in degree between a slowly growing intimation or a sudden impact upon consciousness may rest on the character's ability to recognize accretion in his experience, or his resistance to it. Acceptance may be instinctively held off in defense of illusion, pride, or aversion from commitment; on the other hand, acknowledgment may come slowly only in the usual human way, wherein understanding forever lags behind experience. Most representatively and affectively, in the story as in life itself, at an epiphanal point it may be discovered that all along some not yet identified realization was being sought, or at least skirted, and its factors had been taken in without clear foresight of a relevance they were to assume in the vision, the completed construct and overflow of knowledge. All varieties of progress toward epiphany can occur for a reader, as they may have for the writer in his formative refining of his subject. And *Dubliners* takes on breadth by its epiphanies of several kinds. Of the two "gallants," Lenehan left to himself suffers intimations of futility, though they are too weak for more than passing effect, whereas Corley, figured almost as an automaton, moves in his arrogant cycle impervious to idea or anything other than the most primitive and predatory instincts. The frustrate boy in "Araby" is suddenly stricken with a despairing view of himself; Gabriel approaches his ultimate vision by stages, throughout an evening that garners a lifetime's experiences and leads him to reorient himself to them.

Behind them all looms an adumbration of the young, troubled, but masterfully originative artist. Gabriel and the boy and even Lenehan (together with some other Dubliners, especially Little Chandler) while projected as complete fictional beings, still variously suggest an oblique confession of Joyce's own ambivalence. In *Dubliners* this personal theme is given more perspective and made more representative than in *A Portrait*. Even the three first-person stories of boyhood, though biographically rooted, disclose less of what recognizably corresponds with Joyce's own outward doings in Dublin than pages traversed by Stephen. In general the *Dubliners* narratives seem eclectically synthesized more from the artist's wider observations and reckonings than out of his personal crises. To sustain their themes presentationally while evolving their epiphanies, the stories had to be more objectively controlled than is *A Portrait*. Even so, some of the greatest disclose a Joycean self-knowledge as central and private as anything Stephen tells of, yet throughout *Dubliners* such matter, and especially the factor of ambivalence, is externalized by dramatization, in a mode quite distinct from Stephen's lyricism.

Consequently with *Dubliners* the term "objectivity" must mean something other than a withdrawal to neutrality and a descent to naturalistic recounting. An artist's stepping back for wider view does not necessarily denature him or make his response only a cold enumeration or analysis. Indeed, some distance would seem needed for insight, just as in human affairs disinterestedness and magnanimity depend upon moderation of ego, in measured assertion. Thus the very objectivity of *Dubliners* is ironic counterpart to the artist's complex personal involvement, and the art of the stories is in the framing and symbolizing of a concern both social and internal. While the various Dubliners' lives are acutely viewed, the central subject is Joyce's total response, in which a tension between attachment and rejection seems so pervasive as to be a primary element. If the haunting overtones of *Dubliners* suggest the artist's ambivalence as a determinant, here would be not only an index to the fullest reading of each story, but a defense against minimizing interpretations a sometimes too professionalized criticism has imposed.

Everything which tends to the satiric in *Dubliners,* especially on the recurrent theme of paralysis, seems to imply an author's "There go I but for the grace of my intransigent *non serviam.*" Yet that refusal having had its price, including remorse, and having left its residue of nostalgia, a stress remained which appears, with modifications yet similarly, in various stories. In this respect "Eveline" and "A Painful Case" are at opposite poles in the Dublin Joyce held up a mirror to. Those protagonists represent equally fatal extremes, and Joyce may have felt the threat of either doom, or even to a degree their incursion. However his intuition was come by, he knows the experience of vulnerable Eveline paralyzed in an equivocal yielding to a reductive environment; he also senses calloused Mr. Duffy, irremediably chilled to the bone by his wilful rejection of human ties. Having abjured both such subjection and such separation, the artist still could firmly claim no personal middle ground; ambivalence was a destiny, commingling such extremes, at best to be merely arrested this side of devastation. Consequently *Dubliners* cannot be read entirely in the dim light of Joyce's most acrid contemporary comments about it. He wrote, perhaps with self-directed irony, that the book was only "somewhat bitter and sordid."[70] There is in the stories a great deal besides what he called "the odour of ashpits and old weeds and offal"; there is much the opposite of that. Above all, in 1906 as he drew toward completion of the collection Joyce was not nihilistic and neither did he entirely despair about Ireland, for when he proposed to "fight to retain" censoriously questioned detail in the stories it was because he considered them part of "the moral history" of his country, toward whose "spiritual liberation" he felt he was taking "the first step"[71] in *Dubliners*. In this there was nothing overly sanguine but neither did it lack earnestness, nor had it yet acknowledged futility. In its way *Dubliners* shows the largest commitment of this artist as a man; this faith he was willing to serve, even with the kind of melancholy confession it entailed.

It might be remembered too that Joyce's early diagnosis of the human condition in Dublin did not consider it an outright paralysis but, more precisely, a paraplegia. Nor was this seen as uniform. In several of the most impressive stories, characters achieve a degree of extrication from limiting conditions or else some reconciliation of inner conflict. In either case the advance comes through a deepening of awareness and an enlarged definition of values, a drama played out in a preoccupied consciousness. Since at the core the story is psychological, what is most at issue in the midst of overt action and all naturalistic detail is the progression of sensibility toward some personal outcome. In "The Sisters" the boy, a Jamesian ideal artist in embryo in that nothing is lost on him, holds himself enough aloof from the women's talk in the room and beyond residual influence from the old priest whose ceremoniously arrayed corpse lies nearby, to set his own intention toward an open street. In "An Encounter" this boy, or one very like him or Joyce, moves through romantic illusions and a sensing of real depravity to the saving grace of simple companionship. "A Little Cloud" and "The Dead" each represent a man's penitent growth into fuller realization of primary human claims. "Araby" is a boy's momentary but overwhelming experience of disenchantment, after excessive stretching of expectation; "A Painful Case" shows a middle-aged man's resisted but inescapable realization that he has wasted life, his and another's, by a cold reserve. These, most moving and most profound, are the stories of greatest power, along with those which communicate pity for young Eveline, at last completely paralyzed by her ambivalence, and for old Maria of "Clay," numbed by the meagerness of a life diminished to a timid rehearsing of sentimentalities, under others' condescending toleration.

These two women, both so pitiable, are intermediate between those characters touched by an epiphany and those unvisited by illumination. Eveline, confronting a dilemma grown explicit and crucial, undergoes the most racking experience shown in *Dubliners,* but it stuns her almost to the obliteration of awareness; Maria habitually avoids realization, in order to go on imagining her relationships as more than they really are, and thus to repress the melancholy of a spinster's isolation. If other *Dubliners* characters seem more nearly impervious to self-knowledge than defensive against it (though something is shown of their states of mind, especially in the tendency to rearrange more convenient views of reality) it follows that an extended insight depends chiefly upon the reader, for whom the tenor of these sordid or muted Dublin existences is gradually disclosed through Joyce's more directly satiric tracings. So it is in "After the Race," "The Boarding House," "A Mother," and "Grace," or in the unequal pitting of integrity against proliferating expediency by the dramaturgically objectified "Ivy Day in the Committee Room," or in the utter bitterness of "Counterparts." Thus the narrowly confined matter of *Dubliners,* in which recurs the image of existences turning upon themselves in a closed circle, nevertheless encompasses opposites and extremes, and these as narrative spectacle have been made ready by Joyce's wide, intuitive confrontations, delegated to readers by his art.

Those stories which are primarily satiric render double judgment, upon Dubliners as well as upon Dublin. From his paradoxical vantage of detachment and concern, Joyce glances at the stupidity, irresponsibility, corruption, and occasional brutality of individuals, as they move within a stringent and subtly debasing society, yet each originative of his particular failings. While the sense of environment is constant in *Dubliners,* it is not stressed; instead it is the backdrop to sadly isolate lives, wilful self-defeat, and stupefying fates. The Joyce of *Dubliners* was sufficiently philosophical to distinguish between mores and morals, and enough of a humanist to view behavior as conduct, and to sense the pity of it in its shortcomings. Even for those characters with whom Joyce and his readers can have little or no sympathy there is at least some understanding, as of that adult truant Farrington's compulsive alcoholism and compensatory savaging of his little son, or impoverished Henchy's opportunism in "Ivy Day," or Mrs. Kearney's rampant self-defeating maternal egotism. The *Dubliners* roster, though limited to a lower middle segment of the society, produces a considerable range of men and women, exceeding that of *A Portrait* and comparable at this or that page with *Ulysses.* The greater significance, however, is qualitative; *Dubliners* stands second to nothing else of Joyce's for its sensing of personalities in several sorts. All the epiphanies, of whatever nature and degree, have been gathered up in a regard as intuitive as it is scrupulous.

There is thus a vision which unifies *Dubliners,* going beyond the local setting and basic sociological theme, permeating each of the stories despite their differences in scope and penetration. The constant factor is Joyce's creative command, which not only sustains pointed narration but involves the artist with his characters in a mood he never again expressed with quite the same fusion of detachment and compassion. The theme of ambivalence, rooted in the artist himself, is enacted through a variety of external instances, a multiple faceting, whereas in *A Portrait* the protagonist's struggle is explicitly autobiographical. In *Dubliners* Joyce approached his subject discreetly but in quiet candor, treated it with evaluative selectivity, yet based the fictional bodying forth on personal realizations as well as close observation. Even in their just severities the stories are never cold, and many disclose a private imperative for all the compassionate pondering a judicious scrutiny could allow.

Nor does their economy or their inconclusive structure prevent implication of values. In these stories epiphany, which is like the opening of a door or a flower, has also its closing, whether quickly or in a falling away, yet more strongly figuring life as a continuum with points of realization than is seen in many lengthily sustained narratives. The restrained voice comes to no emphatic climax but simply ceases and does not resume. The whole story is not to be told, and the gist of it, its human source and its indications, cannot be spoken at all but only shadowed forth. The reader of *Dubliners* can have the sense not so much of being led as of following, seeing nothing of his guide but a silhouette as he precedes, yet coming out after him onto the same open ground, but left to himself there. Sometimes the epiphany is only an emanation to be apprehended, such as what in "Grace" is suspended like another odor than incense beneath the flow of the preacher's yet unfinished discourse, or as with the women's talk that closes "The Sisters," where it is not in what they are saying but what the reader may now suppose the listening boy is making of it. Even when the epiphany is plainly glimpsed by the protagonist, it can be felt only through the narrative substance in its whole progress, calling for a reader's conserved responses and growing affirmation. Though this is what some readers may fail to accord, that is the hazard taken by the open-structured short story; and Joyce risked it fully, for the high stake of a permissive communication. His is a conscious art, but its apparent ways are not obtrusive, its composition unbrokenly sustains implicative overtones; and technique is always servant to an evaluation animated through the characters' vital experience and permeated by the artist's paradoxical involvement and transcendence.

5

If the man behind the art was so intimately knowledgeable about many in Dublin's peopled world because he knew himself likewise beset, that private issue, though it made him rebellious to the point of arrogance, did not immediately separate him from all others. He sensed how some among the humble and meek knew agonizing struggle toward a degree of self-possession. Above all in *Dubliners* he avoided modern literature's two offenses against the spirit—the first a pseudo-aristocratic or coterie presumption that acute awareness is the prerogative of an elite, however constituted; or secondly, a fictitious repeopling of the world with jerky automata to enact the artist's delusion that his own absurdity is universal but a comprehension of it is his unique gift. (One can imagine Eliot's condescension toward Eveline, placing her as of a class whose "souls" are to be categorized as "damp," and his considering the "odour of dusty cretonne" window curtains fastidiously rather than with Joyce's sense of the girl's plight. And while Beckett might have taken note of Eveline's final catatonic state, would he not have found it too absurd to consider how she had humanly come to that?) Joyce in *Dubliners* is not just more discriminating but more discerning and committed. If consciousness is his primary subject, that is always in its context of objective realities, and with regard for its individual operations, whether in some assertion or a falling short. Every Dubliner in every story ultimately is tested as to his responsiveness, in its unique nature, degree, and effect, whether more or less continuously manifest; and Dublin is judged for its imposition on individuals at their most private and determinant levels of experience.

Since the recording of such matter exceeds the range of a strict literary naturalism, and also lies beyond the writ of merely sociological readings, criticisms which are thus oriented may fail to grasp *Dubliners* fully. Other approaches resting chiefly upon archetypal symbolism or Christian and Homeric analogies may also stop short of what the stories more largely signify, a young artist's knowing judgment of an immediate reality and his flexible responsiveness. While the variety of *Dubliners,* with its close observation and generally sure command, clearly marks Joyce's genius in fiction, its full evaluation will depend upon discernment of its hidden personal sources. Moreover, the underlying subjectivity of *Dubliners* is of its own kind, not duplicated in the later works, and not definable as prelude or practice for them, but a unique achievement. Twisted into rebellion and then haunted by nostalgia, the ambivalent Joyce was still an extraordinarily dynamic being, capable in his youth of a certain self-knowledge, and prone to relate this not only to himself in Dublin but more subtly to vicissitudes in other lives, however obscure, confined, and submerged. Joyce's unique affiliation with the *Dubliners* subject matter, in that period of his life and in what was then his mood, is as important an aspect, critically, as is the narrative mode of the stories.

To see one's own tendencies for what they are and wherein they have arisen, and then to imagine where they might lead, and to extend such projections by concerned awareness of persons of all sorts and conditions, is a way the fictionist has for multiplying and refining his experiences. While such intent gives narrative scope and may reach to others' extremes of behavior, it can still retain the artist's feeling as a man himself beset and blessed. Indeed, for him to abdicate from that would be to lose creative impulse itself and its esemplastic use. Stephen's agenbite of inwit had been Joyce's own, and it taught him in turn to write of "tears of remorse" in the eyes of the Little Chandler whom too he had with reason satirized, this too possibly with private acknowledgment. Levin's frequently quoted observation that the protagonist of "The Dead," Gabriel Conroy, "is what Joyce might have become, had he remained in Ireland" might also be taken as resonant of ambivalence, in that Gabriel is much of what Joyce himself not only had been but to some degree remained, although it entered into his writing less and less directly. Possibly contributive to this sense of the matter is Levin's terming "the closing paragraphs" of the story "a valedictory."[72] "The Dead" was indeed Joyce's farewell not only to the short story form but to the *Dubliners* mode, with its particular distancing of a temperamental view. Gabriel's epiphany could have had no other source but Joyce's closely prompted intuition, including compassion for Gretta that extended into a sorrowful but saving identification with mankind. For the moment Joyce-as-Gabriel, like the directly confessional young Wordsworth, had felt "A weight of ages . . . descend upon" his "heart" but also "Power growing under weight." It was young Joyce's progressive self-awareness which endowed that great story with its lasting validity. Thus ambiguities are linked in the fancying of a Gabriel-Joyce who had "remained" in Ireland; Joyce did remain, in spirit, while writing "The Dead," and what he otherwise did "become" by not "remaining" so closely thereafter may be glimpsed in a connected view of his whole life and all his works, with comparative regard for *Dubliners*.

For there is no end to a deeply rooted ambivalence, and an artist so possessed can choose only to project further expressions of it, and, if it be his need, to cloak more elaborately any confessional element. In *Dubliners* the theme is still directly transferred to many of the characters, and the underlying personal admission is submerged, but scarcely further than for creative composure and pure fictional effect. Analysis can detect the private element variously projected in such stories as "An Encounter," "Two Gallants," and "A Little Cloud"; in "A Painful Case" it becomes the essence of the matter, concentrated to the point of anguish. If in fact and of necessity in the short stories dilemmas are never resolved, at least experiential quality is as directly bodied forth as fictional convention allows, and is not desiccated by an exile's compensatory cunning. The tincture of a privately confronted ambivalence keeps the most satiric *Dubliners* stories from bitterness and infuses the others with their pathos, which in turn is contained by the kind of objectivity that judicious commitment can empower. Thus even if Joyce's latter-day trend is not definable as a painful case, but as autonomous advance, *Dubliners* still is primary and of a unique excellence never superseded.

Considering who the young artist was and had been, what he had then found to be his subject, and how at that point he had come to view it, *Dubliners* is an eminent example of a poised engagement, concerned and controlled. That performance is as dynamic and balanced as tight-wire walking—instinct serves intent, and the essentially simple act bears the unremitting consciousness of issue. Joyce was to proceed to larger and more daring displays, but where else was he more nearly the epiphanal artist the young man aspired to be? *Dubliners* is, finally as from the first, his greatest act of piety, in that judgment and compassion, service and freedom were combined with some approach to perfection, in full acceptance of vocation and with as yet no tendency to pass by on the other side. Nor was Joyce ever to remove himself so far in later works that traces of this essential original man were not still to be felt. Which makes the technically objective *Dubliners* paradoxically the most intimate approach to its begetter, as well as something to be relished as a completely achieved thing in itself.

6

In that the stories are unities within a unity, *Dubliners* well exemplifies, by its instances and as a collection, a right fictional ratio between concept and embodiment. The work as a whole was avowedly intended to present a widely comprised matter from a sustained particular view, but this was not allowed to harden into ideology or deteriorate into overt demonstration. Each tale realizes its personages, however scantly seen and whatever their limitations, as human beings. Given a small piece of a world which still suffices for them to turn around in, they may be regarded in aspects, with relative implication. All this is projected in a subdued and tentative but solicitous fictional art, most scrupulous in its provision for intuitive response.

Awareness of effect in each of these stories is to be felt as crescendo and reverberation. Reading can view and sense, and onwardly adumbrate the fictional entity, as the artist has found his way to do. Factors concretely provided for the reader are to be reconstituted as means of approximating the matter, in a reciprocal yet spontaneous exercise of knowledge, judgment, and sensibility. Criticism, more particularly, can report such responses to a fiction's substance and qualities without posing as revealer of effects hitherto undiscovered, but merely aspiring to verify these through identification of elements and their shadings and aesthetic disposition. No analysis of techniques should finally fragment the work, or even dally too minutely this side of regard for composition, its whole substance as viewed from its begetter's grounds, and its vision conserved in the autonomous mediating work of art.

Since *Dubliners* read throughout must remain a series of readings, close sustained attention to each story is not superfluous; it is the only way the creation as such may be known, and *Dubliners* can be rightly evaluated only as the sum of fifteen evaluations. Certain critics have recognized this, by commenting on the stories seriatim, even if briefly. Detailed explication is justified, since the qualities permeating a work of art inhere in particulars modified by their play in what they become part of, thematically and aesthetically. Yet explication (even if not perverted by zeal) has its limits too; the aggregated effect of a fictional work of art is not only intrinsic but irreducible. Obviously it is indefinable in completely equivalent terms, and that not only because every individual response will be privately conditioned, but because to name and describe any organic entity must fall short of duplicating or even clearly mirroring it. Here a baffled critic may be tempted to borrow (Polonius-wise) the scientist's method, classification, but to say one work has a trait recurrent in other works does not describe any work as organic entity—and may even largely ignore it as such. Nevertheless, with such fictions as the fifteen in *Dubliners* with their integrated effects readied to be sensed, criticism may attempt at least to scrutinize these, to acknowledge the artist's discerning regard for living reality, and to ponder the art which not only makes a particular view apparent and credible but can evoke corresponding awareness in others' imaginations.

Under such a criterion, to speak of *Dubliners* as one of Joyce's "works," to set it as a whole beside *A Portrait* or *Ulysses,* can be ventured only with duc sustained consciousness of the stories, each as well as all. And here in *Dubliners* these items are to be seen as divers variations on a conceptualizing for which *theme* becomes almost too blunt a word, so intricated are the data, the artist's insights and predilections, and his devisings. Joyce in his letters did define a pervading intention for his book, but it is hazardous to read any work primarily in terms of what its author has said about it, and with Joyce it could obstruct comprehensive criticism. Admittedly certain generalizations may be abstracted from the collection at various points—paralysis, habitual drunkenness, simony, improvidence, "odour of ashpits," superstitious religiosity, pretentiousness, self-deception, environmental and familial confinement, rebellion, alienation, and ambivalence. Still, while such threads cross and recross into a fabric, each story is less a formal unit in a larger construct than another chord struck in a key grown familiar.

Dubliners does not survey a city entire; what the stories glance at is the variously enforced struggles, assertions, and ambiguousness of a few lesser Dublin folk. The first story contains a superannuated priest; the last has as protagonist a teacher and book reviewer among other teachers, but this story is at the highest socio-professional level shown in the book. The scene of the Polly Mooney – Bob Doran idyll is a boarding house. A census would turn up ordinary office clerks there and in several other stories. Eveline is a store clerk, involved with a sailor; Maria of "Clay" helps in an institutional kitchen. In "Two Gallants" and "Ivy Day" the men are economic hangers-on at the brink of indigence, and in "A Little Cloud" Little Chandler, husband and father, is a clerk with the furniture still to be paid for, and the journalist Gallaher's air of having got on seems spurious. The young fool in "After the Race" who can gamble away large sums is a self-made merchant's pampered heir, but such an economic level is scarcely approached by the solid bootmaker who supports a socially ambitious wife in "A Mother" or even by the sea captain incidental to "A Painful Case," where the protagonist is a bank teller. In "Grace" Power and Cunningham are minor government employees, M'Coy has lived by his wits and after other tries is secretary to the City Coroner, Fogarty is a grocer who has failed as a publican, and Kernan is a "commercial traveler" dealing in tea. There is one reputable singer in "The Dead" and lesser ones in "A Mother," one disreputable priest in "Ivy Day" to match one notoriously successful one in "Grace," but no physicians, no men of letters, no lawyers, no figures in public life above the cut of the disparagingly mentioned "Tricky Dicky" the publican, Corporation candidate in "Ivy Day." There are no personages such as those friends of Joyce's university days, Gogarty, Kettle, and J. F. Byrne, and there is no social setting like that Joyce had been welcomed into by the Sheehys. True, there are no thieves or murderers in *Dubliners,* no prostitutes except redeemed ones, laundry workers in "Clay," and but one case of morbid sexuality, the exhibitionist in "An Encounter." There are no still-fervent post-Parnellian rebels, either, but a lone nostalgic man of fixed principle, Hynes in "Ivy Day," where the others, like the prospering government-contract dealer in "After the Race," have found it expedient to moderate political ardor.

In sum, since *Dubliners* offers such narrow grounds for sociocultural generalizations, when those are essayed they might well be retested and qualified as to each story. Such procedure would properly subordinate over-all abstractions to the special tangent and potency of the particular tale, recognizing its people as proper fictions, separately representative. It would also go just far enough beyond a deterministic naturalism to discover in *Dubliners* instances of ordinary good will and right behavior, of human aspiration against the grain of environment, and some few of achievement of transcending insights. Such arrivals by characters at further awareness and deepened view of self and surrounding reality is a trait related to another aspect, the stories' open structure. Since in *Dubliners* this technique, though variably applied, is recurrent, expressing Joyce's psychological-aesthetic concept of epiphany, it might seem that the effect of manifestation would be not only climactic but conclusive, making for dramatic finality rather than the suspension typical of the

Chekhovian-Joycean open-structured tale. However, the central and most dynamic factor in Joyce's work was a pervading and indeed unrelenting sense of consciousness as process. Such a concept is not modernity's discovery or new in literature—the sun also riseth and hills peep o'er hills—but in this century both literature and psychology have enforced a denial that personality is static, making stability accessible. Even at the source of Joyce's term *epiphany* Yeats envisioned the tension of inconclusiveness, through the Magi, who "now as at all times" are "hoping to find once more" the "mystery" that has proven "uncontrollable" and was manifest further in "turbulence." Joyce made, so to speak, no eschatological extrapolations; he saw only cyclical recurrence, varied by perturbations. Yet these, the extremes of consciousness, are the peaks of realization. To picture approach to them is a higher realism, faithful to individual life as fluctuant process, in which generally little more than episode is isolable as a unity, and that only selectively. While the stories scarcely forbid intimations of subsequent progress or disaster in the lives they represent, they quite properly pose no finalities, and hardly open up a wide way to comprehensive abstractions, especially about the collection as a whole.

In the segments of existences otherwise unrevealed, with only glimpses in which outcome is merely of the instance and moment, that is often for the protagonist alone. What denouement there is may affect other characters, but such extensions are not traced out, as might be in more fully and objectively dramatized fiction; and even within the close grounds of each story the characters relate only with difficulty and imperfectly. In this aspect *Dubliners* is less a view of a society than a revelation of separate fates, with these seen only in passing, their further passage an enigma. The stringency of solitude as man's common lot, further intensified by a culture's fixations, may be what is most often echoed in *Dubliners* and the quality which lifts it furthest above locale and period into wider typicality. Since what activates drama is not merely an irksome and irritant social influence but the tracing out of its psychological effects, these may be sensed in the stories as cries beyond words from the encircled and frustrate, whose appeal may seem most of all for something beyond compassion, a commemoration in a larger understanding than the character himself is capable of, or at least able to maintain.

Such comprehensive exercise of the reader's as well as the artist's empathy is possible only from a point of detachment, but this side of aloof censoriousness or indifference. And as to fictional art it requires consent to inconclusiveness, in that solution cannot be imposed upon unamenable realities, and what may be glimpsed as desirable cannot be stabilized. These, Joyce's first completed readings of signatures, beyond static portraiture or a naturalistic mapping, are sensings of the ebb and flow which were the secret life of his little people, and which had some correspondence in his own "pros and cons." Looking outward in *Dubliners,* Joyce saw through appearances to an ultimate "ineluctable modality," the inwardness of any human fate, especially if a confinement to the circuitous and repetitive, socially and self-imposed. Therefore his narratings, alert to sorts and conditions of men and women as they lived, pass beyond observation to intimations of states of being. Forgoing the intently introspective or its obverse flight into casual association, and aspiring toward a fully controlled art, Joyce nevertheless imbued each piece in *Dubliners* with his mood as of that time—a reticent empathy which, with its tincture of distaste and even revulsion and its traces of *mea culpa,* is quite as complex as the fictional situations he pictures, yet stands comparatively freed while still involved.

In these envisionings in *Dubliners* of his own world too, and of others warpingly constrained in it in ways he himself apprehended, the outlook is that of an older, more engaged young man than Stephen, but also of one younger, less sardonic and crafty (and possibly more poised and consistently intent) than the creator of the multifariously dynamic *Ulysses*. Thus the art of *Dubliners* is all its own, not merely by more severe technical practice but in its unduplicated immediacy and commitment, unique even in each story, and asking a reading as such. Beyond self-portraiture yet this side of the stasis of a comic masking, it fixes its gaze upon points where for various beings existence comes upon real issue. Then and there an ordinary gesture may be telling, whether in one more step unsurely taken or in a confused turning aside. However intense the moment or defined the motion, its meaning will be permeated by its actual transience, and only through art is it suspended beyond its time. The aesthetic pause creates further paradox through light cast upon the troubled lives of Joyce's Dubliners, propelled by necessity in its classic sense or its more modern guise of determinism, yet seen, beyond such generalizations, as individuals agitated by their own instability and tending to quiescence only in a drift toward fatalistic passivity.

Despite Joyce's formal protestation that *Dubliners* constituted a first step toward spiritual liberation of his country, it scarcely can be supposed that this already alienated and artistically preoccupied young man saw himself as reformer and deliverer or would have accepted ordination to any such role. There are indications, besides, of a deputed history of revolt and discovery in some stories, and in others a veiled confessional element in representations of ambivalence, as of one knowing almost too well whereof he spoke. Still, in *Dubliners* this infusion of the privately subjective does not yet go beyond the conventions of fictional art, wherein Joyce found it his calling to witness, sense, and represent, vis-à-vis human idiosyncrasy and some major factors in a people's environment. For this little while, in these fifteen stories one by one, he stood his ground, though he too like his *personae* knew himself swayed and felt himself beset. In his first completed enterprise he bent art to a primary purpose, to extract disclosures from observed reality's passing moments, and from these envisionings to conserve aesthetically some lingering awareness. Such insight, humane in its attitude and import, is vitally and fluently embodied in the stories, with melancholy acknowledgment of mankind's fallibility, peril, and inquietude, yet recognizing the august contingency of moments of insight, and representing some of these with regard for the human potential they imply.

THE SISTERS

Joyce carefully arranged the order of stories in *Dubliners*. To end with "The Dead" was obviously right in terms of magnitude and synthesis; where to begin involved a subtler choice. Within the trio which had primacy as first-person accounts of boyhood "The Sisters" has a special validity. Its original draft was Joyce's first published story, in the *Irish Homestead,* but it was extensively and pointedly revised, as Hugh Kenner, Marvin Magalaner,[1] and others have noted, and in its final form it transcends juvenile substance with implications basic to the whole book. Its quietly resonant theme of disengagement establishes Joyce's vantage ground. This is to be seen if the boy's arrival at detachment is recognized in the dramatic use of narrative point of view. In the story's concluding pages Joyce has taken his stance, with his mirror, at a comprehensive distance. A reader's way to this story's revelation is not through prescribed procedure but by direct response to the substantiated work of art.

"The point of it still eludes me," surprisingly confessed Frank O'Connor.[2] Others have searched for the story's meaning in its supposed symbols or with reference to themes developed in its author's other works, such as his condemnation of the Church. And there is some agreement, variously expressed, about the story's inconclusiveness; Ellmann says Joyce "lets the effect seem to trail off,"[3] while Magalaner puts it that the story "is allowed to trail off as inconclusively as possible to fit in with the ambiguous position of the boy and the Priest."[4] Truly the priest's life has been an unresolved ambiguity, as has been his relation with the boy, but the boy's experience, beginning in ambiguity, has proceeded to clarification, and his achieved detachment at the story's end is not just a dramatic finality but a premise for much which follows in *Dubliners*.

The young narrator-protagonist is seen in the midst of his onward life and at a crisis. The death of his "old friend" exacts increased awareness, not only as death usually does, but because of strange particulars, past and present. These he reviews, in hesitant but progressive reappraisals. Along the story's brief main chronological thread are varied recurrences to what has gone before, and (in characteristic Joycean mode) intentional repetitions, even of words. These reiterated details take on changed coloration and weight; they are to be seen for what they were and then become in the boy's enlarging view, as he emerges from his circuitous pondering onto his own tangent.

The two Flynn sisters' down-at-heel presence and rambling impercipient discourse are the naturalistic stuff of the last scene, but the story is of a boy, in whose right it is told, while it concerns an old infirm priest who was his equivocal mentor in life and, ironically, in death. Him the boy finally assesses, not in words, but with an observant, thoughtful lad's intuitions of his possible autonomy beyond the mold which elders, semi-paralyzed by dogma and habit, would impose. He has not understood them, and they have plagued him, and not even through the priest's death does he discover answers, much less formulate counter-declarations. He merely holds his peace, such as it is. However subtly reconstructed, this is a boy's experience, and it communicates no incredibly precocious philosophical break-through, but the verisimilitude of a dawning awareness, a gradual, hushed, yet decisive epiphany. Passing somewhat beyond dependence and subservience, the boy realizes his identity just that much more, and with it his secret isolation, which he accepts as a condition of freedom. He makes no dedicatory vows, nor feels then or later that any were made for him, with some great forward step in maturation. The sum of it is that in his separation he senses and shows a greater self-possession.

Thus a reader's primary need is to locate precisely the narrative point of view and its variables—here and in the two other first-person stories of boyhood as well. Such technical practice as Joyce's has become conventionalized in modern fiction, but it takes some doing, and it risks misapprehension as well as misuse. With psychology's increased reference to childhood as a period of decisive conditionings, often centering in crucial discoveries, there have been many stories in the vein explored in "The Sisters," "An Encounter," and "Araby." The core of all such narratives is a recollection, reassessed maturely; the artist's problem is to couch this in a style that, while allowing implicative reflection, will also represent the child's immediate sense of the original experience, without smothering it in a subsequent analysis and abstraction. Kenner has noted relevantly Joyce's struggle with a phase of the style, for instance, in the revision from "the ceremonious candles in the light of which the Christian must take his last sleep" to "I would see the reflection of candles on the darkened blind for I knew that two candles must be set at the head of a corpse."[5] Besides such verisimilitude, however, this fictional first-person point of view must have stylistic range beyond pure boy's talk, such as Huck Finn's, if remembrance is to imply deeper insights than those of a grown but still naïve narrator like the one in Sherwood Anderson's "I'm a Fool." Such a sentence in "The Sisters" as "It was an unassuming shop, registered under the vague name of *Drapery,*" sounds the quiet presence of the reminiscent adult. And he is heard more definitely with this sentence:

> It may have been these constant showers of snuff which gave his ancient priestly garments their green faded look for the red hankerchief, blackened, as it always was, with the snuff-stains of a week, with which he tried to brush away the fallen grains, was quite inefficacious.

Not only "ancient priestly garments" and "inefficacious" go beyond a boy's way; the sentence is the opposite of colloquial, and by its prolonged, almost struggling construction it is loaded with kinesthetic suggestion, disclosing a sophisticated consciousness not only charged with recollection but in charge of an evaluative evocation. In short, art has entered in and at a more than naturalistic level.

"The Sisters" is anything but what Henry James castigated as "that accurst autobiographic form which puts a premium on the loose, the improvised, the cheap and the easy."[6] James's justified desire for "a particular detachment," from which distance "the observant and recording and interpretive mind" can have "intervened and played its part," is answered in all three of Joyce's first-person stories. The thing to see in "The Sisters" is the boy's beginning to see into himself as to the life around him. As for an artist's "particular detachment," that is fully risked by Joyce in the climactic close, where it is arranged for the reader to be conscious of the boy's diffidence and comparative silence as indicative of a separation toward which he has moved throughout the story. This progress was by a series of dawning apprehensions, implied in a first-person account tinged with reassessment but dominantly presentational, not analytical. It is the early establishment of this compounded point of view for a knowing central intelligence in "The Sisters" which enables Joyce to modulate the tone in the last episode, the prolonged conversation that lends the story its intriguing title. That objectified scene, with the boy now functioning as a capable witness whose reactive insight has been established, makes the point which seems to have eluded Frank O'Connor.

The closing pages of the story extend the skilful dramaturgy of the earlier episode in which the boy at home listened noncommittally to his elders' conversation about the just-dead priest. Corresponding to a cinematic fade-out on an action still in progress but completed in its implications, the ending of "The Sisters" resembles the conclusion of "Grace," but with the significant difference of the quiet boy's acutely attending presence in this first-person story. That presence adds a significance beyond fact; he is there with what he now knows, though he does not speak it fully even to himself. In "Grace" it is easy to see and see through the perfunctory Father Purdon and to postulate the fixity of his hearers in their closed circle of subservience and self-deception; what has dawned on the boy requires a closer look.

Joyce's art asks that "The Sisters" be read in its own right, which would be overshadowed and even falsified if the story is used to plot the direction taken by Joyce's later books or is made the field for a hunting-down of archetypal symbols, or is called up for examination under a predetermined category of Joycean themes. Father James Flynn's paralysis is not a parallel to Ireland's paralysis as defined by Joyce, and this priest cannot be taken to typify the Church, of which Joyce found for *Dubliners* what he considered better images in Father Purdon and Father Keon, and whose representative clerics he treated more broadly and tellingly in *A Portrait* and *Ulysses*. To stress the connection between Father Flynn and the boy as a reciprocal search for father and son is to reduce an unusual and, for the boy, a progressive relationship to one of criticism's most shop-worn stereotypes. And to focus conveniently on the wine and the cream crackers in the last scene as symbolic of communion may obscure the subtler suggestion of what this boy is experiencing in this situation, and thus may pass over an implied epiphany, tellingly related to *Dubliners* as a whole. With nothing "loose" or "improvised" about it, "The Sisters" brilliantly shows that an open narrative structure, while not supplying finalities, nevertheless allows implication of both character and theme in a dramatic-psychological continuum inclining toward the great human event of a further awareness. And when the open-structured narrative, as is usual in the modern mode, restricts itself to the presentational with no expository intrusion, the matters of selection, proportion, ordering, and connection call for ingenious and exact practice. Which "The Sisters" shows, to a high degree.

It begins in the midst of things: "There was no hope for him this time: it was the third stroke." Then one masterly loaded paragraph establishes the narrator, at that point of experience, as a schoolboy—"it was vacation time"—who "night after night," in some concern, has passed the house where lies someone who has been intimate enough to have often told him "I am not long for this world." In that world are certain customs and regulations; the boy "knew" that candles "must" be set at the head of a corpse. But beyond such facts received as having authority there is other and different knowledge, mysterious, fascinating, disturbing and at last liberating. The boy's growth in such knowledge is the story. In the penultimate paragraph he is to say again "I knew," yet now he has in mind not just a pious rule about obsequies but something independently observed and privately estimated. Readers have shared what the boy witnessed, through his noncommittal narration of it; but as to the few surprising bits of new knowledge—the broken chalice and pseudo-laughter in the dark confessional—the boy's intimation from this must be sensed through an implied aloofness in his neutral account of Eliza's talk and his own clear but unexplicated memory of the priest "as we had seen him, solemn and truculent in death, an idle chalice on his breast." As the story ends with one of the sisters still talking on, the reader should be able to hear as the boy would have been hearing her by that time. This is to realize that though her words are about the priest, Joyce's story is of the boy at that point, silent and still but brimming with insight. Here an epiphany, as a total experience, shows its intellectual factor, when a few additional facts consolidate intimations toward which the receiver has been intuitively groping. The boy has heard and also overhears; being informed, he becomes self-taught.

Every night as he had gazed at the window where the light was not yet that of ceremonial candles, he "softly" said to himself the word "paralysis," which "had always sounded strangely" in his ears, "like the word gnomon in the Euclid and the word simony in the Catechism." Paralysis suggested "the name of some maleficent and sinful being," yet though it filled him with fear, he "longed to be nearer to it and to look upon its deadly work." Here in nineteen lines, deliberate and even casual in tone, is given a sustained view over a bookish schoolboy's shoulder and a sense of his ranging thought, with its variableness and conflicts of mood. There follows a specific scene, of two pages, largely dialogue among adults, when the boy comes in to supper. The reader too may overhear a great deal. Some of it is sheer data incidentally dropped, some is naturalistic detail, including grown-ups' speculations that lead nowhere; some of it is quietly dramatic, through the boy's reactive separation from his elders; much of all this is thematically implicative. The boy has something less close than a son's status, living with uncle and aunt, and his comparative isolation is apparent from the first. A neighbor, "old Cotter," sits by the fire visiting, and the gossiping in the past tense is of someone about whom "there was something queer . . . something uncanny." The boy, like the reader, not yet knowing the subject of talk, feels that old Cotter is tiresome, though on earlier acquaintance his references to the distillery in technical terms ("faints"—the impure spirit coming over first and last in distillation, and "worms"—the still's spiral tube in which vapor is condensed) had rather interested this young fancier of words and what they conjured up. Now what comes out is that the boy's "old friend," as the uncle terms him, "is gone," the Father Flynn who, the uncle tells Cotter, had "taught" the boy "a great deal" and was said to have had "a great wish for him." Meanwhile old Cotter, who has called Father Flynn's a "peculiar" case without defining it, keeps his eye fixed on the boy, who responds by forcing silence on himself despite anger at Cotter, whom he thinks of as "Tiresome old red-nosed imbecile!"

The next paragraph has been referred to in some readings as a dream,[7] but it must be carefully noted as something more complex and more real, a wakeful passage through rational reflection to fantasies of association. It begins with the sentence, "It was late when I fell asleep," but obviously it was before doing so that he puzzled over Cotter's unfinished enigmatic references to the priest. Then he visualized what he knew so well, "the heavy gray face of the paralytic," and seeking childlike escape from that presence, he drew the blanket over his head and "tried to think of Christmas." Here he is still awake, but as the image of the face persists, the boy grows receptive to the notion that "it desired to confess something," and there begins his drift into drowsy and increasingly fanciful reverie. It is not unlike another child's meanderings between two worlds, when Coleridge, recalling himself at school thinking of home, tells how "oft/ With unclosed lids, already had I dreamt," till "soothing things" had "Lulled me to sleep, and sleep prolonged my dreams!/ And so I brooded all the following morn."

The boy of Joyce's story is perplexed rather than soothed, but perplexity stimulates him the more strongly. While his suppositions become extravagant, and closer to a dream's grotesque mixture of the strange and the familiar, they grow also more alertly intuitive. The passage becomes a document in imagination. His puzzling over Cotter's "unfinished sentences" leads on not to their completion but to a naming of what the smiling old priest might need to confess, and to the boy's sense of complicity, by his "smiling feebly" too, "as if to absolve the simoniac." It is the next morning, after the boy has come to the house of the dead but has turned aside and walked away from it, that he again "remembered old Cotter's words and tried to remember what had happened afterwards in the dream." Obviously Cotter's words pondered by the wakeful boy had not been part of the dream, nor had his covering his head and trying to think of Christmas, to escape the imagined face of the dead priest, which was also part of an open-eyed reverie. Perhaps it continued to be that, on to the identification of "the simoniac," in the boy's dim sense of what had been in a way confessed and in a way accorded absolution. The accompanying phrase, "some pleasant and vicious region" of the boy's "soul," has a conscious morbidity as well as perhaps more of conscience than a dream. Then when that next morning the boy on his way beyond the house of death recalls "what had happened afterwards in the dream," he does not summon up the old priest's face nor any of his bedtime responses to it, but something not mentioned thus far—"long velvet curtains" and a swinging antique lamp, and the feeling that he "had been very far away, in some land where the customs were strange." He has indeed, and awareness of it has come not by analysis but by intuition, released through severance of his subjection to the old priest. That the land of strange customs was "Persia, I thought" is only his boyish way of naming its exotic quality—such as may have been imaged for a Dubliner of that decade by Araby, the "Grand Oriental Fete," which came to the city in May, 1894[8]—and while the dream has not specified customs, his feeling they are not those he knows is the important matter here. Finally, as he "walked along in the sun," he "could not remember the end of the dream." And in a sense he has not yet come to it, or even to the end of what preceded it. Wrapped as he is in recollection of the old priest—his untidy snuff-taking and morbid lassitude, his perfunctory rehearsing of liturgical detail, and his smiling debilitated nodding over unanswered doctrinal cruxes—this boy too "brooded all the following morn" as he walked on toward the evening of that day. Not until his visit with his aunt to the Flynns' house is he to sight certain implications for himself, in a further wakefulness. In short, the reverie in bed had been increasingly fanciful yet more and more open-eyed; the subsequent dream is an excursion into the altogether foreign and derivatively tinged, perhaps in unconscious attempt at escape from the strange reality he had half-sensed concerning his association with the priest. Though by next daylight the boy makes an orderly return to that immediate past, he does not again enter into it, but instead curiously reviews it in memories tending to substantiate the previous night's waking vision that had identified the simoniac, and himself as collusive absolver. This had been no dream, and its mystery was merely that of any still amorphous intuition as it rises out of enigmatic experience.

Such is the central mode of that passage of about three pages in which action, memory, and speculation mingle as the boy goes his way alone on that next morning. He first "went down to look at the little house," and the very phrase suggests a compelled but still cautious approach, in a concern he cannot define; its meanings come to the reader only as reverberations from the play between the boy's past docility and his emerging detachment.

His reading the card pinned to the crepe on the door-knocker is the first full identification of the shadowy character opposite whom the boy is playing out a decisive experience:

July 1st, 1895
The Rev. James Flynn (formerly of S. Catherine's Church, Meath Street), aged sixty-five years.
R.I.P.

This sight intensifies the boy's awareness of an habitual association ended, and he calls up a scene often repeated, his bringing a gift of snuff to the tremulous untidy old man in "the little dark room." The boy admits a wish "to go in and look at him" but "had not the courage to knock," and so "walked away slowly." However, it is "along the sunny side of the street." In one of his Epiphanies young Joyce had written "O, the beautiful sunlight in the avenue and O, the sunlight in my heart!"—this following his prayer to the Virgin in a "quiet chapel where the mass has come and gone so quietly"[9]—but on this morning this boy's state of mind is not single. As he went he read "all the theatrical advertisements in the windows," and considering it "strange" that neither he nor the day "seemed in a mourning mood," he felt "annoyed" at his sensation of having been "freed from something" by the priest's death, and "wondered at this," remembering that, as the uncle "had said the night before," Father Flynn had "taught" him "a great deal."

Which lingering ambivalence leads the story directly to the priest, and indirectly to just what he had been teaching the boy and how it was being learned. As seen here Father Flynn can scarcely be read to figure the Irish Catholic Church. For one thing, his simony, while perhaps typical in essence, is more subtle than most. He is, first of all, a failure, not "a very great success"[10] like that Ulyssean cleric Father Bernard Vaughan, not a supremely assured procurer of complacent conformity like Father Purdon of "Grace." But neither is Father Flynn in disgrace like that "black sheep" Father Keon; he is, as far as Dublin knows, only physically incapacitated and relegated to retirement.

Nor had he been a bog-trotter ordained to minister among a parish of peasants; his birthplace in Irishtown, his former parish, and his final home on Great Britain Street (now properly Parnell Street) are all close to the city's center, but he "had studied in the Irish college in Rome." So one of the things he had taught the boy was "to pronounce Latin properly." And what else? Stories "about the catacombs and about Napoleon Bonaparte"; besides that, "the meaning of the different ceremonies of the mass and of the different vestments worn by the priest."

When the boy remembers his uncle's saying "the night before" that the "old chap" had taught the boy "a great deal," he does not also recall (or at least does not verbalize) the rest of the uncle's sentence—"and they say he had a great wish for him." This isolated report of what "they say" is the only basis, and it seems insufficient, for Magalaner's statement that "the old man had ended by trying to make a priest of him."[11] What the boy himself now recalls of his visits with Father Flynn does not confirm this but may imply something quite different. As the account goes on from such oddments as catacombs and Napoleon and ceremonies and vestments of the mass, the boy remembers that sometimes the priest "had amused himself by putting difficult questions to me." Thus the boy had been shown "how complex and mysterious were certain institutions of the Church" and how "grave" are the duties of a priest "towards the Eucharist and towards the secrecy of the confessional"—matters about which, he learns, the Church Fathers had written thick and closely printed books. Several considerations bear on this passage, at this point and as it continues. First, if the priest were trying to lead the boy to awareness of a vocation for the priesthood, it is unlikely he would begin with the greatest theological complexities. Moreover, while not until the last scene do the particulars of Father Flynn's disability emerge, with implications of its extent, the early conversation between Old Cotter and the boy's uncle has made the priest suspect; therefore any eccentricities in him may be clues for readers, as it seems they were to the boy, though slowly noted and scarcely defined.

The images accumulate. Told of all those bulky books and beset by the "difficult" questions it had "amused" the old priest to put to him, the boy often "could make no answer or only a very foolish and halting one," and then the old priest's response would be scarcely that of a single-minded mentor; he would "smile and nod his head twice or thrice." Similarly, when for occupation (and perhaps to give practice in Latin) he would put the boy through the responses of the Mass, "he used to smile pensively and nod his head," meanwhile stuffing his nostrils with snuff that dribbled upon the "ancient priestly garments." In his pensiveness is the suggestion of nostalgia, which, as Joyce well knew, can coexist with separation and even with disenchantment. The old priest's smiles, taken with his nods at the boy's foolish and halting answers, may not be just those of a superannuated man reminiscent about his life's work, they may have to do with a more drastic retirement. This telling passage about Father Flynn and his unvested acolyte closes with one more image, connected with the amused nods at the boy's inability to answer and with the pensive smile during the boy's pattering of the memorized responses—"When he smiled he used to uncover his big discolored teeth and let his tongue lie upon his lower lip," not only a man semi-paralyzed but gone slack in spirit, a winded old dog. This habit had made the boy "uneasy" at first, before he "knew him well." Yet evidently the boy accommodated himself somewhat to the curious companionship Old Cotter found questionable. Conversely, the boy's casual but habitual attendance on the old priest is perhaps what allows growth of awareness which is to carry him not only beyond Cotter's insinuations but out of the dark little room and onto the sunny side of the street.

For what altogether had been inculcated, during that odd extended association? In detail, factually, a pronunciation of Latin, some historical data, the text of liturgical responses, the symbolism of rituals and vestments. More broadly, the arduousness of priesthood, and difficulties of the Faith, and the voluminousness of patristic scholarship's endeavors to cope with intricacies and mysteries. But further still, the boy had absorbed something of even larger extent, uncertainty itself; and what the priest actually had prepared him for was withdrawal. However, it scarcely can be assumed that this was the priest's conscious intention. The implications of the account are subtler than that, and the situation more complex. When the boy remembers the priest had "amused himself by putting difficult questions," it is for want of knowing a better word that he calls it amusement, yet at least he sees it not as sober purposeful instruction but as a kind of personal indulgence. He would have to be older, and sufficiently troubled, to know how an isolated adult can use an attentive but naïve child as a sounding board, with no intention to be completely candid, but merely in a kind of talking to oneself, when this evades the urge to an open acknowledgment. Similarly a father may speak darkly to his young son, and abruptly stop, or a mother make veiled lament to the child still small enough to hold; and one might even see a trace of magic in all such cryptic indirection, a charm, an inoculation against some known unnamed evil, which the mind acknowledges the more by circumlocution. If the sense of fate is subjectively colored by feelings of guilt, grown morbid through concealment and even repression, then to skirt the edge of revelation may become a compulsive melancholy game. This is one the artist can play too, with pensive amusement or more grimly; Thornton Wilder found it in *Finnegans Wake,* which he describes as Joyce's "confession at a very deep and agonizing level," calling such an unburdening wonderful but difficult, as "the subject longs to tell his charged secret and not to tell it."[12]

With the boy, at least, Father Flynn may attempt to release a longing "to tell" and yet "not to tell." It is improbable, however, that he discerns in the boy's compliance any beginnings of complicity. The priest is too old, isolated, turned in upon himself, and burdened with basic concealment, and too dulled by his ailment to scrutinize his unofficial disciple and estimate his status and progress. Instead he "amused himself." Yet the amused old man smiled "pensively" too, with the melancholy of one who knows the loss of his hold on what he had committed his life to. The ill, enervated, "disappointed" old man, still a priest but without a curacy except this odd accidental one, can communicate his failure only by implied reference to the larger fact that the Church has failed him. So he goes no further than to put unanswerable queries and then tell the schoolboy how thick and closely printed were the books by "the fathers of the Church . . . elucidating all these intricate questions." Not any answers, and not whether the elucidation was of more than the intricacy. Granted that such subjects were beyond a schoolboy's mind, why should the priest raise the questions if only to tell his pupil of the thick and closely printed books? Hearing of them, the boy "was not surprised," and it is in this situation that he ceases to be uneasy at the laxness of the old priest's half-open mouth when he smiles. The boy is beginning to be touched by dim notions of what it is to let go, in a lapse of certainty. The story does not, however, suggest a lad's awareness of a man's ordeal, caught between commitment and questioning, or of a possible veiled appeal for pity.

Further, the still frocked but idled snuff-stained priest who raises questions he presumably cannot answer does by example teach one thing, the meaning of equivocation. Perhaps it is first in himself that the boy senses simony, by his attendance upon one whose authority has dwindled to fragmented knowledge perfunctorily rehearsed, and to the supererogatory citing of gaps in the system he formally represented. Then piecing it together in the crisis of memory on the night of the priest's death, the boy could imagine the old man's "grey face," murmuring, desiring "to confess something," smiling "continually," and so the boy felt himself too "smiling feebly," as if "to absolve" one he can now identify as "the simoniac." But that was the nocturnal fancifulness which had then deepened into strange dream. Next morning as the boy "walked along in the sun" he reviewed his intimacy with the priest, the bringing of the gift of snuff and the receiving of miscellaneous instruction, but he did not probe further its meaning for him. He cannot reach far enough into himself to assess all that is dawning on him, but significantly the stream of his association is from Cotter's vaguely ominous enigmatic remarks to the indeterminately exotic details of a half-remembered dream. Lying between these poles is everything he had experienced with the priest, but for the moment all he can make of it is that it has been increasingly suggestive, in ways he is yet to assimilate. Seldom have the intuitive gropings of an acute, independent young intelligence been as subtly sketched, with regard for their complexity, yet without exaggerating their reach.

Old Cotter had been right as to the obvious, that children's "minds are so impressionable," but he is invincibly ignorant as to the nature of the impressions this boy had received from the priest. Cotter had added uncompleted but repeated hints of some perversity in Father Flynn—"something queer . . . something uncanny," one of those "peculiar cases." As to one kind of peculiarity there is implied agreement in the uncle's prescription against all that—cold baths and exercise; the aunt wanted to know more, understanding nothing, but the men did not tell her. There at home that night the listening boy had been essentially as alone as he is in the morning, walking away from the dead priest's house; then he would not meet the despised Cotter's gaze, and now as he takes the sunny side of the street, he carries the ambivalent mood of one in transition. Though the word paralysis had "filled" him "with fear," he had "longed to be nearer to it and to look upon its deadly work," had "wanted to go in and look at" the dead man but lacked "the courage to knock," had "found it strange" that neither himself nor the weather "seemed to be in a mourning mood," and felt "even annoyed at discovering" a sense of having been "freed from something" by the priest's death. This tentative and troubled reaching for what it is he has learned and has been prepared to learn from Father Flynn is indeed complicated; the boy's intimations not only oppose the pressure of his environment in general, they conflict with what he himself as well as others might have assumed was to be absorbed from a priestly guide. In the truest sense this story becomes immediately existential, with a dramatic movement no less intense for being discursively subjective and largely dependent on half-submerged implications. Joyce does not cause this lad to state a conclusion; neither does the author set it forth for the reader, even to the degree that a boy is made to formulate it in "An Encounter" or "Araby," or a man in "A Little Cloud" or "The Dead." Joyce does present the boy in the process of coping with influences manifest in his ambivalent reactions before being more clearly recognized by him, presumably, and so by the reader.

If in the central passages there is some chronological manipulation and much return upon details, especially with the boy on his way to sleep and in the street next morning, such an eddying narration is not without design or effect. His recalling at random but collectively the visits with Father Flynn conveys the boy's confused awareness of their unsettling effects. Yet by turning all this over and over he sorts it to some end. His bedtime reverie has groped through to an intimation of simony; it is his morning choice, though hesitantly and still in ambiguous mood, to turn from the crape-hung door and escape along the sunny street. So even before he learns the most indicative facts about Father Flynn he has intuitively fathomed the matter sufficiently to react, and he is already on his way toward separation. Thus all is set for that remarkable closing scene in which the boy, outwardly submissive, silently accompanies his aunt on the ceremonious call upon the bereaved sisters. Here his recollection tells the reader very little except what he saw and heard, yet his unvoiced responses color the overt action with his secret mood, while the stereotyped melancholy talk goes on till Father Flynn's disaster is at last more fully revealed. Then apparently what the boy has already apprehended grows clearer to him, though full assimilation of it may be long in coming, in his progress to manhood's identity.

So in reading "The Sisters" it does not go far enough to name the priest as a father-figure and then take that as a conclusive symbol. Even though the boy had attended upon Father Flynn with some regard, whatever was dutiful in it does not survive the old man's death and the further awareness then precipitated. Bearing the periodic gifts of snuff his aunt supplies, the boy had approached Father Flynn as both his cleric and tutor. In the first aspect a change is perceived, corresponding to the "green faded look" which "ancient priestly garments" had taken on under "showers of snuff." If the old man figures as the Church in his attendant's eyes to begin with, he does not remain so as the boy passes beyond uneasiness at his mannerisms and begins to be more aware of the priest's own distance from what he spoke of. As teacher, Father Flynn performs ambivalently; by precept he inculcates precision, as in pronouncing Latin and making the set responses; but with a larger effect he loosens the reins. The more the boy is informed the less is his certainty and attachment; he is playing out in miniature the typical progress from enlightenment to agnosticism and stoic autonomy. But he only faintly senses the change in himself, and it is thus that he grows disturbed by ambivalence, as when dropping into his dream he had felt his "soul" to be "receding into some pleasant and vicious region," or the next morning, walking away from the house of death along the sunny street, was "annoyed at discovering" his "sensation of freedom." He learns how complex is liberty, and how to be free is often to be adrift. Yet it appears he also knows that what he is discovering is for him, and is not to be surrendered.

In the final episode, his going with his aunt to call on the sisters, he is clarifying his awareness of the situation, and the resolution of his own uncertainties about the priest is conveyed through a crescendo of implicative detail registered in the boy's quiet awareness. He is no longer subordinated in his immediate environment; a larger world is very much with him. "It was after sunset; but the windowpanes . . . reflected the tawny gold of a great bank of clouds," and when the visitors go into "the deadroom," he sees that "through the lace end of the blind" the place "was suffused with dusky golden light amid which the candles looked like pale thin flames"—sunlight itself contradicts these brief particular observances, as earlier it had touched him to mundane freedom on the sunny side of the street. Kneeling with his aunt and the sister Nannie, the boy "pretended to pray" but was "distracted" by "the old woman's mutterings" and "how clumsily her skirt was hooked" and how her boot-heels were "trodden down all to one side." While this could be called sheer naturalism it is also implicative; what distracts him is not these details themselves but their suggestion of the way this old Irish Catholic woman's life has gone, and what he is distracted from is prayer, there beside the corpse of his "old friend." Into his freed consciousness enters a significant image—"The fancy came to me that the old priest was smiling as he lay there in his coffin." But he was not, as the boy saw when he rose from his knees: "There he lay, solemn and copious, vested as for the altar, his large hands loosely retaining a chalice." (Magalaner has helpfully pointed out the importance Joyce must have attached to this image, since in the *Irish Homestead* magazine draft the dead priest held a rosary and in a second draft a "cross.")[13]

For the boy, however, and for readers, whose only access in this story is through him as central intelligence, the full symbolism of that loosely retained chalice is yet to be revealed, through conversations to come, which the boy listens to, unobtrusively but responsively, though from his just-acquired distance and detachment. There are several gradations in the last scene, when the three have come away from "the dead-room" to join the other sister, Eliza, where she sits in the priest's arm-chair. First is a passage of almost pure naturalism, as Nannie serves sherry and cream crackers and then Eliza and the boy's aunt rehearse the clichés of "gone to a better world . . . quite resigned . . . such a beautiful corpse . . . no friends like the old friends . . . gone to his eternal reward." Then Eliza's reflections give a glimpse of the priest in his decline, "with his breviary fallen to the floor, lying back in the chair and his mouth open." But despite his illness "still and all" he had "his mind set on" one thing, an excursion by hired carriage "before the summer was over," and not to St. Catherine's on Meath Street but to the other point of a triangle that had bounded his life in central Dublin, "the old house . . .

down in Irishtown" where he and his sisters had been born. Then follows the women's circling, considerately understated, and actually impercipient discussion of poor Father Flynn's troubled life. "The duties of the priesthood was too much for him," Eliza says, and that is as close as they come to it. "And then his life was, you might say, crossed," she continues, and the boy's aunt agrees that "He was a disappointed man. You could see that." After a silence has possessed the room, Eliza continues, explaining that "the beginning of it" had been "that chalice he broke." She reiterates what "they say," that the accident was "the boy's fault"—the acolyte's, presumably—and she remembers too that "poor James was so nervous," yet she shows no real sense of what may have made him so. A possible symbol, though import does not hang solely on it, is in what else is said about the priest's case. Eliza quite faithfully feels the mishap with the chalice was minimal, since "they say it was all right, that it contained nothing, I mean." Still she has assumed the accident was "the beginning of it," whereas the priest who was "so nervous" that he broke a chalice may have been already emptied of real faith.

Ellmann calls the sisters "well-informed,"[14] and they are, concerning details, as discursive Eliza shows and as deaf, tired, silent Nannie doubtless shares, but they can scarcely be credited with "acuteness."[15] In their complacent ignorance which uncritically lives and endures by half-answers they illustrate a classic form of the paraplegia Joyce diagnosed in Dubliners and sought to hold a mirror to. They have memorized all the set responses, but have heard none of the real questions, not even concerning their own unfortunate brother. It is in such benightedness that Eliza makes the vague understatement which closes the story: "So then, of course, when they saw that, that made them think that there was something gone wrong with him. . . ." What his clerical associates had discovered one night was the missing priest "sitting up by himself in the dark in his confession-box, wide awake and laughing-like softly to himself." Eliza has words for it, but no intuition of the priest's ordeal.

Implication of what that has been is thus given the reader in one of those gradual disclosures which can make an open-structured story definitely conclusive. However, "The Sisters" is not primarily about the sisters (unless reading reduces it to a naturalistic document) and while it concerns Father Flynn, that is as to the progress of his effect on the boy, not by precept or overt example but by subtler influence. While the boy is the direct narrative medium throughout, this is most suggestive in the last scene, where fuller disclosures that presumably filter through his awareness seem the more telling because he remains so carefully quiet. For all his youth, he is by past experience and present curious alertness a peculiarly qualified witness, and as near an expert on the isolated ambiguous old priest and his obscure case as could be found. Through the boy's remembrance of snuff-stained Father Flynn nodding over unanswerable questions the reader can imagine what stumbling along the way and loosening grasp preceded his breaking the chalice. And at the end of Eliza's fragmented account the boy could have some inkling of the double darkness pressing upon the priest "laughing-like to himself" in his confession-box. Something had been dawning on this boy all along; the priest's death had precipitated further intuitions, looked upon in his bedtime reverie and on next morning's ramble. Now in Eliza's released talk he hears, presumably for the first time, the factual details of the priest's collapse; and listening to that and to the silence of the house, he "knew" certain things, with a sudden definiteness as at the drawing aside of a window-curtain. Readers are to have come by this present knowledge in the boy along his same route, and to see that for him the trembling scale, upon which more and more had been put from time to time, has turned. Thus recurring details in "The Sisters" are not superfluous but increasingly weighty with revelation. Modified in their successive contexts, yet recognizable as are variously reiterated phrases in music, they support the nuances which compose a tale of a boy's advancing and finally resolved experience.

The detail of the ceremoniously proffered wine and crackers is what chiefly draws the silently listening boy into the last scene, but probably with further implication than what is sometimes alleged in citing a supposed symbol of religious communion—and just that, as if in itself it were exemplary. Actually, when Nannie pressed the boy to take some cream crackers, he declined because he thought he "would make too much noise eating them." It could be supposed he wants to avoid unseemly sounds in the house of the dead; perhaps beyond that he wishes to escape attention, which is indeed a withdrawal from communication. The boy has moved throughout toward detachment; at this point presumably he wants not just disengagement but perspective in which to resolve his ambivalence. Which he seems to do, finally; but before that the business of the wine and crackers has entered two passages significantly.

When old Nannie, the boy, and his aunt came down from their devotions in "the dead-room" and found Eliza in Father Flynn's armchair, the boy "groped" his way (this is the priest's "little dark room") toward his "usual chair in the corner." Seated as often before, he faces a different instructor, who from that same armchair is to complete his factual knowledge of the priest's failure and also, though unconsciously, will allow him to clarify apprehensions which have plagued him contrarily. Nannie, at Eliza's bidding, poured sherry into glasses she had set out on the table "and passed them to us," the narrator remembers. The first of several implicative moments of silence falls upon them—"no one spoke: we all gazed at the empty fireplace." Then while Nannie "seemed about to fall asleep," the conversation between Eliza and the aunt runs on lengthily through funereal clichés. Finally Eliza hesitates and again there is silence, "under cover" of which, says the now completely unobtrusive teller of this tale, "I approached the table and tasted my sherry and then returned quietly to my corner." Presumably when Nannie had filled the glasses "and passed them to us," the boy had received his glass, while being "pressed" to take some cream crackers "also." His aunt had "sipped a little" and then after some talk had "sipped a little more from her glass," but the boy does not speak (except if he did more than shake his head in declining the cream crackers) nor is it told that he partook of the sherry until, having approached the table, he "tasted" it there, as if avoiding too open a refusal, and perhaps then set down his glass. Plainly there is suggestion of a minimum gesture and a calculated withdrawal in his approaching and tasting "under cover" of silence and his returning "quietly" to his chair in the corner, to hear out the rest of a conversation he takes no part in but presumably responds to privately. Even if more explicitly the images of table, wine, an approach in silence, a sip, and a quiet retiring were seen as symbolic of making a communion, the communing was with himself, the whole course of the boy's observings and implied reflections is the central line the story has taken to give its dominant tone, and all this is to determine what he at last understood unambiguously, at the close of Eliza's account.

It has been an ironic communication, in that her vague and impercipient talk precipitates the boy's lucid realization. This epiphany is sounded by a single note, a sharpened awareness of smiles and silence, related to other images, remembered or fancied, which gather several strands of impressions into what he finally "knew." In the telling, moreover, the artist's presence is felt through a restraint that holds the climax within the pure *claritas* of the boy's reminiscent-attentive-pondering consciousness. As aloof as his fictionalized character, Joyce here is almost as silent. This story provides no formal conclusion, and what it discloses is to be come upon only by going tentatively all the objective-subjective way with the intuitive boy.

When Eliza had come to the somber heart of her tale, describing how the priest had been found "in the dark in his confession-box, wide-awake and laughing-like softly to himself," she then "stopped suddenly as if to listen." The boy followed her one step further: "I too listened." But there was no sound, and the boy now "knew that the old priest was lying still in his coffin . . . solemn and truculent in death, an idle chalice on his breast." He had just seen this, the "large hands loosely retaining a chalice," but what in life was insecurely held by the priest is now conceived of by the boy as "idle." The chalice thrust into a semblance of being grasped by his dead hands suggests others' attempt at a larger restoration and reinstatement, but it seems too like a toy returned to a child who cannot hold, much less make proper use of it. Yet that the priest's fate is summed up in such telling imagery is only adjunctive, narratively, to the boy's increase in a somber yet liberating wisdom.

His visualizing the priest lying "solemn and truculent" proceeds from an earlier progression of awareness, for while he had knelt pretending to pray, a "fancy came to" him that the priest was "smiling in his coffin," but upon rising the boy had seen "he was not smiling" and instead "His face was very truculent, grey and massive, with black cavernous nostrils"—perhaps still snuff-stained. Earlier in the story there have been smiles, but all of them sicklied, as different from any genuine kind as "laughing-like" is from laughing. Three times in seven lines describing the "amused" old priest the phrase "used to smile" recurs. To suggest a dawning realization which the narrating persona himself could not define, Joyce used the concrete yet implicative device of fanciful images which persistently haunt to demand interpretation. When the musing boy had felt that he "was smiling feebly" in return, that too is ambiguous, as between the "pleasant" and the "vicious," but out of it had come insight, "the grey face" had become "the simoniac," its murmuring desire "to confess" completes the boy's intuition of the sin. Man and boy had smiled and smiled, being ambiguous, but all smiles have stopped together with death and its revelations, first obscurely sensed and then confirmed in fact.

Julian Kaye, citing Eliza's description of the priest in his confession-box, proposes that "what he is trying to confess is . . . the sin of simony."[16] But was he then trying to confess or was his "laughing-like" the hysteria of one who, seeking by habit his proper place, knew himself lost where he should have been most at home, in a priestly function, hearing others confess? And was his pseudo-laughter, like the loose-lipped smiles the boy had observed, a form of that melancholy compensation to which

Joyce himself was more rationally prone, a wry derision of a lost belief? But whether or not he was trying to confess at the time his breakdown was discovered, the priest did not confess, then or later; and the sister Eliza and the boy's aunt rehearse the glosses still put upon the matter—"too scrupulous," duties "too much for him," a life "you might say, crossed," a "disappointed man." Behind this veil the real story turns upon degrees of reticence in Father Flynn and progressive discoveries by the boy. While the priest's risky questions and ambiguous nods and smiles seem an adult's toying with a still secret unrest, in the paradoxical companionship of an uncomprehending child, the boy, though intellectually baffled by cruxes in doctrine, is not only "impressionable," as old Cotter has said of all children, but is especially intuitive and innocently curious for the truth. Thus he comes to the heart of the matter, for himself as well as about the priest, and it is the child who names the man's sin, and gives him whatever absolution inheres in understanding.

When in that bedtime reverie at the verge of his dream he "understood" the dead priest "desired to confess something," and the troubled curious boy feels his way, through impressions that have sunk at random into his unconscious, toward identifying the flaw, he finds his catechism had given him a name for it. Seized upon with a precocious child's avidity for words as fit keys to further awareness, there had been not only *faints* and *worms* from old Cotter, but more closely *paralysis*, *gnomon*, and *simony*. While paralysis is not only central in this story but the announced emblem of Joyce's view in *Dubliners*, he makes it, precisely, paraplegia. His Dubliners are only partially paralyzed, yet radically limited and incapacitated, and figuratively their motions are halting, their utterances muffled. So it has been with the old priest, already having suffered strokes preceding that third which carried him off, and still earlier stricken in the vocational breakdown that necessitated retirement. The word paralysis "had always sounded strangely" in the boy's ears; he must have been hearing it specifically of Father Flynn before the final illness. As for "the word gnomon in the Euclid," it can of course be read symbolically, whether with reference to the index of a sundial, or any object which marks by its shadow, or (obsoletely) as a rule or canon of faith, or directly from geometry as the remainder of a parallelogram after removing a similar smaller parallelogram containing one of its corners, and thus leaving an asymmetrical part of a former whole. Gerhard Friedrich, citing this Euclidian meaning of *gnomon* and admitting also the sense of a shadow cast as on a sundial, sees here a clue to the *Dubliners* stories as "gnomonic projections."[17] Certainly the partial, reduced lives of Joyce's Dubliners do adumbrate a potential, something larger and more symmetrical. Father Flynn is such a gnomonic shell of his earlier self, and he casts an indicative shadow, too, and to note this would be no false sighting of implication. However, a different kind of fictional artistry may be involved here, at once simpler and more subtle, in the use of related but not primarily significant details for a diffusion which will keep one central item from being too conspicuous prematurely. Under the aspect of a lad's fascination with the sound of novel words, *gnomon* takes some share of the emphasis in association with *paralysis*. Thereby the word *simony* is less pointedly planted in the first paragraph, and that it too is book-derived from his studies makes it seem the more casual and loosely associated. At any rate, no more is heard of *gnomon*, but when the boy abed muses upon old Cotter's insinuations and fancies the grey-faced, moist-mouthed, smiling paralytic as desiring to "confess something," the boy's responsive feeble smile is "as if to absolve the simoniac."

However "strangely" the word simony had sounded to the lad, he had been hearing it, and would have had some definition of it. If his source there in the 1890's was a Maynooth Catechism (like that on Mr. Duffy's shelf), it might have given him a specific and authoritative statement, but could not have gone to the lengths or involved the distinctions that could have been found in numerous "closely printed" pages of learned doctrinal wrestlings with this ubiquitous and protean sin. What, though, is Father Flynn's simony? Certainly something beyond the receipt of snuff on behalf of a boy to whom he teaches the responses of the Mass, correctly pronounced. The identification of simony, begun by this boy, is also a concern of those two young men (or that young man twice born) of whom the child in "The Sisters," "An Encounter," and "Araby" may be considered prototype. Stephen Dedalus, when the director is asking him to consider whether he may have a vocation for the priesthood, feels that "through the words he heard even more distinctly a voice bidding him approach, offering him secret knowledge" so that among other things, he "would know then what was the sin of Simon Magus."[18] The Ur-Stephen had been assuredly discursive on the subject. Lynch, learning of the Heroic "adventure" with Emma—Stephen's bluntly proposing that they "live one night together"—terms this certainly "not the way to go about it." Answering Lynch's mild enough statement, Stephen defends himself with naïveté and arrogance, supplemented by scholarly reference to the Book of Common Prayer and Goethe, and to simony, under which heading he is disposed to include the convention of matrimony. "These people count it a sin to sell holy things for money. But surely what they call the temple of the Holy Ghost should not be bargained for. Isn't that simony?" Analogically he puts it that a woman's body is "a corporal asset of the State," and argues (in one of *Stephen Hero's* "slashed" passages) that she may "traffic" with it, may "sell it either as a harlot or as a married woman or as a working celibate or as a mistress." But since a woman is also "a human being" and "a human being's love and freedom is not a spiritual asset of the State," these presumably cannot be bought and sold —all of which leads to his declaration that "Simony is monstrous because it revolts our notion of what is humanly possible." Stephen is made to "deplore the fact that the solution of moral problems should be so hopelessly entangled with material considerations."[19] His phrase "what is humanly possible" may suggest that under his definition simony is "monstrous" both because it narrows human realizations and entails inordinate demands.

This perhaps shadows forth the plight of Father Flynn, who had taken vows more stringent than those of matrimony, promising not only as exclusive a devotion but a subservience not required of a husband, and a lifelong faithfulness not just to one chosen person but a whole establishment. If allowance were given Stephen Hero's diatribe, including that "A man who swears to do something which it is not in his power to do is not accounted a sane man,"[20] then Father Flynn's aberration would date from his first vows. At any rate, for him it has not been "humanly possible" either to withstand skepticism or to confess his infidelity. While his nods tacitly admit that the hard questions are unanswerable, he continues to rehearse the boy in the liturgical responses, reducing them to bits of professionalism which are the remaining props of his still privileged status, with its levy not only in gifts of snuff but on the boy's attendance and deference. Which latter the boy in turn finds is not "humanly possible," in the sober course of his memory-saturated musings after the priest's death. The boy's aloof silence first and last is eloquent of a dark apprehension he is stumbling toward, not only the mystery of the priest's life, but the dim vast enigma of service and freedom. To choose absolute commitment out of relative knowledge in a fluctuant and largely inscrutable existence is to attempt the humanly impossible and to incur enslavement and diminution; to avoid engagement and communion is to fall short of the perhaps possible human realizations. Simony is then definable as the monstrous paradox of these inseparable irreconcilables, as Joyce's characters man and boy glimpse it. The lad of the first story takes the first step toward Stephen's *non serviam*, beyond which lies the Daedalian young man's discovered vocation as artist, to be continued in Joyce's unique practice, which rejected external authority and put on the habit of sympathetic alienation.

The wonder is not that the boy comes to no more than shadowy apprehensions and an instinctive withdrawal; what is remarkable (yet a credible foreshadowing of Stephen Dedalus) in his acuteness in identifying his "old friend" as "the simoniac."

As to Simon's sin, the Church itself had long been troubled, not for lack of examples but being much exercised over shapes and shades of this abuse. Such could have been among the "intricate questions" Father Flynn, in his pseudo-confessional chats, had given the boy some notion of. Certainly the artist as a young man, in his peculiarly avid way, would have looked further into scholastic struggles with the problem. The *Catholic Encyclopaedia* states as a usual definition "a deliberate intention of buying or selling for a temporal price such things as are spiritual or annexed unto spirituals."[21] Thomas Aquinas called simony "the deliberate will to buy and sell spiritual things," in the sense of privileges and rights and "their appurtenances,"[22] and here, as Stephen Dedalus learned, simony is to be associated with sinning against the Holy Ghost. Thomas Aquinas attempted the difficult distinction between any specific buying and selling of priestly services, especially as to the sacraments, and the necessary support of the clergy.[23] The identification of kinds of simony was part of the problem; Pope Gregory the Great was active in opposition to ordinations not only for money but because of influence or entreaty.[24] He defined several intents of simony—*munus a manu,* money or other direct material advantages; *munus a lingua,* oral advantage, by commendation and public support; and *munus ab obsequio,* homage, subserviency, or rendering of undue service.[25] And of course in each such purchase of advantage there also would exist the probability of a "deliberate will" to make the sale. Given human selfishness and leanings toward expediency and rationalization, the possible varieties of simony seem endless. Nor is it just an ecclesiastical problem. Stephen Hero saw simony in secular aspects of marriage but proposed a defense of his art against the charge of simony, while expecting payment for his verses. As Father Flynn "amused himself" in equivocal talks with the boy, he may have told him of the tradition, beyond the New Testament account,[26] which represented Simon Magus as a false messiah who not only pretended to magical powers but attempted to set up a rival religion;[27] this could figure the demagogue and also the varied scramblings for a portion of benefit in any organizational structure. Simoniac is the layman who, having lost belief in what religion he once professed, still conforms, perfunctorily, for status, access, or protective coloration. In the secular world the extensions of masked trafficking for advantage are almost as numerous as mankind, and if statesmen are not always innocent of such simony, neither are artists.

It is a basic and universal issue the boy has come upon, in the "pleasant and vicious region" he had felt his soul receding into. Father Flynn undeniably had used his clerical prestige to exact a kind of homage and subserviency from the boy, not, as was thought, to make a priest of him, or to bestow any grace beyond a right pronunciation of Latin, but to have an attendant, a possible commender, and the safe comfort of a naïve auditor. While the old man was pathetic, his status was equivocal and his behavior with the boy had been even perverse, not in a sense old Cotter may seem to suspect, and not with direct intent, but far more subtly, in taking the risk involved in pseudo-confession. Some may read the story another way, to show Father Flynn calculating the boy's gradual liberation from dogmas his mentor could not openly disavow, but such interpretation would not accord with major themes, including identification of simony as a corruptor of human relations, and it would reduce the priest to a grotesque anomaly, something less representative of Joyce's overview in *Dubliners*. The extent of Father Flynn's offense against the boy is that while still in orders, though retired, he raised questionings and nodded that they were unanswerable, knowing them not as beautiful mysteries but as blind alleys in the maze of doctrinal problems that presumably had broken him. Beyond this, his scrupulousness has extended to keeping his doubts to himself, an act tinged with simony in that he thereby conserved some clerical privilege. Only with his pupil did the pensive old man let down his guard, and that but partially and without aim except his own relief, who must still be priest, most of all to his one remaining and unofficial acolyte. So he is to be seen lying at last in his coffin "vested as for the altar" and still "loosely retaining" a chalice in his hands, though in life he had lost grasp on the substance of his hopes.

Hence the potent denouement. Intuition has shaped itself more and more clearly in the boy's mind: in his bedtime reverie that fancied the priest's desire to confess and passed into awareness of the sin; in his quick change at the crape-hung door from being "disturbed" at finding himself "at check" to his departure down "the sunny side of the street" with "a sensation of freedom" and his feeling "even annoyed" at that sensation; in his separation from the others at prayer beside the corpse; and afterward in his silence while he listened, learned, and realized. Through all this his responses have varied between extremes, and he had journeyed by stages before at last he "saw," he "knew." At first there is the acute ambivalence of the "pleasant and vicious region" entered through his reverie, and the "smiling feebly as if to absolve the simoniac" whose imagined face had "smiled continually" while it desired to confess. Next morning on the street he counts it "strange" that neither he nor the day "seemed in a mourning mood." Then in the house of death, kneeling, he merely "pretended to pray" while distracted by sister Nannie's "mutterings" and by the sight of her run-down heels, and he finds time to fancy "the old priest was smiling as he lay there in his coffin."

It is just here, with recall of this suggestive image, that the turn seems to come, marked by the abrupt emphasis of Joyce's next paragraph: "But no. When we rose and went up to the head of the bed I saw that he was not smiling." There follows the description of the dead man "vested as for the altar, his large hands loosely retaining the chalice," but the face "very truculent." In death he has passed beyond the ambiguities of his life, and there is an end to nods that affirmed nothing but uncertainties. Despite the chalice thrust back into the semblance of his grasp, the priest is no longer to be seen as the simoniac; the dead are beyond sinning, as they are beyond grace in the mind unable to pray for them. This is merely the "very truculent" face of one old man who has departed with his unstated doubt still unresolved. They came away, the boy's aunt and Nannie and he, to join Eliza in the familiar room below, and the women's platitudinous conversation ensues, euphemistically skirting the gravity of Father Flynn's collapse, while the boy sits withdrawn but alerted. Then when Eliza stops as if to listen he too listens, but "there was no sound" and he "knew" that the old priest, "solemn and truculent in death," was "still in his coffin," with "an idle chalice on his breast." In the new word *idle* the boy's intuitions have come to the surface; now he begins to understand more than his elders do, and passes beyond the ambiguities of his attendance upon Father Flynn. Earlier, standing outside the house of the dead, he "knew that two candles must be set at the head of a corpse," but this he had received on authority; when at the end he "knew" that the old priest lay unsmiling, "solemn and truculent in death, an idle chalice on his breast," this was not only by observation but a discovery. And Joyce, his story told, lets it fade out into Eliza's repetitiousness and the understatement that ironically marks how little she has apprehended of the priest's long journey into darkness before his death: "Wide-awake and laughing-like to himself.... So then, of course, when they saw that, that made them think that there was something gone wrong with him."

In its final form in *Dubliners* this first story is a fullfledged example of what Gorman defined as Joyce's "disciplined aesthetic ... based on the precision of words, the harmony of parts, and the completeness of apprehension."[28] Beginning in the midst of things, it smoothly alternates economical summary and extended scene. It modifies chronology to project emphasis and provide orderly penetration in depth. It evolves implication by a variably reiterated imagery. It balances substance between the fact of past event and the truth of subsequent assessment, modulating the tone between a boy's fresh immediate response and the mature artist's discreet arrangements. Why, then, reserve insight for the reader alone, overlooking the protagonist's crucial formative experience, as Kenner seems to in predicting the boy will "most probably" remain "a cheerful habitual inhabitant of the boot-heel world," that of the sisters themselves and "the less scrupulous clergy."[29] Is that quiet lad merely acquiescent, or is not his silence a cunning, in preparation for escape? It would seem the story is shaped thus throughout to the point where the character's epiphany provides the reader a like consolidation of insight, not just a progressive consent, but of the same essence. "The Sisters" makes no stand-and-deliver demands upon sympathy, but it is all or nothing as an exercise of the reader's intuitions. The boy knows what he sees, and simply that is recounted, from which is to be seen all that the boy has come to know.

The first three stories of *Dubliners,* in first person and referred to by their author as "stories of my childhood," also have priority as a group in the chronological order Joyce gave—though not for autobiographical but for a more general thematic progression, from "stories of my childhood" to "stories of adolescence . . . of mature life . . . of public life in Dublin."[30] It is of more special significance that "The Sisters" comes first. The perceptions of Father Flynn's attendant are more complex than those in the other boyhood episodes, and allow deeper resonances in their recollection. While "The Sisters" is the most substantial of the three and most intricate in its structure, its real primacy is in its breadth. It sets forth observation basic to the whole collection, and if "The Dead" by reason of its greater inclusiveness is capstone, it also remains antiphonal to "The Sisters," leaving that foundational to the whole book. Its implications are something more than those often stated, as that Joyce's Dublin is fatally diseased and the ailment centers in the moribund but still demanding Church. "The Sisters" is really Joyce's manifesto, autobiographically based but psychologically evolved, and committed in a confrontation. Yet it remains an artist's utterance, what it manifests is not defined but revealed, and its underlying facts have been transmuted through all the devices of bodying forth a presentation. Joyce began by risking everything on the art of it.

It is possible to consider "The Sisters" as a *Portrait* in miniature—and in estimating the analogy it might even be hazarded that the short story is the more controlled and subtler work. The boy as nephew is removed one more degree from family; similarly Stephen felt that he was "hardly of the one blood with them [mother, brother, and sister] but stood to them rather in the mystical kinship of fosterage."[31] If in the director's suggestion that he may find a vocation for the priesthood Stephen hears a simoniac voice "offering him secret knowledge and secret power,"[32] in his earlier reveries he had seen himself not as celebrant but in "the minor sacred offices,"[33] with an awe like that Father Flynn's young auditor had felt, in wondering "how anybody had ever found in himself the courage to undertake" the duties "towards the Eucharist and towards the secrecy of the confessional." Finally, most subtly but most significantly, the boy prefigures the acceptance instead of the artist's vocation, by his withdrawal to a point where, without simony, he can integrate his slowly gathered, tentatively held insights. And when at last he thinks of the priest's "loosely" retained chalice as "idle," he is the artist, revising his terms to suit his clarified vision, and applying the word that will occur to Stephen when the director's voice, "urging upon him the proud claims of the church ... repeated itself *idly* in his memory ... and he knew now that the exhortation he had listened to had already fallen into an *idle* formal tale."[34]

"And he knew now ...," thinks Stephen; "I too listened," the boy tells us, "and I knew. ..." In the idle chalice loosely retained and in the dead man's unsmiling face the boy has not only verified his nocturnal imaginings about Father Flynn but has sufficiently added to Eliza's impercipient account. Within the scrupulous art of this frugal, steadily controlled narrative is to be sensed a refining backward look, but it is not an ironic adult correction of a child's naïveté. The cool detachment arrived at and the almost muted tone throughout do not depend entirely upon judicious reconsideration but are of the action itself, the very substance of the boy's passage and access to awareness. Beginning with his silent evasion of old Cotter, it continues through these crises of ambivalent feeling in which he always finally tends to his own defense and moves further toward separation and liberty. It culminates decisively in what he "knew" for himself, by himself. This acutely apprehensive child, facing emergent awareness in which earlier confusions are resolved, is indeed father to the writer of the *Dubliners* stories. Here at the book's beginning Joyce, through his persona, claims the grounds from which he will proceed. Had he let himself be blunt he could with reason have called the story "Silence, Exile, and Cunning," but it was not his way to label. "Counterparts" is not a typical title, and Joyce preferred either something merely nominal, such as "Eveline" or "A Mother," or else the citing of a facet which when examined leads to the matter's other planes and to the further dimensions of the implied, as does "Clay" or "A Little Cloud." Such is "The Sisters" as a title. It points to Nannie and Eliza for what they represent of pious Ireland's impoverished existence, down-at-heel and semi-paralyzed in impercipience. Beyond that, it is not just the sisters and the aunt who play the last scene to round out the story; it is this as witnessed by one who has been prepared at length to know it beyond its own manner, and in a perspective secured through withdrawal.

If then the abrupt presumptuous question is asked, "What is the story about?," the answer is neither in the title nor in a view of the last scene as pure naturalism, perhaps garnished to taste with one of criticism's stock bits, a "symbolic" communion. Nor can "The Sisters" be adequately evaluated only in terms of what the boy came to see and know. Its fictional essence is of how he came to know it, and that not just by the series of experiences he confronted but by the fluid operation of consciousness, his sensing of complexities around and within him, and his receptiveness to intuitions through which he resolved ambiguities by separating himself from their sources, though these have been the points of his compass. Joyce never wrote anything more deeply psychological. Perhaps too this story hints most clearly how Joyce could come to be so masterful an artist while still so young a man.

There was a priest on Joyce's mother's side of the family who "became harmlessly insane and lost his parish,"[35] and since for the story's first printing the editor of the *Irish Homestead* changed the name of the parish,[36] this priest may have been a contemporary, but it is not recorded that Joyce as a boy bore snuff to such a person or was taught Latin by him. It would have been enough if Joyce knew that the priest had become demented; beyond that he could imagine a partially paralyzed, incapacitated character who had lost his grip upon his vocation and himself and who—as did Joyce more openly throughout life—could continue to toy with what was "logical and coherent" in what he had come to feel an "absurdity."[37] More largely, whatever its biographical roots, the story is a real fiction, a general representation of the almost instinctive counterassertion by which the wily young can emancipate themselves from authorities. That the boy in "The Sisters" is not a son but a nephew may let some critics isolate the theme as a father-quest, in terms of the lad's attendance upon the priest, but the story corresponds to a larger yet more common reality (and one closer to the man Joyce himself): the variable tactics by which typically a growing boy takes whatever he can learn from his elders without necessarily enlisting under them. It is a crafty process, and it tells in advance which boys will grow into autonomous manhood and which will remain boyishly dutiful. Conversely, a father-quest, though so dear to fanciers of the archetypal, is anti-heroic, or at least retrogressive into the nostalgia of myth. In its dependence it is perhaps even more suspect than a retreat to some womb-equivalent, for while this seeks only shelter and comfort the other craves to submit to a precedence with some flavor of the hierarchical. Society repeats the paternal, by its prescriptive fostering, with a larger and looser but more persistent entanglement, through institutions beyond the family—the school, the city and state, employment, the church, and all the mores that expediently close up any gaps in the net. Boyhood may be an initiation into such rituals of obedience, but it also may tempt toward riskings for freedom and further knowledge.

This was what Joyce saw, and what he shows Stephen in his twin embodiments confronting. That young man remained faithful to his preceptors at least in that he analyzed his situation; he ticked off *seriatim* what he would not serve. But the boy who had waited on the priest as listener and antiphonal server then listens to the sisters silently without assent, knowing only that the man in the coffin is not smiling, but truculent-looking, and able to know the priest is posed in death as something he had ceased to be in life. Stephen merely wears his rue with a difference, having refused to be priest so that he might be artist, but still under ordination by Aquinas; the boy, who has never understood clearly either what old Cotter was driving at or whether there were or could be any answers to the priest's most difficult questions, at least has the sense of relief on the sunny side of the street, and later, by silently watching and listening, he attains, in terms of a noncommittal receptiveness, the further gift of a sufficient intuition. Whatever sunrise of definition is to follow, this is the dawning of awareness, diffused but pervasive, over the world of experience, and promising increase into a total light to be lived by, though its source is not to be stared into.

If "The Sisters," though so explicitly detailed, is reserved in its tone, this is not only dramatic as a trait of the aloof juvenile narrator; it is an artist's deference to the reader's intuitions. The story's greatest technical achievement is in a merging of its realistic substance with its implicative mode. The subtle art through which it holds forth its intimations is vitally distinct from a naturalism inert beneath loosely aggregated fact; it is also aesthetically superior to any symbolism which edges too insistently toward a sly kind of definition. Derivatively, a blind compulsive critical search for such symbolism when it isn't there, to the neglect of what may be substantial, is not just perfunctory but intrusively irrelevant. An instance, from among many such, is an equating of the saving grace of baptism with the alleged efficacy of cold baths for adolescent lads.[38] Actually in "The Sisters" as dynamic narrative what is juxtaposed concerning the priest's relation with the boy is Old Cotter's groundless insinuation of perverse sexuality as against the more subtle actual influence toward agnosticism. Joyce's first story, neither naturalistic nor mechanically and affectedly symbolic, allows readers to learn as the boy-narrator learned how to see and hear; it also invites readers to realize the nuances of that maturation as the artist maturely conceived and creatively projected them. Then the title, apprehended as antithetical, will confirm readers in their imaginative exercise and involvement, so that over and above what is being said at the story's end there will be heard the boy's listening. Reticence can be a form of cunning, and for Joyce cunning was craft, a careful art in no way artificial, but a communication proffered with the aesthetic measure and decorum which allows an intuitive response both judicious and empathic.

AN ENCOUNTER

Another first-person story of childhood, "An Encounter" is closely representative of boys' life, showing them at play, in school, and two of them truant, seeking a romantic goal and seizing small adventure along the way. That the narrator and Mahony arrive at both less and more than they sought is not the main point; this lies in the narrator's ambivalent reactions and his passage to one clearer insight. Full of detailed overt action, the story is essentially subjective, and the protagonist's encountering is multiple, not only with the crowded busyness at the Liffey's mouth or with a pervert, but with his own confusions and realizations. Yet thematically as well as structurally it is simpler than "The Sisters." While it too is suffused by reminiscence enhanced in the refracted light of style, its perspectives are not as detached and sophisticated, it is contained within briefer chronology, and its less complex matter is more immediately accessible.

Still this has not obviated the avid searching-out of symbols. Since the boys propose to "walk out to see the Pigeon House"—the electric power station on the harbor breakwater—it is an easy exegetic leap from light plant to mystical illumination, and after this the simple good sense of Mahony's belief that they were not likely to encounter Father Butler there can imply the benightedness of the Church. "His mind fascinated by correspondences, Joyce saw many literary possibilities in the Pigeonhouse," writes a leading Joyce commentator. " 'Pigeon' brought to mind 'dove' and dove recalled the Holy Ghost."[1] Here the critic admittedly is remembering Stephen, in *Ulysses,* seeing the pigeonhouse and saying to himself, "Que vous a mis dans cette fichue position?"

together with the answer, "C'est le pigeon, Joseph." This was simply Stephen's freely associative process, humorously irreverent, but while pigeon and Holy Ghost may have been connected in Stephen's mind through French, there is no evidence this was Joyce's intent in "An Encounter." The critical procedure cited shows what violence can be done when Joyce's later works are used not just as complement but as gloss upon *Dubliners*. Once started, the process easily runs on to the absolute conclusion that "The Pigeonhouse, then, is identified in Joyce's mind with the 'father' of Christ and with fathers in general." (It is perhaps unfair to summarize this critic's prodigal argument so stringently; he does note also that the Pigeon House structure can furnish a phallic and that way too a father symbol.)[2] "But turn we from these bold, bad men," the haunted by archetypes, for a closer look at the story, in and of itself. And if one must look for abstractions in "An Encounter," it would be more to the point to see what light dawns on the narrator well this side of the Pigeon House.

The story begins with Joe Dillon's teaching the boys to play Indian, under the inspiration of his "little library" of penny dreadfuls. The boys are banded together by "a spirit of unruliness," which the narrator shares, though diffidently, as a "reluctant" Indian, afraid to seem too studious or lacking in robustness. Joe Dillon has no such lack; he plays fiercely and always claims victory, which he celebrates with a wild war dance. His reported vocation for the priesthood astonishes "everyone," but it may be read as not unconnected with his vigorous assured imitativeness and his reassuring environment. He is no loosely aligned nephew, like the lad in "The Sisters" and "Araby" and presumably the same one in this story; Joe's parents go to mass every morning, "and the peaceful odour of Mrs. Dillon was prevalent in the hall of the house." Here is a rare glimpse, in Joyce's work, of Catholic piety as a serene and steadily effective influence. The well-intentioned aunt who takes the boy along to visit the Flynn sisters and who chides the uncle for delaying the boy's trip to the bazaar cannot create the like of this with no more help than is to be got from a mate who merely advocates cold baths for boys and comes home late for dinner, drunk. And the Joe Dillon who plays games hard seems not inclined to play truant.

In both Joe Dillon and Mahony is a degree of integration which the first-person character lacks. When Joe's fat, clumsy brother Leo is caught at school reading a story, "The Apache Chief," Father Butler's reproof triggers an ambivalent but progressive reaction in the narrator. The voice of clerical-academic authority "paled much of the glory of the Wild West" for him, and "one of" his "consciences" was "awakened," yet out of the schoolroom he longed "again" for "escape," while finally he wants more "real adventures" than those offered by the juvenile magazines' "chronicles of disorder." Reflecting that "real adventures . . . must be sought abroad," he plans to play truant a whole day, with Leo Dillon and Mahony, for a trip past the docks, and out to the Pigeon House. "Mahony's big sister was to write an excuse for him and Leo Dillon was to tell his brother to say he was sick." There is no mention of any such cover for the narrator, presumably an only child and the ward of childless uncle and aunt, and this is another facet of his separateness, which is to be somewhat mitigated by the story's end.

Leo Dillon did not show up. Perhaps Joe, despite his wildness at games, refused to lie at school, or possibly the influence of the peacefully orderly and pious Dillon household prevailed over Leo too, "the idler" and the "clumsy" one; certainly he had been timorous, "afraid" that they "might meet Father Butler or someone out of the college." After the other two boys have waited a while, it is Mahony who decides they will go on without Leo and consider as forfeited his sixpence in their common fund. Mahony's explicit traits provide a foil to the developing portrait and progressive experience of the narrator, and the story will turn on differences between the two, toward a resultant epiphany for the narrator. Mahony is pure boy; he is being his age and self from first to last, explaining some improvements in his catapult, playing Indian along the way, declaring it would be "right skit to run away to sea," dismissing the pervert at his most perverse as simply "a queer old josser" and renewing his pursuit of a cat. His only dependence on his companion is when he is cheered by the reminder that they can allow themselves a bit more time by "going home by train"—thanks perhaps to Leo's sixpence. Although both boys grow tired, Mahony shows no such fluctuation as does the protagonist. At first he had been "very happy" sitting on the sun-warmed granite of the Canal Bridge waiting for the other two, seeing the sunlight of early June slanting through the "little light green leaves . . . on to the water"; later he suffers not merely the normal let-down after hours of prowling about the lively docks and the squalid streets of Ringsend but also is shaken by the encounter with perversion and its obscurely sensed seductive intent.

Like the young Stephen of *A Portrait,* these boys go venturing down to the quays; they are innocently "pleased" by "the spectacle of Dublin's commerce," while Stephen was to be stirred to "unrest" by "the vastness and strangeness of the life suggested to him."[3] It had taken the dallying boys till noon to reach the quays, and now seeing the laborers eating their lunches, they "bought two big currant buns and sat down to eat them on some metal piping beside the river." In this free-and-easy situation, and looking at the shipping, the narrator feels the "influences" of school and home seeming to "wane" as the scanty geography learned from books is now imagined "gradually taking substance." Here at the harbor this boy bent on escape into novelty is resuming the process which had failed him with Joe Dillon's Wild West tales—the matching of romantic notions with reality. What is to come is no such fulfilment, however, but a harsh contradiction. He has set out with one scheme for adventure; the adventure that awaits him on the other side of the Liffey is of another order. And in his escape from that he will know a truth come upon more closely and perhaps more influentially than all the strangeness he has met with by the way.

By ferry the boys cross to the Liffey's south bank, still in such high spirits that when their eyes meet they laugh, and still bound for the Pigeon House. This structure stands about midway on the long mole which parallels extensions of the North Wall, and thus borders from the south the channel by which shipping proceeds from the bay to Dublin's main docks on both sides of the Liffey. The Pigeon House had been watch tower and later a fort, and once "was for a long period the chief landing and embarking place of Dublin";[4] it became and remains a power station. Having ferried over to the south side, the boys did not set out at once for their goal, but paused again, this time to watch the unloading of the "graceful three-master" they had seen from across the river. Hearing that it was a Norwegian vessel, the narrator tries to "decipher the legend" on her stern but cannot, nor can he confirm his "confused notion" that sailors have green eyes. Not only was his appetite for romantic adventure balked by the indecipherable and the indeterminable, but both boys grew "tired of" the sight itself and "wandered slowly into Ringsend."

This region, on the Liffey's south bank and to the north of lowly Irishtown, was described in the 1880's (just before the probable decade of "An Encounter") as "once a flourishing and much-frequented suburb of our city" but "now so smoky and dingy-looking."[5] In some such aspect the boys saw it as they "wandered" its "squalid streets" eating chocolate and "musty biscuits" that had bleached in the grocer's window, and finding no dairy, settled for raspberry lemonade. The afternoon "had grown sultry," they "both felt rather tired," and so they rested on a bank in the field into which Mahony had chased a cat. Knowing they must be home before four o'clock to avoid discovery of their "adventure," they realized they could not go on to the Pigeon House. Circumstance marks this falling short in their enterprise—"The sun went in behind some clouds and left us to our jaded thoughts and the crumbs of our provisions." The boys' projections have passed a peak; they have moved from classroom unrest to the synthetic adventure of playing Indian and thence to actual truancy and free exploration of the docks, with the Pigeon House still an alluringly remote goal, far out on the breakwater, well into the bay, marking a schoolboy's approximation of running off to sea. All along, however, there has been a fluctuant tension between fancy and fact. The boys' games are not enough, textbook geography takes only partial substance at the sight of ships, the derived notion that sailors' eyes are green finds a semblance in only one among many, and the reality of the docks and Ringsend is so multiform and distracting that their quest loses its singlemindedness, fact defeats the promise of high adventure, Mahony is again reduced to chasing cats, and at last they are weary enough to lie down "for some time."

Thus while the encounter about to follow is the day's central and decisive event for the narrator, what has preceded it was not all of a piece, no simple boyhood idyl to set off against an ugly adult aberration. It is notable that what prevented completion of the boys' quest was not the pervert but their previous daylong dilatoriness, with their attention diffused among many unrelated details as they wandered and lingered in the region of warehouses and along the quays. Had they proceeded directly and expeditiously to the Pigeon House, they not only could have got there, but encounter with the pervert would have been avoided. Yet had they gone straight for their goal they would not have been real boys, making the most of truancy, momentarily, and enacting typically a passage from freedom to aimlessness, nor would it have been so jadingly impressed upon them that there are no infinite days, even for truants. Romance boyishly conceived of as an absolute, unified and durable—simply running off to sea, out and away, among hardy shipmates all with strange green eyes—is denied by reality's variations. Time itself shows them its two faces, as the whole free day they have seized and squandered brings them round to the hour when they must think of returning.

An image recurrent in varied contexts, after Joyce's fashion, connects the story's disparate halves and marks out the sustained themes of objective multiplicity and ambiguous subjectivity. As the narrator goes along, he observes that the one color green is of many shadings. At the beginning of his venturesome day he admires the sunlit "little light green leaves"—the living color of vegetative growth. At the docks the sailors' eyes are variously "blue and grey and even black," and the only one whose eyes "could have been called green" is more cheerfully comic than exotically romantic. A third image of green is pivotal and prophetic; while the yet unknown man approached them in the field, the narrator, "lazily" watching, "chewed one of those green stems on which girls tell fortunes." The man's clothes, at the other end of this spectrum from the "little light green leaves" of that morning, are "greenish-black." Finally, at the crisis of the pervert's circling sadistic talk the boy "glanced" into "a pair of bottle-green eyes," from which he turned his own "away again."

This encounter is not the end of the matter; it makes way for a further recognition, and an approach to a more representative reality, in the story's epiphany. In this the boys are most closely connected, and this too effects a structural completion, since they have hitherto been shown of different natures and ways. Mahony, smiling and strenuous, the improver of catapults, has been decisive about not waiting longer for Leo and appropriating his sixpence; he had the common sense to ask the timorous Leo "What would Father Butler be doing out at the Pigeon House," and with a high opinion of running away to sea, he remains opportunistic chaser of cats. An almost altogether "flat" character, simple and totally naïve in the narrator's view, he becomes a saving point of reference for his diffident and reflective companion, who is subject to stresses of ambivalent reaction. Afflicted as this young protagonist is with a plurality of "consciences," playing Indian reluctantly, still he craves the "real adventures" which "must be sought abroad." Such a complex of traits tends to identify this boy with the one of "The Sisters" and "Araby," and indeed connects him with some of the ambivalent men in the later stories, especially Little Chandler and Gabriel Conroy.

Of first importance is the complexity of the narrator's responses to the ambiguous man who stops to talk to them. To Mahony apparently he is little more than another curious member of the inexplicable, eludible, and negligible adult world; the other boy is too precociously sensitive to the nuances of the pervert's gambit to maintain such innocent self-possession. The man at once distinguishes between the boys as "bookworm" and one who "goes in for games." When the man leads the talk to sweethearts, Mahony "lightly" claims to have "three totties" and "pertly" asks the man how many he has himself. Presumably the brash and innocent Mahony does not recognize the evasiveness in the man's answer that at their age "he had lots of sweethearts." The narrator "wondered why" the man "shivered once or twice as if he feared something or felt a sudden chill," but while the boy cannot recognize this as a symptom of sexual excitement, he is aware of conflict in his feelings about the man's talk. The declaration, "Every boy has a little sweetheart," seems both "strangely liberal in a man of his age" and "reasonable," yet the lad "disliked the words in his mouth." As the man goes on and on about girls' soft hair and white hands and "how all girls were not so good as they seemed to be if one only knew," the narrator's impression is of something "learned by heart" and repeated by a mind "circling round and round in the same orbit." Meanwhile the boy does not face him but does attend, continuing "to gaze towards the foot of the slope, listening to him,"—a simple but absolute image of ambivalence.

Thus when the man says he must leave them "for a minute or so, a few minutes," the narrator "without changing the direction" of his gaze can see him "walking slowly away . . . towards the near end of the field"—close enough for the boys to watch. What is plainly implied is an extreme form of exhibitionism. That Joyce meant an overtly indecent act was indicated when in his altercation with Grant Richards, trying to refute certain criticism, he tactlessly cited other details he considered more extreme—"Why do you not object to the theme of *An Encounter*, to the passage 'he stood up slowly saying that he had to leave us for a few moments &c . . .'?"[6] Mahony watching exclaims "I say! Look what he's doing," but his companion, already looking, does not answer that nor raise his eyes, and the verdict is left to

Mahony: "He's a queer old josser." The afore-mentioned critic calls *josser* pidgin English for God;[7] more properly, joss is pidgin English for idol (supposedly by way of the Portugese *deos*) and in nineteenth century Australian slang *josser* meant *padre*. However, this is the Dublin boy Mahony speaking, and he no doubt is using the word in the more general sense of a simpleton, or merely fellow or chap, nor is his using *queer* to have its special present connotation. At any rate, Mahony's companion does not commit himself on that. Instead he suggests that if they are asked for their names, Mahony is to be Murphy and he will be Smith. Nothing further is said between them, and Mahony may be wondering what this is all about, while his companion, despite this preparation for further encounter, is ambivalently "still considering" whether to "go away or not," when the man returns and sits down beside them. At that moment Mahony spies the cat and once more takes up the chase, while the narrator stays on, despite what he is now aware of about the man. This boy is not perverse, but he has come out for adventure and it turns out to be this; in that field he has scented what he knows as the flowers of evil, and they have the fascination of strangeness; like himself in "The Sisters" he finds his awareness capable of receding into "some pleasant and vicious region." His ambivalence continues; when the man called Mahony "a very rough boy" and asked whether he was often whipped at school, the narrator's first impulse was to "reply indignantly" that they were not National School boys, but he "remained silent," not identifying himself as a Catholic pupil, and listened on.

Now the pervert's talk, though still circling reiteratively, has found a "new centre," has turned from a fetishism for girls' hands and hair to the sadism of "a nice warm whipping" for unruly boys, especially those who have sweethearts. This reversal of attitude so "surprised" the boy that he "involuntarily glanced up." It was then he "met the gaze of a pair of bottle-green eyes peering . . . from under a twitching forehead"—the shiver of sexual excitement has become spasmodic. Though the startled lad turned his eyes "away again," he is still listening as the man now describes how he would whip a boy who lied about having a sweetheart, and how he "would love" doing that "better than anything in the world"—all this in a voice that "grew almost affectionate and seemed to plead" that the boy "should understand him." The tracing of abnormality is deep and particular here. It runs through the man's change of attitude and his rising insistence, from a use of heterosexual interest as a first step to his reversal of mood and need, perhaps brought on by his exhibition; it culminates in sadistic-masochistic dualism, the ultimate ambivalent mockery of love.

But Joyce is steadily concerned with the one whose story this is. The boy does understand, well enough, and finally he does respond, by flight. Indecisive no longer, he stands up "abruptly" and then delays only in pretence of fixing his shoe, lest he "betray" his "agitation." Even so he carried out an orderly retreat, saying he was "obliged to go," bidding the green-eyed man good-day, and starting "up the slope calmly," but with heart quickly beating in apprehension of being seized by the ankles. So he does escape from this most sordid aspect of the multifarious reality he has come upon by having "sought abroad" for "real adventures." Still another encounter is in store for him, however, and it carries the narrative from a picturing of the abnormal to a glimpse of the representatively human. Yet a critic strangely sees the story ending on a "dead and inconclusive note."[8] Such a reading fails to hear the narrator's voice with a full sense of what it reveals subjectively.

When the man calls Mahony "different," one who "goes in for games," he is seeking a special connection with the protagonist as "a bookworm like myself." This possibility has arisen when the narrator "pretended" to have "read every book" the man mentioned, while Mahony was merely regarding these other two "with open eyes." As the man led on by saying "there were some of Lord Lytton's works which boys couldn't read," presumably the narrator didn't know a reason but he probably senses an insinuation, whereas Mahony in his direct naïve way asked "why couldn't boys read them," and the narrator was then "agitated and pained" for fear he would be thought "as stupid as Mahony." Mahony, practical and active according to his lights, is not obtuse; as ignorant of Lord Lytton's works as presumably his companion is, he is also innocent of pretense about it. He is candid and unequivocal, as his more imaginative companion cannot be, subject to intuitions he feels impelled to explore, even by the tactic of pretense. The episode with the pervert continues to employ this difference epitomized earlier in the day, when at sight of "the big white sailing vessel" Mahony's response was explicit and pragmatic—"it would be right skit to run away to sea"—whereas the narrator, "looking at the high masts, saw, or imagined" the geography learned from books "gradually taking substance." And Mahony, protected in the later encounter by his ignorance and unimaginativeness, at least had enough self-possession to answer "lightly" and "pertly" in the talk about sweethearts. Moreover, the stranger's exhibitionism, while startling, strikes Mahony as a plain oddity by which he is so little affected that later he seems to have forgotten his companion's craftily suggesting he go under the false name of Murphy in this dubious presence.

The critic who somehow hears the story ending on a "dead and inconclusive note" blurs certain crucial detail when he puts it that "The boys, worried by the tone of his conversation, depart hurriedly."[9] They do indeed, but not together, nor for the same reason. There is no indication that Mahony has worried about anything, all along, except making the most of their truancy and still getting home soon enough to conceal it. While he does remain sitting there with his companion when the pervert returns from his demonstration at "the near end of the field," what makes Mahony spring up and "depart hurriedly," so to speak, is sight of "the cat which had escaped him," and which he now pursues to "the far end of the field." It might be possible to read this as a conscious removal of himself to the greatest possible distance from corruption, but there seems to have been previously no need for ulterior motive in Mahony's simple, sensuous, and passionate chasing of cats. Then when his friend, in panicky flight from the pervert's seductive talk, called "Murphy!" it was only after that name was called again and when Mahony saw who was calling that he simply "hallooed in answer," evidently not thinking it needful to call out "Smith!" or perhaps so little concerned that he did not even recollect his companion's scheme.

The other boy is still caught in a complex of attitudes; he is "ashamed" of the "paltry stratagem" of an assumed name, in the use of which his voice "had an accent of forced bravery." The stratagem is paltry not in itself but in having arisen from his ambivalently considering whether he "would go away or not" when the exhibitionist returned. A false name could be an unforcedly brave device in a determined cause; moreover, had he gone with Mahony after the cat he would have had all the stratagem needed for a simple escape. But he has lingered, pursuing another kind of adventure, not gamesome but real, of the kind that "must be sought abroad," with some intuitive response to such reality and with a persistent intent to know. In this he is not unlike the lad in "The Sisters," who repeated the word *paralysis* softly to himself, though it "sounded . . . like the name of some maleficent and sinful being," and who although "filled . . . with fear," yet "longed to be nearer to it and to look upon its deadly work." Now as this boy reaches "the top of the slope" and calls "Murphy!" to Mahony, he realizes how shaken he has been, not just with quickened heart for fear of being seized by the ankles, but by his glimpsing in the bottle-green eyes and twitching forehead what he senses as the face of evil, which he has waited to see at close range.

This realization, with his reaction to it, makes way for another. Still his heart beats markedly, but with a different emotion than fear, as now he watches his summoned companion come "running across the field" to him, "as if to bring . . . aid." The *as if* is to be read not of Mahony's intention but of the other boy's recognizing him as companion, in a responsive relationship, on simple circumstantial terms and yet humanly genuine. For the protagonist this is an advance in awareness, to a moment of revaluation, toward a further insight and maturation. The mark of it as a sudden illumination is that the lad is "penitent," for having feared the man would think him "as stupid as Mahony," and for having in his heart "always despised him [Mahony] a little." The penitence is the point of the story, which has not ended in his evasion from the pervert, but culminates in this epiphany. Its essence is expressed in the fictionally dramatic rather than a more formally rhetorical construction of the story's closing sentence. As it runs it is non-chronological, and in putting first what could be climactic it is not only colloquial but it avoids a kind of emphasis that would be given by a periodic construction, such as *And since in my heart I had always despised him a little, I was penitent.* Joyce orders the clauses the other way around, and in a looser construction: "And I was penitent; for in my heart I had always despised him a little." Instead of winding up with a loud topical boom on the term *penitent,* the sentence dramatizes the feel of penitence, which by nature inheres in the presently continuing consciousness of past offense. This time it is no mortal sin, and he has despised his companion only "a little," but these words at the very end, by their measure, imply a positive realization of companionable interdependence as something to be measured up to.

Joyce set great store by this tale of boyhood, and when the altercations with Maunsel and Company seemed to be centering on it, he wrote Roberts (on August 21, 1912) that he had "very reluctantly decided to consent to its omission, but only if he were allowed to insert a prefatory note: "This book in this form is incomplete. The scheme of the book as framed by me includes a story entitled An Encounter which stands between the first and second story in this edition, J. J." Joyce also reserved "the right to publish the said story elsewhere."[10] His surrender to omission of the story from the proposed Maunsel and Company edition was no doubt enforced by past experience and the present pressure of friends. Six years earlier he had drawn down Richards' objection to "An Encounter" and his repeated requests for its removal from the book as projected for publication in England.[11] In

Dublin Thomas Kettle, according to a contemporary diarist, considered the story "beyond anything in its outspokenness he had ever read," and warned that he would "slate the book" as harmful to Ireland.[12] Possibly H. L. Mencken in turn passed upon "An Encounter" and passed it over. In January, 1914, Pound wrote Joyce that he would send Mencken that story together with "The Boarding House" and "A Little Cloud," for consideration for *Smart Set.*[13] Mencken also was urged by B. W. Huebsch, the publisher, to print some of Joyce's stories, and in May, 1915 "The Boarding House" and "A Little Cloud" appeared in the magazine;[14] but "An Encounter" was not published in the United States until Huebsch issued *Dubliners* in 1916.[15] Whatever Mencken's opinion may have been, those nearer home were earlier of little or no help to Joyce. Though Padraic Colum had accompanied Joyce to the dilatory editor Roberts' office in August, 1912, presumably to assist, when called upon then and there to read "An Encounter" he declared it "a terrible story."[16]

And in the deepest sense it is. Unsensational, too subtly conveyed to be shocking, it is nevertheless in part appalling, not so much because of the pervert's repulsiveness but in the spectacle of the youth's pausing ambivalently under that seduction, fascinated less by the thing in itself than by its strangeness, its allure as variation from the accustomed and prescribed. The story's naturalism is sound; Kettle himself admitted concerning the aberrant man, "We have all met him."[17] More broadly, the tracing of psychological realities in the boy's experience is clinically precise and dramatically adroit. Joyce had these grounds for defense of "An Encounter." And certainly he would have been conscious of its serving his overall intention in main thematic strokes—the unruly urge toward escape, the felt need to seek "real adventures . . . abroad," the sense of encirclement by limitations natural and superimposed, the depressing influence of the sordid, and a defeat in falling short in a quest. All these concepts, however, were set forth elsewhere in *Dubliners,* and in that aspect "An Encounter" might have been deemed dispensable. Why then Joyce's emphasis on the importance of this story; why without it would the book be "incomplete"? And what of his specifying that it "stands between" "The Sisters" and "Araby"?[18]

Obviously Joyce had something more in mind than a frugal gathering of his total production, and something more than a mere placing together, with chronological primacy, of three stories of childhood. Apparently "An Encounter" was intended to operate connectively between the other two. In "The Sisters" escape is accomplished, but the advance while intuitive is chiefly an intellectual emancipation from the ambiguous influence of dogmatists both clerical and lay, and the achieved detachment is also a separation and an isolation very like Joyce's own which he made the grounds for his critical view of Dublin. In "An Encounter" the theme of escape, more simply embodied in a day of truancy, receives nevertheless a more complex treatment; flight and exploration bring their own repercussive threats, all the way from boredom to perverse seduction, from which in turn further escape must be sought. And whereas in the first story the boy has estimated an ambiguous relationship from the likes of which he has then slowly but almost completely withdrawn, in the second, if it is read to the end, the boy is seen not merely fleeing a still inscrutable ambivalence but making further discovery of real human connection. Then in "Araby" themes similar to those in the first two stories are interwoven, more intensely developed, and yet held the more ambiguously suspended. The boy in "Araby" is, like both the others, bookish and imaginative, and like Mahony's companion has outgrown child's play; beyond that he has fixed his steadier affections with a passion that makes the frustration of his quest most severe. Between this ardent fanciful young chalice-bearer and the coolly aloof, tentatively analytical observer of "The Sisters" there stands intermediary the lad whose ultimate encounter on a particular day was in a moment of normally companionable feeling. Within the hour he has thus encompassed knowledge of evil and good.

The lads of the first and third stories are specified as nephews not sons; he of "An Encounter" is not shown in any such connection, but from the impression made on him by the atmosphere of the devout and orderly Mahony household it might be supposed his own home, like those in the other two boyhood stories, made less claim. This perhaps is why he must discover relationship in a crisis outside, and with a playmate, and by accident of circumstance, not a way of life. In the end, however, he is not alone, whereas the boys of the other stories are, each in his own way. The narrator of "The Sisters," conversing with the reader but craftily silent with those about him, stands at last in a self-chosen alienation, which his controlled account obliquely reveals. In "Araby" the protagonist comes to see himself as "a creature driven and derided by vanity," but his "anguish and anger" spring from frustration of his desire to bear a gift that will signify relationship. At the conclusion of "An Encounter" the achieved positiveness appears in the boy's penitence, which admits not only relationship but its reciprocal claims. Beyond adolescence this unites him with Little Chandler's "remorse" and with Gabriel Conroy's "generousness." In spite of a half-concealed supercilious separation from his playmates, the boy of the encounters can waken to a moment of common human response. His progress, once begun and without looking back, is up the slope away from the pervert and the field's near end, and toward the ridge, there to behold a manifestation in simple Mahony. In "Araby" the lad will be stirred more deeply and persistently, to be the more shaken, knowing himself pawn of circumstance, and suffering the pathos of divergence between dream and reality.

Despite the representativeness of this latter vision, and of the arrival at penitence in "An Encounter," both these stories center more definitely in emotions conditioned by adolescence though projected toward growing relationship; "The Sisters," conversely, is not as much saturated with the immediate mood of a reminiscence as it is tinged with more deliberate evaluation, in a withdrawal from relationships, that by implication repudiates explicit commitment. As such it fitly illustrates the premises announced for *Dubliners,* but more unreservedly practiced in Joyce's later works. "An Encounter" and "Araby" express emotions Joyce increasingly left behind to achieve another perspective, and thus they make way for the emergence in some other of the stories of a greater degree of compassion than is found in "The Sisters." Between its cool detachment and the intense emotions of "Araby" the story of encounter, though slightest of these three in substance, is a pivot of the positive, upon which the other two can turn, and which the stories of maturity can follow. Hence, possibly, Joyce's own positiveness that without "An Encounter" his book would be "incomplete."

ARABY

"Araby," wrote Ezra Pound, "is much better than a 'story,' it is a vivid waiting."[1] It is true; the boy, suspended in his first dream of love, is also held up by circumstance, and the subjective rendering of this total experience is indeed vivid. Yet "Araby" is also a genuine short story, moving through determining events to self-realization in a Joycean epiphany.

Every morning the boy kept watch from his window until Mangan's sister appeared, and then with a leaping heart he ran to follow her in the street until their ways diverged, hers toward her convent school. Of an evening, when she came out on the doorstep to call her brother to tea, the boys at play would linger in the shadows to see whether she "would remain or go in"; then while she waited they would approach "resignedly," but while Mangan still teased his sister before obeying, the boy of this story "stood by the railings looking at her," seeing "her figure defined by the light from the half-opened door" and waiting upon a summons of another kind. He must wait too for his uncle's late return and for the money to fetch the girl a present from the bazaar Araby; then the special train, almost empty, waited intolerably and he arrived late. Still he drove toward his goal, paying a shilling to avoid further delay in looking for a sixpenny entrance. Once inside, he found the place half-darkened and the stalls mostly closed. Though there was nothing for him to buy, he lingered still, baffled, stultified, prolonging only pretense of interest. What awaits him as the lights are being put out is a facing "with anguish and anger" of his obsessive mood and its frustration, of himself as "a creature driven and derided by vanity"—like Stephen in *A Portrait* "angry with himself for being young and the prey of restless foolish impulses."[2]

While he waited in all the vividness of his budding sexuality and sentiment, and though the impeding world of uncles and trains and subtler circumstances kept him waiting, he had made reality wait upon his preoccupation. On his Saturday evening marketing trips with his aunt the various, insistent, and vulgar noises from the jostling crowds "converged" for him "in a single sensation of life." His imagination dwelt so continuously on the girl that "serious work" at school was made to seem "ugly monotonous child's play" as her image came between him and the page. For the infatuated one himself there was nothing fatuous about it; he had passed beyond boyhood's neutral casual existence and found that the heart can be completely fixed upon one object, with an unceasing inclination. "Araby" is above all a love story, of instinctive-imaginative passion naïvely held, unavoidably lost, and recollected as ardor and disenchantment. It is everyman's puberty rite, imperious desire blunting itself upon limitations, and fragmenting into an opposite despair.

While "Araby" treats this universal theme, it is also a specifically placed and furnished story, and thereby part of Joyce's evaluative mirroring of Dublin. The train to the bazaar "crept onward among ruinous houses and over the twinkling river." There is the Saturday evening milieu of streets where drunken men and bargaining women jostle, where laborers curse and ballad-singers chant nasally. There are the "dark muddy lanes" through which the playing boys ran, past "dark dripping gardens where odours arose from the ashpits," or "dark odorous stables where a coachman smoothed and combed the horse or shook music from the buckled harness," and so back to their street, where "light from the kitchen windows had filled the areas." This is the world of Joyce's boyhood and youth, viewed not only as the scene of first romance but as what he specified when he wrote Grant Richards "it is not my fault that the odour of ashpits and old weeds and offal hangs around my stories."[3]

Drunkenness, a stigma of Dublin life as Joyce shows it in

several stories, is seen here in the uncle's late return, and the domestic unease it creates. Hearing the rattling key at the latch, the rocking of the hallstand under a coat thrust unsteadily upon it, and the man's talking to himself, the boy, though already so long delayed, dare not ask for the promised money until his uncle is "midway through his dinner." Befuddled, he had forgotten, though only that Saturday morning when the boy had reminded him of the bazaar he had said, curtly, "Yes, boy, I know." Now his evasive response is that it's too late, but under the aunt's chiding he is "sorry" and then grows sententious about "all work and no play," and finally sentimental, proposing to recite "The Arab's Farewell to His Steed," which the aunt is about to be subjected to as the boy hurries off. That she will bear it resignedly may be supposed from her earlier attitude, in a scene with tones not unlike some in "The Sisters." Tea had been "prolonged" for over an hour, while the restless boy "had to endure the gossip" of his aunt's visitor, a garrulous old woman who stays until after eight. When she left and the uncle had not yet arrived, the boy began to pace the room, clenching his fists, but the aunt merely said, "I'm afraid you may put off your bazaar for this night of Our Lord." Here too, apparently, the head of the household, like Eveline's father, is "usually fairly bad on Saturday night," and in one degree or another, whether as in "The Boarding House" or "Grace" or "Counterparts," women and children must suffer for it.

The Church as a factor in Joyce's conception of Dublin life comes into "Araby" only as incidental influence, but it is felt. The Christian Brothers school looses its boys into otherwise "quiet" North Richmond Street. The aunt hoped, with sound denominational antipathy, that the bazaar "was not some Freemason affair." Consciousness of the clergy's prestige and virtue may be seen with the recollection that the "former tenant" was a priest, who had died there "in the back drawing-room," and with the separately added detail that he had been "a very charitable priest," who "had left all his money to institutions and the furniture of his house to his sister." Most tellingly, "Araby" shows a young Dubliner's mind pervaded by ecclesiastical imagery. In those exultant days when everything was made to serve love and even the street noises "converged in a single sensation of life" for him, this realization seemed a "chalice" that he bore "safely through a throng of foes." To his ears the shop boys by the barrels of pigs' cheeks proclaimed their wares in "shrill litanies," the girl's name "sprang" to his lips "in strange prayers and praises," and he wondered how he could tell her of his "confused adoration." The Church's control does come into the story at one point, through the austere practice which stands between the girl and Araby; she "would love to go" to the "splendid bazaar" but cannot, "because there would be a retreat that week in her convent."

All such representative details of Dublin life are, however, subordinated to the love story. The bazaar itself, a real event under that name in Dublin for a week in May of 1894,[4] is incidental to a crisis in the boy's experience, as is the tardiness of the drunken uncle and then the train's delay. So also is the religious retreat which prevents the girl's going to Araby, stimulating the boy's promise to bring her something from it. The first talk between them beyond "a few casual words" is about the bazaar, and the one quoted speech of hers concerns his going: "It's well for you." She has brought up the subject: "It would be a splendid bazaar, she said; she would love to go." Nevertheless her "It's well for you" need not be read as self-pity so much as sympathetic pleasure in his prospect. (It has the gentle Irish cordiality about it like that of the flower-girl's response when Stephen says he has no money: "Well, sure, you will some day, sir, please God.")[5] And the boy responds in kind, and his words too are directly quoted: "If I go, I will bring you something." This proposes the immemorial first act of love, the offering which is to speak as the lover cannot, and beyond words can stand as a token. The possibility intensifies the boy's chafing at school and home; having asked permission to go to the bazaar on the coming Saturday night, he dreams in bedroom and classroom of the girl, now that his inclination has found a thing to do about it.

How the infatuation had dawned upon the sensitive boy has been suggested chiefly in remembered images, such as that of her standing by a "half-opened door" through which light "defined" her figure, showing the swing of her dress "as she moved her body," while "the soft rope of her hair tossed from side to side." The attraction, declares one critic, is "as with a noose,"[6] but Joyce says nothing of the kind, nor does the text suggest it. To see portent of a noose in this swaying soft rope of hair is to postulate a designing woman *sans merci,* or even one doomed to be strangled *à la* Porphyria, whereas Joyce's image plainly serves his theme of pure enchantment. Of course misogyny might read selfish design in her leading the talk to the bazaar, but any noose the boy is caught in, besides his own final extravagance of emotion, is adverse circumstance, chiefly the delays by his uncle and by the train. Often the boy had looked upon the charming sway of her dress and the tossed soft rope of her hair while her brother, as "always," teasingly delayed coming in and she waited by the half-opened door. But on the unique evening when they talked of Araby it was under the illumination from the street lamp opposite his own door that she stood, poised in the intentness of the moment, touched by the partially revealing light. The passage is exquisite in its simplicity and suggestion: "Her brother and two other boys were fighting for their caps and I was alone at the railings. She held one of the spikes, bowing her head towards me. The light from the lamp opposite our door caught the white curve of her neck, lit up her hair that rested there and, falling, lit up the hand upon the railing. It fell over one side of her dress and caught the white border of a petticoat, just visible as she stood at ease."

The image recurs in detail on the night when he waits to go to the bazaar; delayed and irritated, he mounts into an upper part of the house. The "high cold empty gloomy" spaces "liberated" him from the sense of domestic restraint and frustration and let him go "from room to room singing." He is also raised above his companions' play in the street; their cries reach him "weakened and indistinct" as he leans his forehead "against the cold glass" and looks "over at the dark house where she lived." Standing there a long time, he holds in his imagination her "brown-clad figure . . . touched discreetly by the lamplight at the curved neck, at the hand upon the railings and at the border below the dress." In such a glimpse is his own sense of the mystery; the image also tells how selective is idealization, and how love can feed on a particular vision. For that sustained moment the boy has found what young Stephen had longed for in "the unsubstantial image" of the Mercedes whom he has assigned a local habitation and looks to encounter "surrounded by darkness and silence," whereupon "he would be transfigured."[7]

Although Joyce mentioned "Araby" as a story of his childhood,[8] the autobiographical links here, as in the two preceding, are tenuous. The most specific is that the Joyce family did live at 17 North Richmond Street, into which they moved late in 1894.[9] However, the *Grand Oriental Fete, Araby in Dublin* had held forth earlier that year, the week of May 14 to 19. As for the Christian Brothers School, cornering on Richmond Place and North Richmond Street, the increasingly impecunious John Joyce had earlier sent his children there for a brief while, perhaps late in 1892, certainly in early 1893, but then had secured admission for James and Stanislaus, without fees, to the Jesuits' Belvedere College, where James Joyce was entered on April 6, 1893.[10] It was there he was a student during the period, more than a year later, when for a while the family lived in North Richmond Street. This would accord with one detail in "Araby," the boy's following the girl "morning after morning" until their schoolward paths diverged, apparently well away from North Richmond Street and the Christian Brothers School. Otherwise there is little trace of factual connection or of a particular boyhood experience out of which this tale of infatuation could have been distilled. In the more connectedly autobiographic *Portrait* Joyce includes nothing pointing back to the family's brief sojourn on North Richmond Street; in *Ulysses* however there are several connections, as Ellmann shows.[11]

As is typical of significant fiction no less than of other literary forms at their most imaginative and refined levels, "Araby" assembles its material arbitrarily; and here the arbiter is not a naturalist anatomizing Dublin of the 1890's, he is commemorator of the generic adolescent smitten by first love, but more particularly he is this precocious sensitive beset and burgeoning lad who is variously Joyce's alter ego in the first three stories. According to Budgen this fictional character represents some of Joyce's basic and enduring characteristics;[12] according to his English composition teacher at Belvedere Joyce was "a boy with a plethora of ideas in his head."[13] By many accounts he was from the first what different aspects of these three stories show—bookish, keenly observant and intuitive, sensitive but often uncommunicative, already somewhat aloof and of two minds about much that pressed upon him for acceptance, and apparently already fated to pass through a never quite discarded ambivalence into a disenchanted separation. Yet whatever assorted cluster of actual boyhood experiences "Araby" may have been distilled from, even were they known, would matter only as to the final fictional product in its essence, evoked by the protagonist in narrated recall, and set in perspective yet with no loss of clarity.

Here Joyce conveyed a dimensioned effect, communicating the boy's sensibility as of his time and circumstance, but recollectively too. The past made present yet viewed at its real distance, the bones of a memory made into coral, a loss turned to a realization, the dynamic paradox of "emotion recollected in tranquillity"—this is the particular fictional achievement, beyond both lyricism and drama. Joyce's procedure to such a result can be fully seen, for instance, in the very artful first three paragraphs of "Araby," and especially in paragraph two. Paragraph one gives the locale, a blind street, quiet except for schoolboys, with the detached uninhabited house at the blind end. (In the sub-poetic vein of a Little Chandler it docs lapse into the pathetic fallacy that "the other houses . . . conscious of decent lives within them, gazed at one another with brown imperturbable faces.") The second paragraph ostensibly is centered upon the former tenant of the boy's house, the priest who had died there. What it really accomplishes, however, is characterization of the boy—rather solitary, fanciful, explorative, sentimentally preferring a book for its yellowed pages, and discovering in the unkempt garden such intriguing artifacts as the late priest's rusty bicycle pump. Then comes the paragraph's closing sentence, totally given over to data about this priest—he was "very charitable," he "had left all his money to institutions" and his furniture to his sister.

On the surface this sums up the passage as realistic description of locale with its incidental associations, including a glimpse of an Irish cleric typically loyal to establishment. More deeply, by easy transition from rusty bicycle pump to the dead priest's repute it aesthetically masks expository intent and partially veils but does not supersede the paragraph's central import, the nature of this adolescent at the verge of a crisis in maturation. Thus it makes way for that rich third paragraph which, while epitomizing the life of the neighborhood boys, moves subtly from this one lad's intensely conscious part in it to his more private and utterly absorbing realizations. Here in extremes is all the vividness which Pound noted in this story. Boys' play in the street could not be more purely expressed. The houses were "sombre," the "space of sky" an "ever-changing violet," the street lamps "feeble" in the half-light; the boys' bodies "glowed," their "shouts echoed in the silent street," they ran all through the darkening neighborhood and lingered to postpone as long as possible being called in. This boy whose unique story is remembered has been a part of all that, all those sensations were his, it was his uncle from whom they "hid in the shadows" until they "had seen him safely housed," and this boy too has hung back with the others when the Mangan girl called to her brother. But when she remains on the steps and the boys leave their shadow and approach "resignedly" there comes the shift; in three simple sentences the narrative moves from one realm of being to another, as does the boy, so that from this point on it is wholly his story, and a love story. The girl stands in "the light from the half-opened door," and while her brother teased, the boy "stood by the railings looking at her," seeing her in this new and wonderful guise—"Her dress swung as she moved her body and the soft rope of her hair tossed from side to side." As simply as that the arrow has gone through him; and the reader, already by imperceptible degrees acquainted with this boy, can sense what this image embodies and promises, and what it perhaps portends.

That possible portent is disenchantment, the typical fate of the romantic. Since it proceeds from a contradiction of the ideal by circumstance, it breeds melancholy, weakens self-possession, and may induce ambivalence. That the fascination itself is not to be derogated and that its sheer spell remains unforgettable only adds to despair, from which there is only the momentary relief of that mental blankness and paralysis of will which frustration can produce, as when the boy, brought up short at the bazaar by being too late, remembers only with difficulty why he had come. To rouse from that apathy is for him to confront a fragmented existence, in which love absolute and single-minded is parodied by the frivolous inconclusive sparring of the saleslady's conversation with two young men, idly resumed after her perfunctory attention to the boy. His "single sensation of life" has become a disharmony, and like Father Flynn in another context of commitment he has lost hold on the "chalice" he had sought to bear. The "throng of foes" he had imagined have become real, in a multiplicity of mean yet finally insuperable hindrances, and beyond that he has fallen into enmity with himself.

In Ellmann's detailed account of the Joyces' neighbors on North Richmond Street the name Mangan does not appear, nor is there any report of a precocious infatuation at that time in Joyce's life. The story "Eveline," including the detail of involvement with a sailor, evidently derives from a North Richmond Street girl so called,[14] but for Mangan's sister in "Araby" Joyce wrote no name, nor did he have the narrator speak it. It is part of the story's realism to suggest that among the boys she was merely "my sister" or "your sister," recognized only factually, the unwelcome familial voice breaking in upon their play. The one lad, though, came to know her more particularly, having looked at her in a different light. That her name, while "like a summons" to his "foolish blood," is never named maintains her fictionally as the ideal figure of his secret dreaming.

Doubtless too the surname Mangan had special resonance for Joyce, because of his enthusiasm for the Irish poet James Clarence Mangan, twice celebrated in Joyce's critical writings. The second of these was a public lecture, in Italian, at Trieste, in 1907;[15] the first and more enthusiastic was an address read to the Literary and Historical Society of University College, Dublin, in February, 1902, and published in the college magazine in May of that year.[16] To his fellow-collegians the twenty-year-old Joyce described Mangan as one whose "sufferings have cast him inwards, where for many ages the sad and the wise have elected to be,"[17] and in a passage echoed five years later at Trieste, Joyce saw in Mangan's writings an intense concept of love, centered on "the moonwhite pearl of his soul, Ameen."[18] The next two sentences project the essence of the story "Araby"—"Music and odours and lights are spread about her, and he would search the dews and the sands that he might set another glory near her face. A scenery and a world have grown up about her face, as they will about any face which the eyes have regarded with love." Then Joyce spoke of Michelangelo's Vittoria Colonna, and Laura and Beatrice, and "even she," Mona Lisa, connecting them with "one chivalrous idea, which is no mortal thing, bearing it bravely above the accidents of lust and faithlessness and weariness."[19]

The boy of "Araby" has imagined bearing his chalice "safely through a throng of foes," but he could not bear it out to the edge of doom; already he would have sensed the fluctuations of passion, while not faithless he has been unable to keep faith, and weariness has possessed him at last. He has sighted what Stephen sought in longing for Mercedes, but he has not found what Stephen expected, that with it "Weakness and timidity and inexperience would fall from him."[20] Instead, obstructions have checked and encompassed him, and though a resolute lad, he is not strong and knowing enough to circumvent them. Hence his very selfhood is shaken. Hating the world for not maintaining one fixed enchanting aspect, he hates himself for having naïvely expected that, knowing himself "driven and derided by vanity." He has found that there is no isolation more severe than that incurred through love frustrated; and emotion, which had been a "single sensation," becomes multiple in his "anguish and anger."

Palpably and poignantly a story of adolescent love, "Araby" rises to this still larger representation, of subjective division under the clash between the idealist's discriminating ardor and adverse insuperable circumstance. There was in Joyce himself that recurrent bitterness which, beyond redressing the balance of judgment, indirectly punishes the self for overexpectation by derogating the world. This can even be the disappointed romantic's handiest mask, too, and an easy expedient securing of scapegoat. Which may invite some conjectures about "Araby" as a story not merely of Joyce's "childhood" but of the man Joyce, whose most deeply rooted affections and natural pieties were so often affronted, and who in disillusionment turned to vast myths of remote origin, yet furnished them out with singular native memories always more recurrent and vivid than anything his life-long exile supplied. In this process romance is to make way for the grotesque, regarded more detachedly. The extravagances of sentimentality, ultimately found agonizing, are to be replaced by intellectual extravagance, in which cool vanity can be preserved.

But whether or not "Araby" is given any thematic reading with reference to Joyce's ambivalence and his progress under it, the "anguish" it vividly pictures remains representative of common human experience. Thereby the story crowns the *Dubliners* group of three first-person accounts of childhood and lays ground for the veiled but genuine empathy with which Joyce treated many of the sadly beset characters in the narratives to follow. While "The Sisters" shows a degree of affiliation between the boy and the old priest, what this leads to is reactive emancipation, not only from that ambiguous pastor but from the world of all his elders, with whom the boy found even less in common. It suggests, by the mode of its concluding scene, the cold distaste and severe rejection Joyce defined as to the city and society of his coming of age. Father Flynn between pinches of snuff had held the lad with bits of erudition, and the boy is an ingrained word-fancier, gathering in *faints* and *worms* along with *gnomon* and *simony* and "reading all the theatrical advertisements in the shop-windows" with perhaps as much of insatiable logophilia as of released worldliness. Beyond this, as he went "along the sunny side of the street" his emerging urge is that of the separatist. In these ways "The Sisters" casts the furthest implications as to all Joyce's work to come.

The boy in "An Encounter" is more gregarious and shares his comrades' general "spirit of unruliness"; he lingers, more secretly curious and intuitive, in the presence of the obscurely pernicious; and when adventure has disclosed the worm in the apple, he seizes upon the reassurance of simple human companionship and is penitent for previous condescension. In "Araby" the reaction in which the story culminates is most drastic and most acutely felt. A degree of intellectual independence and withdrawal from submissive association is achieved in "The Sisters," some worldly knowledge and social alliance are arrived at in "An Encounter," but "Araby" represents emotions most private and intense, a more decisive turn of events, and lapse into a sad disturbance of equanimity. Any former love looked back on has the pathos of transiency, but here, where the unforgettable dream has been broken off unrealized and the desire for completion has been obstructed by disparities, the result is ambivalence. Vanity that has driven the boy now derides him; that is the complex quiddity of the "creature" he then sees himself to be. But his "anger" is also "anguish"; and it is as one whose childhood had thus tempered him that Joyce the examiner of other Dubliners, turning to the third-person mode and a more objective and critical view, still can accord the poor trapped creature Eveline and some other like victims a quiet but genuine compassion.

More broadly, the three boyhood tales give suitable entry into *Dubliners* because the rest of the stories too, while environmentally contained, are at basis psychological. In its synthesis of these facets and the maintenance of scale *Dubliners* achieved a golden mean. When naturalism excessively materializes setting and social circumstance it may enervate drama by dwarfing the actors; naturalism's antithesis, an ultra-subjective fiction, may distortingly magnify and arrest the protagonist through his too-close self-regard. The representative realities Joyce tried to lay hold on in *Dubliners* are more complicated of outer and inner weather, and in ways he well knew before he transferred their stresses to his little Dublin people. When circumstance impinges abrasively while association still makes sometimes poignant claims, a natural objective-subjective reciprocity can be troubled into ambivalence. Thereby an intense temperament or one just severely beset may develop a love-hate relationship with its world and even in itself. Thus attitudes may grow obsessive, so that confinement by the external is compounded and becomes fixed internally. Dilemma is then inescapable: surrender paralyzes, but revolt impoverishes and bereaves. How this dilemma is contended with marks the degrees of ambivalence Joyce pictured in various *Dubliners* characters, a witnessing based upon the gamut of his own experience.

Perhaps too it was self-knowledge which prohibited Joyce from lifting any of the *Dubliners* characters wholly out of the maze. The boy grown to be Stephen proposed it for himself at the end of *A Portrait,* but later the "Telemachia" shows him having to project all over again the still unaccomplished deliverance; and to imagine the Ur-Stephen of the stories or Stephen himself achieving sure poise and steady relationship requires supposition obviously beyond Joyce's intent as well as the reader's right, in *Dubliners* and thereafter, and perhaps also beyond Joyce's power.

In each of the first three stories the protagonist has felt something more besides environment's ways of impinging and its failures to compensate. The superannuated priest whose paralysis had filled his young pupil with "fear" and a paradoxical longing "to be nearer" had cast the ominous shadow of an absolute but devitalized dogmatism, with its obscure but real hazards of simony, yet beyond the little dark room the boy finds no other habitation, only the miscellanies of an open street. In a different encounter the escape from the pervert is explicit, but the flight is from threat which could recur, and the fugitive's relief and penitence in rejoining his schoolmate may be a fleeting reaction. In "Araby" the boy has been frustrated by externality, in the guises of the tardy drunken uncle and a slow train, but he is more lastingly grieved by discovery of universal ineradicable flaw, the gap between idealization and its confined operation. This also is epiphany, but at first sight almost too appalling for him. So in the ardor and sorrow of his youth he berates both his fate and himself, being as yet at some distance in years and experience from one possible palliative, the discovery that at the heart of a wise self-possession is the stoic's tragic sense of life.

To what degree Joyce ever took hold of any such wisdom, whether in his life or in his works, is a larger problem, but at least in "Araby" a protagonist's overflow of devastating emotion is complementary to a similar protagonist's gradual intellectual advance in "The Sisters." Comparable psychological interconnections are to play all through the remaining twelve stories. In the "stories of boyhood" Joyce's realism is quite as deeply in accord with the verities of promise and ordeal in the human situation, and in this aspect too *Dubliners* was well begun.

EVELINE

In the story "Eveline" a far journey is projected, but the timid protagonist, paralyzed by ambivalence at the moment of embarking from Dublin's North Wall, never sets out. In the three preceding stories lesser journeys have been proposed, from their adjacent locales in one region of North Dublin, and all with a crossing of the river Liffey to the south. ("The Sisters" locates the priest's house in Great Britain Street, now Parnell Street; "Araby" has its base in North Richmond Street; presumably the boys of "An Encounter" live in the same area, since they meet at the Canal Bridge, proceed to the North Wall, and then cross the river.) Father Flynn had "had his mind set on" a drive down to Irishtown—the poor region just south of Ringsend, adjacent to the harbor—"to see the old house again" where he and his sisters had been born, and the unfulfilled wish takes on natural pathos in Eliza's mention of it after his death. The boys of "An Encounter" did ferry across the Liffey but did not make it to their goal, the Pigeon House. He of "Araby" not only crossed "the twinkling river" by train, but got to the bazaar, yet to be the more frustrated by coming so close but failing to secure a gift for the girl. Eveline's crisis, more simply narrated, is most severe. On her proposed journey to Buenos Aires she gets only as far as the dock, and while the boy of "Araby" feels an "anguish" that makes his eyes burn, Eveline's mental "anguish" causes her to cry out, and then reduces her to a state of shock.

This third-person story is continuously sustained in the brooding consciousness of its main character. Of its seven pages, almost six are given over to her eddying recollections as she sits by the window at dusk, and her only overt act there is finally to stand up, with impulse to escape. The last page shows her at the North Wall but unable to go up the gangplank to the ship that would carry her away with her lover. This scene too is realized in her consciousness as she subsides through painfully conflicting emotions into a rigidity that marks the numbing of feeling. At the last it is as if not only self-possession but self-awareness have been drained from her; here the point of view changes from her anguish to the climactically worded image of what Frank saw as he called in vain for her to follow—"She set her white face to him, passive, like a helpless animal. Her eyes gave him no sign of love or farewell or recognition."

Who and what is Eveline that her life, in this most vital sense, should be ending before she is twenty? She is in one way a widely representative figure, in her presumable fate as one of that underprivileged and put-upon minority, the spinsters for whom love's proper tide is reversed and chilled into filial dutifulness, and whose care is required for the offspring of others' passion. More particularly, though, this is an Irish story; most pointedly it is Joyce's Dublin with its special injunctions and encirclements that holds Eveline and will not let her go. Religion is part of it, inculcating the pious obligations of family life, no matter how harsh its demands. On the wall is "a coloured print of the promises made to Blessed Margaret Mary Alacoque" —she who will bless a home where her picture is exhibited— and at the dock Eveline's last act before she lapses into a fixed inaction is to murmur prayers "to God to direct her, to show her what was her duty." The neediness that stalks so many of Joyce's Dubliners is in this story too. "She always gave her entire wages —seven shillings" to the family's support. Family demands in addition almost the whole of her life. Eveline's promise to her dying mother has left the nineteen-year-old girl responsible for two younger children, and subject to a domineering father.

This parental figure, from Joyce's view, is authentic Dubliner. Given to drink, he "was usually fairly bad on Saturday night." Then he would be capriciously tyrannical, first refusing money for the household and finally giving it but blaming Eveline for the delay in buying Sunday's dinner. When as children she and her older brothers had played in the adjoining field, their father "used often to hunt them in . . . with his blackthorn stick," and "he used to go for Harry and Ernest." Now Ernest is dead and Harry, "in the church decorating business," is away from home, and there is no one to protect her from this man who had treated her mother badly and whose threats have "given her the palpitations." Like most autocrats, he is insular, damning the Italian organ grinders for "coming over here," and he plays the proper heavy father, forbidding his daughter "to have anything to say" to that sailor chap, Frank.

Thinking of herself as "over nineteen," Eveline looks back to what in her wearisome life seems "a long time ago," before houses were built on the field where she and other children had played, and before those playmates had died or moved away. Then "they seemed to have been rather happy," she recalls. This moderate memory centers on two things—"Her father was not so bad then; and besides, her mother was alive." Since then Eveline has gone to work in the Stores, to bring back all her wage for the family's support, while it also devolved upon her to see that "the two young children . . . went to school regularly and got their meals regularly." She knows it to be "hard work—a hard life," yet habit has so captured her that "now that she was about to leave it she did not find it a wholly undesirable life." At an enervated pause there by the window in the little brown house, looking about the room, she is reminded chiefly of dutiful toil, regarding familiar objects as things she "had dusted once a week for so many years." It is with such and like details that Joyce has gone on to substantiate the story's remarkable opening paragraph of three sentences:

> She sat at the window watching the evening invade the avenue. Her head was leaned against the window curtains and in her nostrils was the odour of dusty cretonne. She was tired.

The word "invade," especially connoting the dusk, suggests a suspended mood without stressing it; "was leaned" conveys her passivity, and that effect is sustained by the parallel verb structure of "in her nostrils was the odour of dusty cretonne." The rhythms of the first two sentences make way for the epitomizing of her lassitude in the simple brevity of the third.

Eveline's fatigue was more than physical; it was a dreadful weariness of spirit as she approached the verge of impasse. With the odor of dust in her nostrils and with bits of the distant and nearer past alternating in her mind, she was trying "to weigh each side of the question" of leaving her home and family. Against all her hardships she could find almost nothing to persuade her to stay. She made herself recall that sometimes her father "could be very nice." Not long before, when she was ill, he had read her a ghost story and made toast for her; but for more on that positive side she must go back to once when her mother was alive and they went to picnic on the Hill of Howth (her widest excursion, probably, no further than those few miles to the northern tip of Dublin harbor) and the father had donned the mother's bonnet to make the children laugh. There is little enough of past felicity to summon up in the room with the broken harmonium and the yellowing photograph of a priest notable for having gone to Melbourne. Of only one thing is she certain—"She would not cry many tears at leaving the Stores," where her superior is inclined to be severe. Eveline can explicitly reject the impersonal claims of a job, but obligation to family is not to be put aside without painful questioning.

Circumscribed by harsh authority and onerous necessity, in meekly complying she has developed timidity as a fixed characteristic, much like others among Joyce's Dubliners, such as Little Chandler, Maria, Jimmy Doyle, and Gabriel Conroy in their variously diffident ways. But Eveline is not simply timid; she is racked by inner conflict, finally to the point of distraction. Her father's inconsiderateness and the hardness of her laborious life are not, however, primary factors in this ambivalence. Its poles are a young girl's desire for the assurances of love with the security of marriage and, on the other hand, her submission under the weight of a promise made on "the last night of her mother's illness" that she would "keep the home together as long as she could." Furthermore, in her very remembrance of that pledge she is of two minds.

While she continued to sit by the window, though "her time was running out," still leaning her head against the dust-impregnated curtain, a street organ was playing outside, sounding from the world beyond Dublin "a melancholy air of Italy," just as on the night of her mother's death. Under music's spur to association she recalls not only her promise but her mother's "life of commonplace sacrifices closing in final craziness," and with this "pitiful vision" she hears again her mother's insistent cry, "Derevaun Seraun!" The words constitute a puzzle. To an inquiry one Irish scholar said that whatever this is, it isn't Gaelic.[1] Another informally put it that it sounds something like what might mean "one end . . . bitterness" or, more closely, "end of riches . . . bitterness."[2] Tindall, in *A Reader's Guide to James Joyce*, reports that Patrick Henchy of the National Library in Dublin "thinks this mad and puzzling ejaculation corrupt Gaelic for 'the end of pleasure is pain.' "[3] Marvin Magalaner writes that the words "seem to be crazed ravings, the meaning of which I have been unable to determine."[4] The phrase doubtless is to be read as unintelligible to Eveline, but that would have made it the more disturbing to her, and whatever the senselessness, the tone of despair would have been clear. Thus the memory triggered by the street organ's air involves both the solemn promise her mother had extracted from Eveline and the inference that if the promise is kept, she like her mother will be misused and deprived, and perhaps even driven to distraction. And the latter fear, for the moment, tips the scale in this ambivalence. In "a sudden impulse of terror" Eveline stands up, knowing she "must escape!"

She believes too that a way to life and rightful happiness is open—"Frank would save her." He is Irish, but is in Dublin "just for a holiday" in "the old country," from which he had shipped out as a deck boy, to Canada; since then he has seen the world and reports himself "fallen on his feet" in Buenos Aires, where a "home" awaits Eveline if she will go with him. This bronze-faced sailor had been attentive, he would meet her outside the Stores every evening to see her home, and he took her to *The Bohemian Girl*. At first for her there was the excitement of having "a fellow," and "then she had begun to like him." Primarily, though, he is a refuge and her salvation. She believes he "would give her life, perhaps love, too" but certainly "would . . . fold her in his arms . . . would save her."

Such details allow a supposition that Eveline's father might not have been all wrong in forbidding her to see Frank, though the reasons were mean—a stereotyped distrust of "sailor chaps" and an unrelenting claim upon his domestic drudge. As Eveline sees Frank, he is not only spirited but "very kind, manly, openhearted." Yet it is not quite as one reader puts it: "Marriage and flight across the sea promise life and 'perhaps love too.' "[5] For her to be a bride before the flight would require, if not a secret marriage in Dublin, an immediate ceremony in the captain's cabin—a most unlikely thing in the Catholic context of this story, and one which, had it been pending, surely would have entered into Eveline's reverie. Instead this inexperienced nineteen-year-old about to "run away with a fellow" thinks simply that she "was to go away with him by the night-boat to be his wife" and believes that "tomorrow she would be on the sea with Frank, steaming towards Buenos Ayres." However, "the night-boat" from the North Wall is probably the regular one to Liverpool, and while passengers might sail to Buenos Aires from there, Liverpool could be the sordid end of this journey for Eveline; or she could reach South America still unmarried and find Frank's promises false.

Joyce has given no further or more substantial grounds for suspecting Frank besides these slight implications in the details and phrasing. If the inference is made, it merely stresses the pathos of Eveline's situation; and to leave it at that would accord with the narrative's tone and intent. For Frank to have given Eveline more precise assurance or for the hint of possible betrayal to have been stronger would have made it another story, or an infringement upon the integrity of this one. It is one of its many delicate balancings, both in Eveline's mind and in the total effect itself, that Joyce makes it a matter of "perhaps love, too" but allows some uncertainty as to just what kind of escape is open to Eveline. There is a great deal of such selective economy and particular focusing in all the *Dubliners* stories, and in this technique they are still quite modern, sixty years after their composition. Indeed, in comparison it is Joyce's later and more experimental works that may seem "dated" by uniqueness and by a fixity less within the literary period than in the artist's own history.

More to the main point in "Eveline" is the nature of her indecision and her eventual paralysis. This intimidated girl perceives in sailor Frank's vitality and amiability something more pleasing and reassuring than anything in the Dublin life she has known, and it is not implied that she doubts him. What she doubts is herself. Too many burdens and restrictions have conditioned her to abandon hope and merely endure, with those bare consolations she weighs as "shelter and food" and "those whom she had known all her life about her." Ellmann reports, on the word of Joyce's sister, Mrs. Mary Monaghan, that an Eveline of North Richmond Street "did fall in love with a sailor" but "settled down with him in Dublin and bore him a great many children."[6] Joyce did not locate the story on that street or any other but only in a neighborhood where an adjacent field had made a place for the children to play until "a man from Belfast" —a foreign invader of a sort—"built houses in it." Apparently for this story all Joyce borrowed from North Richmond Street was a first name for a Dublin instance of early inescapable stunting, this downtrodden young woman who in her twentieth year already is girded about narrowly by what she "had known all her life." To that dead center she returns from her fluttering endeavor to escape, and there she is left, fixed in a confinement as strict as any in Joyce's several illustrations of Dublin's rigorous effect.

As Tindall has put it of this story, "The end is not a coming of awareness but an animal experience of inability."[7] Thereby "Eveline" sounds a somewhat different note from the three tales preceding it. Derived from Joyce's boyhood and told retrospectively in first person, those all show a "coming of awareness," though with some differences. In the first two the boy knows a liberation—in "The Sisters" from clerical and social domination into intellectual detachment, and in "An Encounter" from the contagious staining of a sense for adventure into a real knowledge of honest comradeship. Something positive is thus achieved in both stories, and they imply that where limitations are incidental and particular they may be evaded or transcended. "Araby," based more deeply on universals in addition to the presence of obstructive environmental factors, suggests that ultimately limitation inheres in the tearful nature of things, discovered between the spirit's inordinate projections and reality's unaccommodating welter. "Eveline" merges such elements, in a most economical and pointed story, toward a most acute crisis. The barely more than one page which is the simple concluding scene sketches with urgent directness her descent through conflicting emotions into an almost cataleptic state, with her hands clutching the iron railing in something like a death grip.

What precipitated this ultimate seizure as Frank tried to draw her with him was the indefinable but terrifying sense that "all the seas of the world" in its strange far regions and ways are only an extension of what she already knows—the multiplicity of the disparate and unamenable which has brought her to a neurotic fatigue beyond any remedy but one, apathy. When she sends her "cry of anguish" from "amid the seas," these are real depths; nor is she out of them. Compared to the anguished boy in "Araby" she is more pathetic, and a much grimmer example of frustration, since her whole life has already fallen into so harshly restrictive a mold. The boy's grief is sharp but not paralyzing; he has a lively anger to arm him for the rebellion latent in his nature; the environmental pressures upon him are less direct and insistent; and he has somewhat more time, since his crisis has come earlier; and as a man-child he has more scope. His frustration is of a kind many have suffered in early adolescence and recovered from; Eveline's moment at the North Wall is crucial, with implication of lasting defeat. Passing beyond stories based in his own childhood, Joyce defined in Eveline not only a characteristically limited Dublin life but traced psychologically the onset of impasse, through conflict to submission, and from the unrest of a divided mind to the barren refuge of inaction.

Eveline's is a simple story, simply told, but it is not slight, nor in any sense skimped. The vividly dramatic closing scene can be brief because it is well based. The preceding pages, concerning Eveline as she muses by the window with the farewell letters to father and brother in her lap, are a masterful narrative deployment to bring a whole life into plain view, and by its own light. The movement is that of casual association, suggesting by its shifts the recurrent alternations in Eveline's ambivalent mood. There are brief passages of chronologically ordered detail, but the total order is that of discursive mental process, for realistic characterization and for thematic penetration. Eveline remembers childhood, then looks at this room now, then weighs the question of leaving home, but from that prospect she returns to her past, caught in an eddy of inconclusive reconsideration. In thinking of what they would say at the Stores, where she works, that more immediate situation led her to suppose "it would not be like that" when she was married—"People would treat her with respect then." The next sentence—"She would not be treated as her mother had been"—carries her back to her father's bullying, but as she thinks of hardships she is about to escape, the habitual makes its claim, for "now that she was about to leave it she did not find it a wholly undesirable life," and the imminence of a decisive break wakens timidity and indecision, sounding again the fatal note of ambivalence. Still she projects "another life" which she "was about to explore" and that returns her to her first meeting with Frank, his continuing attentions, and intimations of the great world his tales brought her; then her mind swings to her father's opposition to the sailor chap, and to her farewell letters in her lap for father and brother, and so to her father's increasing age and dependence, and thus to remembrance that sometimes "he could be very nice," as when "not long before" he had been considerate of her in her illness or when, much longer before, he had been playful at their picnic on the Hill of Howth.

This is the point at which her repetitious medley of recollections is broken into by the street-organ music with its reminder of her mother's death; hence Eveline's wrench, from her remembered promise "to keep the home together as long as she could" to an impulse to escape that brings her to her feet. Yet while her musings have been freely associative and inconclusive, the narrative itself has not lapsed into rambling. The details of Eveline's history accumulate into shape and implication as unobtrusively yet solidly as the silting that shallows a river and underlies its meanderings. Unobtrusive yet crescive as thematic effect is the recurrent sway of Eveline's wavering regard. This prepares so well for the climax that Joyce can move into it directly, to show the pendulum finally stilled at dead center. It is not told what steps Eveline took after her standing up, "in a sudden impulse of terror" with intent to escape her present life, and until she stood in "the swaying crowd" at the North Wall at sailing time. The ellipsis is allowable, for evidently the impulse had sufficed to carry her straight on thus far, and her real story is not of direct progress but of haltings and stalemate.

Earlier in the evening, though she was aware that "her time was running out," Eveline had "continued to sit by the window"; now time has run out, she is at the point of embarcation, physically and psychologically. It is now that "a bell clanged upon her heart" as she feels herself about to be engulfed in "all the seas of the world." Now Frank, who she had thought "would save her," appears as one about to draw her into those seas and "drown her." This cannot be taken to mean she suspects him of bad faith. The story has given no hint that she had ever doubted him, and if she had, the probable reaction would have differed from that which follows, her freezing into a complete negation and unresponsiveness, to avoid taking the finally decisive step. This is marked by the fact that here her consciousness fails as the medium of the narrative. The rest beyond her silence can be said, however, in one paragraph of four short sentences. No longer seeing, she is seen in a helpless isolate animal passivity, with eyes that give her lover no sign, not even of "recognition."

Of all the traumatic experiences suffered by Joyce's Dubliners, this is the worst. Herself, too severely beset, has lost the sense of self with loss of volition. The boy of "Araby" at least can say "I saw myself," though only as "a creature driven and derided by vanity." Old Father Flynn in the double darkness of his confession-box was at least "wide-awake and laughing-like to himself." And even Mr. James Duffy's painful case of isolation is of another order, since as he "gnawed the rectitude of his life" he knows his own coldly wilful withdrawals are to blame for his finally feeling "outcast from life's feast." For Eveline the possibility of "life, perhaps love, too" has been eroded by an exacting sense of obligation. Self-sacrifice, inculcated as filial regard, has undone her even more severely than selfishness did for Mr. Duffy. At the quayside, glimpsing "the black mass of the boat" and hearing its "long mournful whistle into the mist," she prayerfully centers her mind on "what was her duty." This for her is the primary dilemma, of which her timidity is the effect not cause; she shows how frustration can produce indecisiveness. She proves too how the subservient finally have no point of reference except the authority which has dominated them; evil becomes what little good is left them, and their only pleasure, if any, would be a martyr's masochism. Frank held her hand and "she knew that he was speaking to her, saying something about the passage over and over again," but she scarcely heard these promises of liberation, and she "answered nothing," meanwhile silently imploring "God" to "show her" the clear path of "her duty." Hitherto basically guided by her promise to her dying mother, and conscious that her father, aging of late, "would miss her," now while her urgent lover is holding her hand what she thinks of is not love, even for him, but of something owed here too—"Could she still draw back after all he had done for her?"

Thus her life has come at last to nothing but a stark dilemma of duties, and either way will be a self-reductive subordination. Yet not to choose is to remain divided, which in the end is self-annihilating. So her final cry of "anguish" is not to Frank or to mother or father or God; if anything more than the scream of a trapped animal, it is to her dying identity amid those "seas of the world" that tumble in all their smothering contrariety "about her heart." She is paying an ultimate price, in unresolved paralyzing ambivalence, as that may be induced by too severe limitations and exactions. Concerning Eveline it has been observed by Hugh Kenner that "she is not a protagonist . . . but a mirror," placed in a "masculine world (Dublin)" which has "given" what her mind must "feed on."[8] It is a nice point, and the more so if it be allowed that Dublin as a masculine world includes the Church's authoritarian impact, especially on family life. It is also true that in some degree all of Joyce's Dubliners are pseudo-protagonists, in subjection to an environment insular, strict, and dominant. There is neither hero nor heroine among them, but whether or not they may be called "protagonists" they are actors; and all spirits, playing out illustratively Joyce's critical, melancholy view of life in Dublin, where degrees of paralysis are traceable to ambivalence more or less induced by various repressions upon the vulnerable.

The story does not tell whether Eveline's frenzied grip on the iron railing was held until the boat put off, or whether even then she had to be torn away from her clutch on an inanimate stability. If at the very best she could have found her way back to dutiful routines as housekeeper and store clerk, would other Dubliners (themselves relatively passive in a fatalistic acceptance) have seen anything about her "that made them think that there was something gone wrong," as was so mildly observed of Father Flynn? Joyce the artist, who has brought his account to a full stop with terrifying impact, states no prognosis of Eveline's case, but there is dark implication in the descending order of those closing words fixing her at that moment as one in whose eyes is "no sign of love or farewell or recognition." Had love's promise been strong enough and she not too enervated to answer to it, she would have followed Frank up the gangplank to at least something more than paralysis. Had she been capable of an unenforced, self-expressive decision not to go, at least she could have called farewell to the person who had persuaded her this far. The absence of recognition is the death of the heart.

And it is read as such through the eyes of one about to depart from Dublin. "Eveline," the second of Joyce's stories to be published, appeared in the *Irish Homestead* on September 10, 1904,[9] and on October 8 Joyce sailed from the North Wall with Nora Barnacle,[10] on a questing that was also in flight from deadening influence. Degrees of approach to the heart's death by various Dubliners are to be seen and shown by Joyce in the subsequent stories. In placing "Eveline" at their head, as example of the endemic Dublin disease in a classic, extreme, and in one sense fatal form, Joyce prepares for recognition of its less violent but at least partially disabling instances. Besides that, "Eveline" is a high particular artistic achievement of controlled intensity, a clearly implicative document in the onset of apathy, and a tragedy in the modern mode, brimming with the pathos of a little person's defeat under the pressures of an inimical order.

AFTER THE RACE

"After the Race," first published in the *Irish Homestead* on December 17, 1904,[1] was the third and last of Joyce's stories to appear in this weekly paper. It was in July of this year that George Russell suggested Joyce offer them something;[2] "The Sisters" and "Eveline" had been submitted, and were published in August and September.[3] However, when H. F. Norman then accepted "After the Race," he asked Joyce not to send in any more.[4] (Nevertheless, Joyce did try again, later, with "Clay," which was refused.)[5] While conceivably Norman saw that "After the Race" was inferior to the preceding stories, probably his real reason for calling a halt was the one he gave, the written complaints from readers both in Dublin and in the country.[6] Whatever those Irish opinions at the time, "The Sisters" and "Eveline"—subsequently refined but not essentially modified—are among the most significant pieces in *Dubliners*. "After the Race" is not only less penetrating but in parts it is labored.

The second is the serious defect. Few stories can attain the pathos of "Eveline" or the retrospective scope and implicativeness of "The Sisters." The very material of "After the Race" excludes pathos, since Jimmy Doyle is superficial in his aims and a fool in their pursuit, nor are there signs that his disappointment will greatly enlighten him. And of all the *Dubliners* stories, "After the Race" is the least realized, in the fictional sense; it is both the sketchiest and the most over-defined. The first three stories, constituting one main division in the volume, show a mastery of reminiscent first-person narration, in which a character's sensitivity provides aesthetic texture and his growing insights contribute to structure. "Eveline" is masterly in its particular use of third-person narration voiced through the continuum of a protagonist's consciousness. Later, in "Ivy Day in the Committee Room," Joyce was to show equal control of objective dramatic presentation, expressed entirely in scene, speech, and gesture. Other *Dubliners* stories smoothly combine these opposite modes to create that sustained illusion toward which fiction was evolving in the latter part of the nineteenth century.

Comparatively, the narrative technique of "After the Race" is at times awkward. Perhaps the trouble was Joyce's lack of grasp and assured perspective on the materials. The race itself, being international, brought the challenge of Europe to Ireland, and the story epitomizes the desire of certain enterprising Irish to transcend their insularity, although in superficial terms, and naïvely. Possibly Joyce, in weighing such a segment of Dublin life, knew too little of it at first hand, and also shared, if anything, some of its naïveté. In 1903, the year before writing the story, and just before his mother's illness called Joyce back from his first venture to Paris, he had sent the *Irish Times* an interview with Henri Fournier, a Parisian automobile dealer and racing driver who was to come to Dublin in July, with two other French entrants, to compete in the second James Gordon Bennett cup race. Joyce's brief piece, published on April 7, begins with a description of the big roofed-over courtyard which was M. Fournier's crowded display room and lively place of business; it continues as a literal report, factual question and succinct answer, of the interview Joyce finally, "after two failures," secured with a very busy and not too responsive man. This curious piece has been included in *The Critical Writings,*[7] and the editors report that when the race in Ireland took place, Joyce "did not bother . . . to attend," but that in writing "After the Race," a story he "never thought highly of," he "used his memories of Fournier."[8]

If so, they were of the French businessman, not the racing driver. The character Ségouin is in good humor over "some orders in advance." French-Canadian cousin Rivière shares that humor because he is to manage Ségouin's establishment. Only relatively are they "also in good humour because of the success of the French cars." Further it might be surmised that Joyce drew upon buried knowledge of himself in the Parisian situation —the Irish novice perhaps dazzled by French enterprise, given scant answers to his inexpert questions, and uneasily aware of a superior craftiness. Possibly suppressed recollection of this was exculpatively transmuted into satire of Jimmy Doyle. Certainly M. Fournier's last remark when Joyce had pressed him about the probable winner in the race had been equivocal, and Joyce not only closes his *Irish Times* piece with an ironic comment on that but in the short story he pictures Ségouin and Rivière as not entirely candid—Ségouin "had managed to give the impression" that only "by a favour of friendship" would he accept Doyle's investment in his business, and Rivière discusses the superiority of French automobiles "not wholly ingenuously." The story is not, however, a study of international types: French and French-Canadian entrepreneurs of the automobile, a Hungarian pianist Villona, an English Cantabrigian, and an American with a yacht in Kingstown harbor. It is the impact of all this foreign sophistication and worldly assurance on a foolish young Irishman whose father's affluence in trade allows the son to prowl excitedly at the edges of a society too experienced and privately centered for him to understand, much less really enter into.

All this takes some doing to establish narratively, and Joyce fails to create a continuously sustained fictional effect until the last episode. Parts of the first pages, in comparison with his other work, are a too apparent summary and exposition, a labored assembling and pointing up. The opening device of describing the cars after the race as they "came scudding in towards Dublin" along the Naas Road breaks down in the second and third sentences with the obtrusively thematic statements that "through this channel of poverty and inaction the Continent sped its wealth and industry" while "the clumps of people raised the cheer of the gratefully oppressed." The narrative passes to Irish sympathy for "their friends, the French," and so to a description of the occupants of one blue car, four young men "whose spirits seemed to be at present well above the level of successful Gallicism"—a phrase almost Dreiserian in its clumsy pretentiousness. Then comes a paragraph on one of the four, the Irish Jimmy Doyle, "about twenty-six . . . with a soft, light brown moustache and rather innocent-looking grey eyes," and so on to his expedient father's financial rise, and Jimmy's education, in "a big Catholic college" in England, at Dublin University for the law, and then for a term at Cambridge "to see a little life," which had included meeting Ségouin there.

Next, in a narrative return to the speeding car, comes a paragraph fully under control, and now in the Joycean mode of simple image and subtle implication, especially in these two sentences:

> The Frenchmen flung their laughter and light words over their shoulders and often Jimmy had to strain forward to catch the quick phrase. This was not altogether pleasant for him, as he had nearly always to make a deft guess at the meaning and shout back a suitable answer in the teeth of a high wind.

In the paragraph which follows Joyce lapses into overt generalization and almost pedantic analysis:

> Rapid motion through space elates one; so does notoriety; so does the possession of money. These were three good reasons for Jimmy's excitement.

After that, however, the story again gets fairly well into the reality of Jimmy's responses. There has been his day at the race, where he "had been seen by many of his friends . . . in the company of these Continentals," and where Ségouin "had presented him to one of the French competitors." There is the project of investing "the greater part of his substance" with Ségouin, with his shrewd father's approval, and the more immediate prospect of a dinner the Frenchman is to give at his hotel. All in all it has a hypnotic strangeness for Jimmy, wherein mechanism and consciousness are paradoxically reversed and indeed reconstituted, in that "the journey laid a *magical* finger on the *genuine pulse* of life and gallantly the *machinery* of human nerves strove to answer the bounding courses of the swift blue *animal.*" (Italics added.)

There is an interval of lessened immediate excitement as Jimmy and the Hungarian Villona leave the car in mid-town and go to the Doyles' house to dress for the dinner. Here Joyce holds up his mirror to the parents, who, having pronounced the coming event "an occasion," nevertheless feel some "trepidation" mingled with their pride. Like son like father; the elder Doyle tries too, also well out of his depth, and is "unusually friendly with Villona," expressing in his manner "a real respect for foreign accomplishments." Joyce frames and terminates this glimpse by reporting that the Hungarian, at the moment, "was beginning to have a sharp desire for his dinner."

With that event the story hits its full stride. There is condensation, but it preserves the sense of action. Dialogue is in large part summarized, but without losing its drama, which culminates in Jimmy's attempt to argue with the hitherto "torpid" Englishman, Routh. Moreover, Joyce's detached economy allows a deft irony. He reports Jimmy's simple conclusion, after the "excellent, exquisite" dinner, that Ségouin "had a very refined taste." Listening to the others' voluble talk, the awed Jimmy thinks he has hit upon a "graceful image . . . and a just one" in conceiving of "the lively youth of the Frenchmen twined elegantly upon the firm framework of the Englishman's manner." Such clumsy extravagance only emphasizes his Irish deference to Gallic sprightliness and English stability. He admires too their host's "dexterity" in directing the conversation, but when the Frenchman "shepherded his party into politics," Jimmy felt his father's expediently buried Nationalist zeal waken in him, in argument with the Englishman, and Ségouin must propose a toast "to Humanity" to avoid "danger of personal spite."

So they proceed into the street, to stroll along Stephen's Green on this evening when, as Joyce pointedly says, "the city wore the mask of a capital," and to encounter Farley the American and set out for his yacht, for supper, music, cards. And for drinking.

"What merriment!" says the story. "Jimmy took his part with a will; this was seeing life, at least." Here is Joyce at some distance, "paring his fingernails," but not quite indifferent, being so bent on satire. And perhaps haunted by some veiled Irish uneasiness, in the imagined presence of a Ségouin, a Routh, and to a degree a Villona all poised beyond the satiric or at least more knowing glance with which from on high he could regard most of his Dublin characters? In the yacht's cabin, after boisterous dancing to Villona's piano, toasts are drunk to Ireland, England, France, Hungary, the United States of America. Jimmy is moved to utterance—he "made a speech, a long speech, Villona saying: '*Hear! hear!*' whenever there was a pause." Since there was "a great clapping of hands when he sat down," he concludes it "must have been a good speech," and when Farley "clapped him on the back and laughed loudly" he thinks "What jovial fellows! What good company they were!"

So then "Cards! cards!" and more toasts, to the Queen of Hearts, the Queen of Diamonds, with the accompaniment of Villona's piano, he being too impecunious to play, and perhaps too wise. Jimmy is swept along in a current increasingly too swift and turbulent for him. As their wit flashed he "felt obscurely the lack of an audience." He frequently misread his cards and could not "calculate his I. O. U.s" and "he wished they would stop," but it goes on, disastrously for him, until at the end, with "his head between his hands, counting the beats of his temple," he can only be "glad of the dark stupor that would cover up his folly." The only light which penetrates that descending darkness is of a grey dawn as the Hungarian Villona, returning from the deck, stands in the open doorway to announce, "Daybreak, gentlemen!"

While such is the story's focus, "After the Race" contains more of Dublin than a portrait of one more Dubliner, this time a pampered, still provincial young fool with social pretensions, attached to an international group of visitors entirely too fast for him. In special ways it is suggested, not defined, that Jimmy too is product and pawn of Ireland as environment. He too is subject to family, though in a way different from that seen in "Eveline," or in either "The Boarding House" or "The Dead." As to this factor of parental influence, what is most like "After the Race" is "A Mother," but the primary affiliations in Mrs. Kearney's social maneuvers are Nationalistic and ecclesiastical, both of which considerations the senior Doyle has minimized. Jimmy's father is the ubiquitous type, the tradesman become rich enough to be called merchant prince; he is also a special breed of Irish opportunist, not only at a socio-economic level untouched in most of the stories, but differently oriented from most Dubliners. Beginning as an "advanced Nationalist," he had "modified his views early" and, it would seem, suitably, for his rise has come with his securing government contracts to supply the police. Now, wanting what is his notion of the best for his son, he had agreed that Ségouin, "reputed to own some of the biggest hotels in France . . . was well worth knowing, even if he had not been the charming companion he was." Although at the race Jimmy's chief gratification is at being seen associating with "these Continentals," the connection obviously is tenuous and less than reciprocal. Jimmy had met Ségouin at Cambridge, but they are "not much more than acquaintances as yet," and the distance between them is suggested in that the Englishman Routh, who joins the party at dinner, is someone whom Jimmy had merely "seen with Ségouin" at the university. Not only from the back seat of the speeding car but all along Jimmy has strained to catch on and keep up and respond properly to what he does not quite comprehend and cannot hope to cope with.

Joyce's knowledge of Dublin life was immense, but it was not entire, and he was working at its limits and a bit beyond as to the social substance of "After the Race." The story may be tinged too with some of his own ambivalence, manifested throughout his life in efforts to maintain pride of family and in the perhaps compensatory tendency to satirize all such pretensions. Despite Joyce's gifts, Dublin's aristocratic Anglo-Irish society and its most cultivated literary circles were both beyond his limited approach as an impecunious and not very well-bred youth, and as fictionist he made a strict virtue of that exclusion. The closest any of his *Dubliners* folk come to the gentry's Kildare Street Club, for instance, is when those two proletarian gallants Lenehan and Corley go by on their meanderings in quest of whatever they can pick up. The most strenuous social strugglings in Dubliners are those of that militant mother, Mrs. Kearney, whose range is scarcely more than parochial, through the media of the "musical friends and Nationalist friends" with whom she would converse after mass at the pro-cathedral; and the concerts for which her daughter Kathleen is to be accompanist at two guineas a night are promoted by a "novice," while the whole affair (paralleling some in which Joyce himself took part) is not of the first order.

Joyce's instinct was discreet in generally limiting the range of *Dubliners* as he did, to instances he had most directly known or observed and also within the bounds of his own noncommittal aloofness. The stories set forth no young Dubliners with the gifts, cultivation, and dynamism of either of those friends of his youth, Gogarty or Kettle. And the members of the international set, so awesome to Jimmy, seem almost as remote from Joyce's eye, for though he makes them serve his plot, they remain—except for Villona—not merely flat characters but stereotypes. The Doyles, however, father and son, fall easily within the scope of Joyce's satire. For them sojourn in Cambridge and association with French sportsmen-industrialists are devoutly wished and relished, but their pursuit of such distinctions exposes a sense of Irish inferiority and a real ineptitude. Joyce pins down a common specimen of *nouveau riche* in quest of rumored values by putting it that Jimmy's father, seeing him dressed for Ségouin's dinner party, "may have felt even commercially satisfied at having secured for his son qualities often unpurchasable." Within such an obvious general theme the story casts a sharper silhouette of those Irish who fawned upon the foreigner, either as the elder Doyle did in modifying his politics or as Jimmy does, more innocently, in tagging after persons ready to exploit him.

The most genuine recognition he achieved in the company of this group was when the old ticket-collector at Kingston Station, where they got off to board Farley's yacht, "saluted Jimmy" and said "Fine night, sir." And so it seems, until the end of the adventure. This is pointed up with a two-word sentence, "Routh won"—Routh the Englishman, with whom Jimmy, in some resurgence of his father's "buried zeal," had tried to argue politics, until Ségouin tactfully intervened. And now the Englishman has got Jimmy's patrimony too. But as throughout the preceding events in the story, at this point there is little or no pathos, only a caricaturing of intoxicating pretensions and a cool analysis of drunken folly.

Besides the unapproachable sophistication of the Englishman and the Frenchmen (the American was also a heavy loser) there is a point of reference still further removed from Jimmy, but entirely of another order, in the Hungarian Villona. Joyce has made him a man of the arts, a pianist, and an impecunious hedonist, who hums with satisfaction after an excellent lunch and is hungry for his dinner. He sat in the back seat with Jimmy, but self-possessed, without straining forward. Going home with Jimmy to dress for the dinner, he was bland under the elder Doyle's "real respect for foreign accomplishments," and at the dinner he "began to discover to the mildly surprised Englishman the beauties of the English madrigal" and his "resonant voice . . . was about to prevail in ridicule of the spurious lutes of the romantic painters" when Ségouin turned the talk to the more general ground of politics. In the yacht's cabin he played the piano while Farley and the French-Canadian Rivière improvised waltz steps, and he encouragingly called out "Hear! hear!" at any pause in Jimmy's long speech. But when the card game began, he "returned quietly to his piano and played voluntaries for them." And for himself, presumably, on the piano which was essentially more "his" than Farley's. Then as the game grew more intense the confused Jimmy noticed that "The piano had stopped; Villona must have gone up on deck." He had, no doubt for air and a prospect of his own; and it is quite properly he who, "standing in a shaft of grey light" in the cabin door, makes the simple, ironic announcement, "Daybreak, gentlemen!" Whatever identification Joyce has with this story is most direct and strongest here, in the role of the detached man and artist, letting in light on a Dubliner who has a headache of his own making, and yet one classifiable also as a national product.

TWO GALLANTS

This thirteenth *Dubliners* story to be completed ran into bad luck for itself and made more for the book. When Joyce in Trieste sent Grant Richards in England his collection (on December 3, 1905)[1] it contained all of *Dubliners* except the still unwritten "Two Gallants," "A Little Cloud," and "The Dead"—and of the dozen stories seven were product of that fruitful summer and autumn,[2] a sanguine season during which Joyce had written his brother Stanislaus of an "intention" to follow *Dubliners* "by a book 'Provincials.' "[3] On January 27, 1906, in asking Richards for some word, Joyce wrote that he had "now added another story . . . *Two Gallants*" to the book.[4] On February 17 Richards wrote that he himself had read the collection of twelve and thought highly of it, yet he feared it lacked "selling qualities," being "about Ireland" and "a collection of short stories." He would, however, "take the risk of its publication," on cautious terms which included no royalties on the first five hundred copies.[5] Replying immediately, Joyce wrote a characteristic letter, "glad" that Richards was "pleased with *Dubliners,*" saying that as to terms "perhaps it would be best for me to put myself in your hands," and offering to send "the last story I have written ["Two Gallants"]—unless perhaps you have as superstitious an objection to the number thirteen as you seem to have with regard to Ireland and short stories in general."[6] Then on February 22, not waiting for Richards' reply, and almost as if to forestall bad omen, Joyce sent him the thirteenth tale.[7] An unsigned letter of February 27 from Richards said, merely, "Many thanks for 'Two Gallants' safely received."[8] Then nearly two months later came Richards' word that he was "sorry" but "afraid we cannot publish 'The Two Gallants' as it stands." Without reading it Richards had sent the copy on to the printers, there objections had arisen, in fear of the law and public opinion, and then doubt had spread to details in "Counterparts" and "Grace."[9]

Out of that trouble came records of Joyce's opinions about his work, and even with allowance for exaggeration under stress, it remains plain that he valued "Two Gallants" very highly. In his extended (and at that time futile) argument with Richards he wrote on May 20 that omission of the story would be "disastrous," and that he "would rather sacrifice five other stories . . . than this one," which he called "the story (after Ivy Day in the Committee Room) which pleases me most."[10] When on October 22 he finally agreed to its exclusion, together with his still later creation, "A Little Cloud," it was only in an effort to secure at least the publication of "the original book" of twelve, with some previously conceded deletions from "Counterparts" and "Grace."[11] Joyce's linking "Two Gallants" with "Ivy Day in the Committee Room" suggests regard for their focus upon a futile Dublin type, the insecure picker up of trifles, like the leech Lenehan "holding himself nimbly at the borders of the company" in a bar, or the damp disgruntled political canvassers waiting on Ivy Day for their candidate to send the dozen of stout. Among all such, the impairment of personality is less direct and outright but more common than the paralysis which fell upon Eveline; yet it has a common denominator with the other stories, that of confinement within a rigid inverted society, and a consequent personal deterioration.

Although Joyce felt himself something less as well as more than an Irish Zola,[12] in various descriptions and defenses of his stories he repeatedly claimed a sociological foundation for them, implying emphasis on environment as a determining factor. Yet this was only the platform on which he staged his stories, and in him as in many an Irishman rebellion was tempered with relish for types, for "characters" in the colloquial sense. An irreconcilable critic of institutions and customs, he was also a penetrating and not unempathic assessor of men and women—and chiefly men—as he shows in his further deployment of quite a few *Dubliners* personae in *Ulysses*. It should be noted, however, that when Joyce was writing his short stories *Ulysses* existed, if at all, only in embryo as one more tale to concern "a dark-complexioned Dublin Jew named Hunter who was rumored to be a cuckold."[13] The Lenehan of "Two Gallants" is to be read within that entity, in his sorry self as of that evening, and not according to his wider divagations and occasionally firmer assertions in the day of Bloom. So too the other *Dubliners* characters are to be most truly seen each within the particular composition, and here discretion would properly extend even to the excluding of alleged interconnections about chalices and encounters in the first three stories.

Of the two gallants, Lenehan is Joyce's primary subject; the other, a "flat" character though he looms large, is foil to Lenehan's progress, such as it is. Lenehan is with Corley in the first pages and at the end, but for nearly half the story he is alone, waiting for his companion, and this passage gives a rounded characterization as he meanders about killing time and trying to stave off intimations of futility. Corley, on the other hand, is a fellow without qualms. The only passing fear he admits was that his current victim, a housemaid, would "get in the family way," but now he is confident she is "up to the dodge." Corley has the simple success of those who barge ahead, as he does when he makes Lenehan walk "on the verge of the path" and at times to "step on to the road." His craft as gallant reduces need and desert to elementary terms—he has told the girl he "was out of a job," but he has invented a reputable past, "in Pim's," the prestigious department store, so that she thinks him "a bit of class." Joyce caricatures Corley more extremely than any other figure in *Dubliners;* he appears a grotesque repulsive automaton as he "walked with his hands by his sides, holding himself erect and swaying his head from side to side," that "large, globular, and oily head" upon which "his large round hat . . . looked like a bulb which had grown out of another." That he turns his whole trunk when he wishes to look in any direction suggests a kind of total animality.

Here is no painful hemiplegia; the automaton is fully galvanized. And more than adjunctive—Corley's flat invariability becomes a thematic abstraction. Perhaps Joyce wrote with less consciousness of a certain Dubliner than of a mankind sometimes monstrous, and used the grotesque to convey the representative, through the paradox of caricature as a refining of truth, as was increasingly his practice in the later works. At any rate, if Corley's being is to be charged to Dublin, it could only be for a complete domination *ab ovo* that would preclude anything more than brute consciousness and instinct—or else superstitiously attributed to some malignant transformation of original human identity in the cradle. Brainwashing must start somewhere, demoralization presupposes morale, and paralysis is to be defined only as the interruption of a potential. Seeming less than other Dubliners, Corley is also more, being alas an adumbration of a universal figure. Call him Apeneck, one of those whom Nature has passed over but not abandoned and indeed easily permits, the unamenable primitive, as able as a pig to subsist on indelicate feeding, and as gruffly confident. Corley's nearest approach to self-consciousness is in the gestures by which he dramatizes his own stolidity. Asked if he can bring off this evening's scheme, he "closed one eye expressively as an answer." Later when Lenehan took off his cap as he passed Corley and the girl at the corner of Hume street, Corley "returned a salute to the air . . . by raising his hand vaguely and pensively changing the angle of position of his hat." And later still at their reunion when Lenehan wanted to know whether it had "come off," Corley walked on "without answering," his face "composed in stern calm," and halted at a street lamp and "stared grimly before him"; then "with a grave gesture he extended a hand" and only then did he smile, as he showed his "disciple" the small gold coin which was token of his success and the summit of his aspiration.

Lenehan is needed, however, for Corley is not always so successful, and this most primitive Dubliner requires a jester to cheer him as well as a bard to verbalize his triumphs. Corley has reported aggrievedly his spending money on girls he would take out after procuring them "off the South Circular" and, except for one, "damn the thing" he "ever got out of it." This was not because such females were beyond approach. Padraic Colum, calling the region "a likely place for pickups," with "the lonesomeness of the canal banks adjacent," reports encountering Joyce and a friend bound thither, and Joyce's declaring "You see before you two frightful examples of the will to live," but as the three progressed the talk turned to "the world as idea," and when Colum left them at the avenue where he resided, they were, as far as he could see, "still without prospects."[14] Lenehan and Corley are a different pair. Their world is Dublin and the idea is to satisfy appetites as they can by whatever feasible shifts. When Corley recalled his one conquest from the South Circular Road, it "brightened his eyes," he "moistened his upper lip by running his tongue along it," and at this point, gazing at the moon, for once he "seemed to meditate," as regretfully, hesitantly he said, "She was . . . a bit of all right." However, if it is more than animal memory it is only fleeting. When he goes on to say "She's on the turf now," having seen her driving with men on the street, and Lenehan calls that Corley's "doing," Corley says there were others before him, and Lenehan puts it on their level of gallantry with ironic acclaim of this "base betrayer."

Lenehan's is the greater dependence, in an actual subserviency, and it appears to be a deeper, more real need. His acquaintances consider him a bar-fly "holding himself nimbly at the borders of the company until he was included in a round," but here he seems leechlike both for a share in what funds Corley can turn up and to suck upon Corley's vigor and assurance. To maintain the attachment Lenehan must flatter, and Joyce makes him the complete sycophant with such a creature's repulsive jumble of traits, a fawning dependency and a secretly condescending manipulation of another's vanity. The dissimulation infecting this relationship is shown in contrasting styles of speech. Corley, who enters the scene rounding out an extended account of which the reader is to hear only the end, is not reticent when he can talk "mainly about himself" and "without listening to the speech of his companions"; now he is describing his most recent conquest and his expert *modus operandi*. It's a "fine tart" he'd picked up on Dame Street under Waterhouse's clock and has been walking out with, "round by the canal" and "out to Donnybrook and . . . into a field there," and "It was fine, man." She would pay tram fare out and back, and would bring him cigarettes every night, and once "two bloody fine cigars . . . that the old fellow used to smoke"—the master, no doubt, of the Baggot Street house where the girl is slavey. When Lenehan heard of the affair, he "laughed noiselessly for fully half a minute," assured Corley that "That takes the biscuit," then added with still more affectation, "That takes the solitary, unique, and, if I may so call it, *recherché* biscuit!" And when Corley had vouchsafed further details, Lenehan, having "laughed again, noiselessly," finally pronounced on this ordinary, sordid seduction and exploitation that "Of all the good ones ever I heard, that emphatically takes the biscuit." Only Corley's forceful stride acknowledged the compliments he considered his due from this retainer.

Silence can overtake Lenehan too, but of a quite different order from Corley's supreme self-assurance. Lenehan is a flabby oldish young man; his laughing noiselessly is as if for lack of the breath of life. "His figure fell into rotundity at the waist, his hair was scant and grey and his face, when the waves of expression had passed over it, had a ravaged look." For all his pretentiousness with others, he knows. Of what Corley is presently up to he has remarked, "You're what I call a gay Lothario. And the proper kind of a Lothario, too!" but his elaborations cannot disguise the triteness from himself, though it may strike Corley's ears as uniquely his due. Lenehan is not naïvely given to cliché as are the old Flynn sisters; talk being his enterprise, he has consciously used old tools again and again, and indeed this night his "tongue was tired" from a whole afternoon of chatter in a public-house. There he had no doubt displayed his "vast stock of stories, limericks and riddles" and also his adroitness in ornate flattery, such as when with Corley he has made "a tragic gesture" and declared him "Base betrayer!" in praise of an earlier exploit in seduction.

Tonight's project is not defined in the narrative, but Lenehan seems to know of it as something meant to go beyond Corley's previous achievements of *al fresco* amour with tram fare and tobacco thrown in. Corley has talked of it to his attendant as they prowl the city streets awaiting the hour, and Lenehan has questioned, with the timid avidity of the prurient who must take much at second hand. He has also of course a practical interest in any success of Corley's, which may yield if nothing more a spare cigarette, though at this hour it is Lenehan who supplies his leader. Their dialogue further displays Corley's absolute egotistic confidence and Lenehan's nagging uncertainties.

In their meanderings they have gone by the Trinity College railings along Nassau Street and there Lenehan "skipped out into the road and looked up at the clock," in one more gesture of impecunious dependence. Turning off into Kildare Street, they are continuing a circular movement of the kind Brewster Ghiselin has pointed out in *Dubliners* as symbolic of its characters' restrictive containment.[15] Lenehan, left to his own feeble devices, is to wander the city streets still more involutedly, but as always in Dublin he had company. The story's first paragraph, picturing the August Sunday evening crowd that "swarmed" in the central streets, has used word-repetition to suggest a common life turning upon itself. In the "grey warm evening . . . a mild warm air . . . circulated in the streets" that "swarmed with a gaily coloured crowd" where under lamps like "illumined pearls" it became a "living texture . . . which, changing shape and hue unceasingly, sent up into the warm grey evening air an unchanging unceasing murmur." But now the two gallants have moved from those most populous parts, and as they turn this corner their mood is changed. They would know the Kildare Street Club as bastion of another world than theirs of Dublin's pubs and streets; if they were not precisely informed of it as the preserve of Anglo-Irish gentry and the Crown's representatives, and predominantly Protestant, they might at least have heard of it as the abode of swells, who played for high stakes in elegant card rooms from which ladies were without exception excluded, though later they were admitted to other parts of the club, but only by a special entrance.[16] (Writing at the time represented in most of the *Dubliners* stories, Francis Gerard described the Kildare Street Club, founded in 1782, as conservative, influential, and reputedly the main source of Dublin Society gossip;[17] now the better portion and corner of the property, including two-thirds of the pillared portico with KSC monograms, has been taken over by an insurance company, and the fine stone carvings by the famous O'Shea brothers, in a line between floors and on the pediments of window pillars, are weathered and grime-encrusted.) To the two gallants, with Trinity's high railings just behind and the National Library ahead, and the Kildare Street Club still at its height of prestige and affluence, the area was foreign, and there is point in bringing these wanderers up that street rather than another. The story does not tell that they paused with "the little ring of listeners" to whom, "not far from the porch of the club," a street harpist is playing "heedlessly" while "glancing quickly from time to time at the face of each new-comer and from time to time, wearily also, at the sky."

Joyce does pause, however. The melody is that of "Silent, O Moyle" (one of his frequent references to Tom Moore) and Joyce's streak of sentimentality, too strong to be always repressed, emerges in a pathetic fallacy. The harp, "heedless that her coverings had fallen about her knees, seemed weary alike of the eyes of strangers and of her master's hands." Though the gallants walk on, they seem subdued by region and incident, and with "the mournful music following them" it is not until they have traversed all of Kildare street and come to Stephen's Green that they are "released . . . from their silence" by "the noise of trams, the lights and the crowds."

Then out of this eddying dependent existence the transition is abrupt, for Corley at least, as he exclaimed that there she is, the girl waiting on the corner for him, in a blue dress and a white hat, "swinging a sunshade in one hand." Lenehan himself "grew lively" and was all for "a squint at her," which brings a sideways glance and an "unpleasant grin" from Corley and a taunting suggestion that this hanger-on is "trying to get inside" him. Lenehan's reply is in keeping, affectedly bold in tone but meek in its demands. "Damn it! I don't want an introduction. All I want is to have a look at her. I'm not going to eat her." Corley, sustaining his dominant role, answers "more amiably," as if he now understands: "O . . . A look at her? Well . . . I'll tell you what. I'll go over and talk to her and you can pass by." To this conceded one crumb from the other's table Lenehan briskly answers "Right!" It is a telling little passage of dialogue, and it carries directly into the complex of Corley's assurance, the girl's pathos, and Lenehan's dependence and exclusion, with the events which close the story.

Corley had "sauntered" over with "something of the conqueror" in his air; and the girl, as Lenehan could observe, seemed responsive, swinging her umbrella more quickly, half-turning back and forth on her heels, and laughing and bending her head at Corley's more closely directed remarks. Having "observed them for a few minutes," Lenehan walked by to take his one allotted closer look, making his bow in passing and receiving Corley's minimal condescending salute. Then all that remained for Lenehan was to follow at a subordinate distance until he saw them take the tram. As for the girl, the story itemizes only what Lenehan could glimpse in simplest detail, yet it carries strong overtones of pathos. "She had her Sunday finery on," it included white blouse, "short black jacket with mother-of-pearl buttons and a ragged black boa," and "a big bunch of red flowers was pinned in her bosom, stems upwards." A black leather belt with a "great silver buckle" that "seemed to depress the centre of her body" suggests the supple waist of girlhood; and this implication is not effaced but rather made more genuine by realistic detail—a "stout short muscular body" and "broad nostrils, a straggling mouth which lay open in a contented leer, and two projecting front teeth."

This pitiful girl who has decked herself out for such a one as Corley and is to be his complete conquest is of course not just Dubliner but a universal figure, and her story here glimpsed at could be, and has been, unfolded with merely local modification in almost any setting. Yet as she disappears, "climbing the steps of the Donnybrook tram" with Corley, this wry tale becomes Lenehan's alone, and more particularly a Dubliner's progress. Deprived of Corley to cling to and play upon, he turned about and went back the way he had come. He is to turn again and again thus aimlessly, trying to "pass the hours till he met Corley again." He went "listlessly," his fingers plucked at railings in recollection of the harpist's air, he viewed the crowds "morosely" and was averse from any contact, feeling "his brain and throat . . . too dry" for his calling, "to invent and to amuse." He could think of nothing to do "but to keep on walking." Pausing on a "dark, quiet street" whose "sombre look . . . suited his mood," he peered hungrily into the refreshment bar that, however "poor-looking," displayed cut ham and plum pudding beyond his means. Hurrying in "after glancing warily up and down the street," he spoke roughly to counteract what the other patrons, by their "pause of talk" and their scrutiny, seemed to have taken as "his air of gentility." He would be ashamed to be seen entering this place and now he is uneasy in it; he has no firm ground of his own between these simple workingmen and his habitual street and pub companions, who though presumed somehow superior, are also of equivocal status and drifting practice, with himself only their sycophantic jester.

Having had nothing since breakfast but some biscuits grudgingly furnished by bartenders, Lenehan greedily eats his frugal meal, "a plate of hot grocer's peas," and then sat sipping ginger beer and "thinking of Corley's adventure," imagining the lovers in the dark. From this he falls naturally into a keen sense of "his own poverty of purse and spirit." His self-examination at this point supplements what the story's opening passage had more objectively revealed of him—this fellow in yachting cap and "white rubber shoes" (like young Joyce's own affected attire) with a light waterproof "slung over one shoulder in toreador fashion," but with a figure already falling into slackness and a voice "winnowed of vigor," a "noiseless laugh," and a face upon which successive masks cannot always conceal "a ravaged look." Sipping his ginger beer in that poor place, he admits himself "tired of knocking about . . . of shifts and intrigues." He will soon be thirty-one (not relatively old in that day for a bachelor in Ireland, where in 1929 the average marriage age for men still was nearly thirty-five and in 1963 was only just under twenty-seven)[18] but he wants "a good job" and "a home of his own," yet he envisions this with characteristic dependence—"if he could only come across some good simple-minded girl with a little of the ready."

When Lenehan leaves the refreshment bar, it is to wander again, into Capel Street, into Dame Street. He meets friends, they talk compulsively but disjointedly of who had seen whom where, and "what was the latest." Of this the most significant bit is that, whether or not "Mac had won a bit over a billiard match," for certain "Holohan had stood them drinks in Egan's." On Lenehan went alone, evidently keeping to himself Corley's present enterprise and his interest in it, up George's Street and past the City Markets and into Grafton Street, where the crowd of girls and young men was thinning and good-nights were being heard. At Stephen's Green he went "as far as the clock of the College of Surgeons," which was "on the stroke of ten." What time it has come to in his life he has not been able clearly to assess, but as to this night he knows precisely, having an end in view. So he turned back and "set off briskly . . . for fear Corley should return too soon." Waiting at the corner of Merrion Street, in the shadow of a lamp, he allowed himself a cigarette from his slender reserve, and now that Corley may be expected soon, this leech's "mind became active again," and "suffered all the pangs and thrills of his friend's situation as well as those of his own." The natural next step for this timid, servile man is a nervous sensing of how tenuous is his hold, allowing the likelihood that Corley might have "seen her home by another way and given him the slip." Then at last there they came, "walking quickly, the young woman taking quick short steps, while Corley kept beside her with his long stride," but since they "did not seem to be speaking," Lenehan falls back upon the faint-hearted's one negative security—"He knew Corley would fail; he knew it was no go."

Still he follows them, stealthily, to spy on the end of it played out before the Baggot Street residence, where this girl works as servant. She and Corley having talked a few moments, she then "went down the steps into the area of a house"—which would be her prescribed entrance, into the basement. What follows is recounted with significant implications. "Some minutes passed" —something presumably is going on inside. "Then the hall door was opened slowly and cautiously" and from this main entrance to the house "A woman came running down the front steps and coughed." This summons Corley, who had "remained standing . . . a little distance from the front steps," and now "His broad figure hid hers" for the "few seconds" until "she reappeared running up the steps" to the entrance and "The door closed on her." Having entered by the servants' route down the area steps, presumably she has then left the basement quarters to go into the upper part of the house, from which she has hurried out to Corley by the most direct way, through the front hall door. It might be supposed too that this is the same route by which at the end of an earlier evening she had emerged to reward her lover with "two bloody fine cigars . . . that the old fellow used to smoke." Now, as Joyce handles the narrative, when Lenehan watches while Corley's "broad figure hid hers from view for a few seconds" it need not be visualized as more than a last embrace but it could conceal some further handing-over to Corley.

Therefore after the door had closed on the girl, and as Corley moved off "swiftly towards Stephen's Green," Lenehan ran after him, settling his waterproof against the first drops of light rain, panting from exertion, calling to his unanswering friend, approaching and anxious to ask, "Did it come off?" Corley was making the most of the chance to keep his follower dangling and to dramatize himself. Silent still, with features "composed in stern calm," he went up a side street and "halted at the first lamp and stared grimly before him." Still silent, "with a grave gesture he extended a hand towards the light," and only then did he smile as he opened the hand "slowly to the gaze of his disciple." After all this suspense a sentence of eight objective monosyllables suffices to round off the story: "A small gold coin shone in the palm."

If this token were from the slavey's wages, it would be a considerable accumulation; more likely the bringer of "bloody fine cigars" has now been induced to steal money from her employer. This is not her tale, however, and were it to become more so by discovery of a theft, Corley, whose name she has not been told, would no doubt remain as uninvolved and unconcerned as with that other girl he had betrayed to a life on the streets, according to Lenehan's cynically flattering allegation. But a slavey brought to police court through doting on a Corley would have been another story, and here once more Joyce showed himself scrupulous technician with a brief and concentrated narrative. In the extensive gallery of his minor characterizations she stands outlandishly, pitifully bedecked and leering contentedly, and at the Baggot Street house she runs in and out by different ways and in again with implications of the eventful, but as the solid front door closes upon her, she is gone forever, and the story remains that of the two gallants, in their separate yet interrelated roles.

The gold coin which signalizes Corley's sordid success will bind the leech Lenehan to him more closely, and yet ambivalently, in self-dissatisfaction and a sense of inferiority as well as in the greedy dependence which requires that he be "insensitive to all kinds of discourtesy." Lenehan's epiphany over his solitary supper of peas has been, like himself, feeble and transient. What illumination the night has held has been largely local, as from the street lamps shining on their tall poles "like illumined pearls" over the Sunday street crowds, or the more ordinary lamps like the one in the shadow of which Lenehan awaited Corley's return, or that beneath which the two gallants come at last to a halt. There has been also, earlier a more distant and dimmer illumination, "the large faint moon circled with a double halo," and Lenehan had "watched earnestly the passing of the grey web of twilight across its face," while Corley too at one point, licking his lips in bright-eyed recall of a past conquest, had "gazed at the pale disc of the moon, now nearly veiled, and seemed to meditate," over what had been "a bit of all right." Now there is no moon to light the story's end, and a light rain has begun to fall. But one manifestation remains. Now under the street lamp the small gold coin shines in Corley's palm, a hard bright disc, glitteringly explicit in the price it puts on these two Dublin gallants.

THE BOARDING HOUSE

It has been noted by R. M. Adams that an earlier manuscript of "The Boarding House," now in the Yale library, describes Polly's affectedly rolling eye as giving her the look of "a little hypocritical madonna," whereas in its final version Joyce made this phrase "a little perverse madonna."[1] The revision does not point to a change of theme but a refinement of its presentation. The psychological essence and perfection of hypocrisy is its maintenance even to itself. It was a further subtlety for Joyce to have removed from his description the term Polly would never have let cross her mind. And "perverse" was not just handy alternative or even quaint little conceit, but a sure stroke, for the kind of hypocrisy Polly engages in might be called a perverted sincerity. To Joyce's eye Dublin was saturated with this not-to-be-named quality of being, and in "The Boarding House" it is operative force, inescapable determinant, and the most interesting theme.

Polly, "a slim girl of nineteen," is about Eveline's age, but with some differences. She has "light soft hair and a small full mouth," and the habit of glancing upwards through "eyes which were grey with a shade of green," giving her that oddly modified madonna look. She also has, unlike poor Eveline, a mother to guide her, the formidable Mrs. Mooney, proprietress of the boarding house, and utterly adept in that practice of dissimulation Polly is already picking up. The present episode requires delicate co-ordination without overt collaboration between mother and daughter, and their performance in a crisis shows not just rapport but a finesse that in itself almost reaches the level of art.

Picturing complex intrigue making the most of human

frailty, and sketched with sure broad strokes, the story is fundamentally comic, not pathetic. Disaster come full circle later looms plain in Bob Doran as Bloom and others hear from him—drunken, wavering between raw-nerved outcry and sentimental pomposity,[2] but the pathos seen there can scarcely be read back into "The Boarding House" without violating its special tone. Neither should Mrs. Mooney's gaudier coloration in *Ulysses* as "old prostitute . . . procuring rooms to street couples"[3] be superimposed upon the discreetly crafty Madam of the story. A noting of characters' recurrence from one book to another may sometimes be illustrative and even supplementary, but such considerations should never eclipse the substantive autonomy and uniquely fit mode in each work. "The Boarding House," with its controlled focus on the multiple arts of Mrs. Mooney and her daughter, should be credited for a wryness quite different from the fortissimos of the *Ulysses* passages. In instances such as these connections are too slight and incidental to provide broad definition of tendencies or to mark off complete separations, much less to synthesize generalizations about Joyce's art. Recurrence of the same character, or even of the same situation, may serve best by turning attention to the quiddity of each instance. Certainly a look backward from *Ulysses* which would take Mr. Doran's boarding-house predicament quite seriously would almost seem a reduction of Joyce's cool entertainment to an exemplary tract fortifying young men against the world, the flesh, and the devilishness of females. There does stand at the story's edge only subordinately out of the past one quite abject Dubliner, Mr. Mooney the butcher, who had been married by his employer's daughter (perhaps her trial run in such controlled arrangements?), had taken to drink and domestic retaliation with a cleaver, and had been cast off, to subsist as a sheriff's man—"A shabby stooped little drunkard with a white face" and "little eyes . . . pink-veined and raw." That Mrs. Mooney had acquired him and in a fashion finished him off is important chiefly as index of her capacities. This "big imposing woman," having gone to the priest and got a separation from her husband, has "taken what remained of her money out of the butcher business and set up a boarding house," where there are further ranges for her competence, viewed in all its minor majesty from Joyce's aloofness. True, daughter Polly is "in trouble," but in no more than the technical sense, and while there are tears galore, they come with proper effect and are duly wiped away. Having stooped to folly, the girl "looked at herself in profile and readjusted a hairpin above her ear" but had no need to put a record on the gramophone; her mother in the parlor is beating out the tune for Mr. Doran, and Polly is soon to be called to that station in life she and her mother consider meet and right. Not that Mrs. Mooney is a mere schemer; she operates under a complete code and with vigilant responsibility according to her lights, even though, as Joyce puts it, she "dealt with moral problems as a cleaver deals with meat." She has had a hard life, in the way of that marriage which evidently was even harder on Mr. Mooney, but she has never lost resolution; and if she were to be billed as heroine, hers would be a success story of the purest kind, for beyond adversity she can look herself in the eye, in the mirror, "satisfied" with the "decisive expression of her great florid face," and conscious of superiority to "some mothers she knew who could not get their daughters off their hands."

Mr. Doran is in an opposite state and mood. His hand so unsteady he cannot shave, he is depressed by the incontrovertible "notion that he was being had." While he is almost the stock figure of farce, the chap who has had his fling and got caught and must pay up, he is also more particularly another of Joyce's Dubliners. Any strand of pathos in his characterization comes by the trait he shares with some figures in others of the stories, a kind of timidity; and it is in the conditioning of this characteristic that environmental influence has entered—Catholic, mercantile, conventional, ostensibly conforming, gossipy Dublin. Mr. Doran on the previous evening had confessed his fornication, and still suffers from the way his confessor "had drawn out every ridiculous detail of the affair." There had been another confession too on that same Saturday night, Polly's to her mother, and now the maid has brought word that "the missus wanted to see him in the parlour." Caught between the Church and Mother Mooney, he had only two choices, to marry the girl or run away. Despite his indiscretion he is a reputable young man of thirty-four or five (fixed upon by Mrs. Mooney as "serious . . . not rakish or loud-voiced like the others"), and with years of service in "a great Catholic wine-merchant's office," too well settled to skip, as saving instinct prompts, or, on the other hand, to scandalize his employer by attempting to "brazen it out" in this "small city" where "everyone knows everyone else's business." Then besides his normal masculine distaste for the confinement and responsibilities of marriage, he has become disenchanted with the girl herself; admittedly "she *was* a little vulgar," his friends would talk laughingly of the matter, and his own family "would look down on her," with her "disreputable father," and because of "a certain fame" Mrs. Mooney's establishment "was beginning to get." But stern presences hedge him in—his confessor, his respectable employer, the forceful mother, and Polly's bellicose brother with his "thick bulldog face" and "thick short arms" and coldly regarding eye. Finally, Polly has clung to him weeping and said she "would put an end to herself." In other words, Mr. Doran's unhappy situation is classic and complete, and so the tale quite properly is not so much of his doom but of how it was brought about.

"The Boarding House" is comparatively simple, and in no way markedly unconventional in techniques, but it is also skilful, especially in its proportionings and modulations. There is economical but telling exposition, intensified by Joyce's talent for the quick epitomizing stroke. There is tactical ordering of narrative contraction and expansion, in a smooth march containing some detailed glimpses and substantially realized episodes. There is also one extended flashback viewing the progress of the amorous affair, and one deft ellipsis dispensing with what is already implied and thus maintaining a more important thematic focus. The first three pages fill in a background. Mrs. Mooney appears as "a determined woman" who "had married" and then had "got a separation" when "Mr. Mooney began to go to the devil," by the well-worn Dublin route of drink. She set up her boarding house on Hardwicke Street (in that area north of the Liffey where Joyce placed a number of his stories and domiciled Bloom) and here she governed "cunningly and firmly," with a nice sense of "when to be stern and when to let things pass."

With shrewd maternal concern she decided that since nineteen-year-old Polly "was very lively" she should be kept at home "to do housework" and "to give her the run of the young men," the "clerks from the city" who were the resident boarders in this establishment that also catered with some liberality to tourists and transient "artistes" from the music halls. Known sotto voce among her permanent boarders as The Madam, Mrs. Mooney allows that degree of laxity which will best forward her designs while least endangering the appearance of respectability. Father Purdon of "Grace" couldn't have told her a thing about making friends out of the mammon of iniquity; indeed, she might have given him pointers on practical application of the text. She is that rare remarkable parent who can combine unobtrusive permissiveness with precise concealed purpose. Among her clientele she was quite able to distinguish which in their flirtations "were only passing the time away," and which might suit, and on such grounds she had even begun to consider sending her daughter back to a job as typist when she noticed "that something was going on between Polly and one of the young men." And not just any one of them, but Mr. Doran, who now, in his thirties, "had sown his wild oats," had passed through his free-thinking phase, attended to his religious duties and "for nine-tenths of the year lived a regular life," had put in thirteen years diligently at his job as clerk in an eminent establishment, has a good salary, as Mrs. Mooney knows, and, she suspects, "had a bit of stuff put by."

It is in this situation, with "something . . . going on" between Doran and Polly, that the mother displays her peculiar genius, while the girl proves herself a not unworthy daughter. Mrs. Mooney "watched the pair and kept her own counsel." Polly, knowing "she was being watched," did not mistake "her mother's persistent silence." It continues, and still there is "no open complicity between mother and daughter, no open understanding," even though "people in the house began to talk of the affair." The narrative itself takes on a tone of reticent indefinition: "Polly began to grow a little strange in her manner and the young man was evidently perturbed." But whatever that strangeness and that perturbation, they are within Mrs. Mooney's ken. With exquisite precision "she judged it to be the right moment" and "intervened."

So after three swift rich preparatory pages the story passes into a main episode, that wry domestic idyl perhaps describable as Mrs. Mooney's Sunday morning service. The bells of George's Church nearby are pealing (the same which were to be heard by Bloom and Stephen in nearby Eccles Street) but those worshippers now answering the summons, with "their self-contained demeanour" and "the little volumes in their gloved hands" are not Mrs. Mooney's folk and this Protestant church is not for her; she will "catch short twelve" at the pro-cathedral in Marlborough Street, but only when that morning's work is done. While she watches the servant clear off the egg-streaked plates and sees that crusts are collected for Tuesday's pudding, she plans larger economies. For these she has prepared thoroughly the night before, questioning Polly frankly and receiving frank answers, confirming that "things were as she had suspected." It had been somewhat "awkward" for both, but each had preserved the special proprieties of this situation as they saw it, and neither missed a step in the pavane. Mrs. Mooney tried not "to receive the news in too cavalier a fashion or to seem to have connived." Polly too is properly hypocritical. She makes no misrepresentations nor is it told that she concealed any central facts, yet she does proceed as one who "did not wish it to be thought that in her wise innocence she had divined the intention behind her mother's tolerance"—and here the very tortuosity of Joyce's phrasing is suggestive of their subtlety. Bent on the main chance, they not only have preabsolved each other but have maintained a fine feminine instinct for the style of it. This is high comedy, transcending the plebeian milieu itself and the trite farce of Mr. Doran's entrapment.

Now as the bells of George's Church stopped ringing Mrs. Mooney "counted all her cards again" before summoning Mr. Doran, and it is in this rehearsal that her dissimulation rises to the histrionic sublime, and hypocrisy becomes like charity at least in not letting one hand know what the other is up to. Social opinion, Mrs. Mooney feels, will support her—"she was an outraged mother," who "had allowed him to live beneath her roof, assuming that he was a man of honour, and he had simply abused her hospitality." Nor could he plead youth and ignorance as excuses, not at his age and with what he had seen of the world; indeed, it is to be a particular charge that he "had simply taken advantage of Polly's youth and inexperience." So there must be "reparation," and not just money, as some mothers would settle for; with this strict-principled parent "only one reparation could make up for the loss of her daughter's honour: marriage." Thus by a conjuring with unexceptionable conventions Mrs. Mooney transmutes her sham into a gesture of high maternal concern and family respectability. With that form of single-mindedness which makes self-interest so potent she has evoked out of theatric clichés not only a sound legal brief but a whole handbook of etiquette and catechism of morals. She can well await the interview confidently and congratulate herself in advance.

And can do so with something almost like sincerity, though with important differences. Mrs. Mooney is not artless, and as for candor, whether she ever knew its meaning, she has taught herself to forget it. Yet in her way she is genuine, and she has her own formidable integrity. She is a living example that hypocrisy is not always the simple thing melodrama makes of it, but sometimes deeper and darker, and insidiously harder to cope with. A stage villain hissing his asides is himself fully aware of what he confides to the audience; having chosen evil for his good, and never mistaking what means he is stooping to, he makes their masking his conscious art. But an Iago is a simple creature by comparison with a Mrs. Mooney. She has passed beyond duplicity, has escaped from moral ambivalence into an impervious and in its way sincere self-justification. An infinite pity might see this too as human frailty, grown calloused under necessity, but to the ordinary eye which must seek the least hard way in a world of double dealings such an ultimate hypocrisy, passing beyond not just conscience but self-consciousness, is hard to allow. Mrs. Mooney is perhaps bearable in that she has the natural law of marrying and giving in marriage on her side. Beyond that, she is even amusing because Mr. Doran's transparent error, seen at the low level of a sporting chance, is of such an inferior order of concealment that Mrs. Mooney deserves the palm. In any case, it is not only her boarding house and her daughter, this is her story.

When the nerve-wracked Mr. Doran is now brought forward to play out the second of the story's more sustained passages, the detailed chronological flashback to how it had all started achieves a superior kind of dramatic irony. The reader knows all that lies in wait for Mr. Doran and can share Mrs. Mooney's confidence that what must be will be, but here again the story transcends the conventional farce of the naïve victim in for a total surprise and reversal. What is dramatized instead is Mr. Doran's feeble intermittent flickers of regrets which he must admit are futile. Beyond this, what is more broadly shown is the Dublin background as enclosure that from all sides positions Mr. Doran inescapably for Mrs. Mooney's moral cleaver. Pondering his miserable situation, he goes back to the embarrassments of his confession the night before and forward to what his conservative employer would say if the scandal broke; backward from that to "all his long years of service gone for nothing . . . his industry and diligence thrown away!" and then forward again to this girl his family will disapprove of. His thoughts flop about like a landed fish: "He could not make up his mind whether to like her or despise her for what she had done. Of course, he had done it too."

As he sat thus "helplessly on the side of the bed in shirt and trousers," too nearly paralyzed to finish dressing, Polly makes an appearance that has its own nuances; she "tapped lightly at his door" but then "entered" without being asked to, and "told him all." The sequence of these items is a model of strategy. First, she too has made a confession the night before, to her mother. Second, her mother in consequence "would speak with him that morning." Then come the tears, the despairing lament, and the traditional pose, that the only art to hide her shame is to die. The passage shows Joyce's narrative skill at its sharpest:

> She cried and threw her arms round his neck, saying:
> "O Bob! Bob! What am I to do? What am I to do at all?"
> She would put an end to herself, she said.

The drop of that last sentence into indirect discourse is a rhetorical shift of emphasis from what she is saying to what he is hearing. It suggests she is not too utterly distressed to be tactical, and its sound in his ears can be imagined as just sufficiently terrifying. So he made the conventional response; he "comforted her feebly, telling her not to cry, that it would be all right, never fear." He has said the proper thing, and for him there is not a word of consoling truth in it; thus he takes upon himself that chronic ambivalence which goes with any equivocal involvement and which is the doom of several of Joyce's confused, irresolute Dubliners.

As he spoke his forced assurances he "felt against his shirt the agitation of her bosom," and in this pose and proximity he remembered that what had happened "was not altogether his fault." Any man would have to agree. It was "late one night as he was undressing for bed" that she had "tapped at his door, timidly," wanting "to relight her candle from his for hers had been blown out by a gust." In this confrontation Mr. Doran naturally is concerned neither with credibilities nor symbolisms;

there she is, fresh and warm from her bath, in "A loose open combing-jacket." Joyce's conduct of the narrative here is expeditious, sufficiently detailed but also skilfully elliptical while most logically progressive, as in the two sentences which now close this paragraph and open the next:

> From her hands and wrists too as she lit and steadied her candle a faint perfume arose.
>
> On nights when he came in very late it was she who warmed up his dinner.

Polly and her mother know how to take steps and hold to a course. With the rest of the house asleep and her there beside him, he "scarcely knew what he was eating." And in her thoughtfulness "there was sure to be a little tumbler of punch ready for him" whenever "the night was anyway cold or wet or windy." So the nights have gone, and he remembered all that and its consequent "delirium" vividly enough even under his present stress to think "Perhaps they could be happy together." But he has learned too that "delirium passes" and now he can apply her desperate question to himself: *"What am I to do?"* In such a pause at dead center the imperatives of his Dublin environment come into play, under their most august formulations, "honour . . . reparation . . . sin," within the close dimensions of his kind of piety, pretensions to respectability, and modest security as a clerk.

Mrs. Mooney's timing is uncannily perfect; this is the moment when the servant came to say the missus wanted to see him in the parlor. "More helpless than ever," he stood and put on his coat; almost as mechanically he told Polly "it would be all right, never fear"; her impelling send-off is to remain "crying on the bed and moaning softly: *'O my God!'* " Vision troubles Mr. Doran variously as he descends; moisture dimmed his glasses, he imagines the "implacable faces of his employer and of the Madam," and there in fact on the stairs is Jack Mooney, the brother who is "handy with the mits" and who now turns and watches him in a way to make the reluctant lover remember

Jack's proneness to violence in defense of his sister. And with that on his mind, as he goes down the last flight to the parlor where Polly's mother waits, Mr. Doran disappears from the story, which returns to Polly still in his bedroom.

The elision of the interview between Mrs. Mooney and Mr. Doran cannot be judged a dramaturgical flaw, an omission of an obligatory scene. It is, conversely, a further instance of Joyce's practice in the fine art of selection, for a relative emphasis, and not merely on event but on character and theme. The skilful proportioning and ordering of what has gone before fully implies what is to happen in the parlor. In any further rehearsal of it as overt confrontation, all which has preceded as characterization of Mrs. Mooney would be reduced from its level of wry psychological exploration to that of shotgun wedding farce. However, simply to end with a glimpse epitomizing that there goes Mr. Doran ungraced, down and done for, would at least emphatically terminate with if not expand upon the farcical. Beyond that the focus would not be upon the psychological but the sociological, in this instance of how the weight of an authoritative and rigidly encompassing system can reduce a captive to ambivalence, panic, and abject submission. Joyce did announce, reiterate, and practice such an abstract thematic purpose for *Dubliners,* but its incorporation was always subordinated to the concretely fictional, and what is made to dominate the stories is characterization, especially through those nuances of consciousness that describe Dubliners by instances and at instants. So while Dublin looms forebodingly over Mr. Doran, its factor is Mrs. Mooney, given Polly's preceding function; and however genuine their purpose their method is pretense; and the cream of this story's jesting is not in Mr. Doran's archetypal fall but in a mother's and a daughter's practiced hypocrisy distilled into fairly high comedy.

To this central aspect the story therefore returns in its final page. Polly continues to sit "for a little time" on Mr. Doran's bed, "crying," and in that room she is to remain, with some right and with a cessation of tears, until the voice of the mother is heard in the hall. Meanwhile she freshens her eyes with cold water, looks in the mirror and readjusts a hairpin, returns to relax on the bed, and with a seeming share of her mother's assurance, waits "patiently, almost cheerfully, without alarm." Certain "amiable memories" excited by the bed pillows absorb this Lorelei of stair-landings and lead her on to such "intricate" visions of future delights that she no longer thought of the practicalities being arranged in the parlor. "Polly! Polly!" her mother is calling, and the dreamy daughter picks up her practical role with an innocently questioning "Yes, mama?" which Mrs. Mooney caps with a nice blend of unctuousness and finality: "Come down, dear. Mr. Doran wants to speak to you." Thus the lively Polly has been set up for life, Mrs. Mooney can hang up her cleaver, and Mr. Doran, who allegedly "wants" to speak to the girl, while actually in for it, is dramatically out of the picture.

Hugh Kenner has cited the skill with which Joyce revised this passage. Where he had first written that Polly "jumped up" at her mother's call, Joyce put "started to her feet." Furthermore, the original conclusion — "She remembered now what she had been waiting for. This was it" — becomes the single and less assertive statement of the final version: "Then she remembered what she had been waiting for."[4] Collation of the available *Dubliners* versions and manuscripts continues to show the care with which Joyce weighed words and shaped sentences, but nothing can calculate the pains that went into forming the fifteen stories, the retractions and substitutions, the successive trials till the sentence rang true, the looking before and after, and the conjuring of a subject to take a firm, supple shape. Considering the economy, subtlety, and sustained effectiveness of the finished products, it may be assumed that some such care as the discovered revisions show was constant, and that the young Joyce who wrote *Dubliners* was already the extraordinarily scrupulous artist his later work revealed, however different the ends toward which he was to turn.

"The Boarding House" is but one of the examples in

Dubliners of uniquely adapted narrative art that will reward the closest attention. In loading every rift with involutions Joyce has asked for absorption commensurate with his own. At the same time, and throughout as well as especially in this story, he has carefully subordinated texture to composition. Structure becomes a term too rigid for the modulations of his procedure and the pliancies of emphasis. When the omniscient author openly takes charge and summarily blocks in the conditions of his tale, as he does in the first movement of "The Boarding House," he is direct, firm, and expeditious; when he turns to dramatic scene or state of consciousness, the touch is so light as to appear casual, and under anything less than a close reading the event may seem obvious and its actors commonplace, yet it is here, most of all, that Joyce justifies his solemn claim to have written *Dubliners* "with considerable care . . . and in accordance with what I understand to be the classical tradition of my art."[5] For Joyce, in this regard, the classical was not a convention to be merely imitated, and tradition was a living cultural realization to be projected in furtherance of its provings. *Dubliners* was no trial flight but a full acceptance of vocation, by a man of genius and artistic conscience. In this art each little story, by its unique integrity, magnifies and makes representative its immediate subject, and the separate masks of tragedy and comedy, like the streams of satire or sentiment, merge in the pure pleasure of any aspect of reality acutely apprehended and, for all its ambiguities, compositionally encompassed.

A LITTLE CLOUD

Discussions of "A Little Cloud" have left cloudy questions on all sides, and professional symbolists in particular have seen it from several angles. What is it very like, this little cloud, of what shape and what its drift, and what may there be that is let down out of it? Answers must depend on whatever characterization of Little Chandler is accepted, and whether a simple or complex one. The whole matter comes to a crux in one arresting word, when at the end of Chandler's day and his story, "tears of remorse started to his eyes." If there is an epiphany here, what is it? And how define the "remorse"? This asks, of course, the point and extent of its application to the inconstant Little Chandler whom the story has revealed — the law-office clerk, fastidious and punctilious and yet given to gazing out the window; the putative poet; the eager but diffident companion rejoined to a former friend; the meek, lovingly thoughtful, yet restless husband; the inattentive ineffectual babysitter; and finally the figure standing "back out of the lamplight." Concerning Chandler as husband, a whole gamut of attitudes is briefly but clearly comprised in the last episodes. As for the impact of the returned Dubliner Gallaher on Chandler, that is a story in itself, of anticipation, memory and discovery, and reassessment, with Chandler ambivalent between susceptibility and disbelief. A lesser detail, but pointed, and one to be weighed in estimating the total characterization, is Chandler as reader of poetry and assumptive poet.

It has been liberally suggested by Hugh Kenner that despite Chandler's resort to reviewers' clichés in fancying the reception of his imagined first volume of poetry, "given a different ambience, he might indeed have been a sound minor poet."[1] If "ambience" here merely implicates Dublin as total conditioning environment, the point is still hard to determine, but it can open into the question of whether this story contemplates Chandler as anything other than Dubliner, perhaps as more broadly representative of man's condition, even at its extremes. Another commentator has put it that "Little Chandler, who reveals a sensitivity to poetry, discovers too late that he was 'a prisoner for life,' "[2] and while this does not estimate his aesthetic "sensitivity" it does suggest, in terms of the story, that the imprisonment is more domestic than civic and that the chief obstacles to Chandler as poet are his wife and child. This accords somewhat with a most eminent Joycean critic's assertion that Chandler "feels 'shame' and 'remorse,' immediately perhaps for his failure to mind the baby but ultimately for his wasted life."[3] A "wasted" life would be one lost to itself and its own potentialities, in this case presumably a poet's life, together with the perquisites of success, such as Gallaher's boastings of life abroad have conjured up. However, perhaps "remorse" must be given a larger sense than that, considering its weight in the Joycean vocabulary, where it figures as the deep repeated gnawing of conscience, "agenbite of inwit." How severe then is Little Chandler's remorse, and does it reach to an epiphanal experience?

"A page of *A Little Cloud* gives me more pleasure than all my verses," wrote Joyce to his brother Stanislaus in October, 1906.[4] This may suggest his attachment to its significant theme; it certainly implies a regard for prose fiction as a potentially meticulous and penetrating art, permitting favorable comparison with poetry. The author's sense of the matter being, presumably, communicable, that pleasure was first open to Americans in May, 1915, when H. L. Mencken published this story, along with "The Boarding House," in *Smart Set*.[5] Of the two, "A Little Cloud" is obviously the more complex, but that it comes to a greater attainment and indeed strikes a deeper note than is to be heard in any of the seven *Dubliners* stories preceding it seems not to have been fully recognized. To distinguish satire and pathos in their involvement here and to mark the progressive characterization of Chandler will forbid a simplified reading, such as would limit theme to the environmental frustration of a potentially "sound minor poet" wasting his sweetness on a clerkship and a commonplace marriage, and wakened to painful sense of this by reunion with another Dubliner who, having escaped Ireland's nets, has made something of his life. Such capsuling fits so neatly with generalizations about *Dubliners* that it may obviate a close look at the particular Dubliner and the ex-Dubliner who largely play out this story; and it might even (in the arbitrary way of Richard Levin and Charles Shattuck) all but eliminate Chandler's wife.[6]

In "A Little Cloud" there is an anticipated and then realized encounter between an inordinately delicate, timid man and a crudely blatant one; there is Chandler's progression from expectancy to let-down and distaste, and at last from melancholy unrest to something larger and deeper. Both Chandler and Gallaher are satirized, but it does not rest there as to Chandler. Gallaher, after an eight years' absence, reappears in Dublin with a vaporous yet glittering aura of success abroad, in Chandler's romanticizing view, but at moments he does seem much the same, with signs of further wear and tear. Chandler runs through fluctuations of attitude and emotion, with much vague yearning and some attempts at counter-assertion, and ends in "shame," with those "tears of remorse" in his eyes. So Chandler himself must first be seen, and progressively, and Joyce takes some pains and six pages with that, also setting the stylistic tone, entering Chandler's exotic fancies and aloof extravagant observings, yet tingeing this directly presented naïveté with quiet irony. Then Chandler's reunion with Gallaher and the course of his reactions to it are to be traced. And so that readers may see more clearly what Chandler is seeing after decisively shaking his head, Joyce gives the close of that episode entirely to Gallaher, for more than half a page, a brilliant dramatic miniature of unconscious self-revelation, setting up a thematic counterpoint of reference. Finally, by one of his characteristic uses of ellipsis, with maximum effect of sudden contrast, Joyce moves into the concluding scene, Little Chandler at home, still tossed by contrarieties and then brought to the issue and at last suffused with further feeling.

Throughout that preceding afternoon thoughts of Gallaher, just returned to Ireland, and of the invitation to have a drink with him, had preoccupied Little Chandler; and they go with him as he leaves his clerk's desk in the King's Inns, presumably in a law office, and walks to the anticipated appointment at Corless's. There "he had never been" but "he knew the value of the name," as a place where people went "after the theatre to eat oysters" and where the waiters "spoke French and German." Corless's was in fact a notable establishment; it stood in the very center of things, opposite St. Andrews at the juncture of Dame Street and Nassau Street, and, according to Stephen Gwynn, in the latter part of the nineteenth century it had "the best oyster bar in Dublin."[7] But even as Chandler walks toward his meeting with flamboyant Gallaher in this glamorous place, other musings enter, relevantly at first in contrasting Gallaher past and present, and himself and Gallaher now, and then digressing with a fascination of their own as Chandler "pursued his revery so ardently that he passed his street and had to turn back."

This little fellow is a prodigious dreamer, wistfully imagining himself as perhaps a poet. That envisioning becomes a veil between him and the physical-human realities of Dublin through which he moves. The recurrent self-dramatization is not only heady enough to make him miss his turn toward Gallaher and Corless's, but later in the midst of his home life it continues to distract and even divide him. In the story's title many cloudy symbols have been descried. Some find Little Chandler resembles a cloud; others see the cloud passing over him or looming to pour down upon him. Truly as dreamer he is self-levitated above the common matter of his life. In floating he also drifts and is borne hither and yon, by his own veerings and by the huffings and puffings of others. He is also easily overshadowed, as modest clerk, as Gallaher's partially dominated auditor, and as husband-father momentarily relegated from the circle's center. Most to the point, something does strongly come over him at the story's end, a suffusion of shame. Whatever figure is seen in the cloud, what happens to Chandler in the last scene has been plainly named and must be explicitly read, with relevance to all the story, one way or another. And while Gallaher has been immediate cause of the unusual turmoil in this day in the life of a Dublin clerk, the story is also of Chandler before and after the hour at Corless's, and something more significant and enduring than Gallaher's influence is catalyst to Chandler's culminating vision of himself in the midst of his life.

This relation of factors and not simple narrative convenience explains the story's plain chronological order (so different from that in "The Sisters" or "Eveline" or—as to its main episodes—"The Boarding House"). It is necessary that Little Chandler's complexity be established before the scene with Gallaher can be read aright; then the domestic scene concluding the story will cast its proper light back upon Little Chandler versus Gallaher, and Chandler in himself, as nearly as he can be glimpsed. Although "ever since lunch-time" the thoughts of this somewhat idling clerk "had been of his meeting with Gallaher," he had found moments to muse on other extra-clerical matters. He gazed into the King's Inns' autumn-tinted gardens, "thought of life," and was possessed by "a gentle melancholy," which told him "how useless it was to struggle against fortune." When Joyce calls this "the burden of wisdom which the ages had bequeathed to him," it definitely fixes the long view in which Little Chandler is to be held as he walks across central Dublin. His wistful notion of superlative achievement in being a poet revealingly involves his conceptions of poetry itself. What is here unmasked is so weakly sentimental and childishly naïve a little man that it not only prepares for his diffidence with Gallaher but complicates the judgment to be made of him at the story's end.

A typical subordinate, "When his hour had struck he stood up and took leave of his desk and of his fellow-clerks punctiliously." Passing under "the feudal arch of the King's Inns," he "emerged . . . a neat modest figure, and walked swiftly down Henrietta Street." Joyce, with his ever-present minute and vivid sense of Dublin locale, strikes a thematic chord in that emergence of his little actor through the towering massive gateway out of the law's fixed proprieties and into that downward sloping street which now showed a descent from better days. For Little Chandler, however, these are not compass points. His escape from a clerk's desk and the copying of documents is not into this other area and aspect of Dublin reality but into that presumed poetic career which by its fancyings insulates him from the very substance of literature. The children he passes are "grimy," a "minute verminlike life," in hordes that "stood or ran in the roadway or crawled up the steps before the gaping doors or squatted like mice upon the thresholds." He "gave them no thought," either in themselves, or in comparison with his own infant son, or in their contrast with other lives that had played themselves out along this same street. A genuine poet who really "thought of life" and not first of himself as its melancholy prisoner might have considered these children whose "struggle against fortune" was indeed more severe than his. He might too have been more aware here of the rude wasting of time, since these "gaunt spectral" slums had been "mansions in which the old nobility of Dublin had roistered."

The eighteenth century had seen those fine Henrietta Street houses built, from plans drawn in 1720; and in 1798 within this block that gently slopes from the King's Inns' imposing entrance there lived five peers, one peeress, one peer's son, one landlord member of parliament, a judge, a bishop, two rectors, one doctor, plus one presumably prosperous publican, according to Stephen Gwynn. "By 1910," he continues, "ten of the houses were tenements; Sisters of Charity had No. 12, where 'the most gorgeous Lady Blessington' once received."[8] And where, as Frances Gerard recounts, her body lay in state for eight days, in an improvised chapel, at a cost of £4,000, a detail in the Earl of

Blessington's spectacular progress to financial ruin, so that Blessington House had to be sold, and then was resold for chambers to accommodate barristers attending at the King's Inns, and so finally came into the hands of the Sisters of Charity,[9] of whom by this time the street had need.

Little Chandler, as he "walked swiftly" out of Henrietta Street, is not only ignoring its present squalor, and not "touched" by a sense of its different past, he is looking toward the excitement of joining Gallaher at Corless's. It is a glory dimly conceived, since he had never entered the place, but had only seen "richly dressed ladies" being gallantly escorted out of cabs and into its door, while he himself would pass swiftly without turning his head, in that ambivalence of curiosity and timorousness with which he sometimes haunted the darker streets by night, "apprehensively and excitedly," troubled by silence, courting "the causes of his fear" and trembling at the "sound of low fugitive laughter." But this afternoon, in expectation of what awaits him, he feels for once superior to passers-by; "for the first time his soul revolted against the dull inelegance of Capel Street," and he sounds to himself the theme of escape in absolute terms—"There was no doubt about it; if you wanted to succeed you had to go away. You could do nothing in Dublin."

That this is a general Joycean theme does not preclude its being read here as a particular gibe against the escapism of an arty poseur, for it is in this guise that Little Chandler continues to show himself. Crossing Grattan Bridge and looking "down the river towards the lower quays," he "pitied the poor stunted houses," and from that springboard of sentimentality he launched himself into an extended pathetic fallacy:

> They seemed to him a band of tramps, huddled together along the river-banks, their old coats covered with dust and soot, stupefied by the panorama of sunset and waiting for the first chill of night to bid them arise, shake themselves and begone.

From there on it is up and away for Little Chandler. Wondering "Whether he could write a poem to express his idea," he soars in a further speculation—could Gallaher "get it into some London paper for him?" Yet even in his conceit Little Chandler lapses into timidity, and even in recovery from it shows the ambivalence of a doubtful dreamer. "Could he write something original," he wonders. Admitting himself "not sure what idea he wished to express," he is still carried forward by "the thought that a poetic moment had touched him." Joyce's treatment becomes almost clinically satirical of the type, the femininely intensive fellow with "so many different moods and impressions that he wished to express in verse." Admitting, in what is typically a morbid claim, that melancholy was "the dominant note of his temperament," he saw with a kind of snobbish modesty that he "would never be popular," and "could not sway the crowd" but "might appeal to a little circle of kindred minds." Perhaps the English critics "would recognize him as one of the Celtic school by reason of the melancholy tone of his poems," and "besides that, he would put in allusions." With all that settled so reassuringly, he can proceed to imagine phrases from the reviews "his book would get"—"Mr. Chandler has the gift of easy and graceful verse . . . wistful sadness . . . Celtic note." This leaves only one slight problem; he feels it "a pity his name was not more Irish-looking," and he thinks he could make it so by inserting his mother's name, or, "better still," signing himself "T. Malone Chandler." He would consult Gallaher about that, he decides, and so discovers his "revery" has carried him past the way to Corless's.

It has been one of Joyce's most extended satires, this caricature of a compensatory day-dreamer, affecting literary aspiration. Nevertheless, within the sketch occurs one note unmistakably different, and perhaps finally more significant of Chandler. It has been struck relatively, indeed subordinately; it shows a precise touch with preparatory detail, strategically planted but not prematurely emphasized; yet merging as it does, it is to allow a further reverberation, and a clearer one. In trying to dream his way out of "his own sober inartistic life" and weighing his soul for its poet's qualities, Chandler has not only considered melancholy "the dominant note of his temperament," but he believes it "a melancholy tempered by recurrences of faith and resignation and simple joy." Can this too be part of Joyce's caricature, or does it represent a moment of fuller recognition by Chandler? Some may read "recurrences of faith and resignation and simple joy" as merely more satire by cumulative clichés, yet who is to deny that Little Chandler may have experienced such insights, and may feel himself open to their further recurrence? The reading of "A Little Cloud" can turn upon this as a main point.

First, however, Little Chandler is to find his way to Corless's, having overshot that proper turning, and then find how to deal with Ignatius Gallaher, the former acquaintance he naïvely admires, for reasons almost as unsubstantial as his own dreams of poetic success. Gallaher at the bar—"with his back against the counter," in fact, and "his feet planted far apart"—unhealthily pallid, with slate-blue eyes, and flaunting a vivid orange tie in the face of Catholic Dublin, is strenuously jovial, compulsively talkative, and heavily condescending to Tommy Chandler, whose travels have been no farther than to the Isle of Man. It has been eight years since Gallaher, then himself really under a cloud, had sailed from Dublin's North Wall, seen off by Little Chandler. "Gallaher had got on," the story's second sentence has stated, but this is Chandler telling himself. He had thought so "at once," finding it in Gallaher's "travelled air, his well-cut tweed suit, and fearless accent." Still, Chandler's review of the past, which now lets him "remember many signs of future greatness in his friend," has also some coloration of dubiety. Gallaher in the old days had been "wild . . . did mix with a rakish set . . . drank freely and borrowed money on all sides," and had been "mixed up" in such a "shady affair" that his leaving Dublin had been a "flight." However, "nobody denied him talent," and he had "always a certain . . . something" that "impressed you in spite of yourself," and even "out at elbows and at his wits' end for money he kept up a bold face," for which Chandler "couldn't but admire him." This is the undue deference accorded the arrogant by the timid, but here too is hinted Little Chandler's ambivalent attitude which is to settle at one point into a firmly negative shake of the head.

The irony with which Joyce introduces Chandler as the untraveled man overwhelmed by Gallaher's brashness and yet not quite credulous of him should allow some question as to just how successful is this Gallaher (he of this story, of course, without regard for the figure he is to cut in *Ulysses*). Gallaher puts on a front of worldliness, calling the bartender *garçon* and then François, but there are traces of exertion in his poses. Life on the London press "pulls you down," he admits, with its "hurry and scurry, looking for copy and sometimes not finding it." Then in talk of the old gang Gallaher touches on extremes, O'Hara's seeming "to be in a bad way" and Hogan's having a "good sit"; and there follows a remark with an enigmatic pause —"I met him [Hogan] one night in London and he seemed to be very flush. . . . Poor O'Hara! Booze, I suppose?" Perhaps Gallaher's pause in this weighing of cases is to let Chandler appreciate the hint of high living abroad, but it could mean Gallaher changes the focus to O'Hara while remembering that Hogan flush in London paid for the drinks, or perhaps had been good for a loan. At any rate, Gallaher has reverted to O'Hara, someone apparently worse off, but only a more extreme case of the typical Dublin way he himself had known and may have felt himself still not too securely removed from, especially in comparison with Hogan and his "good sit." Finally Gallaher says he's "over here with another fellow, clever young chap he is too, and we arranged to go to a little card party," and this could mean Gallaher had been brought by a smart English gambler to set up a game, or that Gallaher was making a gull of some traveling companion.

There is no indication that Little Chandler suspects any such thing, but in the drift of their conversation he does pass from thinking of Gallaher as "a brilliant figure on the London Press" to a practitioner of "mere tawdry journalism"; and not without reason Chandler has begun to "feel somewhat disillusioned" by "something vulgar in his friend." Gallaher, as Joyce puts it, has "upset the equipoise" of Little Chandler's "sensitive nature." This prompts once more an ambivalent questioning of his own life. Having been thinking to himself, on his way to this appointment, that "if you wanted to succeed you had to go away," Chandler must acquiesce to Gallaher's phrase, "old jog-along Dublin," and supposes his friend must find it very "dull," yet he feels distaste in an awareness that travel has not much broadened Gallaher's interests or refined his appreciations.

When Chandler wants to know whether Paris is "really so beautiful as they say," Gallaher, almost startled by the question, says it is "not so beautiful" and then "of course, it is beautiful . . . ," but goes on to mention the city's "gaiety, movement, excitement" and the "hot stuff" that is not for "a pious chap" like Tommy. The pitch and grounds of Gallaher's lurid gossip is a further measure of him—he "revealed many of the secrets of religious houses on the continent . . . and ended by telling, with details, a story about an English duchess—a story which he knew to be true." Joyce gives the reader sufficient perspective on Gallaher, however astonished Little Chandler is by him. And it was from mention of "old jog-along Dublin" for which nevertheless one "can't help having a certain feeling" that Gallaher passed, perhaps with invidious comparison, certainly patronizingly, to inquire into Little Chandler's status. Boisterously then Gallaher congratulated his friend, "married last May twelve months" and father of a son; but he refused to come for an evening's visit with this little family. Chandler, piqued, "felt acutely the contrast between his own life and his friend's, and it seemed to him unjust," and thus he "wished to vindicate himself in some way, to assert his manhood."

It would seem significant that at this point he does not proffer his recent dream, his imagined poem and volume of poems, nor does he make any lesser pretensions, such as inquiring (as he had previously considered) about publication in a London paper, or consulting Gallaher man-to-man about T. Malone Chandler as a preferable literary signature. Little Chandler has been challenged in terms more actual and on local grounds, and here he makes a stand, on a reality he knows. He also predicts, "calmly" and "stoutly," a similar discovery for Gallaher. He declares Gallaher will marry. This is more than the usual chaff between a recently married man and a companion still a bachelor; neither is it a benedick finally consoling himself that his fate is common to mankind and in due time will be shared by his friends. That would isolate the instance from a larger context and would block awareness of the episode's other aspects. Nothing in Joyce's stories is isolated; extended context is an ever-present complementary function in a fabric without gap or basic contradiction, no matter what the arrangements of chronology or the juxtaposition of contrasts.

This means, as with any highly composed story or poem, that effect remains suspended though implied, and response is to be tentative although anticipatory, until everything falls into relevant formation, not merely as plot but for what is evoked of insight into human existence. Not until then, with details firmly "placed," is the work of art to be tested for its essential unity, that integrity and consonance out of which, in Joyce's Thomistic terminology, arises its luminousness. Then is when the reader of such a work as *Dubliners* is also tested, for his concerned waiting upon revelation, and for those exercises of memory, association, and intuition which make way for evaluative grasp. The possibility of the reader's arriving at the reward of cumulative and culminating vision is what justifies the poet's or the fictionist's special levies upon attention, empathy, and imaginative response. No modern fictionist has laid greater claims upon readers than Joyce, and as he went along he voiced his expectations quite demandingly; in *Dubliners* the texture often is closer than that of the more formally designed later works, the treatment more objective, and in some ways implications are subtler, as in "A Little Cloud."

What emerges in *A Portrait* and *Ulysses* as Stephen-Joyce's ambivalent *non serviam* and agenbite of inwit was the psychological rock-bottom of *Dubliners,* deeply submerged even in the "autobiographical" first three stories, and quite objectified in the diverse players of the other tales. Aesthetic distance, achieved by perfected fictional convention in *Dubliners,* is sought differently in *Ulysses* and *Finnegans Wake,* through structural, referential, and stylistic experiment and gradually a further remove from empathy. The connection throughout Joyce's work, however, even in the antic disposition of *Finnegans Wake,* is ambivalence. In the *Dubliners* stories it is detachedly yet compassionately observed in a variety of rounded characters and implied of them by sustained dramatic narration; consequently self-justifying, self-castigating Stephen may seem easier to measure than Little Chandler, and both Bloom as ever-acquisitive picker-up of odd trifles and the slyly showy Shem the Penman may seem comparatively flat characters when set beside Gabriel Conroy. The underlying but operative ambivalence of the most typical and central characters in *Dubliners* means that they are never seen plain and whole at any one point, but only in this or that aspect, with the shift of mood, in the course of circumstance and behavior. Though Little Chandler pines for what is not, he does so from the midst of his actual life, where he can be seen fabricating illusions and stumbling upon realities progressively discovered. At every instant the reader is solicited to comprehend imaginatively, in an enlarging view transcending the character's own, and comprising obverse factors and contending value-concepts. Such a sustained consciousness of Little Chandler's fluidity will not only allow realization of this living being but will lay open the story's artful unity in containing him without immobilizing and thus denaturing him. Such practice is in some degree common to good fiction, and becomes one measure of aesthetic potency and total effect. Joyce's *Dubliners* folk, as he saw them, required a full use of it, and his skill was generally equal to that technical demand.

Beyond that, these open-structured narratives show that

significant summing-up may be made as of the moment at the story's end yet without the air of a resolution projected to endure forever after. It is not only not told but not suggested (neither precluded) whether and when the lad from "Araby" might once more allow love to possess him, nor is it implied how Eveline's clutch upon the iron railing at the pier was broken, or for how long Mr. Kernan was saved by grace from relapse into drunkenness. It would be even more difficult to say whether Little Chandler's remorse was to have some lastingly transforming effect on him, or to what degree at least it might resolve the restlessness of his ambiguous life. But the ambiguity is there, with the underlying ambivalence, and to read the life exclusively from either of its poles at any one moment is to minimize protagonist and theme. This is not to say that in Joyce's paraplegic and inconstant Dubliners ambivalence is always only a barely perceptible trembling of the scale. The stories are genuinely dramatic in their showing a preponderant shift, one way or another, and often in an intense crisis of realization and emotion, as with Little Chandler. Scales can be turned, and sharply, by something added on the other hand. This vicissitude is the mode of drama, as it must be, with fidelity to the existential fact of man in motion; in a state of fixity there would be no reason to look before and after, and it is flux which induces revaluation. Nor are the *Dubliners* characters, with all their limitations, merely pacing back and forth over the same path to the same extremes like caged animals. Tortured by constraint within painful contradictions, external and internal, which seem to remain largely unresolvable, these little people are nevertheless capable of insights and of some degree of choice.

Even Eveline; her halting is dramatic only because she had already come a certain distance out of her imprisonment and had seemed about to resolve her ambivalence. The paralysis which overtakes her is so acute only because the factors in opposition, while simple, are so extreme. This Dublin affliction Joyce set out to document is always, even in the less severe cases, a product of contradictions, and since in most of the stories both circumstances and character are more complex than Eveline's, they oscillate beyond such fixity as hers and sometimes make an advance. The Little Chandler who feels he must "vindicate himself in some way" has several ways—he is humble clerk but fastidious man, compensatory daydreamer yet easily abashed; he has the diffidence of the stay-at-home in facing the returned traveler, but he has never fled Dublin leaving a rumor of "some shady affair"; he fancies himself as predominantly melancholy, but that, he knows, is "tempered by recurrences of faith and resignation and simple joy." So every word and thought of his is part of the trend of his life, sinuous and sometimes eddying but a current. Confronting Gallaher, he is expressing something of all this. Since Gallaher, in evading Chandler's invitation to visit him at home, has said he may be skipping over to Ireland again next year, Chandler has phrased it that by then he "may have the pleasure of wishing long life and happiness to Mr. and Mrs. Ignatius Gallaher." Gallaher doubts that, and is for a "fling" first, and "seeing a bit of life and the world" before putting his "head in the sack." But "calmly" Chandler says, "Some day you will." When Gallaher, all orange tie and staring slate-blue eyes, says, "You think so?" then Chandler, though repeating Gallaher's derogatory phrase in the common way of argument, "stoutly" adds its opposite, a particular consideration and a factor of another order: "You'll put your head in the sack like everyone else if you can find the girl."

Here is another turning point, and Joyce's indications, while minute, are plain. Chandler "had slightly emphasized his tone" and "was aware that he had betrayed himself" but "he did not flinch from his friend's gaze." (Here certainly *betray* means *reveal, disclose,* as for instance in "An Encounter," in the phrase "Lest I should betray my agitation.") Contextually considered, it is not by the echoing of Gallaher's cliché that Chandler has revealed himself. What he has exposed to this coarse and cynical companion is his experience of love's predilection, upon finding the girl. This is the implication Gallaher replies to—if he marries it will not be for love, but for money. Little Chandler "shook his head" at that. The gesture implies he knows better, for himself at least, whether or not hopefully for Gallaher. The image of a shaken head constitutes the last glimpse of Chandler in this scene, and that contradiction of Gallaher implies Chandler's belief in affinity. Nor is this all. The episode at Corless's approaches an ellipsis in that further passage of half a page given over entirely to Gallaher the self-declared vulgarian, confident he could find a wife "rotten with money, that'd only be too glad," but in no hurry to be tied to one woman, a state he makes a face over, as something that "must get a bit stale." Here it remains for the reader to remember that Chandler has already shaken his head over this man.

The last scene then shows Little Chandler back at home, with his sleeping child in his arms—and yet not entirely at home, again errant in his thoughts and once more prey to ambivalent feelings. He had returned late, forgetful of the coffee he was to bring, and his wife has gone out to the shop at the corner. Now he looks at what stands nearby under the table lamp, a photograph of her in the blouse he had bought her. This calls up a whole history: his nervous shopping for it, her pleasure and grateful kiss but her housewifely outrage at the price, and her proposing to take it back, her trying it on and deciding to keep it, and kissing him again and calling him very good to think of her. But now Little Chandler, unsteadied by his afternoon, finds the eyes in the photograph irritating in their "composure" and cold compared to his awakened fantasies of rich voluptuous women. His little house, with furniture bought on the hire system, now seems "mean" and again he craves "escape," perhaps to London, to "live bravely like Gallaher." Yet like many a wavering little man at a moment of libertine longing, he lets himself feel baffled by a puny fact—"There was the furniture still to be paid for." Thus he does escape issue, but again into his dream. What might "open the way" would be if he "could only write a book and get it published." Meanwhile cautiously, hampered by the sleeping child he is holding, with his left hand he opens a book, Byron, and begins to read the first poem, a piece of juvenilia that reeks with artificial diction: "Not e'en a Zephyr wanders through the grove"—"Within this narrow cell reclines her clay." Apparently Chandler had no notion of what a bad poem this is; he felt its rhythm, and "How melancholy it was!" Indeed, he aspires to "write like that," and again he thinks intensely of wanting to describe "so many things," such as his view of the old houses from Grattan Bridge that afternoon, if only "he could get back again into that mood. . . ." Then the child awoke and cried. While he rocked it Little Chandler still tried to read, but the child would not be hushed, and Chandler's little frustration became the shadow cast by something larger—"It was useless. He couldn't read. He couldn't do anything. . . . He was a prisoner for life." Angrily he shouted "Stop!" and the child screamed and then sobbed convulsively and would not be comforted, though Little Chandler walked the floor with it in alarm. Annie, bursting in, snatched the child from him, her eyes glaring with hatred, and he made his limp excuses—"It's nothing . . . I couldn't . . . I didn't do anything." She gave him "no heed," but speedily comforted the child, her "little mannie," with repeated endearments; and Little Chandler, feeling "his cheeks suffused with shame," and standing "back out of the lamplight," listened as "the child's sobbing grew less and less," while "tears of remorse started to his eyes."

There the story ends, and so remorse for what, that is the question. Richard Levin and Charles Shattuck called Chandler "abashed by his inferiority to Gallaher,"[10] but this only half-reads only one scene. Tindall's previously cited reading—"he feels 'shame' and 'remorse' immediately perhaps for his failure to mind the baby but ultimately for his wasted life"—is substantially the one most often accepted. In more detail Thomas Connolly considers the husband shamed by his wife's comforting her "little mannie," and suggests she had married childish, effeminate Little Chandler to obtain a real man-child. Such speculation probably takes too little account of the story's one extended passage characterizing the day-to-day tone of this marriage, the blouse episode. Of Chandler's suffusion with shame and starting tears of remorse Connolly puts it thus: "He is shamed in his virility and remorseful about the position he has allowed himself to be placed in."[11] This, however, makes Chandler a completely passive person, dominated by how others may estimate him, which he has not been, either in his projective reveries or, more importantly, in his final rejoinder to Gallaher, in which he positively takes his own position. And now, as he stands back, it is not just from his wife's resentment but in what he has been made to see of himself. In reading the word "remorse," consideration might be given to what troubling of mind, chiefly in terms of personal relationship, Joyce himself had known, and had in part passed on to Stephen as the "agenbite of inwit," that phrase which transliterates the insistent sharpness of the Latin root in *remorse* and indicates that the gnawing is of conscience. Not as artist and not as man either was Joyce the one to write "remorse" when "regret" would have done well enough. A man is not remorseful for what fate has done to him, nor because he is abashed by a feeling of confinement. A man feels remorse when in a realization of his aberrance he confronts his ethical self. If here in "A Little Cloud" it is called remorse over having made the baby cry, that must include for the inconstant Chandler all the variables which led up to it, now more clearly evaluated in a moment of fuller insight, an epiphany.

The story has prepared, structurally and substantially, for revelation of Chandler's remorse by showing a pattern of oscillations in this ambivalent man. Within their whole course are three main movements, each containing conflicts of illusion and reality, in alternating preponderances. First there is Little Chandler, moving toward Corless's and Gallaher, mentally and physically, and passing from the monotony of his job and the sordidness of Dublin streets into sentimental reveries so extravagant that he actually loses himself. Then there is his meeting Gallaher, with dazzled Little Chandler at first subject to his friend's pretensions (while still a bit skeptical of this fellow as Dublin had known him) but "stoutly" resistant to Gallaher's cynicism, "calmly" affirming values he has learned something of, and shaking his head over Gallaher's invincible ignorance and unmitigated vulgarity. Finally there is Chandler at home, in a recurrent ambivalence between escapist illusion and domestic realities, which is again resolved, also positively, as in the conviction with which he had opposed Gallaher, but this time as a sentiment, in a fundamental realization. Chandler's naïve romanticizing of Gallaher's alleged way of life has broken down and reversed itself as stubborn counter-assertion; now Chandler's even more naïve romanticizing of himself gives way to a remorse deep enough for tears. These two major changes of mind and heart are related, and that interplay is supported by all the minor alternations which make up the story and lay the basis for Chandler's epiphany. To retrace Little Chandler's meandering moods is to recognize more clearly Joyce's control of texture, structure, theme, and climax.

That climax is to be located along a rising line from the point where Little Chandler on his way to Corless's "passed his street" in his "revery" and "had to turn back," then on through diffident credulity to the emphatic tone and shake of the head with which he contradicts Gallaher, and so finally to the starting of Little Chandler's tears of remorse. Chandler has merely shaken his head at Gallaher, who is allowed the last words at some length in that episode; Chandler was not shown having it out with him, yet not just because Gallaher is obviously incorrigible, and not because Chandler is not stout in his own opinion, but because Joyce's story is to come full circle in Little Chandler's having it out with himself. As the climax is approached in the stress of contrarieties when Chandler tried to read Byron while holding the baby, what appears is not just a frustration of simple choice but a real ambivalence. Opposites have alternatingly dominated, as this little Dubliner went his wavering way. Finally, however, it is not just the baby who has been wakened and shocked and given over to grief. Little Chandler has found that the fault is not altogether in his stars. The sentimental escapist yearner is stirred and stabbed wide awake to confront himself as a neglectfully unappreciative husband and father.

Before "A Little Cloud" is classified simply as one more story of a Dubliner circumstantially restrained from escape into a larger life, due weight must be allowed the strong threads of satire that interweave with the deep sentiment of the epiphany. There is the dramatic irony of Gallaher's unconscious self-revelation, in classic form as the semi-transparent boaster. More importantly, there is the exposure of Little Chandler as pseudo-poetic superficial day-dreamer inattentive to that immediate reality which must be the substance of art because it is the stuff of life. And to measure Little Chandler's remorse it is to be remembered that in his self-assessment, however dreamily oriented, he found his melancholy "tempered by recurrences of faith and resignation and simple joy." These qualities can be taken as genuine, less amorphous than melancholy, more specifically experienced and definable, and it is a part of Chandler's ambivalence to recognize them as tempering factors in his malaise of spirit. The simple joy he had had in bringing Annie the pretty blouse was real, and had he not been so foolishly unsettled by Gallaher's transit of his horizon, he might have had another real joy of a primary sort quietly holding his child for its comfort while Annie went out to buy tea. At the least, coming home late, he might have remembered to bring the parcel of coffee; at the very least he might have refrained from shouting at his child because it interfered with his reading Byron.

Some may consider the characterization of Chandler ameliorated at this point because of Joyce's known and sustained admiration for this great name. Not only does Joyce recruit Stephen Dedalus to Byron's defense,[12] he himself as a schoolboy of twelve had asserted Byron was the greatest poet, nor would he yield that opinion under his schoolmates' drubbing;[13] and when in 1931 he was considering a collaboration with George Antheil to make an opera of *Cain,* he wrote that though he would act as "scissors and paste man" to produce a libretto, he "would never have the bad manners to rewrite the text of a great English poet."[14] Joyce was right, Byron is great; but Joyce's youthful taste in poetry was sentimental, and later he may have held to Byron primarily as arch rebel, just as personal considerations could have conditioned his liking for Mallarmé's indubitably fine line: "Il se promène, lisant au livre de lui-meme."[15] Joyce's poems, by their simplicity and pure lyricism, seem to show a limit he set on the art, at least for himself. Musical and imagistic, but casting deep shadows of implication, as in the subtly perfected unrhymed lines of "Tilly" or the austere euphony of "She Weeps Over Rahoon," they are the very opposite of the inflated or affected. However, Joyce's first and very early attempt, the lost "Et tu, Healy," must have been in a conventionally sentimental-ornate vein like Byron's juvenile poem, to judge by the fragment Joyce reproduced for Harriet Weaver,[16] illustrating its parody in *Finnegans Wake*.[17] If so, it accorded with an endemic taste, which Tom Moore had answered to, and Joyce's father proudly had the precocious effusion printed, but certainly Joyce had outgrown that along with much else. "Et tu, Healy" may also have its echo, along with that of a song composed and sung by Joyce's father,[18] in the sincere but cliché-loaded poem Mr. Hynes had composed and is called on to recite on Ivy Day, but there Joyce obviously knew what he was doing. Can it be doubted that in writing "A Little Cloud" he was conscious of how bad the Byron poem is, how soggy with just the kind of affected sentimentality he had caricatured in Little Chandler's view from Grattan Bridge, and therefore a supplementing effect at this stage of the story. But merely supplementary; Chandler himself need not be capable of literary judgment in order to experience his epiphany of a deep remorse, and his impatience with his child appears the more childish in that his preoccupation was with something inferior in itself.

It is no wonder Annie glares at him, shows hatred in those eyes that in the photograph had seemed so cold, so ladylike and passionless. Mrs. Thomas Chandler is a mother, too, but not necessitously ruthless as is Mrs. Mooney, nor spitefully assertive like the socially aspiring Mrs. Kearney. She is an ordinary young woman whose eyes in the photograph "answered coldly" only when Little Chandler, still under Gallaher's shadow, had "looked coldly into" them. She is pretty, ladylike, self-possessed, and the "composure" in the photograph is precisely what has challenged the discomposed Chandler, to the extent of making him ask not why he had married Annie, but "Why had he married the eyes in the photograph?" He is adrift between two fancies, the coldness he has read into those eyes and the "dark Oriental eyes" full "of passion, of voluptuous longing" which Gallaher had conjured up for him. Annie objectively viewed seems in all probability neither cold nor voluptuous, but rather "a creature not too bright or good for human nature's daily food." When Tommy came home late without the coffee, she was understandably "in a bad humour and gave him short answers," but she didn't throw a tantrum; she went out to the shop herself, first "deftly" putting the sleeping child into her husband's arms and pointedly instructing him: "Here. Don't waken him." Perhaps this Annie is just the girl for Little Chandler, therapeutically speaking; she had been woman enough to be "delighted . . . with the make of the sleeves" in a blouse and to make a to-do over the price, and to kiss her husband repeatedly for the gift; and now is woman enough to comfort a crying child and edify her husband at the same time by "giving no heed to him."

Little Chandler "stood back out of the lamplight" but not into utter dark, not yet "an outcast from life's feast" as Mr. Duffy came to find was his painful case. Instead Chandler can see an actuality still immediate to him, and is it not to his shame, remorsefully felt, that he had let shoddy illusions eclipse this human reality, had let his sentimental reveries and Gallaher's crude swagger come between him and this wholesomeness? In fancying himself poet he had walked by the turn to Corless's; in mooning over Byron's puerile verses he had been distracted from the plain great facts of family and home and a man's responsible and rewarding place therein. Now true emotion, validly centered, significantly engaged, surges through him. In this confrontation and the vision it enforces, the addicted dreamer is for once fully awake. "If you can find the girl," he has told Gallaher; now it is shown Little Chandler that to have found her is to go on finding, in further realizations. In this sense he foreshadows Gabriel Conroy, of whom Joyce was to write not long thereafter, and perhaps "A Little Cloud," the fourteenth of Joyce's stories in the order of writing,[19] was part of Joyce's readying himself for "The Dead." In the former, however, it was his great care not to overplay the climax; there is no such prose-poem as at the close of "The Dead," but only a tableau and one augustly resonant word. The human values are not defined but merely implied in the mention of "remorse," to be seen as an ambivalent man's full return from previous extremes, and, in a resemblance to "The Dead," with a suggestion through the universality of present elements that here is the norm from which Chandler's sentimental dreaminess and susceptibility to Gallaher have been aberrant.

Though Joyce treated this climax sparely, the last episode in its entirety has been sufficiently furnished, as the minutely woven, mildly variegated texture of domestic life, through which there can strike a manifestation of primary truths. That Chandler is such an ordinary little man, except for a certain daintiness, and with perhaps little more than average secret dreaminess, makes his example the more representative. His tangential departures from the orbit of dutifulness are typical; he is not only brother to Walter Mitty but cousin by whatever remove to everyman when fancying inordinate triumphs as he frets against life's routine demands. And when Chandler's compensatory reveries must be compensated for, not merely by a return to reality but by remorse for his infidelity to it, this is true to the vicissitudes of the average man's daily life, with his discovery therein of shortcoming and some saving grace. Finally, Annie is sketched and deployed by Joyce with suitable touches, this side of sentimentality yet with a full range of sentiment and its human significance. She is not the dream-girl half-seen in the half-light of "Araby," nor Stephen's still more elusive and ethereal Mercedes; Annie is neither a broken-spirited Eveline nor a too coquettish Polly; and she is certainly not the Madonna some supererogatory readings would make of her. (There is that *blue* blouse, and so Little Chandler stands back subordinately like St. Joseph, one specialist has been heard to say.) Annie is a pretty, sensible, active, natural home-body; Chandler accomplished one genuine work in the gesture of bringing her the pale blue summer blouse; she was shrewd to call the price a swindle and economical to keep it for her delight, and true when she kissed Chandler and called him "very good to think of her." And though the furniture is not paid for, they have set up an abode, and with the child between them they have turned into life's main path. All this Chandler has known, and this he can summon up as more real than the pseudo-poetic view he took from Grattan Bridge, and of more weight than anything Gallaher has pretended or actually represents.

Though at the close of Chandler's day with all its variable tides his final response may be to a real epiphany, whether that vision will continue to prevail is a question the story does not answer. If, as some see it, his "remorse" is merely for having let the baby cry, and simply a further grieving in a timid melancholy life, then Chandler may be the little cloud, blown here and there in reversals of mood under the force of circumstance. On the other hand, if Gallaher is the cloud which has overshadowed Chandler's day, then Chandler's emerging resistance to Gallaher's vulgarity and his stout rejoinder, "if you can find the girl," may show a developmental experience, preparing him for remorse as a decisive epiphany, through which he could lay steadier hold on chosen values. Between these views in their extremes, and however the title is read, there is middle ground for a receptive but less sharply defined view of Little Chandler's epiphany. In this light he may seem, in his susceptibility to varying moods, capable for that very reason of steps toward further levels of awareness, of which this closing moment in the story is one instance. This would accord to the fluidity and the reverberative inconclusiveness Joyce gave his open-structured stories, yet would allow the magnitude, thematic and dramatic, of that word *remorse*. It would affirm also that the ambivalence which haunts so many Joycean characters and in some degree visits all men does not necessarily prohibit any maturation and may at least allow approach to the dry wisdom and lean virtue which steadfastly acknowledges values it cannot steadily hold to.

Little Chandler, having moved from selfish exasperation to shame, has not measurably increased his stature, but he has had a further and clearer look than from Grattan Bridge and has heard other voices besides Gallaher's. His epiphany is not as profound as Gabriel Conroy's nor as complex, progressively emergent, and comprehensive. Chandler's "remorse" assails him suddenly and acutely, whereas Gabriel's enlarging sense of man's mortal lot grows upon him from passion and jealousy to intuitive compassion. While epiphanies in the Joycean sense and use may be gradual or instantaneous, they also may be of various potencies. Little Chandler's response concerns matters closer home and of more enduring import than the "penitent" reaction of the lad in "An Encounter" who tardily senses his playmate's human worth. Even in this slighter story the grounds of penitence are somewhat defined: "for in my heart I had always despised him a little." There is no comparable explanation of Chandler's "remorse," only its mention at the story's very end. This has admitted readings of "A Little Cloud" by the doubtful method of forcing it or any other story into the mold of critical generalizations about Joyce's works. Yet particular reason enough for Chandler's "remorse" is clearly enough implied by all that the story has built up within and of itself. Though Joyce has left Little Chandler to one side "out of the lamplight," he is perceptible as joined to generous Gabriel and the encountering boy by this, that in the midst of their various unrests, preoccupations, and frustrations all are challenged in an immediate personal relationship. This, though seemingly ordinary, is fraught with those human values which are taken for granted, lost sight of, and then by grace recovered, with an access of vision so acute that the sense of inconstancy to it is humbling. Thereby the heart is revived, and is readied for further growth in love.

This was ground that Joyce trod hesitantly, and, except in "The Dead," with his mask of cynical indifference only half removed and ready in his hand. The lad's beating heart and "penitent" feeling about Mahoney, Little Chandler's "shame" and "remorse," and Gabriel's "generous tears" are there, however, as points in a line otherwise obscurely traced in *Dubliners,* the line of compassion not only for Dubliners paralyzed by Dublin but for that paraplegia by selfish preoccupation which may fall upon any man anywhere. Little Chandler is not merely ridiculous, merely pitiable. He is also somewhat reprehensible, like many other *Dubliners* characters in greater or lesser degree, whether the two preying gallants or cold-hearted Mr. Duffy, brutal Farrington or the corrupt temporizer Henchy, or Mr. Kernan and Mrs. Kearney, gracelessly intemperate in their different ways. Little Chandler is not utterly tragic victim, either, like Eveline, or partially comic dupe, like Mr. Doran. And standing back in remorse, he still is not isolated, as in their various ways are the disenchanted boy in "The Sisters" or little old unclaimed Maria, or Mr. Hynes in that committee room, silent and alone in his integrity. There before Little Chandler in the lamplight for him to see is his world, his wife and child, and his tears of remorse may be of relief, too, as for the time and not without promise of times to be when the trembling scale of his ambivalence settles and steadies on the side of this preponderant reality.

While a page of "A Little Cloud" could give Joyce more pleasure than all his verses, the story as a whole, so finely executed, can thereby give readers pleasure throughout, and then at the end a pause with regard for what may be Joyce's transmuted confession and thereby his largest personal commitment in *Dubliners* this side of "The Dead."

COUNTERPARTS

"Counterparts" follows "A Little Cloud" with some illuminating parallels and differences. Farrington too is a clerk, a copyist, also in a law office, and feels himself caught in his situation, but whereas Little Chandler is precise, punctilious, and neat, Farrington, a tall fellow and muscular, with "heavy dirty eyes," is careless, gross, quarrelsome. He too compensates for his unrest by imaginings, but they are of a primitive order—of crushing the boss's skull, of getting drunk, of clearing out "the whole office single-handed," of rushing out to "revel in violence." Chandler merely shouts at his crying child-in-arms in momentary impatience; Farrington beats his "little boy," in a plain case of transferred aggression. As seen throughout, Farrington seems a totally brutalized man, capable of vanity but not of shame, much less remorse. What fluctuations there are in his behavior arise not from self-realized nuances of experience, but in the almost animal lurkings and chargings of an amoral creature, rebellious against external demands under his own demand for drink.

Although the narrative line follows the irregularly mounting graph of Farrington's rage, this story is not more psychological than sociological. That this was Joyce's intention seems borne out by his remarking in a letter to Stanislaus that "if many husbands are brutal, the atmosphere in which they live (vide Counterparts) is brutal."[1] The reference implicating Farrington must pertain to the "atmosphere" of his life in office and pubs, since any outright brutality in his home is what he brings there. The Farrington menage is almost diagrammatic of Dublin's ingrown sordidness as Joyce saw it. The wife is "a little sharp-faced woman who bullied her husband when he was sober and was bullied by him when he was drunk," and as alcohol is his relief, so her solace is the church. When Farrington, in the depressive state of his drinking bout, finally gets home very late to the dark and almost fireless kitchen where he is to perpetrate his worst brutality, she is "out at the chapel." This sad glimpse into Dublin life also furnishes some special indexes of the Irish as a people put upon—the boss, Mr. Alleyne, speaks on the tube in a "piercing North of Ireland accent," which Farrington has been overheard mimicking but must jump to; and Weathers, the acrobat performing at the Tivoli, who defeats Farrington in a barroom trial of strength, is presumably English.

While Joyce's rendering of the violent Farrington is almost monochromic as to this man's general reprehensibility, the view of a clerk's precarious state under the likes of Mr. Alleyne extends reprehension to a whole segment of Dublin economic life. The point is given ironic stress by the physical disparity between the huge muscular Farrington and the boss to whom he is subject, "a little man wearing gold-rimmed glasses on a clean-shaven face." His "pink and hairless" head is caricatured as something scarcely human, with Farrington's seeing it vulnerably bent in its baldness over the desk "like a large egg reposing on the papers." Joyce extends the caricature, with a final suggestion of the inhumanly mechanical:

> Mr. Alleyne flushed to the hue of a wild rose and his mouth twitched with a dwarf's passion. He shook his fist in the man's face till it seemed to vibrate like the knob of some electric machine.

That Farrington himself is inexcusable does not obviate the element of privileged bullying in this employer's relations with a dependent clerk; it is to be restressed by its differentiated but still paralleled counterpart in Farrington's bullying his son. That conclusion shockingly illustrates how the innocent can fall victim to those who have been brutalized by environment. Sociologically this short and simple annal is one of Joyce's most widely implicative stories. But in contrast to some naturalistic treatments of such a concept, with Farrington it does not falsify a total social reality by sentimentalizing and thus denaturing the underdog; indeed, it still implies his primary responsibility.

The story has three clearly divided parts, correspondingly timed like movements in a suite—Farrington in or truantly out of the office, then at the pubs one after another, and on his late arrival home. The office is all annoyance, which he evades now and then by sneaking out for a drink, to return to further trouble. The ellipsis between this first part and what follows bridges over "an abject apology" he "had been obliged to offer" Mr. Alleyne to keep precarious hold on his hated job, for without it there will be no money at all for drink. It does not appear that support for a family of five children is ever his serious concern, and indeed his behavior throughout the story is inconsiderate of this primary obligation. All his family supplies him, besides a lair to retreat to, is a field for vengeance he is otherwise impotent to deal out.

In the story's second phase, with Farrington released from office hours and onus, he seems able to put aside consciousness of having "made a proper fool of himself," and his mood expands under the stimulation of drink and conviviality. This heavy-footed man is at no point himself a jolly fellow, however, and his greatest approach to liveliness is in telling and hearing retold a flattering version of how smartly he had answered back to the boss, but without mention of the apology it necessitated. Then his evening falls off in a series of further frustrations—his six shillings got by pawning his watch have run out, and therefore he cannot follow after a woman, an *artiste* from the Tivoli, who seems available, and when he is put up against Weathers in a sporting test of muscular strength, he is defeated. The third part, which Joyce begins by showing him reviewing his humiliations while he waits for his tram, describes his coming home in a rising fury that can be appeased only by a cruel reversal of roles, making his son his counterpart in vulnerability to another's command and to another's physical strength.

The scene, though shocking, does not run beyond the

probabilities of parental license. Joyce's uncle William Murray treated his children savagely when he was drunk, and one of them once pled with him on the same terms as does the boy at the conclusion of "Counterparts"—"I'll say a *Hail Mary* for you, pa, if you don't beat me."[2] There was, however, a softer side to William Murray as parent, different from anything conceivable of Farrington, and "Counterparts" is no mere anecdote out of Joyce's early recollections. While it is illustrative of one level of Dublin life in Joyce's youth, at its terrible conclusion it takes on the tone of a fable as Farrington and his son Tom are reiteratively named "the man" and "the little boy," generic figures enacting a typical inhumanity and a typical human attempt to appease fate. When the boy hits hesitantly upon his one offering: "I'll . . . I'll say a *Hail Mary* for you," whether or not this proposed traffic in things spiritual for an immediate material benefit is a bit of simony, it is certainly the only recourse Tom knows of so far, presumably from the example of his chapel-going mother. In Joyce's Dublin, as any lad grew up out of a home like this, the chances were he would have learned from other men (as could the delivery boy in the committee room) of another anodyne, to be had from bottles.

Farrington, as repulsive as Corley and even more reprehensible, claims attention not just by such grossness but by the psychological spectacle of his fluctuant moods, transparent and immediately emergent in rebellious action, and Joyce follows out minutely the waverings on the path to disaster. Farrington's afternoon has gone from bad to worse. First he is summoned and harried by a justifiably incensed Mr. Alleyne for not having a contract copied by four o'clock and for taking too much time at lunch—"Do you hear me now?" says Mr. Alleyne twice, as if cracking a whip, and finally "Do you mind me now?" Farrington feels a "spasm of rage" that can find no present outlet beyond a murderous "gauging" of the "fragility" of his master's egglike bald head, but he senses "he must have a good night's drinking." Caught between the necessitous and addicted phases of his life, the office and the pub, he is thrown into that compensatory reaction almost reflexively, and the rest of the story shows its accelerating process. There are vicissitudes along the way, under which his moods change, but the "barometer of his emotional nature . . . set for a spell of riot" is to go always higher, until pressure breaks through at the end.

Meanwhile, after enduring Mr. Alleyne's just rebukes abusively uttered, the shirker and escapist in Farrington must have some release, and for the fifth time that day, under pretense of going to the toilet, he sneaks out of the office for a drink, to find himself "safe in the dark snug of O'Neill's shop," where he spends his last penny for a glass of porter. A "snug," an inconspicuously accessible, separately enclosed part, in some Dublin pubs could be such a fine private place as would hold only two or three; whatever the size of the "dark" snug in the establishment Patrick O'Neill operated on Henry Street at that time, Farrington's sense of it suggests an almost uterine retreat and marks the regressiveness in this heavy-footed man whose "great body" at the end of a chaotic day's clumsy work is "aching for the comfort of the public-house." When he comes sneaking back, now "wondering whether he could finish his copy in time," he notes the "moist pungent odour" of Miss Delacour's perfumes on the stairs, supposes she has come in to Alleyne's office, and finds indeed that the Delacour correspondence has been called for. Taking the papers in, Farrington can only hope Mr. Alleyne "would not discover that the last two letters were missing." Sent away with a flick of his employer's finger, and given only a glance at "the middle-aged woman of Jewish appearance" who "came to the office often and stayed a long time when she came," Farrington dawdles like an incorrigible schoolboy, though he has pages still to copy. He muses over alliteration in the phrase he has left incomplete; "for a few minutes" he listens to the clicking of the hurried Miss Parker's typewriter. Trying at last to work, he cannot put aside the thought that this "was a night for hot punches." Then when he inattentively makes a mistake, still on the contract that should have been finished by four o'clock, and must start the page over, he is so "enraged" by "the indignities of his life" that he is seized in quick succession by two grotesquely incongruous impulses —"to clear out the whole office single-handed" and to "ask the cashier privately for an advance"—and though he knows he can't hope to get this, he lets himself become so absorbed in thought of "where he would meet the boys" that his name must be "called twice before he answered."

Mr. Alleyne, with Miss Delacour, has come into the outer office asking about the missing letters, and to his "tirade" Farrington can only reply that he knows nothing about "any other two letters." Mr. Alleyne, enraged but also playing the scene by "glancing first for approval to the lady beside him," asks whether Farrington takes him "for a fool . . . an utter fool," and Farrington stumbles upon an apt but hazardous answer, that it's not "a fair question to put to me." This brought "a pause in the very breathing of the clerks," the "stout amiable" Miss Delacour "began to smile broadly," and Mr. Alleyne flushed, twitched, and raged against this "impertinent ruffian," who must apologize for the offense or "quit the office instanter." Here comes the first ellipsis. The next sentence shows Farrington standing outside, watching the other clerks leaving, waiting for the cashier, but then unable to ask him for money because when he comes out he is with the chief clerk. In Farrington's review of his situation, which he finds "bad enough," it comes out that he "had been obliged to offer an abject apology to Mr. Alleyne." Could it be said, then, that Joyce here evaded an obligatory scene? Or at least neglected an opening to probe Farrington further, for instance by showing his surly mumbling compliance, with his bitter sense of all the others listening, and no doubt under more seething comment from Mr. Alleyne in his domineering role?

On the contrary, it would seem that, as with the use of ellipsis in many of the other stories, Joyce's instinct was again acute. He never lingers upon the presumable, for the sake of its mere melodramatic to-do, but vaults the story into the protagonist's further experience, and often with added effect from abrupt contrast. In "Eveline" there was no need to trace her progress across Dublin to the North Wall; and the leap from her feeling while still at home that Frank "would save her" to her inhibiting fears at ship-side confirms the psychological depth of her ambivalence and makes for thematic emphasis in the quick onset of her paralysis. In "The Boarding House" Mr. Doran's fate was predestined; that mother who "dealt with moral problems as a cleaver deals with meat" will not miss, and when she calls to Polly that Mr. Doran wants to speak to her, it is obvious, even though readers have not seen the rehearsal under Mrs. Mooney's direction, that he has learned his lines in a hurry and will deliver them correctly, even if with some lack of style. In "A Little Cloud" the quick transition is from the reader's (and a silent but unconsenting Chandler's) extended view of Gallaher at his most distasteful to the simple image of Little Chandler back at home, "holding a child in his arms"; here instant change to an opposite extreme from Corless's bar yet with some lingering sense of vulgar footloose Gallaher gives basis for that oscillation of moods out of which Chandler's epiphany is to dawn on him. As for Farrington, his apology to Alleyne is as inevitably forthcoming as Mr. Doran's proposal of marriage to Polly. "Counterparts" does not tell of the breaking of a strong man; whatever integrity Farrington might be supposed ever to have had has disintegrated under what he rationalizes as "the indignities of his life." Nor has he, in his puerile evasions of responsibility and generally laggard existence, any honor to be defended by a refusal to humble himself. Moreover, the one fact simple and severe enough to force itself upon him is that economically he is trapped. Finally, just as the issue for Little Chandler is not against Gallaher so much as with himself, so for Farrington the most revealing test, in which this story too has its climax, is not in his performance on the job or behavior in the pub but in his conduct as a father, in which he takes the opposite road from Chandler's, pitiless violence rather than a humane remorse. Even Farrington's apology to Alleyne is scarcely a mark of discretion as much as of desperation; he must hold the job if he can, to have money for drink. There is indeed a shrewd disposition of narrative elements in passing over a Farrington subdued by that one necessity, to focus on Farrington grown the more rampant thereafter. So at the ellipsis, with just a glance back at the apology itself, the action spurts ahead to its second movement, Farrington's compulsively re-enacting a shambling rise and fall in the mean drama of convivial pub-crawling.

The progression of his moods increasingly exposes him. He realizes that he having "made a proper fool of himself this time," now Alleyne would make his life in the office "a hell to him." Yet this morbidly disconcerted man, "savage and thirsty and revengeful, annoyed with himself and with everyone else," turns by another drift of associations which again demonstrates his aimlessness, except for one real desire. Remembering how he has been in trouble ever since Mr. Alleyne "overhead him mimicking his North of Ireland accent to amuse Higgins and Miss Parker," Farrington thinks he could have "tried Higgins for the money"; then in dismissing that as a poor prospect, what with Higgins having "two establishments to keep up," Farrington does not go back to the larger problem of whether he can hold on to his job, much less to the related duty of providing for his family; he continues to wonder about raising money to drink with now. So, "fingering his watch-chain," he recalls Terry Kelly's pawn-office. He sets off quickly, "muttering to himself that they could all go to hell because he was going to have a good night of it." Who "they" are, "all" of them, he doesn't specify. It is the thirsty rebel's defiance of order and obligation, the fist shaken at the sky. Only the story's end is to show how widely and cruelly doom will fall on others besides.

With his watch pawned and six shillings in hand, he is reinstated in his own opinion. He walks along crowded Westmoreland Street "with proud satisfaction and staring masterfully at the office-girls" as "his nose already sniffed the curling fumes of punch." Now his folly in the office becomes something he can brag about to the boys, and he rehearses it up to but neither including nor consciously excluding the apology —how coolly he looked at him and her and back at him, taking his time before saying he didn't think that was "a fair question" to put to him. And it works. Nosey Flynn, in Davy Byrne's, "stood Farrington a half-one" and called the story "as smart a thing as ever he heard," and the flattered Farrington "stood a drink in his turn." It is a clerk's small ground for triumph, retorting to a superior; similarly in "Clay," when Joe tries to be attentive to Maria, he tells what "went on in his office," including "a smart answer which he had made to the manager." Now when O'Halloran and Paddy Leonard came in, "the story was repeated to them," and O'Halloran "stood tailors of malt, hot, all round" and recounted an answer he had made to the chief clerk in an office where he once worked, but admitted "it was not so clever as Farrington's," to which Farrington expansively responded by telling the boys to "polish off that and have another."

Then as they are "naming their poisons" in comes Higgins, from the office, and is asked to "give his version of it," which he does with great gusto especially with a drink in sight, imitating the irate boss and then Farrington, crediting him with being "as cool as you please" under Alleyne's tirade, but evidently leaving the story at that. This spectacle of the spirit of recalcitrance unconsciously editing the event to give a spurious justification turns upon Farrington's having cited fair questioning to his exasperating but justifiably exasperated superior; later that evening Farrington again is to call for fairness, and again in denial of reality, this time Weathers' fairly besting him in equal struggle; finally Farrington is to achieve completely unchecked self-assertion by an act of monstrous inequity, in as unfair an infliction of force upon weakness and punishment upon innocence as could be imagined. Thus out of this shabby life of an obscure, half-submerged Dubliner Joyce evokes a faceted moral fable of wide relevance, including an offender's attempt to rationalize "fairness" into a one-way street.

After that round enlivened by Higgins' version of Farrington's great moment, Higgins and Nosey Flynn drop out for want of money, while the others come along through a drizzle of rain in the cold streets to the Scotch House, at Farrington's prompting. There Leonard introduces them to Weathers, an acrobat then appearing at the Tivoli; and Farrington, still playing an assertive part, "stood a drink all round." As the conversation with Weathers "became theatrical," a livelier form of shop-talk which supersedes Farrington's story of his retort to Mr. Alleyne, O'Halloran stood a round, so then Farrington stood another. Weathers, "protesting that the hospitality was too Irish," promises to introduce them to girls back-stage, and there is jesting about Farrington as a married man, at which his "heavy dirty eyes leered at the company in token that he understood he was being chaffed," but he finds no more apt reply this time. After Weathers has "made them all have just one little tincture at his expense," he leaves but promises to meet them at Mulligan's. There they went when the Scotch House closed, and O'Halloran ordered, and Farrington again, with Weathers entering in time for that round. When "two young women with big hats" came in with another man, Weathers spoke to them and then told his companions they were "out of the Tivoli." One of these women attracted Farrington, she became aware of his gaze, and as she left she brushed against his chair and said "*O, pardon!*" in a London accent. To Farrington's disappointment she did not look back, and he knew he could not follow her, lacking money. To himself he cursed this lack and "all the rounds he had stood," but "particularly" those to Weathers, and he grew "so angry that he lost count of the conversation of his friends."

Here he has passed the peak of his felicity, and now a further descent awaits him. His companions have put him up against Weathers "to uphold the national honour" in a show of strength, that form of wrestling with elbow on the table and opposed hands clasped, each trying to push down the other's forearm. In half a minute Weathers does it. Farrington, angered and humiliated, and again resorting to the line of argument he had taken against Alleyne, accuses Weathers of unfairly using his body weight, and calls for the best two out of three. They try again, and this time it is a long struggle, but once more Weathers wins. And again Farrington's trait of fury tending to run wild shows itself; when the bartender who has been watching approvingly says that "that's the knack," Farrington turns on him fiercely and says, "What the hell do you know about it? What do you put in your gab for?" O'Halloran, hearing this and seeing the look of violence on Farrington's face, discreetly shushes him and proposes as diversion just one more little drink before they go. With this, and its presumed averting of further outbreak from Farrington, the story is brought to its second ellipsis; and here, as in the more extended vignette of Gallaher at the bar in "A Little Cloud," the closing view is fixed on another, O'Halloran, rather than the main character, but only for a diminuendo, a distancing of focus to make way for recurrent emphasis in the break to another scene and time.

In the third panel of this sordid triptych and closing movement in this melancholy suite, Farrington is seen not much later but alone, "very sullen-faced," immobilized waiting for the tram "to take him home," beginning "to feel thirsty again" and longing "to be back again in the hot reeking public-house," but with "only two pence in his pocket." In this enforced pause that allows such reflection as he is capable of he is "full of smouldering anger and revengefulness . . . humiliated and discontented," and worst of all, "he had not even got drunk." He curses "everything," and it is quite a category—the recurring consciousness of his having "done for himself in the office," his watch pawned and the money spent, "his reputation as a strong man" lost. Cumulative fury nearly chokes him as he adds the remembrance of the woman who brushed past him, spoke, and was gone, beyond following. The half-page Joyce gives to this recapitulation is justified not by factual content as such but for the subjective realism of Farrington's brooding and for the indicating of still further rise in the "barometer" of his "emotional nature . . . set for a spell of riot." It was in this state of raging frustration that he arrived home, loathing the return, to find "the kitchen empty and the kitchen fire nearly out."

When he shouted for his wife, "a little boy came running down the stairs," and when Farrington, "peering through the darkness," asked who it was and the boy answered, "Me, pa," the father did not recognize this son's voice, much less this child's implied claim as an individual. Nor could Farrington be certain it was another's voice, for he said, "Who are you, Charlie?" and had to be told it was Tom. This is partly a heavy drinker's benumbed state, but it suggests this careless man's insensitivity to his children. The distance between these abstract parabolic figures, "the man" and "the little boy," is to be bridged this night, but only by physical contact and an infliction that makes still greater the gulf between them as father and son. The child is to become his parent's counterpart as trapped victim of another's wrath which exercises a power more circumstantial than inherent, running beyond the contractual rights of an employer or the disciplinary function of a father, and indulging in a bullying that is a release of sheer ego. The parallel is added to in Farrington's interrupting his son's attempts to answer, as Alleyne had done with his clerk, and also in the sarcastic echoing of phrases, Alleyne's repeating Farrington's "Mr. Shelley said, sir" and Farrington mimicking the boy's "At the chapel," concerning the mother. Here, however, Farrington is also talking "half to himself," adding "if you please," and evidently extending his fury to his absent wife for not being there, waiting to serve him his dinner.

There is also a reversal of roles in another way, in that this irresponsible man who has behaved so childishly is now to be cared for by the responsible child, who answers his call, tells where the mother is, lights the lamp, and is going to cook his father's dinner. Still the spirit of rebellion, thirsting for violence, rages in Farrington, not to be appeased. With any consciousness of relationships he would have remembered that the fire was almost out and the kitchen dark and his wife at chapel because he had not come home and there had been no knowing when he would. But drink, his temporary release, has soddened this man beyond shame; more generally, his is the typical substitution of nihilism for acknowledgment of mutual responsibility. He orders the lamp lit, bangs his fist on the table, demanding what's for his dinner, and then makes the inadequate fire the excuse he craves for beating his son, in a distorted counterpart to the physical defeat he had suffered in fair and equal trial with Weathers. It is an amends possible only to one with no considerations beyond his own thirst, rebelliousness, and savagery. Nor will the promise of a child's prayer for him stay his heavy hand. And for the boy too there is "no way of escape," as for his father before him, caught in the net of economic necessity, the compensatory habit of drink, and the induced spirit of violence. Farrington walks in darkness not of that kitchen only, and he has failed to uphold honor in other ways besides succumbing to Weathers' superior muscles.

Farrington is among those fictitious Dubliners who most obviously and explicitly demonstrate Joyce's announced sociological thesis. Beyond that the psychological profile, though strong in particulars, is of a simple but unhappily common type, and more than locally representative. And the mounting narrative of a slothful bullied clerk's obliquely defiant binge, the typical alcoholic arc of excitement and depression, and the final outlet in tranferred aggression—all this makes for one of Joyce's most effectively conducted stories, so much so that in the end it becomes almost unbearable to read. What emerges in the contrapuntal structure is a drastic variation of theme—or something perhaps comparable to the reversing of the notes of a musical phrase—and a modulation to a most somber key. Alleyne had some rights and reasonable expectations, even though he enforced his demands for them wrongly; Farrington finally becomes, as sheer rampant force, an eruption and extension of chaos. As the tale fades off into this ancient elemental darkness all that is heard is a child's reiterated uncompleted cry, in a futility that makes the prayer he is promising seem itself perhaps futile. Which also would accord with Joyce's view of his Dubliners.

CLAY

In reading "Clay," it is immediately and continuously relevant to sense the particular narrative mode and tone. A third-person story, it nevertheless moves throughout in Maria's presence and almost altogether in her partly veiled consciousness, with a transposing of expository or descriptive matter into her terms. Maria as a central intelligence is also almost a puppet in Joyce's hands, made always to speak and think in her unique way, and most of all about details minute and apparently insignificant, to convey an image of lifelong innocence, timidity, and wistfulness. The result is an artistic perspective that mingles the ironic and elegiac. This story's highly sophisticated technique underlying a seemingly plain texture guardedly conveys Joyce's discerning conception—Maria the physically witchlike but gentle little spinster with her precarious limited relations to life, yet with her moderate *amour propre* and her discreetly sentimental notion of herself—a protective cloak which others instinctively assist her to keep wrapped all around. Childlike, she is treated with kindly condescension, but this she innocently assimilates into her shy persistent sense of her own identity as a special sort of grown-up. In the peculiar course of her life she has nevertheless followed a common way, has come to what terms she can with what she understands of her present self and situation, and has taken on a role enough larger than reality to save her from being overwhelmed by melancholy.

Compassionately conceived of thus, with this made the tenor of her consciousness and the grounds of her slender morale, she is then set forth ironically by way of her unaffectedly, unconsciously childlike way of being. The story has therefore a rare quaintness overlaid by a mild pity; throughout it is kept in a minor key. In no way is it satirical; Maria is too innocent and harmless, and in her minute fashion too good, to be laughed at, much less criticized. Nor is the story tragic; she lacks both stature and history for that. Hers is the quiet pathos of the unattractive, unclaimed woman who must live out her life at the edge of other people's, effacing herself lest she offend by intruding where she is superfluous and perhaps not wanted, yet clinging to whatever attention comes her way and making the most of it, and a bit more, just enough to avoid acknowledging how little it really is. Such persons, though not uncommon, are so inconspicuous and unassertive that they go generally unnoticed, and seldom has one of them been looked at as discerningly as does Joyce in his quiet, careful discovery that for all her witchlike appearance tiny Maria is more like a wren, with her little niche in life and her fluttering excursion from it.

The isolation of such an existence and her subdued notion of it have retarded her at an immature stage, in which after the manner of a child she is a sort of fable to herself, even to an extent, now and then, of seeming to reflect upon herself in the third person. So it must seem, at least, in such a sentence as that at the end of paragraph four—"Everyone was so fond of Maria"—which follows her gratified recollection of the matron's calling her "a veritable peacemaker!" " 'Everyone,' says Joyce, 'was so fond of Maria' "[1]—so one critic puts it, apparently taking little notice of the feminine intensive. That *so fond* is, however, something other than purely objective fictional narration as Joyce would conduct it according to his own sardonic rather than effusive temperament. Is it not Maria secretly allowing herself to think that "everyone" was "so fond of " her? Similarly, later she is conscious, more privately, that for "so many Hallow Eves" Fleming has made the ridiculous joke about the ring. Joyce has also established, with a particular variation of his *Dubliners* style, something of a fable's tone in those few passages of omniscient narration and description which for the moment lie somewhat outside Maria's way of regarding herself—for instance, the first two sentences of paragraph two, especially the first: "Maria was a very, very small person indeed but she had a very long nose and a very long chin"—or for instance with the jesting on Hallow Eve about Maria's getting the ring and a man, while she "had to laugh and say she didn't want any ring or man either," and here Joyce interpolates, "when she laughed her grey-green eyes sparkled with disappointed shyness and the tip of her nose nearly met the tip of her chin"—almost a fairy-tale sort of grotesquerie.

The predominantly childlike tone, then, is the story's ironic medium. It is a complex irony, however, for now and then Maria's consciousness seems to hover at the verge of a truer and more bleak recognition of herself. Always, though, she turns back from any fact that would be fatal to defensive illusion, and keeps the fable of Maria alive in her own mind. But while self-delusion is, and properly, an object of satire in some *Dubliners* stories, "Clay" shows a closer intent. It is rather a compassionate study of these minimal terms on which little old Maria manages to sustain herself, psychologically. In her meek enduring way she does get along, at the laundry, on her eager timorous Hallow Eve journey through the heart of Dublin, and in her diffident sharing of the Donnellys' family party. Joyce does not show her imprisoned in her conventional illusions so much as adapted to determinative circumstance through them. The pity of it runs deeper than a failure of will, such as what may be seen in some other *Dubliners* folk; Maria's is the pathos of a blameless human inadequacy to surmount natural limitation. Despite the adverse weight of environment upon Eveline or Farrington, it is conceivable that with resolution she might have got up that gangplank, though hardly, and he might at least have done his work instead of slacking off; little simple Maria seems born into a class with the woman to whom the reader of palms, after one glance, said, "You have no fortune." For her, circumstance and response can never intersect so favoringly as to grant an extended insight; no epiphanies are visited upon her, and she must find her miniature fulfilments in the habitual—"Then she had her plants in the conservatory, and she liked looking after them"—or from such incidental crumbs as being "glad of her old brown waterproof" this rainy evening. "Clay" does not center upon a death theme, as some readings assert, but on Maria's little life, with gentle regard for its particulars. It simultaneously expresses her subjectively and with perspective, to make this perhaps the most delicately rendered of all the stories, yet at the same time to sustain the narrative as composition.

If Maria is seen in this guise and by the light of such a compassionate irony, it will obviate the strenuous attempts to load this quietly resonant little story with symbolisms of Maria as witch, Maria as the Virgin Mary, or at least as saint.[2] It is no specific symbol but a pervasive tone that Joyce is establishing, and as Tindall has put it, "analogy or parallel does not establish identity. Maria remains Maria."[3] What is to the point is to realize her human situation on the fringe of life. Joe and Alphy (modeled on Joyce's uncles William and John Murray)[4] are not "her brothers," as one critic repeatedly called them in deducing a "death-in-life theme" from the clay.[5] Maria's original in fact was merely "a relative of the Murrays, and one of whom May Joyce was especially fond," according to Ellmann; elsewhere he indicates Maria was "a distant relative."[6] In the story her connection with Joe and Alphy is never defined; though she may be distantly related, that is not specified, but it is evident she is not of the Donnelly brothers' immediate family. This accords with her status on the periphery of all the life she knows and has known. Evidently she had lived dependently with the Donnellys while Joe and Alphy were growing up, and had been their attentive nurse, for now she clings to the memory of Joe's often saying, "Mamma is mamma but Maria is my proper mother." When that home was broken up—probably by the mother's death and certainly after Joe and Alphy were grown—"the boys had got her that position in the *Dublin by Lamplight* laundry," remembering which, she adds in her tactful little mind that "she liked it."

She has told herself too how "often" Joe "had wanted her to go and live with them; but she would have felt herself in the way (though Joe's wife was ever so nice with her)." What "ever so nice" means becomes more apparent when she thinks of Joe's wife as "Mrs. Donnelly" and Mrs. Donnelly emerges in the story as a firm-minded woman who manages the children even in their games and chides her husband for quarreling with his brother till "there was nearly being a row on the head of it." Mrs. Donnelly is polite to Maria, declaring it was "too good of her to bring such a big bag of cakes" and making all the children say thanks; she also offers Maria port wine; but as for the missing plum-cake, she bluntly "said it was plain that Maria had left it behind her in the tram," and she deals strictly with the children over the saucer of clay. She joins in the request Joe makes, as "the children grew tired and sleepy," that Maria "sing some little song before she went"—but perhaps too as a prompting to Maria that the party is over. Mrs. Donnelly plays the accompaniment (as she has played earlier for the children's dancing) and gives the command, *"Now, Maria!"* when she is to begin. Joe's family are all kindly to her (the children had sensed no harm in the game's conventional saucer of clay) but obviously there is no permanent place for little old Maria in this energetic outspoken household with a complete life of its own.

Even on this night of games and warm reminiscence Maria is self-effacing. When the nutcracker can't be found she is doubly so: "Maria said she didn't like nuts and that they weren't to bother about her." Her only assertion comes when, during talk of old times, she "thought she would put in a good word for Alphy," but when Joe cried out against him, Maria "said she was sorry she mentioned the matter." It is here that Mrs. Donnelly takes her husband to task and a row seems imminent, but "on account of the night" and with more stout Joe quiets down and the Hallow Eve games proceed; and as far as wistful Maria could tell, "soon everything was merry again," and she "was delighted to see the children so merry and Joe and his wife in such good spirits." Then later, after the to-do over the clay and the prayerbook in the fortune-telling game, when "Mrs. Donnelly played Miss McCloud's Reel for the children and Joe made Maria take a glass of wine . . . they were all quite merry again," and with Joe "so nice to her . . . so full of pleasant talk and reminiscences," Maria said "they were all very good to her." Here are her oldest, closest remaining human ties, and this an evening of special warmth, but that only emphasizes how tenuous is the connection and discloses her barely suppressed sense of her extraneousness.

Actually Maria seems less at home there with Joe and his family than in her Dublin by Lamplight situation. In the midst of domestic life the single outsider seems the more isolated; at the laundry Maria has her place and a kind of standing as well. Even so, there too she is a stranger; and much of the attention she receives is occasioned, ironically, by the fact that she does not really belong. Not only is she a Catholic in a place under Protestant direction; this modest old spinster, indubitably virginal, works among inmates of a home for the reformation and rehabilitation of prostitutes. In the *Guide to Dublin Charities* of 1884, Dublin by Lamplight Institute is listed in the section on "Homes for Fallen Women."[7] There were then several of such institutions in Dublin, and these altogether could care for 650 inmates, but the need no doubt seemed even greater, since at that period there were reportedly "7,000 young women of the fallen class in Dublin." Refuges for them were philanthropically set up by both Catholics and Protestants; such establishments were made largely self-supporting through laundry-work done by the inmates. Dublin by Lamplight Institute was founded by Protestants in 1856, to be managed by a committee and administered by a chaplain and a matron. The laundry, built in 1877, was one of the largest and best in the city. Inmates were "received on their own application," but what explains the institution's curious name is that "others" were "gathered in after midnight meetings," presumably street evangelism under the lamplight of Dublin's notorious Nighttown or elsewhere in the city. The *Guide to Dublin Charities* of 1884 says of these homes in general that women were "received without religious distinction, though expected of course to attend to the religious instruction given," and at the Protestant Dublin by Lamplight a specific condition was that all "must conform to the rules of the house, and attend daily prayers." This same 1884 report stated that "The conduct of the inmates is good, and not one per cent of those who leave return to their former evil life." It added that "Those who remain two years are placed in situations, or sent to America."[8] That some of the women may have chosen to stay longer, and even to settle in such a haven, is implied in "Clay" when in the joking about the barmbrack Lizzie Fleming's declaring "Maria was sure to get the ring" is something "Fleming had said . . . for so many Hallow Eves."

A more incongruous place for little old Maria could scarcely be imagined, and her connection with it over those "many" years has remained unique, her adaptation partial. She is apparently one of the hired staff, working in the kitchen, not in the laundry itself; she has a "little bedroom" of her own; but as a resident she comes under the matron's supervision and must have "leave to go out as soon as the women's tea was over" this Hallow Eve. Maria had had "a bad opinion of Protestants" but has found them—presumably her associates on the hired staff—"a little quiet and serious, but still very nice people to live with," and the matron "such a nice person to deal with, so genteel." Maria's one dislike, "the tracts on the walls,"[9] is an instance of the isolation she must feel, both among these Protestants who operate the establishment and among the inmates to whom the tracts would be perhaps pointedly aimed. Conversely, her setting her alarm ahead because "next morning was a mass morning"—it would be a holy day of obligation, All Saints Day—suggests a quiet preservation of her own way of life and some respect for that by her employers. Between the "genteel" matron and the "common" inmates who work in the laundry Maria had found her own little refuge; and with considerateness for her naïveté those among whom she works have given her a special role, which she takes up with the utter seriousness of a child playing in a game, or like any socially and emotionally deprived adult shoring up an ego, but tentatively and unpresumptuously.

The story begins with Maria's looking forward to her evening out. To her in her mood of simple expectation everything takes on a glow; the kitchen is "spick and span," with the fire "nice and bright," and cook has made the cheerful communication that "you could see yourself in the big copper boilers." The rest of the opening paragraph concerns the barmbracks—that bread with a light mixture of cornmeal, with raisins, eaten at other times too but on Hallow Eve a ceremonial requirement even in the poorest families.[10] Here in the kitchen were "four very big barmbracks," which "seemed uncut; but if you went closer you would see that they had been cut into long thick even slices and were ready to be handed round at tea." Some one has punctually done a neat job here, so neat "you" would have to go close to see the "even" slicing; and behind the passive "they had been cut" lurks a self-consciousness which comes out in the next sentence: "Maria had cut them herself." These five words, and especially "herself," come to the readers in Maria's own shy tone, tinged with her diffidence and pride. It is almost like a child's clapping her hands over a successfully accomplished surprise.

In the second paragraph, after Joyce has described her with a child's storybook language of "a very, very small person" with "a very long nose and a very long chin," the narrative drift is again into her consciousness, of herself as "always sent for when the women quarreled over their tubs," and always succeeding, so that the generously condescending matron has called her "a veritable peace-maker!" The conclusion of the matter is that "Everyone was so fond of Maria," and this intensive is overtone to her pleased awareness that "the sub-matron and two of the Board ladies had heard the compliment." To suppose, though, that timid little old Maria is a skilled and forceful arbitrator is impossible; what is shown in this introduction is her holding to any minute assurances she can find to give her a sense of belonging and being recognized, as in her "veritable" role as peace-maker.

Specifically there is the matter of Joe and Alphy. Their quarrel is between mature men and presumably of recent occurrence, since just five years earlier the brothers had "gone to Belfast on a Whit-Monday trip" together—the excursion of which Maria's purse from Joe was a memento. Maria naturally dislikes quarrels, but she is especially disturbed by any breaking apart in what is her nearest thing to a family. So in the mellow mood of Hallow Eve by Joe's fireside Maria attempted to "put in a good word for Alphy," but when "Joe cried that God might strike him stone dead if ever he spoke a word to his brother again," Maria not only desisted but meekly "said she was sorry she had mentioned the matter." What then presumably did she accomplish at the laundry? If she quieted the worldlywise inmates of Dublin by Lamplight, it must have been by the persuasion of her innocence and sensitivity. The roughest people can sometimes be gentle with children, or with the childlike; the quarrels of those coarsened women, and especially their vocabulary, would not be for Maria to hear. So they have spared her and made a sort of pet of her, it seems, and thereby allowed her a role to play.

Thus "Ginger Mooney was always saying what she wouldn't do to the dummy who had charge of the irons if it wasn't for Maria." Magalaner reads this literally, saying Maria's "calm moderation alone keeps Ginger Mooney from using violence against another worker."[11] But Maria could scarcely have prevented it had Mooney "always" or even ever have been bent on a real assault, rather than the kind of facetious abuse manual workers sometimes affect to lighten monotony. Here the common game has an added fillip. If it is a repeated jest for Mooney to declare she is about to batter another inmate, and the dummy at that, the jest is crowned by pretense that only timid, self-effacing little old Maria has power to prohibit it. Maria accepts that fiction, with wistful belief. Her recollection of the matron's compliment and Mooney's suspended threat is followed by that telling sentence: "Everyone was so fond of Maria," which is true, yet not quite in the way she is allowed and allows herself to suppose. If she is veritably a peace-maker, it is by no strength except the passive appeal of her own vulnerability.

She must wait till the cook said "everything was ready" but then it is her no doubt cherished function to "pull the big bell" summoning the women. They come in, "wiping their steaming hands in their petticoats and pulling down the sleeves of their blouses over their red steaming arms," to settle before "huge mugs" which the cook and the dummy fill with hot tea from "huge tin cans." Yet how nicely and surely little Maria moved among all this heavy heartiness; she "superintended the distribution of the barmbrack and saw that every woman got her four slices." In the midst of "a great deal of laughing and joking" Lizzie Fleming predicts, as on other Hallow Eves, that Maria will get the ring (presumably in the barmbrack, in one of Ireland's Hallow Eve games) and it is here Maria "had to laugh and say she didn't want any ring or man either," her grey-green eyes (Joyce interpolates) meanwhile sparkling "with disappointed shyness." Then how loudly the women "clattered with their mugs on the table" when Ginger Mooney proposed Maria's health, though "sorry she hadn't a sup of porter to drink it in." Maria laughs so hard that nose and chin nearly meet and "her minute body nearly shook itself asunder"—the excessive laughter of the unsure and embarrassed, but ostensibly, in her own guarded mind, "because she knew that Mooney meant well though, of course, she had the notions of a common woman."

After this social scene—("But wasn't Maria glad when the women had finished their tea . . .")—she is alone, dressing for her evening out, first remembering to set the alarm at six for "a mass morning." Changing her blouse and standing before the mirror, "she thought of how she used to dress for mass on Sunday morning when she was a young girl," then no doubt with natural girlish hopes. Now, though, "she looked with quaint affection at the diminutive body which she had so often adorned" and "found it" despite its years "a nice tidy little body." It has come to that; and since it has, Maria has come to certain terms with it. In her timidity she has not been without fortitude; she is of that scantly considered innumerable ubiquitous band—"the disregarded multitude of the bewildered, the simple and the voiceless,"[12] Conrad called them—who make do and, in Faulkner's word, endure. And make the best of it, as when sitting in the tram with her feet barely touching the floor, planning her evening, Maria "thought how much better it was to be independent and to have your own money in your pocket" —her "two half-crowns and some coppers" she has in that purse labeled "A Present from Belfast," which she is "very fond of" because Joe had brought it for her. So throughout she incants a sense of identity and sufficiency while clinging unobtrusively to her few, tenuous human relationships and a meager status therein. She is simply unaware of this polarity, but it intensifies the story's pathos, ironically enhanced through narrative keyed to a childlike naïveté, closely according with her nature and consciousness, in one of Joyce's most subtle devices of characterization.

To "the Pillar" she rode (Nelson's Pillar, now no more, in O'Connell-then-Sackville-Street) and in that busy district she got out to do her shopping for goodies to take to Joe's children. Like others of Joyce's Dubliners, she moves about the city, but within routines and confines. She has come from the Ballsbridge area, at some distance south of the Liffey (which straitly bisects central Dublin, flowing east into the bay) and having crossed over, she will go on to the Drumcondra area. This is at the further edge of that region north of the lower Liffey where Joyce himself had lived, in North Richmond Street as a boy and at several other addresses thereafter—"Joyce" says Padraic Colum, "was a north-side man"[13]—and there he domiciled several of his characters, not only the lad of the first three stories, and the folk of the boarding house, but Leopold Bloom. It is in general a more ordinary region than the south side (where Joyce was born and from which the family had migrated by degrees northward as John Joyce's status worsened), but the vicinity of the Pillar was and remains one of the city's handsomest, and full of enterprise. Little Maria is not quite lost sight of in the crowds of shoppers, but at Downes's cake-shop "it was a long time before she could get herself attended to." (Every word in *Dubliners* is worth noting for its scrupulous use and implicative weight; here Joyce could have written *served* or *waited on,* but in this characterization *attended to* is more distinct and resonant.) At last Maria got "a dozen of mixed penny cakes" and "came out of the shop laden with a big bag." Next, a use of Joyce's stylistic device of repetition—here the word is "buy"—suggests Maria's simplicity and intentness, and how in her limited view small matters are magnified:

> Then she thought what else would she buy: she wanted to buy something really nice. They would be sure to have plenty of apples and nuts. It was hard to know what to buy and all she could think of was cake. She decided to buy some plumcake. . . .

What re-enters the story and is to continue in the Drumcondra tram is a central theme, consciousness of spinsterhood. It has figured in Fleming's annual jest about getting the ring and, more delicately, in Maria's thought, before the mirror, "of how she used to dress for mass on Sunday morning when she was a young girl." Now it appears by implication in the episode at the cake-shop in Henry Street, where she has come because "Downes's plumcake had not enough almond icing on top of it." Here she is attended to, but "she was a long time in suiting herself and the stylish young lady behind the counter, who was evidently a little annoyed by her, asked her was it wedding-cake she wanted to buy." It might be suggested that the clerk is being sarcastic with a hesitant elderly customer who, whatever she wants, would not be needing a wedding cake. This is in itself implausible; a busy clerk and stylish young lady would not waste so much wit (even in Dublin) on such an insignificant little old body. It can be supposed, though, that Maria's glance has half-strayed half-consciously toward wedding cakes, and that it is her being made conscious of this and not just the clerk's sharpness which now makes her "blush and smile at the young lady." Such a reading seems supported by the clerk's matter-of-fact way; she did not return blushing Maria's smile (which like her excessive laughter with the laundry inmates and later with the children is a cover for embarrassment) but "took it all very seriously and finally cut a thick slice of plumcake, parcelled it up and said: 'Two-and-four, please' "—an abrupt termination which sets off the relative emphasis given this little episode as a whole.

The next paragraph finds Maria in the Drumcondra tram, where room is made for her by an elderly man with "red face and a greyish moustache," whom she naïvely considers "a colonel-looking gentleman." (Tindall, reading a word rather than in Maria's mind, makes him "a British colonel.")[14] He chatted with her about Hallow Eve and the rainy weather and "supposed the bag was full of good things for the little ones," which phrasing could imply that Maria has a family of her own, with children and perhaps grandchildren. She does not answer until he goes on to say "it was only right that the youngsters should enjoy themselves while they were young," at which she "agreed with him and favoured him with demure nods and hems," and considering he had been "very nice with her," she "thanked him and bowed" as she left the tram. He had "bowed to her" in return "and raised his hat and smiled agreeably," and so as she goes along "bending her tiny head under the rain," she was thinking "how easy it was to know a gentleman even when he has a drop taken." She had not found in this an explanation of his genial volubility; she had felt simply that he had been "very nice with her."

How agreeably flurried and also perhaps half-consciously disturbed she had been by this elderly man's casual assumptions and courtesies becomes apparent when at the Donnellys'—almost immediately after "Everybody said: 'O, here's Maria!' "—it is found she had left the plumcake behind. Maria's reactions, the strongest she displays in the story, are nevertheless muted by her minimizing the crucial factor, her unexpressed consciousness of spinisterhood together with her pleasure in attentions from the colonel-looking gentleman. Now she recalls the episode only in terms of "how confused the gentleman with the greyish moustache had made her" and again she blushes, "with shame and vexation and disappointment." Is all that only for the wasted expenditure and the defeat of her intention to bring "something really nice"? Perhaps her "shame and vexation and disappointment" include more and run deeper and more persistently, but she reduces it to the immediate, at least in her conscious definition of it, when "At the thought of the failure of her little surprise and of the two and fourpence she had thrown away for nothing she nearly cried outright."

With this indirect preparation for its climax the narrative passes into that series of little doings in which Maria's moods alternate from quiet pleasure to apprehension, while the tide of a family's vigorous life flows around her and the reader has an ironic view of the Donnellys' careful yet casual regard for this childlike little old woman. Soothing her for the loss of the plumcake (and as if made half-aware associatively of the irremediable lacks in her life) Joe says it doesn't matter and makes her "sit down by the fire" and is "very nice with her," but he can offer little except an account she scarcely understands of "a smart answer which he had made to the manager" in the office where he works. She remains self-effacing, as in denying any liking for nuts when the nutcracker can't be found, and being "sorry" for having attempted to patch up the brothers' quarrel by putting in a "good word." And as in the laundry, she is shielded like a child. In her accustomed way, she seized upon the illusion offered her, and while the "next-door girls" arranged for the Hallow Eve games, Maria felt that "everything was merry again." These are timid Maria's alternating masks, to make only small demands on life, discreetly, and to magnify what little assurances she receives. That appreciation of a minimal subsistence as human being and its defense against further attrition constitutes the fable of her self-dramatization, which the story's tone subtly embodies. Others' kindly uncritical acceptance of Maria as the least troublesome way of dealing with her creates the story's mild irony, the medium of an almost lyrical characterization, with this slight protagonist become an abstract of the humanly underprivileged.

Hence Mrs. Donnelly's severe reproof to the next-door girls for putting the saucer of clay into the fortune-telling game, and hence Joe's crisis of emotion over Maria's song. At each point the truth about Maria is too closely approached for that slim comfort maintained by her modest persistence and by others' connivance in sustaining the fiction of her importance. Both Mrs. Donnelly and Joe are protecting her from the fact that life has long since passed her by and she has already come most of the way toward her death. They succeed, and perhaps not just because of Maria's simplicity, but since she is always so ready to accept and even amplify what assurances she can find. About the saucer with something she recognizes only as "a soft wet substance," she merely "understood it was wrong that time and so she had to do it over again." When she repeated the first verse of the song instead of going on to the second, "no one tried to show her her mistake" and there is no indication she was conscious of it. Here the reader may go beyond what the Donnellys were witness to; they would have attributed to an old woman's forgetfulness what in longer perspective may seem a summary instance of Maria's defensively repressing into her unconscious the fact that she, unlike the woman of the song, had remained unclaimed.

That such an implication was intended is not demonstrable, but the possibility is there, and close reading will not only admit this but will obviate certain errors that have sprung up around this story, out of a criticism in every sense too partial. It is scarcely possible to assume, as one critic does, that the children trick blindfolded Maria into choosing the clay; she is merely told "to put her hand out in the air"; she then "moved her hand about here and there" and it "descended on one of the saucers." It is more to the main point of the story to assume that the girls who "arranged" the game knew what it traditionally required, and that when Mrs. Donnelly quickly and sternly overruled it by saying "that was no play," she is really considering Maria's vulnerability, though ostensibly the girls are blamed. There is nothing whatever in the text to support the critic's further statement that "Joe scolds the children" nor for supposing "he and his wife arrange that on the next try Maria will choose the prayerbook."[15] In any case, get it she does, whether by happy chance or not, and after Mrs. Donnelly has shifted the mood by playing a reel for the children and Joe has "made Maria take a glass of wine" and in Maria's view "they were all quite merry again," Mrs. Donnelly is still emphasizing the comfortable omen, saying "Maria would enter a convent before the year was out because she had got the prayer-book."

It is not told that Joe and his wife play the game, and presumably they do not, for why should they, since they have marriage, and presumably will neither travel by water nor enter a religious order, nor at their age is death within the coming year likely. That Maria is drawn into the game, blindfolded and "led . . . up to the table amid laughing," is an attention to a guest but also a wry token of her childlike status, not only in her simplicity but in that she is one to whom, despite her years, nothing much has yet happened. Her laughter "while they were putting on the bandage" seems excessive, like that at the laundry when Mooney toasted her, and the phrase "till the tip of her nose nearly met the tip of her chin" is exactly repeated; the parallel, besides indicating the nervousness of a timorous person, may suggest that in this place too and by these people her uniqueness is being considered, playfully but also with regard for her sensibilities. Then when the game's prediction accords with the actual probability that what awaits Maria is nothing but death, Mrs. Donnelly overrules it as an intolerable threat to the fabrication concealing who and what Maria really is—a concealment from herself by her own weaving, and accepted by others as the ready way of being kind to her.

This instinctive protection accorded the childlike Maria comes out most strongly at the story's end, in a scene with the children in the background, tired and sleepy, but still so lively that their mother must tell them to "be quiet and listen to Maria's song." Joe has asked for it, "some little song . . . one of the old songs" and his wife said *"Do, please, Maria!"* and "so Maria had to get up and stand beside the piano"—and in that phrasing again her consciousness is to be felt, her timidity and also her veiled pleasure in being wanted are implicit. The complex implication is continued as Mrs. Donnelly, having played the prelude, must say *"Now, Maria!"* and Maria is "blushing very much."

Like the aging Miss Julia Morkin's "old song" in "The Dead" —"Arrayed for the Bridal"—Maria's offering is incongruous. Joyce, in recounting her forgetful repetition of that first verse of Arline's ballad from *The Bohemian Girl,* gives it in full, with all its ironic unreality as to Maria—the dream of dwelling "in marble halls." Discussing this incident in the story, Phillips George Davies has asserted that the marble halls symbolize death, and finds in Joe's supposed consciousness of this a clarification of his emotional response to Maria's performance.[16] This seems a fragmenting reading, in a too microscopic pursuit of symbols. The marble halls as dreamed of in the song are said to enclose the felicitous life of one who was attended by "vassals and serfs," was "the hope and pride of all," possessed of "riches too great to count" and "a high ancestral name." In the opera itself, which presumably Joe knew, since there is "no music for him like poor old Balfe," the dream has basis in reality; Arline, now grown, has lived for twelve years with gypsies who had abducted her; she is really the daughter of an Austrian count, and the images of that dream are drawn from buried early impressions. That second stanza, which Maria does not go on to, continues Arline's dream, now enlarged by her present sensibilities, of how "suitors . . . knights upon bended knee" had "sought" her hand and "one of that noble host" had "claimed" it. Maria's tolerance of spinsterhood has required her to relinquish any hope of being claimed. Lizzie Fleming in her hearty common way was only joking with the little old maid in predicting for "so many Hallow Eves" that Maria would get the ring from the barmbrack, and Maria's disconcerted laughing until her little body shakes is her attempt to bring the matter down to the level of humorous indifference. So quite possibly her not going on to the second verse is not a simple senile forgetfulness, and in the considerate Donnelly household it is certainly not what one critic suggests, a conscious choice to avoid exposing herself to any danger of "ridicule,"[17] but rather a repression, a subconscious censoring, a willing to forget. In any case, the story as continuum, as composition focused on a characterization, reveals in Maria's uncompleted song of marble halls not a foreshadowing of her end but a suggestion in lengthy retrospect of all that had never begun and come to pass for her. Even so, Maria has more life than is allowed her by some readers too intent on symbols of the "death theme," or that of witch or Blessed Virgin.

In the story of *The Bohemian Girl* there is a further detail as to the song. Both stanzas end with the same lines:

> But I also dreamt, which pleased me most,
> That you loved me still the same.

The situation in the opera is mysterious and hyperromantic: Arline is singing to Thaddeus, high-born Polish political fugitive, also living with the gypsies, and he had been Arline's rescuer, years earlier, from a wild boar. This was in her early childhood, and adjacent to her father's castle, none of which she consciously remembers, nor does she know of Thaddeus except in his present station as the gypsies' associate and one who loves her. At the conclusion of her song-confession of her dream, "Thaddeus presses Arline to his heart," and she asks "And do you love me still?" and he (stout fellow) answers, "More than life itself."[18] The only parallel that a love "still the same" could have now in Maria's subdued reveries would be in the frail but long-standing connection she claims with Joe and Alphy, whom she had helped rear and who had seen her settled in the Dublin by Lamplight Institute. And had not Joe brought her that purse from Belfast, and had she not been invited to the Donnellys' this night? It would seem that the pathos of her dependence, along with the poverty of her life and her forgetfulness in old age, rather than the association of marble halls and death, is what moves Joe through that song. And is not his attributing his emotion so largely to Balfe's music a disguise for his real feelings, which he has come closer to naming in his preceding phrase, "no time like the long ago." Richard B. Hudson, in *The Explicator,* mistakenly (and exaggeratedly) speaking of Joe as Maria's drunken brother, says "he weeps sentimentally for the old days, not for Maria or for himself."[19] But who weeps for the long ago except also for himself in and of it, together with those he knew then? It has been the "talking over old times" with Maria in terms they shared, and Maria's disappointment over the lost plumcake, and then her unconscious mishap with the clay, and finally her singing that song which cumulatively has brought in the note of sadness for Joe as he too knows it in the common involved way of life. In *Dubliners* Joyce unostentatiously sketched the complexity of simplicity, but nowhere with steadier attention than to Maria in "Clay," where even Joe too is to be glimpsed in a nebular swirl of feelings.

With Maria's repetition of the ballad's first verse, now given in full as a transition, the story passes out of her consciousness into simple narrative statement, and perhaps the collective consciousness of the others, in that "no one tried to show her her mistake." Thereafter that final paragraph uses Joe as the medium—another instance of Joyce's practice of diminuendo and withdrawal in these reverberantly inconclusive compositions, yet here too in a way that harmonizes with the whole story, since Joe too, like Maria, seems to be arranging some acknowledged perceptions to keep a screen between him and a fuller, more painful knowledge. The story tells that "when she had ended her song Joe was very much moved," but then it does not veer deeply into his consciousness; what follows is only what he said about "the long ago" and Balfe's music. When he declares his absolute preference for these, "whatever other people might say," he is not posing as antiquarian or musicologist; he is indirectly acknowledging how genuine and profoundly personal is his experience at that moment.

Joe may or may not have read the omen from the saucer of clay with full credence. It is doubtful that he would have attributed Maria's repeating the first stanza to a subconscious evasion of the second, rather than merely an old person's typical lapse. That in itself, however, coupled with the evening's reminiscing and the stout, could have made his eyes so fill with tears "that he could not find what he was looking for." Perhaps he, like most mortals when the pathos of life is brought home in particular terms, is really groping for a principle to connect this instance with the human condition, in which nothing remains "still the same," and at least to see solitariness mitigated in terms of a common fate. But Joe is no tragic poet, nor is little old Maria a heroine of tragedy. So it is to "poor old Balfe" that Joe sentimentally attributes his tears, and what he asked his wife to tell him was "where the corkscrew was," for that too, along with the nutcracker and Maria's plumcake and who knows how much of wistful expectation, seems to have been mislaid during this little segment of devouring time. It would be difficult to conceive a more masterful yet quiet extrication from a scene of great pathos to a point of detachment where all is drawn together thematically, in perspective and with diminution, to let the curtain fall slowly upon a slight but epitomizing effect. Fiction in its essence as a pure art has scarcely gone beyond this.

A PAINFUL CASE

Joyce considered "A Painful Case" one of his two weakest stories, along with "After the Race," and in August, 1906, soon after moving to Rome to clerk in a bank, he set about revising these.[1] Would that he had done a bit more pruning and apportioning, for this story, like the other, is marred in its earlier parts by too heavy-handed presentation of its chief character and his doings. Examined as to alleged sources, especially data concerning Joyce's brother Stanislaus, it also shows lumps of unassimilated and indeed inconsistent detail, and makes suspect the impulses for such inclusions. While "After the Race" carried Joyce into segments of Dublin bourgeois society he knew too little about, "A Painful Case" may have come all too near home. Seen in its possible connections with the man James Joyce rather than Stanislaus, the story may seem in part a protective shield for an uneasy author rather than a proper mask in the fictional presentation of human behavior. The shield is lowered as the story proceeds, as if the artist at last feels Mr. Duffy safely objectified and distanced as a fictional entity, and then the painful case becomes fully that of the protagonist.

Far below the general level of *Dubliners,* the first three pages of "A Painful Case" are a hodgepodge. The most conspicuous flaw is a too obviously calculated attempt to project. In its biographical context this appears an anxious dissociation, irrelevantly extending in certain details to a caricature of Joyce's brother Stanislaus. Yet despite deviousness and ineptitude there does emerge if not quite a portrait at least a fictional silhouette of Mr. James Duffy, the withdrawn and disengaged man. Thereafter the composition moves into a series of actions, his various meetings with the woman he has encountered casually, and their growing association. The continuing story is still largely abstracted, though perhaps with some propriety, since Mr. Duffy's life is by design a flight from the personal and its particulars. After an inconclusive relationship, despite its possibilities, he and the woman part, on his initiative. Four years pass; summarized in one paragraph, they show a further hardening of habits by which Mr. Duffy guarded his solitariness. Finally comes the evening when he reads in his newspaper of the woman's death and the painful manner of it, and at last her case becomes his (under the ambiguous title) as he realizes his life's dead end. Therein the story takes on power, having mounted to a real climax, under the artist's psychological rather than cultural scrutiny, and with a negative epiphany and the onset of a special kind of paralysis for the protagonist.

The plot's precipitating event, Mr. Duffy's meeting Mrs. Sinico at a concert and subsequently seeing her, does have remote biographical connection with Stanislaus. He did converse with a woman at the Rotunda, but he was then seventeen, she between thirty and forty. Their conversation was about music, she having noted his enthusiasm for the performance, and at the concert's end she shook hands and "smiled placidly." Later when the woman met young Stanislaus on the street she stopped him and asked "some conventional questions" about his studies.[2] It is a nice little anecdote of incidental cordiality, but it was also a male-female encounter, and mischievous James claimed a wider use for the matter, after snooping in his brother's diary to read about it. According to Stanislaus, when Joyce came to write the story he attempted to implement ridicule by making Mr. Duffy what he "imagined" Stanislaus "should become in middle age."[3]

Joyce's prophecy was false not only to his staunchest ally but to all further fact. Stanislaus Joyce became a respected teacher, a husband and father, and remained from youth on a more consistent rebel against clericalism than James Joyce, and so unequivocal an opponent of Fascism that he suffered expulsion from Italy and temporary loss of his professorship. "His Triestine friends," says Richard Ellmann in a biographical introduction to *My Brother's Keeper,* "thought of Professor Joyce as like Cato, and there is something of Cato's monumental integrity in his life."[4] Joyce's derogatory forecast about his brother may disclose his own unrest in his lack of geniality and generosity, and the narrative lapses may have come of an ulterior attempt to project such flaws onto a Stanislaus-Duffy in the story's first pages and at points thereafter. Whatever a brother's privilege to pry, the artist had every right to start with Stanislaus's experience and—noting that whenever male and female strangers begin casual conversation, some consciousness of sex may enter—to make Duffy middle-aged and the woman "a year or so younger," and not only married but accompanied by her daughter. From there on the transmuted situation belonged to the realm of fiction, and in the light of the artist's concept, imaginatively composed beyond the initiating fact. However, no such fictional projection could support the satiric notion that Stanislaus would in fact follow Mr. Duffy's course. Here arrogance may have tripped up creativity, for by holding factual source too dearly in mind a fictionist may cling to incongruous detail, and the hazard is more severe if the factual, being colored by animus, is included raw, unassimilated rather than dissolved into the conceptual-aesthetic vision.

Since "A Painful Case" becomes a powerful story, finally appalling in its revelation of the evil done by a leaving undone, some irrelevancies and a recurrent laboriousness in the first pages become the more glaring. Once Joyce got under way, forgot about factual instances and, escaping himself as a sardonic uneasy young man, became himself an engaged artist, the work clarified into its essences. But its beginnings may seem an awkward attempt at disguise, not quite carried off, showing how painfully close was his knowledge of aloofness and withdrawal, and suggesting a fear that fictional display of it might become too openly confessional. Basically James Joyce, though imaginative, was a colder man than Stanislaus, who while more rationally self-disciplined and even pedestrian at times, was also more generous-minded. No one could have known this better than James, who from youth on to well through the period of writing *Dubliners* quite callously profited by his younger brother's firm regard and tolerant loyalty. Aspects of "A Painful Case" may seem to echo this association. Joyce cannily involves himself by oblique use of only a few autobiographical bits. Not only is "A Painful Case" based to begin with on Stanislaus's encounter; Joyce interjects some irrelevant details drawn from his brother, as if to implicate him through the case of Duffy. In many instances from their youth on, Joyce vented a curious tendency to victimize and satirize Stanislaus, in what might be suspected to be a selfish man's compulsive self-exculpation. Joyce was not altogether cold, and indeed there was much evidence in him of deep emotion still more deeply repressed; he was moved to repudiate Mr. Duffy's inhumane detachment, the awful price of which he knowingly describes; but this may have required some self-defensive suppression, and besides Mr. Duffy there was Stanislaus, to be made scapegoat.

Of Mr. Duffy an introductory passage tells that on his desk "lay a manuscript translation of Hauptmann's *Michael Kramer* . . . and a little sheaf of papers" into which "a sentence was inscribed from time to time." Here Joyce touches on both himself and his brother. Joyce had translated *Michael Kramer* and *Vor Sonnenaufgang,* in the summer of 1901;[5] and in "The Day of the Rabblement," in October of that year, he had announced that Ibsen had "already found his successor in the writer of *Michael Kramer*."[6] To align an interest in this play with the "saturnine" nature of Mr. Duffy is not easy, however, whether *Michael Kramer* is read for its glorification of the insurgent and exclusive life of the artist, its example of parental pressure, or its implication of an artist's possible failure to realize and respond to the personal. The first two of these have little or nothing to do with Mr. Duffy, he being neither artist nor parent, nor is his role as son referred to. In the play the neglect of immediate relationship is associated with the intellectual's or artist's withdrawal to a vantage point; Mr. Duffy can figure only as amateur intellectual, a fancier of books, music, and his own dry thoughts, and a habit-bound bank clerk. Moreover, while he is to experience an epiphany in these matters, it comes only at the story's close and is not part of an extended dramatic interaction. If analysis of aloofness were what had interested Duffy enough to lead him to translate the play, could he still have been so impervious to the claims of life that only tardily and under shocking stimulus would he begin to sense his failure? It is as if Joyce struggled to clear himself by secret confession under an alias, despite its lack of sufficient credibility.

As for Duffy's "little sheaf of papers" in which "a sentence was inscribed from time to time," this is drawn from Stanislaus, and Joyce puts two of his brother's aphorisms into the story.[7] One is that "Every bond is a bond to sorrow"—and indeed young Stanislaus had reason to believe so, in his filial and fraternal roles. Mr. Duffy is made to speak the sentence to Mrs. Sinico the night they "agreed" at his insistence "to break off" their relationship. As for the other sentence, Joyce's cribbing it suggests the deplorable fact that people sometimes steal things they don't really need, perhaps under deep compulsion, possibly retaliatory. "Love between man and man is impossible because there must not be sexual intercourse and friendship between man and woman is impossible because there must be sexual intercourse," which young Stanislaus thought worth putting down, is noted also by Mr. Duffy, two months after he parted from Mrs. Sinico, in avoidance of her gesture of affection. Whatever either of the home-grown axioms may have meant to Stanislaus as he struggled into maturity, Joyce's borrowing them for Mr. Duffy in his arid prime suggests ulterior motive, however little realized. Furthermore, a real confusion of purposes enters with use of the phrase "Bile Beans." Not only had Joyce read in his brother's diary "without asking 'May I?' or even saying 'By your leave' "[8] but for that collection of sententious entries which Stanislaus had made on those "loose pages pinned together" James contemptuously suggested "Bile Beans" as a title.[9] Then he transferred the phrase to the story, making it "the headline of an advertisement" which Mr. Duffy —presumably it was he—had cut out and "pasted on to the first sheet" of his notes, and while it is told that this had been done "in an ironical moment," irony is just what rigid, negatively doctrinaire middle-aged Mr. Duffy would seem incapable of, above all at his own expense. Joyce was perhaps conscious of risky deviousness here, which may have prompted the passive statement of the detail: "the headline . . . had been pasted."

To many readers that passage apart from its factual source must have seemed to be sounding a false note, even if unidentifiable. Joyce may be suspected here of clinging too fondly to a relished phrase, superciliously used against Stanislaus. That this indulgence threw him off his narrative stride appears in the next sentence, which is not pointedly relevant, and in the next paragraph, in which resolute resumption of the theme becomes perhaps too obvious. The sentence which trails on after the thrusting in of "Bile Beans"—"On lifting the lid of the desk a faint fragrance escaped—the fragrance of new cedarwood pencils or of a bottle of gum or of an overripe apple which might have been left there and forgotten"—is not impeccably grammatical, but apart from that there is the sense of an effort to get back to the solid desk itself and yet a lapse into what is almost always a weakness of fictional procedure, the indecisive furnishing of this or that or the other—odor of pencils, gum, apples?—which the reader must sort out. The succeeding paragraph, taking determined grip, offers generalizations about Duffy and encloses some description. "Mr. Duffy," it begins, "abhorred anything which betokened physical or mental disorder"—but that makes the overripe forgotten apple in the desk an incongruity.

While it was characteristic of James to make presumptuous use of his brother's diary, and to imagine disparagingly his brother in middle age, nevertheless to take such sharp pleasure in his own phrase "Bile Beans" as to let that irrelevance creep into his story as an uneven characterization was an unusual artistic lapse. Behind Joyce's tensely assumed superiority lay a lack of composure, and beyond that, in "A Painful Case," there seems a perhaps instinctively defensive transfer of blame for coldness to a confusedly fabricated notion about his closest ally. Stanislaus, the first man in the world to recognize and unquestioningly serve Joyce's genius, and one who endured that bond through their most sorrowful youth and early manhoods, was ill-used whetstone, and his stability and forthrightness, as well as his large personal sacrifices, were by implication a reproach to his mercurial, irresponsible, and sometimes equivocal brother. (Ellmann has treated this relationship fully and judiciously.) It was Joyce's imperious need to avoid serving but to be served, and it was his brother's strong fraternal attachment and discerning admiration, together with certain economic and social limitations on both their lives, that kept the connection. Stanislaus Joyce merely put it that Duffy was "a portrait of what my brother imagined I should become in middle age"; hence the comment that Duffy "in most respects was modeled upon Stanislaus"[10] may lead on, if isolated from Ellmann's contexts, into a cliché that will not only be misinformative about Stanislaus but may seem to cover up some of Joyce's fumblings in the characterization of Duffy, whose inconsistent traits should not be mistaken for a close life-study of an actual eccentric.

As for Mr. Duffy's youthful socialism, that too seems swept up into the story through insufficiently controlled associative process beginning with a defensively projected caricature of Stanislaus. Here though the sources are reversed, from Duffy-Stanislaus to Duffy-James, (as with the Hauptmann translation). His brother tells of the times when young James "frequented meetings . . . in back rooms in the manner ascribed to Mr. Duffy," accompanied to "these dimly lit, melancholy haunts" by Stanislaus, who found the socialists' arguments "unconvincing."[11] This rejection was not, however, a withdrawal from political concern; as time showed, it was Joyce who washed his hands of society (though "At Trieste he still called himself a socialist")[12] and it was Stanislaus who endured hardships for his resistance to both monarchical and fascistic politics.[13] But here again the question is not whether a fictionist may borrow, rearrange, and modify; that is his unlimited privilege. Still he may carry into the story only what is relevant to it as it is objectively conceived. Hence his most vexatious problem in using factual sources is to eliminate the casually associated but extraneous, and above all to exclude the incongruous from infiltrating on a tide of personal feeling, especially if self-defensive. Of Mr. Duffy as drawn it is hardly conceivable that he had had such past political interests. If they are postulated it would seem obligatory to show by what drastic impingements his character had been modified. But except in the concluding episode there is no personal progress in the story. While Mr. Duffy may live "at a little distance from his body, regarding his own acts with doubtful side-glances" (in this too the opposite of Stanislaus Joyce), he is at no distance from the dicta he even writes out for himself, and in his equally rigid existence his only apprehension (up until the dark hour of his epiphany) concerns the danger of commitment.

Mr. Duffy's affixing the label Bile Beans to his own aphorisms "in an ironical moment" might seem traceable simply to Joyce's petulant tendency to deride his brother, even to this extent of allowing the extraneous and psychologically incongruent to intrude upon fictional concept; Mr. Duffy's improbable past as socialist, however, having some factual source in Joyce's own youthful ardor and activity, is perhaps a subtler incursion at a deeper level, a drifting closer to fictionally transmuted confession. By this time Joyce had turned his back upon the claims of home, church, and nation, had gone some way in the exemplary dramatization of Stephen's *non serviam,* and, having involved himself with Nora, had also found extremely difficult the challenges of closest intimacy and a steady commitment. In the first pages of "A Painful Case" the unusual ineptitudes and disruptions (beneath which were tangential attempts, now known of, to transfer some sense of fault to a Stanislaus-to-be) suggest a writer not at ease with his subject, in an anxiety more personal than artistic. By this time ambivalence was already Joyce's inescapable doom, and the divided mind was to be discernible in other works of his. That complication is not unique among fictional artists; occasionally their concern with aesthetic distancing may be first of all for their own sakes, and invention may be a paraphrased confession, for a secret self-absolution. What is requisite here is a hand steadier than the heart behind it, and this Joyce usually achieved, in *Dubliners* and later. If the conceiving of Mr. Duffy out of issues of human existence all too closely known caused Joyce to tremble and seek a scapegoat and even so to fumble some early passages, it could have been from the weight of his subject, and terror enough to make possible its sustained intense representation in the story's last pages.

Had the story been more consistently contained, it could scarcely be called a failure of the artist's obligation if nothing were shown of how Mr. Duffy, man and boy, had arrived at his aloofness. That an ingrained and seemingly fixed attitude could abruptly suffer conversion is not incredible, nor without precedent; and in a fiction such reversal supplies a sufficient action. "A Painful Case," without its unassimilated excursions into a past for Mr. Duffy, could then merely define an extreme of the allowable tendency in *Dubliners* to settle on fixed present traits, as well as to enclose the narrative within a limited field of action, as in "Two Gallants," "The Boarding-House," "A Mother," and even "Clay." Seldom does Joyce examine personal development causally in detail and in depth, except for the great dramatically epiphanal stories—the first three and "A Little Cloud" and "The Dead." It is true that in *Dubliners* Joyce's arrested characters are wonderfully each of their own kind, a type and yet fictionally alive, and Joyce is estimable as the painter of idiosyncrasies against a solid background of environment. Such portraiture suits Joyce's concept of Dublin's stagnant, static life. Even the arrivals at epiphanies—usually against the grain of unmodified surroundings—do not promise continuing personal growth, not in the boy of the first three stories, nor in Jimmy Doyle, Little Chandler, or Gabriel Conroy. The improbability of lasting reformation and the likelihood of return to a closed cyclic pattern is the satirical point of "Grace." The ungallant Lenehan and Mr. Doran the incautiously amorous boarder, along with little old Maria, are in decline on a figured gradient; and other Dubliners—Lenehan's leader Corley, Henchy in the committee room, Gallaher at home and abroad, and the brute Farrington—have the awful consistency of the incorrigible. Perhaps with Eveline and Mr. Duffy, despite their differences in age, circumstance, and human qualities, and despite Joyce's different success in objectifying them, he has come to the logical ultimate of his depiction, in these Dubliners' arrival at nothing but a final total apathy. And still, even in its brevity, "Eveline" shows a more consistent evolving of character than can be assumed of Mr. Duffy.

For some readers, a sensed inexplicable discordance in the characterization of Mr. Duffy may have put off recognition of what power the story finally attains and the surer skill as it progresses. It is worth noting blemishes if that can clear the way for sight of the ultimate achievement. Nor are the first pages without some merit. They have, as portraiture, what Joyce spoke of to Stanislaus as "the grim Dutch touch."[14] Mr. Duffy is a roomer in "an old sombre house" well away westward from Dublin's center and from those suburbs he considers "mean, modern, and pretentious." He himself has furnished the room, barely, without carpet or pictures, with bedstead and washstand of iron. His books are shelved "from below upwards according to bulk," with a martinet's superficial notion of order. Their range is from a complete Wordsworth to a Maynooth catechism. (Maynooth, just west of Dublin, is seat of the National Synod; its seminary is a center of theological studies in Ireland, and this catechism would be one prescribed for general use.) Books being often such fortuitous possessions, as accidentally and remotely surviving some break-up as pieces of driftwood, a catechism and a Wordsworth may vaguely hint a past but seem less instructive about that than a present frame for Mr. Duffy, set as he is in dead center at some distance from what each implies, for he had "neither companions nor friends, church nor creed." Now and then, with what is indeed "an odd autobiographical habit," he would compose "a short sentence about himself" but "in the third person and . . . the past tense"—seemingly combining a child's egoistic self-dramatization and a valetudinarian's detachment. "He never gave alms to beggars and walked firmly, carrying a stout hazel." For "many years" a bank cashier, he always lunched at the same place, on lager beer and arrowroot biscuits, and he always dined at "an eating-house in George's Street where he felt himself safe from the society of Dublin's gilded youth." Of an evening he played his landlady's piano or roamed about the city's outskirts; his furthest excursion beyond his routines was to an opera or a concert, especially to hear Mozart.

This then is the man, now middle-aged, who is casually addressed by the elder of two ladies sitting next to him at a concert at the Rotunda. They converse and he attends; in Joyce's floundering description of what Duffy sees, "the grim Dutch touch" becomes a large smear:

> The eyes were very dark blue and steady. Their gaze began with a defiant note but was confused by what seemed a deliberate swoon of the pupil into the iris, revealing for an instant a temperament of great sensibility. The pupil reasserted itself quickly, this half-disclosed nature fell again under the reign of prudence, and her astrakhan jacket, moulding a bosom of a certain fulness, struck the note of defiance more definitely.

Whereupon Joyce escaped to a new paragraph and a later time. Meeting the woman at another concert, Mr. Duffy "seized" the opportunity "to become intimate." How he goes about it is not shown; no dialogue is reproduced, and the summary of conversation is limited to essential data. It is as if Joyce, ostensibly to show Mr. Duffy's aridity, but possibly for more personal reasons, tends to keep the reader too at a little distance. However, the story does progress, and the substance of the episode though sparse is credible. The woman has a husband (captain of a merchant vessel plying between Dublin and Holland) whom she mentions but not in a tone to warn off Mr. Duffy. Perhaps he saw her as not inaccessible, for when he encountered her a third time "he found courage to make an appointment," and thereafter they walked together often, in the evenings, in quiet regions. To avoid stealth, he insisted on being asked to her house. "Captain Sinico encouraged his visits, thinking that his daughter's hand was in question," and moreover, he "had dismissed his wife so sincerely from his gallery of pleasures that he did not suspect that anyone else would take an interest in her." This plainly implies the double loneliness of a woman whose husband is absent much of the time and shows no intimate concern when at home; it makes more pitiable her turning to another, and it adds a cruel irony in that the one turned to is essentially a more distant man than her husband.

Neither she nor Duffy "had had any such adventure before and neither was conscious of any incongruity," Joyce writes, still struggling with this ambiguously conceived subject matter and not always making it real. As the story moves into episode it becomes more credible, though scene is still compressed and dialogue summarized. When "in return for his theories she gave out some facts of her own life" (an epitome of their antithetical natures) she could then urge him to reciprocate. He is led to tell of former association with the Irish Socialist Party, in which he had considered himself "a unique figure," and from which he had dissociated himself when intimate group discussions began; now he can proclaim that Dublin would see "no social revolution" for some centuries. She listened; she suggested he "write out his thoughts." With the "careful scorn" of the cynical and self-isolated he refuses to "compete with phrasemongers" or "submit himself to the criticisms of an obtuse middle class which entrusted its morality to policemen and its fine arts to impresarios." Yet even this intransigent man seems gradually touched, in evenings alone with Mrs. Sinico in her "cottage outside Dublin," speaking "little by little . . . of subjects less remote," in a mode that "wore away the rough edges of his character, emotionalized his mental life," as Joyce curiously defines it. Now sometimes "he caught himself listening to the sound of his own voice." Yet on this verge of self-examination and possible epiphany, and while he consciously "attached the fervent nature of his companion more and more closely to him," what he heard was "the strange impersonal voice which he recognized as his own, insisting on the soul's incurable loneliness." (This could shadow forth Joyce, who attached many to him but remained aloof from most.) And on this theme Mr. Duffy had discoursed more than once, but then one night the woman, as if in positive contradiction, made a passionate gesture of affection, pressing his hand to her cheek.

Mr. Duffy was "very much surprised" and also "disillusioned" by her misinterpretation of his words; this suggests not only feebleness of impulse to begin with but in the progress of events a dull lack of intuition. Nor is his reversal made on moral grounds but in defense of his isolation; this is the man who has admitted to himself that "in certain circumstances he would rob his bank," but had preferred tidier arrangements, for their inconspicuousness and avoidance of any more drastic involvement than that through a cashier's guarded window. So after the woman's sudden display of emotion he waited a week and then wrote to arrange what he intended should be "their last interview." Here narrative compression, with a few select details, more strongly suggests his withdrawal to remote and neutral ground; it is told merely that in "cold autumn weather . . . they wandered up and down the roads of the Park for nearly three hours." What they agreed upon was "to break off," on the basis of the principle Mr. Duffy lays down—"every bond, he said, is a bond to sorrow." In his anxiety to extricate himself he was despicably inconsiderate; as they walked to the tram she was to take "she began to tremble so violently that, fearing another collapse on her part, he bade her good-bye quickly and left her."

Mrs. Sinico having sent back his books and music, Mr. Duffy "returned to his even way of life," which is not to be interrupted for four years. He has proceeded to Nietzsche—whom Joyce had discovered while a young Dubliner and probably drew upon, according to Ellmann, "when he expounded to his friends a neo-paganism that glorified selfishness, licentiousness, and pitilessness, and denounced gratitude and other 'domestic virtues' "[15] —but what Mr. Duffy made of Nietzsche is not told. Infrequently he added to his sheaf of aphorisms, and on this point too Joyce's odd intent to make wry use of Stanislaus diverted him, to what is filched from his brother's notebook and propounded as Mr. Duffy's reflection two months after his severance from Mrs. Sinico: "Love between man and man is impossible because there must not be sexual intercourse and friendship between man and woman is impossible because there must be sexual intercourse." This piece of juvenilia, shakily antithetical and denying the possible coincidence of love and friendship, nevertheless does not exclude friendship between men nor love between man and woman, neither of which Mr. Duffy will have. And the most incongruous thing about Stanislaus's aphorism as Mr. Duffy's product is that it is saturated with strong sexuality. In Mr. Duffy there was no such urgency; had there been, a woman's pressing his hand to her cheek, after prolonged and agreeable acquaintance, would have brought the most proper response. Instead, after the breaking-off he had even "kept away from concerts lest he should meet her." Otherwise during those four years he had held to his regularized way of life, "and every evening walked home from the city after having dined moderately in George's Street and read the evening paper for dessert."

With that simple fact Joyce finds a neat narrative transition into the last episode, that night when the customary newspaper jolts Mr. Duffy out of his fixed habits of mind. A paragraph arrested him, he read it "attentively," pushed aside his plate, reread the account "over and over again." He ate no more of his dinner; he walked home, going rapidly and then at a slackened pace. In his room he "read the paragraph again by the failing light of the window." Now Joyce reproduces the painful story, to the extent of over two pages, concerning Mrs. Sinico; she had tried to cross tracks at a station and had been killed by a train. Testimony by her husband and her daughter revealed that for two years she had been "rather intemperate in her habits" and of late would go out at night "to buy spirits." The Deputy Coroner, having heard witnesses of the accident, and after due expressions of sympathy, had declared in conclusion that "No blame attached to anyone."

The "Death of a Lady at Sydney Parade Station," so headlined, was subheaded "A Painful Case," and it becomes that for Mr. James Duffy too, by several stages which constitute a document in psychosomatic response and dramatize a moral crisis wherein the Joycean themes of epiphany and paralysis are merged. Mr. Duffy's first reactions are on two levels, incredulity and loss of appetite. He does not care for the rest of his corned beef and cabbage and he reads the newspaper account over and over. However prompt the involuntary visceral reaction, his conscious defenses are at first in good working order. Whether or not the coroner was right that "no blame attached to anyone," Mr. Duffy is not going to let any attach to him. He is "revolted" by this "commonplace vulgar death" and by the recall of previous intimacy with this woman so evidently "unfit to live, without any strength of purpose." In this vein he the habit-ridden man is made to condemn her as "an easy prey to habits." Feeling "degraded" and "deceived" by his association with her, he now "interpreted . . . in a harsher sense" her emotional gesture toward him, and "had no difficulty now in approving the course he had taken."

But later as he looked out from his bare room into the failing November light his desperate self-justification failed, and as "his memory began to wander he thought her hand touched his." (Here Joyce, again too anxiously expository, thinks it necessary to say that "The shock which had first attacked his stomach was now attacking his nerves.") Escaping from the house, Mr. Duffy was met by cold air; "it crept into the sleeves of his coat." He took refuge in a public-house and had a hot punch and then another, sitting aloof from the workingmen drinking from "huge pint tumblers" and smoking and "spitting often on the floor." Now there sets in for Mr. Duffy a gradually intensifying ordeal of self-examination, and for the reader a dreadful spectacle of shamed confession and useless regret, with its still more appalling sequel. Its stages and steps are narrated closely and with psychological penetration. At first Mr. Duffy evokes alternately his memories of her and the derogatory image he had tried to substitute, but with the fact of her death increasingly realized, he "began to feel ill at ease," and then at last to interrogate himself—"what else could he have done" and "how was he to blame"? Now he senses "how lonely her life must have been," and thereby he begins to glimpse the barrenness of his own.

Leaving the public-house, going into the cold gloomy night, he took the paths in Phoenix Park "where they had walked four years before," and with a growing sense of her nearness, almost of her voice, her touch, he must ask himself "Why had he withheld life from her? Why had he sentenced her to death?" At this thought he "felt his moral nature falling to pieces." Since that moral nature has been constituted of little but caution, abstention, and negation, he can realize that he has also withheld life from himself; and when "he saw some human figures lying" in the shadowy park, their "venal and furtive loves filled him with despair," as one "outcast from life's feast." Agenbite as well as famishment is suggested in the phrase, "He gnawed the rectitude of his life." From himself his thoughts go back to the woman he had "denied . . . life and happiness," and seeing her as the one human being who "had seemed to love him," he saw in himself the one who "had sentenced her to ignominy, a death of shame." Now this man who had chosen isolation could not escape from it. He was aware that "the prostrate creatures" in the shadows "were watching him and wished him gone," and again he knows himself "outcast from life's feast," feeling it as he sees these others making love, and a second time sensing that lovers would reject him as he had rejected love.

Mr. Duffy is to go one more step, from an empty epiphany to a kind of paralysis. The laborious rhythm of a train leaving Dublin reiterated for him the syllables of her name, but as "he turned back the way he had come" he "began to doubt the reality of what memory told him." The suppressed acknowledgments which had struck first his stomach, then his nerves, and finally his full consciousness had become so painful that they must be put down once more, with that selective amnesia which is the ego's defense and in which he was already so practiced. Halting, he allowed the train's rhythm to "die away." Now he "could not feel her near" nor hear "her voice touch his ear," and having waited "for some minutes listening," he "could hear nothing." In the "perfectly silent" night "He felt that he was alone." He has accomplished the death of his own heart. Epiphany so illuminating can leave blank dark behind, especially for the mind already as bent toward negation as was Mr. Duffy's. Eveline, with her cataleptic grip upon the iron railing at the North Wall, is shown as victim of environment; Mr. Duffy's painful case furnishes no data on his earlier conditioning, and so his end, with the self-defensive erasure of memories and the onset of silence and solitude, seems more fully what he has willed, repeatedly, out of original pride, in all his sinnings against the spirit. The tale, so broadly admonitory as to hardness of heart and separation by self-righteousness, seems to have so touched Joyce himself as to disconcert him in the writing of it. No other story in *Dubliners* so exposes its author's ambivalence, and in its essence—not clear-cut dilemma but that troubled oscillation between repression and recognition that can tend to neutralize emotion. Sardonically Joyce the young Dubliner had prophesied a grimly barren future for his brother, but there could well have been at the back of the artist's mind an apprehension of such a judgment upon himself. Was it the anxious attempt to project this fate upon a Stanislaus-Duffy which so troubled the story in its course and at points so muddied its surface? But the story's imperfections are transcended by the sustained power of its somber denouement.

Taking its place with the more profoundly psychological and emotionally resonant stories, "A Painful Case" also supplies a counterpoint in the relatively unified collection. It reinforces especially the great epiphanal pieces, "A Little Cloud" and "The Dead," by citing in its extremity the fatal impoverishment which their protagonists rise above, and by embodying the humanistic view that the ultimate hazards are moral. Joyce did remain in Ireland, in spirit at least, and enough to envision a boy "penitent" for superciliousness toward a playmate; Joyce remained to sense and show the deep springs of Little Chandler's "remorse"; he remained to believe the splendid woman Gretta Conroy was not deceived when she called Gabriel "generous" nor Gabriel wrong either in "shameful consciousness" of himself or in his accepting involvement with mankind, comprising "all the living and the dead." Whether Joyce thereafter escaped a more stringent net than any Stephen named is a question in psychography; but that he knew it was there, this other net, not just in Ireland but in the human situation, and knew it could enfold and gradually deaden, is painfully told of in Mr. James Duffy's case.

IVY DAY IN THE COMMITTEE ROOM

Joyce incidentally but clearly cited "Ivy Day" as a favorite. In a letter on May 20, 1906, during contentions with Richards about the proposed publication of *Dubliners,* Joyce defended "Two Gallants" by terming it "the story (after *Ivy Day in the Committee Room*) which pleases me most."[1] Robert Scholes has indicated "a letter not yet published," also to Richards, of October 22, 1906, in which Joyce again gives "Ivy Day" highest place by repeating the comparison.[2] It was made, according to Scholes's brief report of the passage, as "among the first thirteen stories," which leaves out "A Little Cloud" and "The Dead." The latter was not written until after Joyce left Rome in March, 1907, but "A Little Cloud," according to Ellmann, had been "inserted" into "the whole manuscript in a slightly altered form" which Joyce sent back to Richards on July 9, 1906,[3] with "The Dead" still to come. However, Stanislaus Joyce makes the preference completely inclusive: "Of all the stories in *Dubliners,* 'Ivy Day' was the one my brother said he preferred."[4] Whether Joyce put it first among the whole fifteen of the finally published collection or only among thirteen or fourteen of them, such a striking preference perhaps suggests something about his attitude toward his work at this stage, and even about the man himself.

Surely Joyce had a right to be well pleased with "Ivy Day." It revealingly deploys a considerable cast of Dubliners, it epitomizes the post-Parnellian decline of Irish politics, and technically it is an almost perfect piece, significantly expressive too of major Joycean themes. It could be speculated further, though, that Joyce valued it for its uniqueness in its complete independence of the characters' subjective life, which in most of the other stories is not only insistent but more or less tortuous. Here is another sort of fictional composition, never extending into the dimension of unvoiced thought or feeling. It is largely conversation, and less in the Joycean short story mode than that of the one-act play, but with quite enough description and narrated action to "produce" it in the mind's eye and ear. The only considerable lapse in this scrupulously objective dramatic presentation is in the paragraph which tells why Mr. Crofton remained silent, one reason being that "he considered his companions beneath him."

In particular, Joyce may have felt more at ease with this story because he was quite removed from its source. "My brother," writes Stanislaus Joyce, "was never in a committee room in his life." All the story's substance "except the poem" was furnished him, in a letter and in conversation, by Stanislaus, who had served as clerk to his father, "temporarily engaged as election agent and canvasser for a candidate in the municipal elections" in the autumn of 1902.[5] (This further indicates a factual frame; King Edward VII did come to Ireland in July, 1903, after postponing a proposed visit in 1902, and in general he was received with a full measure of Irish warmth, yet less than three weeks before his arrival the Corporation of Dublin had voted down, 40 to 37, the much disputed proposal, touched on in the story, to present him with a municipal address of welcome, a refusal repeated when the King came again in the spring of 1904.)[6]

Of more import as to the work of fiction is the contrast between Stanislaus Joyce's severely matter-of-fact observations and the artist's intuitive transmuting and dramatic formulation of the material. Tindall, in suggesting the poem in the story may resemble the famous lost "Et tu, Healy" Joyce wrote at the age of nine, calls Hynes's effusion "tawdry" yet "well-meant,"[7] and Joyce has made Hynes's intentions creditable throughout, but Stanislaus still saw him as a "wastrel," and calls all that he himself had witnessed a "many-faceted squalor, its personages below human interest." He finds "tolerance" and "compassion" in Joyce's fictionizing of the account, but considers this not for its deep empathy with Hynes but only as a rising above "the contagion of that experience."[8] Stanislaus was not to be the only reader who has tended to see Joyce's "Ivy Day" as all of a piece and neglected the implied thematic stress between extremes in Henchy and Hynes. A sufficiently close viewing of the story might well trace repetitiously over its course, following through each character, to identify him as a human type, an individual Dubliner, and a separate factor in the eddies of this seemingly so casual and inconclusive action. Such systematic examination of the *dramatis personae* one by one, returning to given points to recognize each in his uniqueness then and there, can enlarge awareness of how brilliant, technically, is Joyce's easy yet weightily implicative deployment of the numerous, minute, and disparate details. At the least, it might help any who, like Frank O'Connor, could not "profess to understand" the story[9]—though he nevertheless presumed to discuss it.

Like a one-act play, "Ivy Day" has complete unity of time and place. Both are important, for this is the anniversary of Parnell's death, the sixth of October (apparently in 1902, since the king has not yet visited Ireland but there has been talk of his coming) and the scene is an ill-lit, inadequately heated room used as base by an odd lot of needy hangers-on canvassing in a municipal election, besides others who stray in and out. The Nationalist candidate for the Corporation (the body composed of Lord Mayor, Aldermen, and Councillors, who elect a new Lord Mayor each year and act upon other civic matters) is Mr. Richard J. Tierney, P.L.G.—which stands for Poor Law Guardian and indicates a fellow already in the political swim. He is also, it appears, a publican. The territory being canvassed in his behalf is the Royal Exchange Ward, in the very heart of Dublin. That Joyce was intent on thus centrally locating the story is implied by his writing Stanislaus to verify that Aungier and Wicklow streets are in this area.[10] The ward's northern boundary extends along the Liffey's south bank inclusively from

Essex to Aston's quays, and a suggestion could be derived from its bordering the deep tidal basin in the river below Grattan Bridge from which the name Dublin can be derived, through the Gaelic *Dubh Linn,* dark pool;[11] but Joyce probably was more concerned with immediate actualities. Royal Exchange Ward included busy Dame Street, the Bank, and the Castle, seat of English authority, and around these were streets crowded with Dublin's commerce. Just to the east of the ward are Trinity College (Protestant), the public buildings including the National Library, to which Joyce and his friends and Stephen likewise resorted, and St. Stephen's Green, and University College (Catholic) and, a bit beyond, fashionable Merrion Square; just west of the ward are the two old cathedrals, both Church of Ireland—St. Patrick's, where Swift was Dean, and Christ's Church—surrounded by one of Dublin's oldest and most dilapidated regions. Aungier Street, which the character O'Connor had been diffidently canvassing until the rain drove him in to steam his leaky shoes by the low fire, is a sort of spine to the ward, a main thoroughfare north and south; the committee room is close to the center of affairs, there on Wicklow Street just to the south of Dame Street and southwest of College Green, in the midst of a Dublin of differences.

Some sense of these will contribute to a full reading of the story. Too often it is seen as a naturalistic monochrome, all in a sort of dull dirty Dublin sepia. But there is both dark and light here, and the glossy green of the ivy leaf is disclosed, in its minuteness and isolation the more striking, like a touch of red in a Corot. Actually no piece in the collection shows greater interplay of opposed forces within what on the surface looks like a fairly unified Irish scene. The deep stresses, though primarily political, penetrate to socio-ethical issue. This little play has its modest hero too, a quiet man, circumstantially beset, but unbroken. He is Joe Hynes, and even his antithesis, the completely opportunistic Henchy, has to concede that he's "one of them . . . that didn't renege him." This is Parnell they are then speaking of, and while it is hazardous and may be presumptuous to propose a defining connection by following any Joyce character from one book to another, perhaps with the steadfast Joe Hynes it is permissible. In *Ulysses,* a couple of years later, he is seen at the cemetery, the same man: "Let us go round by the chief's grave, Hynes said. We have time." If he still had time, it was not because he had nursed illusions; when Mr. Powers mused that "Some say he is not in that grave at all. That the coffin was filled with stones. That one day he will come again," Hynes "shook his head." But he does not pronounce, as had Henchy in the committee room, that Parnell "is dead," implying that's that, and what's next and what will be in it for us. In the cemetery that day Hynes spoke the relinquishing but still loving elegy: "Parnell will never come again, he said. He's there, all that was mortal of him. Peace to his ashes."[12]

Bloom had reflected, a bit earlier, that "People talk about you a bit: forget you. . . . Even Parnell. Ivy Day dying out."[13] But Joyce never quite forgot what was perhaps his boyhood's one lasting parental inculcation, an apotheosis of Parnell. The force of that uncompromising attachment was translated into the brilliantly dramatic scene in *A Portrait* which recalls the Joyces' Christmas dinner in 1891, a few weeks after Parnell's death, and reflects the actual tears of his father and his father's friend John Kelly,[14] in the violent altercation with that female relative Stanislaus called "the most bigoted person" he "ever had the misadventure to encounter."[15] The boy Joyce declared allegiance to his parent's hero in the lost precocious poem, "Et tu, Healy," denouncing the disloyalty of Parnell's associates.[16] This youthful involvement in his father's and fatherland's political conflicts could have added to Joyce's morbid tendency to distrust his Irish friends; it may have been too the real beginning of a general detachment and skepticism. Padraic Colum has remarked: "What passion a boy of ten or eleven must have known as he watched Parnell's downfall! Was it this that separated him from all political interests?"[17] While such pinpointing of the conditioning of a fixed outlook is perhaps an oversimplification, Parnell as great historic reality was a weighty influence.

Moreover, Joyce, who seems to have remembered everything and to whom in his studied detachment still nothing was negligible, assimilated his memories subjectively in a range from utter antipathy to self-identification. Stanislaus reports that while Joyce "stood aloof" from a national struggle of which "Parnell's name became the symbol," he sensed the man as heroic figure in "the tragedy of dedication and betrayal."[18] Moreover, Colum's question about separation from political interests might as well have been extended to Joyce's separation from the Church, since in part his father's denunciation of Parnell's enemies extended to the hierarchy, as the scene in *A Portrait* implies.

At any rate, "Ivy Day," beneath the factual substance Stanislaus had furnished him, has roots deep in some of Joyce's most enduring memories and their severe emotions. All the more remarkable, therefore, is his coolly objective representation of the matter. That objectivity, however, is confined to an aesthetic technique. Conceptually the story is not neutral; it not merely invites but necessitates discrimination among the actors and as to the variegated texture of this slice of Dublin life. That oppositions are only guardedly revealed and never come decisively to an issue is of special importance in this defining of Dublin's paralysis as a strained impasse rather than mere stagnancy. Joyce's Dubliners here revealed in passing are not placid robots dominated by a strictly stabilized culture; they are restive men evasive along the vague boundaries of an obscure interminable cold warfare, or are glimpsed sniping from one sector and another. Dublin early in the new century was still caught up in the last decades of the old; it was ground of all too many inherited beliefs and interests and complex hostilities in pursuit of them. The meandering talk in the committee room crackles faintly but continuously with these stresses, and the conclusion is no mere tableau of Irish sentimentality, it is a ranging of several representative men at some distance from each other, incompatibly and irreconcilably, under the pretenses of a shabby *modus vivendi*. Indeed, what Joyce wrote in Trieste in the summer of 1905 about Dublin on Ivy Day in 1902 might even be read as a transcription of ancestral voices of a sort, prophesying war and more war, by implication, and all in a murky atmosphere of making do.

Realization of the story's dialectical structure and its thematic filaments can be strengthened, therefore, by tracing out each profile among the main actors. The time is the latter part of an inclement day, a meager fire is burning low in the committee room in Wicklow Street, old Jack the caretaker is there with one of the canvassers, O'Connor, "a grey-haired young man," who has come in out of the wet with his leaky boots and his lack of present conviction. Yet when he lights a cigarette, with a strip indifferently torn from one of his candidate's canvassing cards, the flame shows up "a leaf of dark glossy ivy" in his lapel. Tierney, the candidate, hasn't said "when he'd be back." Later the talk is to recur not to his coming but to something of more concern, whether and when he's going to send along the promised dozen of stout and pay their much-needed wages. Meanwhile between the two of them old Jack continued to complain about his son, nineteen, irresponsible, already given to drink, and inclined (not surprisingly) to assume "th' upper hand" whenever he sees his father has "a sup taken."

Hynes enters, "a tall, slender young man with a light brown moustache," but with no protection against the rain except his soaked hat and turned-up coat collar; he calls out before the others can see him, jestingly asking, "Is this a Freemasons' meeting?" and, with dramatic irony, he twice inquires "What are you doing in the dark?" He is not a Tierney man, but supports Colgan, "a good honest bricklayer," who will "represent the labour classes," those who produce everything, who are not just "looking for fat jobs" for relatives, and are not "going to drag the honour of Dublin in the mud to please a German monarch" —which Hynes then translates to the old man as no "address of welcome to Edward Rex if he comes here next year." Hynes communicates his poor opinion of "Tricky Dicky Tierney" to O'Connor, who is reduced to the simple hope of being paid, at least. Then, with a suggestive parallelism, another ivy leaf is revealed; O'Connor's had not been lit up till he put the flame from the torn canvassing card to his cigarette; now Hynes's comes into view when he turns down his wet coat collar. He points to it and says, "If this man was alive we'd have no talk of an address of welcome," and O'Connor says "That's true" and the old man laments: "Musha, God be with them times! There was some life in it then."

Here there enters another canvasser and a key figure, Henchy, who nods "curtly" to Hynes, asks for more coal on the fire, and speaks abusively of Tierney for postponing payment. Hynes leaves; Henchy thinks him a spy for Tierney's opponent, but O'Connor mildly defends Hynes, and Henchy's charges against the opposition become more generally insinuative. In comes Father Keon, looking for the politician Fanning; and goes again, and his obscure status as clerical black sheep is discussed with the peculiar delicacy accorded such cases. Henchy has obsequiously carried a candle to light him down the stairs. (This is an upper room, as certain symbol-fanciers will not fail to note, but it might be more broadly considered how any of these men are to find their way out of all this.) Henchy shows a wry kind of feeling in his remark about the priest's entry—"God forgive me, I thought he was the dozen of stout." Its delay leads to more derogation of Tierney, but then it arrives and Tierney is not so bad, and the main problem is the borrowing of a corkscrew from next door. In come Lyons and Crofton, two other canvassers; Crofton, though, has come over to Tierney only after the Conservative candidate withdrew. The borrowed corkscrew has been returned, so their bottles of stout are set by the fire to pop the corks, while the talk drifts from canvassing to the question of welcoming the English king, which Henchy favors for its bringing an "influx of money" but O'Connor and Lyons oppose. They variously introduce the name of Parnell—O'Connor on principle, to which Henchy answers abruptly that Parnell is dead, while Lyons disparagingly attempts a parallel between the King's and Parnell's scandalous private lives.

At this point Hynes returns, Henchy offers him stout, and

O'Connor says they were just talking about "the Chief" and asks Hynes to give them "that thing you wrote." Reluctantly, saying "O, that thing is it. . . . Sure, that's old now," and no doubt feeling this is scarcely a fit place for it, he solemnly recites his florid verses on the death of Parnell. Silence follows, then clapping, the popping of a cork, and conventional commendations, with which the story closes. That is all there is to "Ivy Day in the Committee Room" by way of action; it is open-structured, desultory and inconclusive. Some people have come and gone, others have come and stayed, and one, Hynes, has come and gone and returned—as has the name of Parnell. There has been political gossip, personal innuendo, and some argument, but to no end; and the story ceases with a principled man's reciting a deeply felt even if mediocre poem of his own writing about the hero dead and gone, and an insincere opportunistic man's affecting an enthusiastic response, while the most nearly neutral one among them covers all over with a safely perfunctory remark of approval. Even at this point theme is not made explicit, but there is a gathering up of implications accumulated about these Dubliners, all more or less of a class, but diverse individuals, projecting from their variance the paralyzing disharmony that further stultifies a disillusioned, semi-paralyzed people.

On this chilly wet day, in this temporarily occupied room with bare walls "except for a copy of an election address," the fire has a special meaning. One critic connects it with hell,[19] but this seems almost a conditioned professional reflex rather than a reading of the story. Recurrently the fire glows as quite other than hellish; by igniting the torn Tierney card for O'Connor's cigarette, it lights up the ivy leaf in his lapel. The "whitening dome of coals" is fanned as best he can by old Jack, whose "crouching shadow ascended the opposite wall," almost a form of Ireland with his anger at his son for drunkenness the father himself is prone to, and his lamenting the days of Parnell and the "life in it then," while wondering "what kind of people is going at all now?" One pervasive kind going at a great rate is

Henchy, the unprincipled man, who at one point "spat so copiously that he nearly put out the fire." The stingy provision of coal, far from symbolizing hell's decline, is a measure of the canvassers' not impecunious but ungenerous employer, the publican Tierney. There is little warmth and less illumination in this place, but what burns so low is still a fire, and when candles are lit they only bring the cold bareness of the room into view. What prompts the old man to fetch them is when Hynes, the man of principle, comes in and asks and asks again, "What are you doing in the dark?" He might have added that there was no human comfort in what these candles illuminated. Physical comfort is what Henchy demands on entering, rubbing his hands over the fire "as if he intended to produce a spark from them." And he makes practical use of the fire to pop corks from the bottles of stout.

Of this utilitarian gesture, with its display of petty officiousness, Frank O'Connor wrote that "There is no doubt this episode has been contrived to suggest the three volleys fired over the dead hero's grave."[20] Himself a practiced narrator, O'Connor could have done better than to pose as a newer critic. The so-called "episode" in its contexts is not "contrived" in any such artful sense; the poppings occur at irregular intervals in the course of realistic drama, not with anything like a rhythmic ceremonious formality, and Lyons and Crofton must wait on them. Most significantly, at the story's end when the cork flew out of the bottle set there for Parnell's steadfast disciple and elegist Hynes, he "did not seem to have heard the invitation." This plainly separates him from the others, but most of all from Henchy, who in his "trick" with the bottles is the merely expedient and pretentious man. O'Connor's symbolical reading of the popping corks (which he repeated in another book)[21] can scarcely stand up against the telling detail of Hynes's seeming not to hear.

Over this committee room and what transpires therein hang the shadows of two men. One is Parnell, whose day it is—the anniversary of his death on October 6, 1891, more than a decade before these events. It is also in an obverse sense the day of a different man, the candidate Tierney. He is silhouetted as a substantial person, a publican, with "three places of business" and "extensive house property in the city"—which guarantees that he will "keep down the rates." But he does not have the unqualified regard of his canvassers, who judge him pragmatically by the low supply of coal and the delay in the arrival of the stout. Henchy in his assertive way is most outspoken against him, and calls him "little shoeboy" and "mean little tinker," who "hasn't got those little pigs' eyes for nothing," a "mean little shoeboy of hell," and the abusive term recurs when Henchy says he "asked that little shoeboy three times" about sending the stout, but "he was leaning on the counter in his shirt-sleeves" (no doubt in his pub) and talking to an alderman, leading Henchy to suspect some sort of deal, perhaps involving election as Lord Mayor. Henchy's vocabulary, which besides "tinker" and "shoeboy" includes "little hop-o'-my-thumb," is plainly abusive, as is apparent from Hynes's refusal to let him apply one of his words, "tinker" (gypsy, clumsy mender, bungler), to the other candidate, the "honest bricklayer" Colgan.

Amazingly, one prominent Joyce scholar has thrust a supernumerary adolescent into this story, remarking that "Even the teen-agers are flippant and disrespectful to their elders. Mr. Henchy, seeking the support of the shoe-boy, is told: '. . . when I see the work going on properly I won't forget you, you may be sure.' "[22] This failure in reading not only neglects the context and mistakes a condescending and soothing tone for flippancy, it passes over the question of what "support" a political canvasser would be "seeking" from a minor, or indeed who is to give whom what kind of "support." What Mr. Henchy was after at that point was a day's pay and the dozen of stout for the committee room; he sought it from their candidate-employer, the publican Tierney. When the stout comes, Henchy pronounces Tierney "not so bad after all," although like most minor politicians apparently his soul is mortgaged, since "Fanning has such a loan of him"; thus Henchy cannot apply a stock phrase of liberal allowance without further derogation—Tierney "means well," but "in his own tinpot way."

That Tierney is the typical opportunistic politician is implied by Henchy's reported method of canvassing for him—"He's in favour of whatever will benefit this country." To Henchy's mind this includes supporting the proposed address of welcome to the English King. O'Connor and Lyons, although working for Tierney, are against the address; and Hynes, aligned with the opposition, has rhetorically declared the Irish workingman, represented by the candidate Colgan, "is not going to drag the honour of Dublin in the mud to please a German monarch." Finally when Lyons puritanically suggests that the scandal in Parnell's life could be found paralleled in the King's, the analogy is rejected outright by Henchy as an irrelevance. As the episode now evolves, both the "little shoeboy" Tierney and the naughty King as topics are eclipsed by the shade of Parnell. Mr. O'Connor would not have "any bad blood" stirred up on this anniversary; Mr. Crofton, who is not of the inner circle, having come over to Tierney in the absence of a Conservative candidate, announces that his "side of the house" respected Parnell "because he was a gentleman." Later, when O'Connor calls for it and Hynes recites his poem, "The Death of Parnell," under that evocation the presence is complete and commanding, and O'Connor and Hynes himself are deeply touched. But then the august shade is dissolved as Henchy with pat enthusiasm calls on Crofton for his opinion, and "Mr. Crofton said that it was a very fine piece of writing."

One scholar has critically termed this "an anticlimactic, inconsequential remark."[23] Padraic Colum, in his introduction to the Modern Library edition of *Dubliners,* sees it as indicative of Crofton's "fine reserve," and suggests that as "a former canvasser for the Conservative faction" he "must have felt a taint of treason in the verses," but as " a man of the world" he attempted to be "tolerant." Colum adds that "his aloofness is felt."[24] R. M. Adams, however, sees Crofton throughout "in the role of a silent, stupid, and somewhat arrogant hanger-on."[25] Whatever Crofton may be, Henchy has had to admit that "he's a decent chap" even though "not worth a damn as a canvasser," and when in the story "Grace" his Protestantism is referred to, Kernan called him "a damned decent Orangeman" and reported of him in that character—"*Kernan,* he said, *we worship at different altars,* he said, *but our belief is the same.*" This ecumenical platitude has struck Kernan as "very well put"; as a supplementary glimpse it may strike the reader of "Ivy Day" as characteristically "tolerant," in Colum's terms; but rather than in Colum's way of seeing Crofton's "aloofness" as a "fine reserve," it seems the ordinary caution (or perhaps the buried irony) of a man of the minority, now in an especially equivocal position.

None of this would, however, make Crofton's remark that closes the story "anticlimactic, inconsequential." It is loaded with import, and aesthetically is one of Joyce's most successful diminuendos and narrative resolutions. Colum, however, seems not to have read it quite closely; he puts it that "Had Joyce given Mr. Crofton's words, his barest words of appreciation, he would have wronged that gentleman's fine reserve."[26] Perhaps Colum was overanxious to discover traces of Irish gentility in this committee room. But hasn't Joyce given Crofton's words, merely transposed into indirect discourse? What else can be supposed but that when asked and asked again by the bustling officious Henchy, Crofton merely said "Yes, it is a very fine piece of writing." This does something other, however, than just reiterate Henchy's term when he asked "Isn't that fine?" As to any fineness, it evades the substance of the poem (and passes over Hynes's genuine feeling in reciting it) and talks only of a "piece of writing." It parallels the tactic of Crofton's earlier remark that his side of the house respected Parnell "because he was a gentleman," which smoothly evades a stand about Parnell the statesman. Crofton has twice obscured and avoided the central issue, first making it a matter of manners, then a matter of rhetoric. To call Parnell a gentleman and Hynes's poem a fine piece of writing comes near, in a subtler way, to echoing Henchy's earlier outright dismissal: "Parnell is dead." Joyce has prepared very well for the effect of Crofton's curtain line. The poem is shoddy though unquestionably sincere, and Hynes, in preparing to speak it (taking off his hat and standing) and in his preoccupation with the mood of it afterwards ("sitting, flushed and bareheaded on the table" and seeming not "to have heard the invitation" of the popping cork) is to be seen as the one unequivocally committed man in this dingy room. The only "fineness" that has come into this place is with Hynes himself, at this moment. But the story shows too, and with conclusiveness, his isolation and the practical futility of his devotion, through Crofton's cautious commendation of the poor verses as a "piece of writing," following in the mode of Henchy's more voluble and even more perfunctory lip-service.

Not that Hynes is quite alone in his honest grief. O'Connor has spoken to the point—"Good man, Joe!"—while "taking out his cigarette papers and pouch the better to hide his emotion." O'Connor is an intriguing and edifying figure in this playlet. If he is less markedly sketched out than some of the others, perhaps that is because there is nothing extreme about him; thus he may represent a kind of median in this Irish group, and a complex of common traits, good and bad. Along with old Jack the caretaker he is there from first to last, and despite his lack of force he has some word on everything that comes up. Sometimes he is naïvely not in the know, sometimes easily swayed; yet more than once, in his mild way, he puts in the good word, for others and for what is right. He is unprepossessing, young but grey-haired, pimply-faced, speaking in "a husky falsetto." He must take two tries to roll his cigarette and can't find a match in his pockets. Yet using a scrap torn from one of Tierney's election cards for a light from the fire, he also lights up the ivy leaf he wears; he has remembered and signifies his remembrance. He responds sympathetically to old Jack's worry about an intemperate son. When Hynes comes in and asks how it goes, O'Connor only shakes his head, and his more immediate concern is whether Tierney will pay him, on which the realistic satiric Hynes is no comfort. When old Jack has spoken scornfully of the other candidate,

Colgan, and Hynes defends him as a representative of society's basic class, labor, rather than a mere job-hunter, O'Connor, roused to honest judgment, says, "I think you're right." As to the proposed address of welcome upon the King's visit, O'Connor naïvely says Tierney won't vote for it, since he "goes in on the Nationalist ticket," but when Hynes suggests "Tricky Dicky" will, O'Connor loses his vague conviction and says, "By God! perhaps you're right, Joe," and falls back on the lesser hope of the day's pay. At least O'Connor can agree with Hynes that if Parnell were alive there would be "no talk of an address of welcome."

When Henchy comes, O'Connor searches his pockets for memoranda and reports vaguely on what must have been an ineffective job of canvassing. When Henchy's complaint that Tierney hasn't paid up expands into a sneer at the publican-candidate's father as former keeper of a "hand-me-down shop" with "a tricky little black bottle up in a corner," O'Connor, innocently yet perhaps warily too, says "But is that a fact?" and returns to the real point, the "nice how-do-you-do" it is that Tierney hasn't paid them. Hynes, to whom Henchy has only "nodded curtly" and who has not spoken except to enforce Henchy's admitted low opinion of Tierney with a "What did I tell you" to O'Connor, now laughs and leaves with the ironic remark that "It'll be all right when King Eddie comes," and O'Connor alone, and only as the door is closing, says, " 'Bye, Joe." Immediately Henchy, while admitting Hynes's father had been "a decent respectable man," berates Joe as a "spy," and old Jack agrees; but O'Connor answers them, several times, mildly yet with conviction—"poor Joe" is "hard up like the rest of us," he's "a decent skin," he's "a straight man," and "a clever chap, too, with the pen," which leads to mention of "that thing he wrote," a preparation for recurrence to it at the story's end. Henchy, who is to be ostentatiously effusive about "that thing" later, now has no time for it, but turns from his attack on Hynes (perhaps because of O'Connor's steady defense) to dark insinuations about "some of those little jokers" as "in the pay of the Castle," half of them, particularly "a certain little nobleman with a cock-eye," judged "a lineal descendant of Major Sirr" (a Corporation officer of a century before who had put down a conspiracy for insurrection that had been denounced by informers).

Into this atmosphere of cynical distrust comes the ambiguous Father Keon, with his "discreet, indulgent, velvety voice," but will not stay, being in search of Mr. Fanning, whose man Tierney is; after Henchy has lighted him down the dark stair, O'Connor, who has been silent, is again the questioner; but now Henchy mutes the gossip, putting it that Father Keon is "what you call a black sheep" but minimizing that to "an unfortunate man of some kind." O'Connor shrewdly observes that "Fanning and himself seem to me very thick," and Henchy speaks of Tierney's "having a deep goster with Alderman Cowley." O'Connor suspects "some deal on in that quarter," having seen "the three of them hard at it yesterday" on the street, and Henchy thinks he knows "the little game they're at," the financial fixing of the election to Lord Mayor. Cynicism, presumably well enough founded, turns for relief to grotesque jesting; Henchy fancies himself in that office, driving out "in all my vermin," with old Jack behind him in a powdered wig, and Father Keon his chaplain; and O'Connor enters into it, laughing, and thinks Henchy would do for the job "so far as owing money goes," and wants to be his private secretary.

When the dozen of stout has arrived at last, O'Connor only says that "Anyway, it's better than nothing." When Crofton and Lyons come, O'Connor laughs at Lyons for spotting the drink first thing. As the two late-comers wait intently for the fire's heat to open their bottles, the talk turns to canvassing and Henchy takes over with his boastful account of "the way to talk to 'em." Then Lyons raises the question of the address to the king, on which Henchy is voluble with expedient defense, in the face of which O'Connor makes his key speech. He asks why they should "welcome the King of England" and is continuing, "Didn't Parnell himself . . ." when Henchy interrupts:

" 'Parnell,' said Mr. Henchy, 'is dead.' " He continues to override O'Connor, in a domineering passage of some style.

> Now, here's the way I look at it. Here's this chap come to the throne after his old mother keeping him out of it till the man was grey. He's a man of the world, and he means well by us. He's a jolly fine decent fellow, if you ask me, and no damn nonsense about him. He just says to himself: 'The old one never went to see these wild Irish. By Christ, I'll go myself and see what they're like.' And are we going to insult the man when he comes over here on a friendly visit? Eh? Isn't that right, Crofton?

Crofton merely nods to it all, but then Lyons resumes the objecting, on grounds of sexual morality, extending the criticism to Parnell, and after Henchy argumentatively denies any analogy, O'Connor quietly but effectively intervenes, with reminder of the anniversary, and urging that they not "stir up any bad blood." Hynes's coming in then allows O'Connor to continue in that ameliorative vein by saying they were "just talking about the Chief" and by asking Hynes to give them "that thing you wrote." Twice more he urges it—"Go on. Fire away, Joe."—"Out with it, man!" After Hynes has recited, O'Connor says "Good man, Joe!" and is much moved. Not a very forceful fellow, unsure of himself and of things about him, O'Connor nevertheless has a key position in the action, caught as he is, like the Irish of his times, between conviction and necessity. To earn what he can, he tries to aid a candidacy in which he has less and less confidence. He copes with Henchy as well as possible without either giving ground or intensifying argument. But it is Hynes he is most naturally responsive to, and to the memory of Parnell, for whom he also wears the ivy leaf this day. Comparatively unassertive though he is, he is not only spectator but advocate and judge in the running contest and basic conflict between Henchy and Hynes which makes this story a miniature of history and something of a morality play.

Henchy is one of Joyce's most substantial creations, and the satire of him is indeed severe. He is the unprincipled man, the temporizer, with expediency his first rule. If there is any excuse, it is his poverty; he admits he expects "to find the bailiffs in the hall" when he goes home. But he is not, like O'Connor, a subdued man. Quickly officious, he not only has the gift of gab, he assiduously talks his way to a petty dominance, and he alternates between rough and smooth to keep the upper hand. Profession and act are not always consistent; when the old man cedes him his chair he says, "O, don't stir, Jack, don't stir" and then sits in it. His offering a drink to the boy who delivered the stout and then fetched a corkscrew from next door seems less a liberality than a gesture asserting his pre-eminence here. When the boy, drinking, has responded properly with "best respects, sir, to Mr. Henchy" and has gone, and the old man in disapproval of giving drink to a seventeen-year-old says, "That's the way it begins," then Henchy shifts to another stance as ready talker and comes up with a phrase for it—"The thin edge of the wedge." From the time he enters, "a bustling little man with a snuffling nose . . . rubbing his hands as if he intended to produce a spark from them," until the end of the scene, when he is pretentiously prompting Mr. Crofton to agree that Hynes's poem is "fine," he struts and pronounces. He gives to every utterance almost the same air of mastery as that over opening the stout—"Wait now, wait now! Did you ever see this little trick?" Yet he is also capable of obsequiousness, though in this committee room it is elicited only by Father Keon, clerical black sheep but colleague of the local operator in politics. (Here Joyce has epitomized a whole pattern of traits in the man and the society—a working alliance of political and ecclesiastical powers, in a reciprocal tolerance of each other's oblique craft, and with an unctuous mutual deference so habitual as to have passed beyond hypocrisy.) It is after Crofton and Lyons have entered and Henchy has a greater audience than just the old man and O'Connor that he becomes most expansive. Having put the two bottles of stout on the hob for the fire's heat to open them, he first gives a sample of "the way to talk to 'em" in canvassing—Tierney is "in favour of whatever will benefit this country" and "doesn't belong to any party, good, bad, or indifferent." When Lyons asked what about the address to the King, Henchy says "Listen to me;" he repeats what he has said in canvassing, that the King's visit will bring money into the country, and elaborates that, but superficially. It is then that O'Connor brings in the name of "Parnell himself" and is not allowed to finish. Here Joyce's use of total sentence rhythm notably suggests the accent of abrupt and final dismissal: " 'Parnell,' said Mr. Henchy, 'is dead.' " Then he goes on volubly to "the way I look at it," which is with jolly tolerance for the King, as between men of the world. However, Henchy makes another shift, to keep on top of the tide of talk by going along with it. When Lyons had insisted in moral censure that includes Parnell as well as the King, and O'Connor asked that they not be provocative on the day of a man they "all respect . . . now that he's dead and gone," and Crofton conceded respect from his "side of the house" because Parnell "was a gentleman," then since this is what the talk has come to, Henchy takes it from there. "Right you are, Crofton!" he says, but "fiercely," and then he forces upon the theme of Parnell's gentility his own crude notions—Parnell "was the only man that could keep that bag of cats in order. 'Down, ye dogs! Lie down, ye curs!' That's the way he treated them."

At this point Henchy catches sight of Hynes in the doorway, and continuing as self-appointed man in charge, calls expansively to him to come in and order him a bottle of stout. In view of what has preceded, the temporizer is disclosed in this, for when Henchy had first entered the room and found Hynes there, he had merely "nodded curtly" and had directed all his talk to O'Connor, on the meanness and base heredity of "the little shoeboy"; and then when Hynes left, Henchy voiced his suspicion that he was the opposition's spy and wondered (with supreme dramatic irony) why Hynes couldn't "have some spark of manhood about him." Only O'Connor's insistent defense of Hynes diverts Henchy to more general (and still dramatically ironic) speculations about political treachery. Now, when the others have turned the conversation to Parnell, Henchy is chiming in to retain control as Hynes reappears. When O'Connor, having invited Hynes to sit, says "we're just talking about the Chief," then Henchy says, "Ay, ay!" and when Hynes sits but says nothing (for what is there to say, here and now?) Henchy launches into a eulogy of Hynes as one "that didn't renege" Parnell but "stuck to him like a man!" This lets O'Connor ask Hynes for his verses on the death of Parnell, and Henchy, who had passed over O'Connor's earlier mention of it, now is all for it —"Give us that"—and urges Crofton to listen to this "splendid thing" and even makes himself the master of these ceremonies —" 'Sh, 'sh,' said Mr. Henchy. 'Now, Joe!' " Hynes recites, there is "a silence and then a burst of clapping," then O'Connor's brief, sincere commendation, and finally Henchy again, crying, "What do you think of that, Crofton? Isn't that fine? What?" Which continuation of Henchy's calculated effusiveness leads into the story's diminished closing note, Crofton's discreet classification of the poem as "a very fine piece of writing." From Hynes to Crofton, by way of the ever-obtrusive Henchy as pivot, the story in its last few words passes from a point of honest commitment through pretentious expediency to a passive neutralism, in the graph of a society's desolation, across which strike the diverse tangents of these separate personalities—contrasting threads in a close narrative texture.

For all the talk there is imagery too, the immediate patterned substance of a dramatic action, strongly sustaining the scenes, especially the last. Hynes, who after removing his hat and standing has said his piece, now sits on the table, bareheaded, flushed, indifferent to the "Pok!" that says his bottle of stout is open for him. (The image takes on more force by contrast with earlier instances: Lyons had asked which bottle on the hob was his, the quicker to claim it, and Crofton had "looked fixedly at the other bottle.") Hynes, in his immobility and detachment at the last, his flushed face signaling a suffusion of a deeper feeling than has hitherto been shown in this room, is epitome of the honorable man mourning the defeat of a cause and a hero he has remained unchangeably devoted to. His integrity has been manifested before in a certain ease and firmness as well, and Joyce's establishing this earlier in the seeming drift of events is fine strategy. On his first entry Hynes had jestingly asked these indubitable nominal Catholics whether this is "a Freemason's meeting" and had been ironic about the certainty of Tierney's paying up; but he is quick and convinced in his defense of Colgan as representative of the workingman, and openly against any address of welcome "to Edward Rex," in the firm faith that were Parnell alive, "we'd have no talk" of such a thing. When he goes out midway in the action he is again tautingly ironic to the other more ambiguous men, telling O'Connor and Henchy, in their worry about Tierney's dependability, that "It'll be all right when King Eddie comes." In the final scene, however, he is at first aloof and silent, presumably because he is not at ease in a discussion of Parnell in this sordid room and situation. When he acknowledges what they're asking him for as "O, that thing is it. . . . Sure, that's old now," it is not just that Parnell has been dead for over a decade, and obviously it is not that Hynes's own devotion to the Chief has waned. His superficially deprecating remark suggests instead this honorable man's melancholy realization of the shabby state to which politics have declined. However it has gone with the others, he has not forgotten nor has he compromised, and as he sits there in his latter-day isolation it is to him the focus is drawn, beyond Henchy's prattle and Crofton's safe evasions, beyond Lyons' negative morality, and beyond the well-intentioned but less than forceful O'Connor, who being thus most like and most unlike Hynes, must wear his ivy leaf with a difference.

In the brief but variegated continuity this story enacts, the state of a nation is so concretely reported and with such clear, rapid demonstrations of its contradictory elements that it is almost a surprise to look back and see how few have been required to play it out and how ordinary have been the circumstances that have sufficed for revelation. Despite its pondering of issues and values, the action is quite casual, and though its incidents are tightly knit in a progressive development, nothing is forced, nor do the artist's calculations obtrude. Though the apparent pace is deliberate throughout, the actual thematic development is steadily accelerated. Meanwhile, as a crowning artistic grace, although the players are analogous to tendencies within the body politic, they are realized and sustained as individuals. Read as pure naturalism, the story is arresting in its kaleidoscopic detail. Its cataloguing of traits in gradual substantiation of each personality is evocative of recognition if not always of empathic regard. But any reading, if it be careful enough to note the separate cumulative characterizations and connect what has been furnished, can scarcely avoid the judgment Joyce evidently made, and suggests the reader make, between Henchy and Hynes. Whatever Joyce's aloofness in later life, here is his alliance, intellectually and morally, in the confusion that was the Irish political situation at the turn of the century. What so terribly came thereafter he washed his hands of, but here he draws the line, and stands with Hynes, with no perceptible hope but without surrender of principle or diminution of fidelity. Perhaps Joyce gave first place among his stories to "Ivy Day" not merely in satisfaction with its accomplishment as objectified, sustained drama but for its positiveness in delineating issues and declaring values, all within the medium of a scrupulous and yet lively art.

A MOTHER

"Ivy Day," "A Mother," and "Grace" make up a special group in Joyce's collection, since they explore the culture of Dublin in three broad but quite specifically treated categories—politics, at a ward level but with national and historic reverberations; art in a dominant local phase, ambitious musical performance; and religion, at once serious and perfunctory, and contributive to the vain repetitiousness of Dubliners' confined circling lives. Nationalism, inescapably a felt force in "Ivy Day" and seriously treated there, is also a factor in "A Mother," but here in its minor aspect as a social affectation. The satire in "Ivy Day" and "Grace" runs deep and is unrelentingly severe; that in "A Mother," though broad, is lighter in tone; from Joyce's view here less is at stake. In "Ivy Day" a cynical, self-seeking expediency is seen at work in the body politic; in "Grace" the Church is presented as it is ignorantly conceived of by some of its unstable adherents and as in itself an actual purveyor of simony. No such grave issues arise in the other of these three stories; the mother of Kathleen Kearney, however rampant, is not going to subvert the arts in Dublin, not even in such a minor manifestation as the concert she interrupts only briefly.

Stanislaus Joyce calls this piece and "An Encounter" the "only two of the stories" based on Joyce's "actual personal experience," and adds that "A Mother" describes "a concert at which my brother sang with John McCormack."[1] (This "Grand Irish Concert" was on August 27, 1904; Ellmann's biography reproduces the *Freeman's Journal* announcement of it.)[2] The occasion doubtless provided some of the substance to be woven into the short story (but the admired McCormack is not translated into this cast, nor Joyce himself, apparently.) According to Joseph Holloway's diary, as quoted by Ellmann, the incompetent management delayed starting the concert, making the audience impatient; the accompanist (at whose home Joyce had rehearsed that morning and whose mother had given him whisky) "left early," though Holloway does not say why, and the substitute "was so incompetent that one of the vocalists, Mr. James A. Joyce, had to sit down at the piano and accompany himself."[3] The *Freeman's Journal* praised his "sweet tenor voice" and his feeling performance, but noted that "Mr. J. F. M'Cormack was the hero of the evening."[4] Certainly in that admired presence Joyce would have done his best, even under difficulties. Therefore it must have been a different instance that Judge Eugene Sheehy reports of the youthful Joyce: "Once, when paid to sing at a Dublin concert, he walked off the stage because he did not like the accompaniment,"[5] and thereby forfeited the badly needed fee. Psychographers of the creative process might see a hint that Joyce was obliquely confessing and absolving himself of haughtiness by satirizing it in Mrs. Kearney. What this incident and other similar ones more plainly call to mind is that Joyce did know at first hand the Dublin world of professional and semiprofessional concert performance, and could have observed the idiosyncrasies of "*artistes*" and their promoters as well. If besides there is any ambivalently felt autobiography in "A Mother," it is deeply buried. Joyce's view of his characters here is so detached that it would scarcely claim a fictionist's embodying attention were he not so coolly amused by absurdities in general and so disdainful of his chief character.

Taking that point of vantage, and seeing Mrs. Kearney's life as a sustained energetic affectation, he makes her almost a grotesque, but one neatly carved, with a deft touch. In working at some remove from his subject, he gives less dialogue, compared to its extended use in "Grace" and the major dependence upon it in "Ivy Day." Here instead much is epitomized, in the language of the omniscient interpretive teller of the tale, bending it to his judgment and taste by indicative summary. Indeed, at the crisis of Mrs. Kearney's conflict with the wills of others, she is for the most part not heard but merely seen across the room in a dumb show of voluble protestation. Whenever her words are given, she speaks in character, but that has been sustained all along by the narrator's shaded descriptions.

Nationalism in its socially fashionable aspect being one target of the satire, the focus on that is broad and the brush-strokes quick and firm. The concerts for which Kathleen Kearney is to be accompanist are sponsored by the Eire Abu Society, a fervidly Irish organization, and at the final concert when Kathleen "played a selection of Irish airs" and another young lady, one who "arranged amateur theatricals," delivered "a stirring patriotic recitation," these were "generously" and "deservedly applauded." People of this persuasion, the Kearneys' "musical friends or Nationalist friends," customarily gathered after mass for gossip, would shake hands across a circle, and "said good-bye to one another in Irish." Nor do they lose touch; they send "Irish picture postcards" back and forth. Joyce had early paid his harsh disrespects to what he considered a backward-looking cultural insularity, and later he imported a more particular attitude, along with Kathleen Kearney herself, into *Ulysses,* where she is briefly glimpsed among other young ladies seen as "a lot of sparrowfarts skitting around talking about politics."[6] In this story the superficialities of an affected nationalism are satirized chiefly through the Eire Abu Society's officers. There is the assistant secretary, limping Mr. Holohan, whom Mrs. Kearney "helped" with a "tact" at first concealing the force that was to become tactless, then ruthless. Another telling figure, the Society's secretary, Mr. Fitzpatrick, comes into view as the trouble mounts—"a little man with a white vacant face," he "held a programme in his hand and, while he was talking to her [Mrs. Kearney], he chewed one end of it into a moist pulp." He was one who "seemed to bear disappointments lightly," this perhaps because he "did not catch the point at issue very quickly." It is little wonder that under such auspices the concerts begin badly and the third is canceled to allow a greater effort for the fourth and last. This one comes off fairly well and is still successfully in progress when the raging Mrs. Kearney leaves the field, defeated, deploying an embarrassed husband and daughter with her in the retreat.

Only incidentally then is Joyce satirizing nationalistically oriented artistic pretensions; his main target is one woman's use of such a movement as means of social climbing. Tindall alludes to the possibility of considering Kathleen as Ireland and her mother as the Church but adds the cautious reminder that in *Dubliners* Joyce was not writing allegories.[7] What to make of Mrs. Kearney should be no problem, since her story is given, in summary but definitely enough to show her motivation and even to account for her moods. It would be possible to see pathos in the life of this woman whose artificially cultivated expectations, the product of a special conditioning within Dublin's larger containment, have been doomed to frustration; but Joyce looks more steadily at the other side of the matter, the ridiculousness of her ambitions, her fantastically compulsive pursuit of them, and her disastrous impingement on others in her clumsy destruction of the possibilities she herself was aiming at. That even this calamity has an air of the bizarre is due to Joyce's subtly droll tone in recounting what went before. Still Mrs. Kearney is maintained as a plain target of satire in that she has played her roles as woman, wife, and mother with calculating presumptuousness, as Joyce envisages it.

The first paragraph sets the tone in a gradual approach and then a sudden confrontation. Mr. Hoppy Holohan "had been walking up and down Dublin for nearly a month" on his game leg, "with his hands and pockets full of dirty pieces of paper, arranging about the series of concerts . . . but in the end it was Mrs. Kearney who arranged everything." The next two pages round her out in detail, together with adjunctive husband and daughter Kathleen. Economy is not Joyce's aim in "A Mother"; it depends in part for its effect upon an extended, deliberate display of rather trivial events. Considering the slightness of the central incident—the quarrel over whether accompanist Kathleen is to be paid in advance—the action is made to yield a full effect, even with the climax of Mrs. Kearney's tirade largely in pantomime rather than heard. She has said enough, however, to accomplish her own frustration, and that comes in terms which ironically contradict all her pretensions.

Though in details the account lingers on the grotesquely idiosyncratic, at bottom this is deservedly a *Dubliners* story, since here too is the theme of persistent environmental influence, and resultant compulsion and self-defeat. Mrs. Kearney had been conditioned in girlhood, and confined thereby, and is now compensating, ostensibly seeking her daughter's advancement yet really feeding her own hungers. In this typical situation all that obviates sympathetic response is that she, herself blindly foolish, so relentlessly troubles others. She differs from Mrs. Mooney, whose life as boarding-house keeper was not easy, and who with such a lively daughter had to accomplish what she could, and promptly, and make it stick for Polly. Mrs. Kearney, on the other hand, is using a compliant husband and daughter in vain pursuit of her own superficial aims ingrained even before her marriage.

Joyce begins to delineate her with an unendearing stroke; she "had become Mrs. Kearney out of spite." Her assets as a young woman were some knowledge of French and music learned in "a high-class convent," a pale complexion, and "ivory manners." She gave "no encouragement" to "ordinary" men but awaited the "offer" of "a brilliant life," meanwhile "trying to console her romantic desires by eating a great deal of Turkish Delight in secret." Finally, to silence those who were beginning to predict spinsterhood, she married Mr. Kearney, "a bootmaker on Ormond Quay," and "much older than she." Joyce immediately sounds the tone that relegates him to an auxiliary yet not unsubstantial position like that Mrs. Kearney herself assigned him: "His conversation, which was serious, took place at intervals in his great brown beard." He is "sober, thrifty and pious"—another kind of Dubliner from the sometimes confused, ambivalent, or even distraught ones who appear in some of the other stories. He provides summer vacations for his wife and two daughters at nearby coastal resorts (which Mrs. Kearney does not neglect to report to her friends) and he is laying up "a dowry of one hundred pounds" for each girl. Apparently too in this area he is amenable, for presumably it had been at his wife's direction that Kathleen had been sent "to a good convent, where she learned French and music." In this continuity with Mrs. Kearney's own girlhood is evidence that the mother "never put her own romantic ideas away." Yet she was, in her fashion, "a good wife" to her unromantic husband. A single sentence epitomizes her determined performance in the role of one who comforts and commands: "At some party in a strange house when she lifted her eyebrow ever so slightly he stood up to take his leave and, when his cough troubled him, she put the eider-down quilt over his feet and made a strong rum punch."

Mrs. Kearney's greatest purposefulness, however, is not conjugal but matronly. In quite the modern sense she promotes Kathleen, not without self-interest. Having "determined to take advantage of her daughter's name," she arranges for her to have lessons in Irish. Joyce's skill with the right word is to be seen here; Mrs. Kearney had made this calculated move "when the Irish Revival began to be appreciable." The mother is "well content" with results; "people said" Kathleen was "very clever at music and a very nice girl and, moreover, that she was a believer in the language movement." In consequence of this created reputation Mr. Holohan comes proposing that Kathleen be accompanist at "four grand concerts" the Nationalist Eire Abu Society would sponsor in the Antient Concert Rooms. Mr. Holohan was to have reason to regret this step, but at first it must have been a relief, after limping about on his game leg "for nearly a month," when Mrs. Kearney repeatedly "pushed the decanter towards him" and daily "advised and dissuaded" concerning *"artistes"* and programming. One outcome of such conferences was the contract promising Kathleen eight guineas for her services at the four concerts.

There were related matters for the mother to attend to, and in one brilliant paragraph Joyce summarizes this, in almost objective language yet tinged with Mrs. Kearney's resolution, precision, and self-satisfaction. Such overtone of the character herself is to be heard concerning her purchase of "some lovely blush-pink charmeuse . . . to let into the front of Kathleen's dress," in the belief that though it "cost a pretty penny" still "there are occasions when a little expense is justifiable," as also with the "dozen of two-shilling tickets for the final concert" which she took and sent "to those friends who could not be trusted to come otherwise." In this fashion "She forgot nothing, and, thanks to her, everything that was to be done was done." (Is there to be heard in this last sentence a satire of the preposterously high and mighty Mrs. Kearney by impish parody of an august passage in the first verses of the Gospel according to St. John, with which the celebration of the Mass is concluded, in particular its third verse, *Omnia per ipsum facta sunt, et sine ipso factum est nihil quod factum est*—or as the King James Bible has it, "All things were made by him; and without him was not any thing made that was made.")

In his introductory pages, then, Joyce has Mrs. Kearney idiosyncratically established in the generic title role and in her familial-social situation. Now he can let the story proceed and ramify, and it does, through almost fifteen more deliberate pages, intent not so much on dramatic crisis (though there is one) as on an ironic view of the amateurish cultural enterprise and particularly of Mrs. Kearney's discomfiture through her own excesses. The first concert, with generally poor *artistes,* begins late, to a scanty and gradually decreasing audience; the second night has a larger crowd, but mostly on passes, and it behaves "indecorously," which Mr. Fitzpatrick, the Society's secretary, abets by sticking his head out beyond the screen and having "a laugh with two friends in the corner of the balcony." (Such an adventitious detail, so immediately contributive to effect, perhaps derives from a trifle picked up by young Joyce during some Dublin experience as a concert singer; in its credible oddity it makes for realism more than a greater fabrication might do; and this can be assumed to typify how the observant artist, retentive of memory, substantiated his fiction at innumerable points by detail simple in itself yet with the double force of unique concreteness and peculiar relevance.)

With the way things had gone at the first two concerts Mrs. Kearney was in no mood to accept quietly the news that Friday night's concert would be canceled, to bolster Saturday's. She presses the contractual issue: four concerts, eight guineas. Getting no satisfactory answer, only with difficulty does she restrain herself from asking a question in a mocking manner she knew "would not be ladylike." Before the time of the last concert she has "thought her plans over." She had also told something of her "suspicions" to her sober-minded husband, who "listened carefully and said that perhaps it would be better if he went with her" that night. She is glad he suggested it, and Joyce, in a sentence, sums up her evaluation of her mate: "she respected her husband in the same way as she respected the General Post Office, as something large, secure, and fixed; and though she knew the small number of his talents she appreciated his abstract value as a male." That he perhaps understands her better than she knows is suggested by the part he discreetly undertakes later. It is narrated only as an action seen across the room, but it adds to the judgment upon Mrs. Kearney that her quiet and deferential husband is moved to suggest she restrain herself. Her failing to do so does not invalidate his good sense, but only shows how the wilful run on beyond the reach of those most inclined to guard them.

The story having come to the episode of the last concert (and Mrs. Kearney with daughter and husband having arrived at the Antient Concert Rooms three-quarters of an hour ahead of time) two narrative matters must be interwoven—the general goings-on backstage, introducing the various performers and others, and Mrs. Kearney's endeavors to bring the Society's officials to terms in the matter of eight guineas in advance. Joyce does this in a smoothly running, skilfully modulated narrative. There are mere glimpses of some characters—little, oldish-faced Miss Beirne of the Committee, with her air of "trustfulness and enthusiasm," or

Madam Glynn, the faded soprano from London—and extended glances at such others as Mr. Duggan, the professionally successful bass whose manner has not quite transcended his humble Dublin origin, and Mr. Bell, the nervous second tenor, winner of a bronze medal on his fourth trial, at the Feis Ceoil, the annual music festival, or Mr. O'Madden Burke, delegated to "write the notice" for the *Freeman,* and instinctive in his discovery of the room where bottles are being opened. Meanwhile Mrs. Kearney is searching the hall for Mr. Holohan or Mr. Fitzpatrick and, finding neither, is baffled by the uselessness of making her complaint to the vague Miss Beirne. Returning to the dressing room, Mrs. Kearney passed by Mr. Duggan and Mr. Bell, but "brought her daughter over" to the more prestigious first tenor and baritone and "talked to them amiably." She did not, however, forget her business with Mr. Holohan and soon followed him out of the room to press it rigorously in "a discreet part of the corridor." Here her insistence and Mr. Holohan's evasively referring her to Mr. Fitzpatrick are in part condensed through indirect discourse but partly rendered directly as increasingly curt exchanges.

Mr. Holohan having "distantly" put her off, she came back to the dressing room with cheeks "slightly suffused." With her fixed in this heightened state, Joyce gives several paragraphs to the general scene in the now lively room, noting especially "the *Freeman* man" in his ocular dalliance with Miss Healy, and introducing his substitute who "will write the notice," Mr. O'Madden Burke. While Mr. Holohan was being courteous to the *Freeman* man, Mrs. Kearney "was speaking so animatedly to her husband that he had to ask her to lower her voice," and as others in the dressing room began to take note, conversation grew strained. They did not need to hear; across the room they could see, and so can the reader—Mr. Kearney, poor fellow, looking "straight before him, stroking his beard, while Mrs. Kearney spoke into Kathleen's ear with subdued emphasis," and while the impatient audience clapped and stamped to demand that the concert begin. Then Mr. Holohan is seen speaking "earnestly" with Mrs. Kearney, becoming "very red and excited," talking "volubly" and pointing "desperately towards the hall," where the noise is growing louder. Briefly is heard the voice of Mrs. Kearney, reiterating that Kathleen "must get her eight guineas" and "won't go on without her money." Here it seems plain that Mrs. Kearney's concern is not money but status; the baritone, for instance, "had been paid," and whether or not Mrs. Kearney knew this, she probably was aware of such consideration for professionals.

Again the story becomes a pantomime as Mr. Holohan "appealed to Mr. Kearney and to Kathleen," but the husband "continued to stroke his beard," and the daughter "looked down, moving the point of her new shoe." At this juncture Joyce wavered, not quite trusting a purely objective and mainly visual method of narration, for he notes Kathleen's consciousness that "it was not her fault." Then (in objective view again) Mr. Holohan, after the "swift struggle of tongues," had "hobbled out in haste," while noise from the audience rose "to a clamour" and the *artistes* waited in a "silence" grown "painful," with Miss Healy heard tactfully trying to make cultural shop talk about Mrs. Pat Campbell. Mr. Holohan brings back Mr. Fitzpatrick, who, promising "the other half at the interval," counts out four bank-notes into Mrs. Kearney's hand—pounds, not the guineas demanded, and this implacable woman declares it is "four shillings short." But here Kathleen acted to avoid impasse; she "gathered in her skirt," said, "Now, Mr. Bell" to the quaking second tenor, and went onto the stage with him, to get the first half of the concert under way. Kathleen's move could have been merely a diplomatic *démarche,* to keep the peace by pretending the dispute was settled, but it may also suggest the beginning of Mrs. Kearney's real defeat, in a daughter's conscious separation from her.

Except for Madam Glynn's mannered performance "in a bodiless gasping voice" that "the cheaper part of the house made fun of," the concert up until its intermission was well received, including Kathleen's playing of Irish airs. Backstage, however, there was great discussion among the Society's officers, the baritone and bass, and Mr. O'Madden Burke; he summed up their condemnation of Mrs. Kearney's behavior—a "scandalous exhibition." In another part of the room the rampant mother continued her tirade, and the narrative indirectly reports her declaring "she would see that her daughter got her rights" and "would make Dublin ring" if she weren't paid "to the last farthing." When she declares too that the committee "thought they had only a girl to deal with" and "wouldn't have dared to have treated her like that if she had been a man," Mrs. Kearney exposes another facet of her obliquely conditioned personality, in the obsessive demand for equality paradoxically made by a woman who really disdains men and sees them as subjects for regulation, whether by finesse or opprobrium. Now she is told that "the other four guineas would be paid after the Committee meeting on the following Tuesday" but that if Kathleen "did not play for the second part" of the concert, they would "consider the contract broken" and pay nothing further. Mrs. Kearney stands her ground, cites the contract, and says her daughter is to get the remaining "four pounds eight into her hand or a foot she won't put on that platform." She and Mr. Holohan exchange heated words, she mimics him and he rebukes her, and now she is "condemned on all hands" as again in the long view, in pantomime, she is seen at the door, "haggard with rage, arguing with her husband and daughter, gesticulating with them." When she realizes the concert is to continue with Miss Healy as accompanist, she commands her husband to get a cab, wraps the cloak around her daughter, whom she has failed to make secure in more important ways, and leaves with a final threat to Mr. Holohan. He retorted in kind, while helpless Kathleen "followed her mother meekly" through the doorway.

Mrs. Mooney was the better mother, at least pragmatically. She had engineered an arrangement which Polly found an agreeable prospect, and while the two of them were hypocritical about it, they had proceeded in view of certain realities and in accord with each other, and had made something of a situation.

(That it would, as glimpsed in *Ulysses,* drive Mr. Doran to drink is not relevant within the unities of "The Boarding House.") Mrs. Kearney, more cultivated than Mrs. Mooney, and of a more secure and privileged social stratum, professes devoted concern for Kathleen's progress, yet her maternal solicitude turns out to be sheer parental vanity and self-compensation through her arrangement of modish activities for her daughter. But in the altercation, alleging defense of Kathleen, she is really embarrassing her and alienating people who might have been congenial friends. (And who knows, there was the nervous second tenor, the fair-haired little man with his bronze medal on a fourth try, whom Kathleen might have chosen to take in hand further, as easily as she had said "Now, Mr. Bell" and got him and the concert started.) But every prospect is devastated by Mrs. Kearney's rage. While Joyce sharply individualizes her, he also makes her something more than unique—a type of those who are defeated in attempting to impose on outsiders the same egotistic domination which a too deferential family endures.

Even in that private area of her absolute matriarchy Mrs. Kearney's power begins to suffer some erosion, as is seen in the running conflict backstage, when neither her husband nor her daughter remain fully aligned with her. Theirs are but two, and the least severe, of judgments upon her, and Joyce arranges all these in a pattern of rejections that closes around Mrs. Kearney with a thematic as well as narrative finality. Mr. Kearney's asking his wife to lower her voice and his noncommittal attitude thereafter suggests he had come along fearing the worst and now recognizes it. Kathleen's independently starting onto the stage with Mr. Bell to begin the concert while her mother is still demanding an added four shillings foreshadows Mrs. Kearney's imminent full-scale social failure. Later when Mr. Holohan appeals to Kathleen and her father, her looking down and moving the point of her new shoe (like her father's stroking his beard) suggests a neutrality bordering on aversion, while her thought that "it was not her fault" marks an aloofness not unlike the beginning of alienation from her mother. Even the baritone, who with his money in hand would "be at peace with men," will go so far as to say that "Mrs. Kearney might have taken the *artistes* into consideration," and thereby in a sense excludes her from the professional world into which she would force entrance for her daughter. Even little Miss Beirne, as cited approvingly by Mr. O'Madden Burke, has decided despite her general "trustfulness and enthusiasm" that Mrs. Kearney should be paid nothing. Miss Healy, the contralto, and one of Kathleen's Nationalist friends, is swung about in the controversy, and Joyce's mentionings of her typify his balanced economy and cogency in the use of adjunctive characters. She has chatted with Kathleen before the concert, she tries to make casual conversation to divert others' attention from Mrs. Kearney's behavior, and she stood with the Kearneys' group during the fateful intermission "because she was a great friend of Kathleen's and the Kearneys had often invited her to their house." However, she then consents "to play one or two accompaniments" so that the concert may go on; and Mrs. Kearney, still waiting for the committee to yield, sees the tide turned against her when she "had to stand aside" to let Miss Healy and the baritone "pass up to the platform." Though composition becomes contrapuntal in this formalizing of aggressive strategy and a hardening defense, it remains realistically detailed.

It is Mr. Holohan who, having borne the brunt of vituperation, gives Mrs. Kearney her final and tellingly severe dismissal. At the second concert, when she heard the third was to be canceled to strengthen the fourth, she had stipulated that this did not alter the contract for eight guineas; Mr. Holohan, with an appearance of haste that made her suspicious, had passed her on to the secretary, Mr. Fitzpatrick, who said he "would bring the matter before the Committee." It had been "all she could do to keep from asking: 'And who is the *Commetty,* pray?' " but that time she had restrained herself from what she knew "would not be ladylike." Later it is this same impulse to mimic that bursts out. When she would not allow Kathleen to continue for the second half of the final concert without payment in full, Mr.

Holohan himself had become somewhat more personal, was "surprised" that Mrs. Kearney would treat them "this way," and even said she "might have some sense of decency." Not surprisingly, the suggestion had a negative effect; Mrs. Kearney plunged on, complaining that she couldn't "get a civil answer," and assumed "a haughty voice" and evidently a mocking one—"You must speak to the secretary. It's not my business. I'm a great fellow fol-the-diddle-I-do." This was too much for Mr. Holohan; he said, "I thought you were a lady," and walked away "abruptly."

A sharper denunciation and dismissal would be hard to imagine, for Mrs. Kearney has thought herself indubitably and even superlatively a lady, from her young womanhood on. But an excess of artificiality has come full circle; the lady overreaches and betrays herself, and destroys a lifelong fabrication, her pose of gentility. It had been in terms of this that she was "well content" when her daughter's studies (of French and music and of Irish as it "began to be appreciable") brought Mr. Holohan and the contract. Later it is not the eight guineas itself that she cares about but the certifying of her daughter's achieved position as a cultivated young lady, in the pattern set by her mother. At the height of the trouble, when Mrs. Kearney declared "the Committee had treated her scandalously," she claimed aggrievedly to have "spared neither trouble nor expense," but she could afford both and would have minded neither if the elder Kearney daughter, musically trained and with fashionable Nationalist associations, could be advanced in the public eye of middle-class Dublin. Her reiterated complaint is legalistic, but though eight guineas is her battle-cry, behind that is a complicated matter of prestige, for she herself had negotiated this agreement involving her daughter's status in Dublin's musical world. More representatively, she is the woman so accustomed to having her way absolutely in her domestic realm that she cannot desist when she finds the outside world not so easy to dominate. Like many a social climber, she is defeated by her egotistical lack of social sense. This is utter failure, her being found deficient in the one thing she has most pretended to. So Mr. Holohan can utterly dismiss her—leaving, she glares and says, "I'm not done with you yet," and he answers "But I'm done with you."

So were the others. After her mimicry of Mr. Holohan, she was condemned "on all hands" and "everyone approved of what the Committee had done." Though for finality nothing could surpass Mr. Holohan's "But I'm done with you," Joyce did not stop there, nor with the general expressions of disapproval which epitomize Mrs. Kearney's self-defeat. There is atmosphere as well as theme to convey, and unity of action in this composition is more than dramatic, it is tonal. By way of the flushed Mr. Holohan's ironically repeating "a nice lady! . . . a nice lady!" after her departure, the focus comes round to Mr. O'Madden Burke for the final word and the posture from which it is promulgated, renewing the mode of coolly controlled grotesquerie with which the story began. Joyce has carefully established this spokesman—later termed by Lenehan in *Ulysses* "that minstrel boy of the wild wet west who is known by the euphonious appellation of the O'Madden Burke."[8] He appears first under the auspices of "the *Freeman* man,"[9] Mr. Hendrick, who "had come in to say that he could not wait for the concert" but that "O'Madden Burke will write the notice." After Mr. Hendrick had paused to enjoy Miss Healy's coquetry and outstanding feminine attributes, and when he then accepts Mr. Holohan's invitation to "have a little something" before he goes, and proceeds with him "up a dark staircase . . . to a secluded room," there already is Mr. O'Madden Burke, having found his way "by instinct." Here Joyce furnishes a telling and compositionally provident look at him, "suave," "balanced . . . upon a large silk umbrella," and balancing "the fine problem of his finances" upon his "magniloquent western name," a "widely respected" man. Obviously this is a fit person to utter the properly attuned judgment of Dublin's cultural circles upon Mrs. Kearney's uncouth behavior. He states the first items of his findings during the furor at intermission time, and Joyce gives this in two skilfully constructed sentences of indirect discourse, enclosed first and last between "Mr. O'Madden Burke said" and "he said," in a way to suggest sustained discourse and final pronouncement: "Mr. O'Madden Burke said it was the most scandalous exhibition he had ever witnessed. Miss Kathleen Kearney's musical career was ended in Dublin after that, he said." Then as the conversation among the *artistes* and the Eire Abu Society officers continues, he is heard directly, magisterially: " 'I agree with Miss Beirne,' said Mr. O'Madden Burke. 'Pay her nothing.' " Finally, after Kathleen has followed her fuming mother out of the room, and while Mr. Holohan is exclaiming "a nice lady!" and pacing up and down to cool off, he is offered endorsement by this assured voice from this steady presence: " 'You did the proper thing, Holohan,' said Mr. O'Madden Burke, poised upon his umbrella in approval."

With this idiosyncratic figure, as pre-established and in this posture, Joyce comprises the story within the frame and key established for it by the first two paragraphs, which introduced Mr. "Hoppy" Holohan in his particular enterprise "with his hands and pockets full of dirty pieces of paper," and Mrs. Kearney as one whose chilly young womanhood had been consoled by Turkish Delight eaten in secret and who had married "out of spite." Grotesquerie of this sort excludes a great deal—and not only terror but pity, except in that purely charitable view which would even forbid any sardonic look at Mrs. Kearney. Kathleen's situation was uncomfortable, but the story leaves it relatively unexamined, and all that is seen at last is Mrs. Kearney's ironically inadequate protective gesture of wrapping a cloak about the daughter she has embarrassed socially, and Kathleen's "meekly" following her mother out of that place, with nothing to do but forbear, as anyone must with a relative on a rampage in public. Still, Kathleen is no Eveline, nor will be a Maria, and her whole life will not necessarily be shadowed by this debacle, since people will know what she knew—"it was not her fault." "A Mother" does not consider either Kathleen or Mrs. Kearney herself in the most comprehensive and soberest aspects.

In this it is, along with "After the Race," the "lightest" of the

Dubliners stories. But "A Mother" is furnished and controlled and effectively set forth throughout, which "After the Race" is not. Yet even "The Boarding House" is more penetrating than "A Mother" in its realism and representativeness, and this not just because it shows Dublin society at a more ordinary level, but because there certain stern necessities, the commonplace dilemmas of the less than middle-class, are confronted—a seduced and probably pregnant girl's redemption into a forced marriage, a man's tardy discretion in the hard choice between his freedom or his retention of good name and a job, a mother's manipulation of persons and events in fulfilling what she conceives of as her duty. Perhaps some will not quite agree with Richard Ellmann that both "The Boarding House" and "A Mother" portray "mothers who fail in their role." True, their force marks "a type Joyce could never endure,"[10] but it is differently motivated, differently exercised, and only in "A Mother" is Joyce severely satirizing unendurable aggressiveness. Furthermore, as for the madam of the boarding house, she has no sense of having failed in her maternal role; rather, she takes pride in bringing off the scheme (with Polly's ardent connivance), and indeed according to her lights she has done right well by her daughter.

As for pity as generally accorded, though Kathleen Kearney is at the moment implicitly deserving of it, the indiscreetly amorous and then panicky boarder Mr. Doran is not. By general consent women probably would condemn his type, especially in its wavering between forwardness and hesitancy. Men will laugh at him, for even if Mrs. Mooney's sugary "Come down, dear. Mr. Doran wants to speak to you" may give certain males a retrospective shiver, this can yield to the amusement felt over others' disasters. The women who would condemn Doran would not be exceedingly merciful to either Polly or her mother, whose operations run beyond the rules a bit too crassly. Pathos is hardly a problem, then, in "The Boarding House." Pathos was an inherent something to be excluded from "A Mother," and that was done by cool detachment, a skilful superficiality, and a bizarre tone, largely achieved by a wry diction.

What Joyce had most strongly on his side for these chosen treatments was that while his Mrs. Mooney is understandable, his Mrs. Kearney is insufferable. Mrs. Mooney may even win that sidelong glance of partial approval accorded the truly formidable matriarch in the hour of her relative success, whereas the defeat of Mrs. Kearney is to be fully approved of, especially for its kind of poetic justice in the ruination, by her own excesses, of the very ambitions she most sought to advance. It is a satiric not a tragic justice, however. Hence the story's slow drift to a close, like a boat with engine stopped coming to rest at dockside, while lesser gestures secure it. There is not enough at issue in "A Mother" to require that the conclusion be intensely, centrally pointed, as in "Araby," "Eveline," "A Little Cloud." So behind Mr. O'Madden Burke officiously poised upon his large umbrella is the artist more purely poised, with an equanimity that has never wavered in the apt but always easy conduct of his story.

GRACE

Writing of "The Background of *Dubliners*," Stanislaus Joyce referred to the use in "Grace" of a tripartite division analogous to Inferno, Purgatorio, and Paradiso in the *Divine Comedy*.[1] This has been much noted, though not always in the most pointed aspect suggested by Ellmann, that of parody.[2] It is but a mean little inferno, that Dublin pub's basement gents' room into which Mr. Tom Kernan literally has fallen; the purgatory is only a malodorous bedroom crowded with Kernan's consolatory and benevolently scheming visitors and filled moreover with what R. M. Adams well describes as their "chuckleheaded collective woolgathering;"[3] and as for these creatures' paradise, it is of parochial dimensions, a "retreat" for businessmen in a Dublin church under a fashionable hearty Jesuit preacher who instructs his masculine congregation in easy means of passable compliance with the teachings of Jesus Christ. (Joyce calls him Father Purdon, from the old name for a Dublin street of brothels, and Stanislaus indicates this as an intentional expression of "contempt.")[4]

Mock-epic analogies extend further; this story begins in *medias res*—"Two gentlemen who were in the lavatory at the time tried to lift him up: but he was quite helpless." There "at the foot of the stairs down which he had fallen" Kernan has hit bottom. Moreover, that first sentence shadows forth the story: there will be other attempts to lift him up and presumably he will coninue to be unredeemed. As will his associates. This presently anonymous damned individual prefigures them all, whatever their superficial differences. Joyce shows them as typical *gens de Dublin,* economically beset, culturally restricted by rigid conventions, liable to domestic discord, dependent on drink and masculine fellowship and a naïve allegiance to an ecclesiasticism tainted with simony. Dublin, epitomized in this pub, is the more general backdrop for the specialized purgatory of Kernan's bedroom with his four associates there, but then they are to conduct him into the final episode, where again the scene will widen, even beyond that of the pub, to include the large congregation of men shepherded by Father Purdon in their "retreat."

The pub incident with Kernan prostrate at its center, first in the lavatory and then on the floor of the bar to which they carry him, offers some paradoxes relevant to Joyce's theses. Dublin is gregarious, yet in the stir the individual is essentially isolate. Dublin is humane in its immediate responses, yet it is also hypocritical, covering up its failings rather than naming and grappling with them. Bystanders attempt to aid the fallen, semi-conscious Kernan, but no one knows who he is. Two gentlemen had been with him (presumably in the bar upstairs before his descent), but no one can say who they were or where they are now. The constable (whom Joyce pinpoints with a quick Dickensian caricature) wants first things first—the facts he "made ready to indite" in his notebook, but a well-meaning "young man in a cycling suit" sees the injured man's need at the moment, washes the blood from his mouth, and gives him brandy, which brings him to.

He tried to stand up; he was helped to his feet, and "the battered silk hat was placed on the man's head"—he is still just that, an unnamed graceless figure. Nor does he want to confess his identity and home address in response to the constable's routine questions. Saying "Sha, 's nothing" and twirling his moustache, he asks them to get him a cab. At this point "a tall agile gentleman" enters, greets him as Tom, and wants to know what's the trouble; the constable knows the newcomer as Mr. Power and deferentially turns the soiled and incapacitated man over to him. The considerate young man in the cycling suit still assists, and outside the pub the injured one thanks him again, says " 'y na'e is Kernan," and again regrets they could not have a little drink together. To which this person who is not to reappear in the story makes nevertheless a thematically significant reply —"Another time."

Within the fully circumstanced opening passage of accidental injury and rescue are other darker tones, implicative and thematic. After the fallen one is carried upstairs and laid down again in the barroom, "a dark medal of blood had formed itself near the man's head on the tessellated floor." The word medal is emphatic in this context; beyond shape it seems ironically to suggest something of heroism, something of piety. Then that image is erased; as soon as Kernan has been led out a "curate"—a bartender—"set about removing the traces of blood from the floor." While this is only routine housekeeping, it accords with other cleaning up that has been going on. Despite his bitten tongue, Kernan is still capable of glossing over the matter; he repeats his statement, "Sha, 's nothing." Mr. Power's question, "How did you get yourself into this mess?" is by implication far-reaching, but the helpful young man in the cycling suit gives the simple answer that "The gentleman fell down the stairs." The manager and the constable "agreed that the gentleman must have missed his footing."

He has indeed. And that his thick speech is not due just to his bitten tongue is confessed by his inquiry: " 'an't we have a little . . . ?" Saying he "must have missed his footing" is even wider of the whole truth than Eliza's remarking that Father Flynn's "laughing-like to himself" in the confessional "made them think that there was something gone wrong with him. . . ." But Eliza was naïve, whereas the commentators on Kernan's mishap are tactfully evasive. It is thematic; at the story's conclusion Father Purdon is to be heard in a professional job of glossing over. Between such a beginning and ending the central scene pivots on an amalgam of fact and falsehood, and in certain larger matters confusion is compounded.

The widely current view of "Grace" as a Dantean triptych should at least allow in passing that the story actually has four developed scenes—the pub, the home and family to which

Power returns Kernan, Kernan's bedroom crowded with his four visitors, and the Gardiner Street church filled with "business men" at their "retreat." It is not difficult, however, to lump pub and home as complementary diurnal aspects in Joyce's view of a sordid even if scarcely infernal Dublin. The two are not as starkly separate and fatally conjoined as in "Counterparts," but there is a markedly inauspicious relation in Kernan's case, and Mr. Power's concern over it makes for design and progress in the story. Happening to come upon Kernan in the pub, Power not only took him out of the constable's hands but saw him hoisted onto an "outsider" and rode home with the miserable fellow, who pulls his "filthy coat" about him in the cold. It is high time for his return, nine-thirty. Like the uncle in "Araby," like Eveline's father, and like Farrington of "Counterparts," Kernan had lingered too long. He is still evasive, though, about his behavior and situation; when Mr. Power again asks "how the accident had happened," Kernan pleads that his " 'ongue is hurt." That it is; he's bitten off a minute piece; yet when Power inspecting it says it's "ugly," Kernan says as before, "Sha, 's nothing."

At this point in the journey from pub to home Joyce interrupts the straight narration for an account of Mr. Kernan and, less lengthily, of Mr. Power. Kernan's pretensions and gradual decline are ironically summarized. He wears "a silk hat of some decency" (it is to be "rehabilitated" by Mrs. Kernan for his attendance at the retreat) and gaiters too, in token of the "dignity" of his "calling" as "a commercial traveler of the old school." He deals in tea, which he tastes and grades in a little office where he spits forth the samplings into the grate, there behind the window displaying the name of his London firm. Thus Mr. Kernan's injury is more than just physically painful, it is at least temporarily disabling to his vocation. His wife, though, sees it in another light as curiously appropriate—"but that she did not wish to seem bloody-minded," she might have told her husband's visitors "that Mr. Kernan's tongue would not suffer by being shortened," and no doubt she has in mind not only his palaver with her (seen when she brings drinks for his visitors) but also his inordinate conviviality exercised in Dublin's pubs for the amusement of those who "esteemed him as a character."

Mr. Power is "a much younger man"; he, like Cunningham, is "employed in the Royal Irish Constabulary Office in Dublin Castle," which explains the constable's deference. Power has his own "character" as a "debonair" fellow with "inexplicable debts"; he is on the rise and somewhere along this line he has met Kernan in that gradual descent of which the fall in the pub was only a sharper instance. Mr. Power is also a good-hearted man, as he shows in this second scene, Kernan's home-coming. The fallen one's dependents are waiting in the "small house" for "the money" he has been spending for more drink than he could hold, and he already in debt to the grocer. Mr. Power notes that the children are ill-trained and unruly, and he hears further of the state of things from Mrs. Kernan after she has put her delinquent husband to bed. Kernan had been on a protracted bout, "since Friday," she said, and "never seems to think he has a home at all." Mr. Power, seriously concerned, promised help. He would "talk to Martin" and they would "make a new man" of her husband. Which sets the stage for the purgatorial episode in the bedroom, two nights later, when Mr. Power returns, with Martin Cunningham and Mr. M'Coy, to be joined by Mr. Fogarty the grocer and to set working their strategy for bringing Tom Kernan into a state of grace.

First there is inserted a wryly humorous vignette of a Dublin wife, in the person and domestic history of Mrs. Kernan, and especially as to her faith in general and its limits concerning any possible reform of her husband. Puzzled by the assurances that Kernan could be made to "turn over a new leaf," she watched Mr. Power drive away and then asserted her practicality as one twenty-five years married by going in and emptying her husband's pockets. But courtship had had its flavor of romance for her, and she was still woman enough to be a fancier of weddings, remembering "a jovial, well-fed" Mr. Kernan on their own occasion, "dressed smartly in a frock coat and lavender trousers" with "a silk hat gracefully balanced" on one arm and she leaning on the other. In three weeks "a wife's life" had become "irksome," and later, "when she was beginning to find it unbearable, she had become a mother." She had "launched" two elder sons, now fugitive from Dublin, clerks in Glasgow and Belfast, who write regularly and sometimes send money; she has two younger girls and a boy at home still to fend for. Her situation, however, is not quite desperate, nothing like that in the Farrington family, nor does she seem in danger of such extremity as befell Eveline's mother. Mrs. Kernan has adjusted herself to her portion of reality and has even accommodated her religion to a life with "very few illusions left." She is not, like Eveline, stricken, nor does Joyce make her pathetic, like Maria. Moreover, while she is not without device in her role, she has not become the tyrannical matriarch, like Mrs. Kearney.

One of the least extreme of Joyce's characters, Mrs. Kernan warrants the attention he gives her as perhaps a more representative Dubliner, surviving vicissitudes but still a less than fortunate person, and one at least partially paralyzed, conditioned not only by Kernan's unreliability but by rigidities in the social order and the Church. She has "kept house shrewdly for her husband," has both fed and scolded him, has made religion "a habit." Kernan's "frequent intemperance" she "accepted . . . as part of the climate," and she is sensibly doubtful that "a man of her husband's age would . . . change greatly before death." That doubt of hers comes as close to the plain truth as the story's irony allows, and its medium is this representative Dublin wife whose formal orthodoxy is tempered by a fatalistic realism. Consequently though Joyce smiles at her, she is not the target of his satire; that falls rather upon the less realistic, more pretentious men, and more especially upon the Church insofar as it is represented by Father Purdon. The scheme conceived by Mr. Power and administered by Mr. Cunningham is to see Mr. Kernan gathered, by way of the businessmen's retreat, back into the arms of the Church, to which he had come over at his marriage but from which he had lapsed, even to the lamentable extent of "giving side-thrusts at Catholicism." Mrs. Kernan reflects that Mr. Power's plan "might do good and, at least, it could do no harm"—which typifies a life more accustomed to prudence than to hope. Beyond that, she considered Mr. Cunningham "capable," and besides, "religion was religion."

By summarizing what this comes to for her, Joyce sets limits on the characterization as a complement to the story as well as an item in his category of Dubliners: "Her beliefs were not extravagant. She believed steadily in the Sacred Heart as the most generally useful of all Catholic devotions and approved of the sacraments. Her faith was bounded by her kitchen, but, if she was put to it, she could believe also in the banshee and in the Holy Ghost." The extended treatment of Mrs. Kernan, together with briefer but detailed glimpses of such others as those minor apostles M'Coy and Fogarty and even the constable and the "Irish Jew" Harford, puts "Grace" in a category with "A Mother" as more deliberately and fully told, with more summary narration and exposition and longer pauses upon lesser characters than in some of the other *Dubliners* stories. The difference is sharpest in contrast with the first three stories, as they are held in the consciousness of a first-person narrator, and also with "Eveline" and "Clay" in their nearly complete containment within the protagonist's awareness and mood. "A Mother" and "Grace" also contrast as markedly with the perfected dramatic objectivity of "Ivy Day." They are less highly tuned aesthetically, less continuously resonant; nevertheless they proceed effectively, without lapse into such obvious flaws of narrative method as intrude by way of the too desultory and too openly explanatory opening pages of "After the Race" and "A Painful Case."

Two nights after Mr. Kernan's mishap Mr. Cunningham and Mr. Power, with the hanger-on Mr. M'Coy, come visiting and find him still in bed, in a disordered room "impregnated with a personal odour," but in a mood that has something of "a veteran's pride." Kernan knows nothing of the reformatory scheme, and its strategy will be to let him move to get in on something already covertly under way among the others, their plan to "make a retreat." Mr. Cunningham, as the story tells it, "was the very man for such a case." He is experienced in another problem of intemperance, as victim of a wife who is "unpresentable . . . an incurable drunkard," who had "pawned the furniture" all six times he had "set up house for her." He has everyone's "sympathy," but also their "respect." He is "an elder colleague of Mr. Power"—that is to say, a Castle employee; he is also recognized in his own right as "a thoroughly sensible man, influential and intelligent." Having told this, Joyce metaphorically adds a tinge of irony, to set in perspective the oracular role Cunningham is to play: "His blade of human knowledge, natural astuteness particularized by long association with cases in the police courts, had been tempered by brief immersions in the waters of general philosophy." Consequently friends "bowed to his opinions and considered that his face was like Shakespeare's."

Mr. Cunningham is not alone, however, in the tendency to parade what knowledge he thinks he has. So does Mr. M'Coy. He has had to live by his wits, and in ways that Mr. Power might well consider a "low playing of the game," if, as may be presumed, the valises and portmanteaus recently borrowed "to enable Mrs. M'Coy to fulfill imaginary engagements in the country" were for pawning. M'Coy had gone from job to job but is now secretary to the City Coroner, and with an air of challenge he supplies such technical terms as "mucus" and "thorax" to illuminate Kernan's description of his symptoms. When in the discussion of the various Popes' "mottoes" Mr. Fogarty proposes *Lux in Tenebris,* Mr. M'Coy says "O yes, *Tenebrae.*" When M'Coy's fragmentary knowledge runs out, he grasps for more, repeatedly asking "Is that so?" The least of this group of Dublin men, he still is typical in his insecurity and consequent expediency, and in his talkativeness. Thus he rounds out the demonstration of one of Dublin's most depressing aspects as Joyce pictured it, the random, roundabout, stereotyped, and forced conversation of commoners heard in any extended dialogue, as at the close of "The Sisters" or in "Two Gallants," "A Little Cloud," "Ivy Day," and portions of "The Dead."

In the purgatorial bedroom scene the story's plot runs along with characterization, centering on Mr. Kernan's evasiveness and the stages of pressure applied by his friends. Even as the talk increasingly tends to muddle over questions of fact, it centers on the Church and its great figures with ulterior intent of impressing and then persuading Kernan. He is a slippery fellow, but they haul him in, and there is wry comedy in this struggle of clumsy wits and in Kernan's final gasp of Protestant recalcitrance, his barring "the magic-lantern business" of carrying a candle, a defiance the others laugh off as face-saving bluster. There has been satire as well in Kernan's gradual surrender not to basic argument but to superficial aspects of the Church's prestige; he will give fit audience to the simoniac man-of-the-world, Father Purdon, as is suggested in his phrasing: "I'll do the retreat business and confession, and . . . all that business." But to bring so evasive a man this far has taken some doing. When he complained of feeling sick and Cunningham firmly told him, "That's the boose," Kernan said, "No, I think I caught cold on the car." When Cunningham inquired who were the two he was with at the time of the accident, he concentrated on the "little chap with sandy hair" whose name he can't remember until Cunningham closed in, asking "And who else?" and he had to admit it in one word, "Harford." To which Cunningham said "Hm," while the others were silent, doubtless remembering not only Harford's notorious "manners in drinking" but the man himself as usurious money-lender, often bitterly spoken of as "an Irish Jew," though as the story puts it "he had never embraced more than the Jewish ethical code," (and indeed he is to be seen later at the retreat, sitting "some distance off" from more reputable Catholics). Kernan tries to evade the fact that Harford had deserted him in his need, and wants it thought the two of them had "missed each other" by "some mistake." Mr. Power, having tactfully said "All's well that ends well," says it again, but Kernan is not ready to leave the topic of his sorry exploit or otherwise be led and turns the talk to "a decent young chap, that medical fellow" who had administered brandy. Only Power's reminding Kernan that he might have got a week in jail stirs his memory of a policeman, and after fending that off by wondering "How did it happen at all?" he finally must admit Cunningham's direct charge that he had been "peloothered."

Yet the mention of the policeman has provided a diversion for them all. Mr. Power resents M'Coy's familiarity in suggesting he (as employee of the Constabulary office) had "squared the constable," and so addresses his reply to Kernan, in words not given, but evidently touching upon the oafishness of the young fellow with the provincial accent who had "made ready to indite" it all in his notebook. Mr. Kernan, again evasive of his own fault, grows indignant that Dublin citizens and rate-payers should be affronted by "country bumpkins . . . ignorant bostooms." Mr. Cunningham, though a Castle official, shows an after-hours joviality about such rustics on the metropolitan force and tells the "65, catch your cabbage!" story. Mr. Kernan, relishing a digression, can be enough wrought up to speak of writing a letter to the papers about the "yahoos coming up here" who "think they can boss the people." Though Mr. Cunningham, in full resumption of his specific gravity, comes up with another judicious pronouncement—"It's like everything else in this world. You get some bad ones and you get some good ones"—still Mr. M'Coy, clinging to the edge of the conversation, opines that "It's better to have nothing to say to them." In a typical instance of compensatory group animosity, as Joyce sees it, these Dubliners so confined in the rigid mores of a sluggish metropolis have bolstered their self-esteem by disdain for provincials, and meanwhile for the moment Kernan has been let off.

Mrs. Kernan rescues them from preoccupation by entering with some bottles of stout, but nothing for her comically pleading husband except the wry offer of the back of her hand, and after some merriment, the conspiracy for redeeming Kernan is again set in motion. The three visitors talk mysteriously of their plans for Thursday night, where to meet, and not to be too late, "because it is sure to be crammed to the doors." Kernan finally has to inquire "What's in the wind?" and Cunningham still puts him off—"It's only a little matter that we're arranging about for Thursday"—and no, not the opera, "just a little [and he pauses reticently] spiritual matter." Mr. Kernan says "O," with what shift to a less eager tone may be imagined; there is further silence, and finally Mr. Power, with an air of "point-blank" admission, says they're going to "make a retreat." Then, giving Kernan time, they concentrate on themselves, owning up to each other that "one and all," as Cunningham puts it, they're "a nice collection of scoundrels" and are "going to wash the pot together." Only now, and as if the thought had just struck him, Cunningham proposes that Kernan join them, which Power amplifies as "Good idea. The four of us together." Kernan remains silent, and his resistance is described as of a familiar kind —"understanding that some spiritual agencies were about to concern themselves on his behalf, he thought he owed it to his dignity to show a stiff neck." So "for a long while" he listened silently, "with an air of calm enmity," while his friends, refraining from any direct pressure upon him, "discussed the Jesuits." Presumably this talk is laudatory, for "at length" Kernan admits he hasn't "such a bad opinion" of them, since they're "an educated order," and he believes "they mean well too."

With that much consent from him his friends can proceed, in a drifting conversation sampling Irish Catholicism among such a class of men, but it also differentiates them personally and develops into a nice play of characteristic assertions and responses, and a cumulative mood. Mr. Cunningham at once took up Kernan's tolerant remarks about the Jesuits and termed them the Church's "grandest order." When M'Coy would reduce it to a matter of power, and was about to cite proof that "they're the boyos have influence," Mr. Power cut in with another respectful generality, "a fine body of men." The Jesuit Order, Mr. Cunningham continued, "was never once reformed" because "it never fell away," and to M'Coy's almost reflexive "Is that so?" at any glimpse of information, Cunningham said "That's a fact. . . . That's history." The pragmatical M'Coy's further remark that the Jesuits "cater for the upper classes" led Kernan, with his flimsy pretensions of gentility, to say this was why he had "a feeling for them," as contrasted to "some of those secular priests, ignorant, bumptious—," whereupon Cunningham interrupted with plenary tolerance, to assert that "They're all good men, each in his own way. The Irish priesthood is honoured all the world over." "O, yes," Mr. Power agreed, and though M'Coy reduced national pride to insular chauvinism, derogating "some of the other priesthoods on the continent, unworthy of the name," Kernan had taken the main point, and has relented enough to say, "Perhaps you're right." To which Mr. Cunningham not only says "Of course I'm right," but asserts his reliability as "a judge of character." Kernan, impressed by him, "asked for particulars" about the proposed retreat; the benevolent scheme is beginning to work.

In the next passage talk passes from Father Purdon, who "is giving" the "retreat . . . for business men"—("Fine jolly fellow! . . . man of the world like ourselves . . . won't be too hard on us") —to another noted pulpit orator, Father Tom Burke. Him Kernan has heard, and indeed he is "nettled" at Cunningham's question that perhaps suggests Kernan has been too far out of touch to know about such an eminent preacher. Kernan also recollects that Crofton (though a Protestant, "a damned decent Orangeman,") was along on that occasion, and this leads to a trial flight of broad-mindedness which is brought back to orthodox grounds by Mr. Cunningham, to which Kernan consents, and thereby pulls himself a step further on the way his friends have chosen for him. As Kernan told it, after Father Burke's sermon, he and Crofton had gone "into Butler's in Moore Street" —Kernan being "genuinely moved," he confesses, and here is implied the Irish mixture as before of sentimentality and stout. Kernan recalled Crofton's "very words," that though they "worship at different altars" their "belief is the same," which Kernan considered "very well put." Power admits "There's a good deal in that," but instead of saying how much, he adds there were always "crowds of Protestants . . . when Father Tom was preaching." M'Coy, struggling to have his word, says, "There's not much difference between us. We both believe in—" and hesitates, then adds "in the Redeemer," but he touches base again by saying "Only they don't believe in the Pope and in the mother of God." The conversation by this time apparently seems to Mr. Cunningham to need some regulating, and "quietly and effectively" he declares, "But, of course, our religion is *the* religion, the old, original faith." To this Mr. Kernan now warmly assents: "Not a doubt of it," he says; the round-trip excursion in amateur theology appears to have had a bracing effect on his lapsed convictions, and he seems ripe to be gathered in.

At this point the group is augmented. Mr. Fogarty, a "modest grocer" but "not without culture," and enough of a Joycean Dubliner to have failed once in business, arrives to inquire politely about Kernan (who owes him a small account) and to proffer "a half-pint of special whisky." Before any of the talk deviously intent on reformation of a drunkard is resumed, this gift is portioned out to the five of them; then Mr. Fogarty, "sitting on a small area of the chair," listens with special interest as Cunningham continues his discourse. From here on the conversation produces a tangle of historical data, chiefly because Mr. Cunningham, always positive, is often wrong, but also because no one else is exactly right. Joyce, who was scrupulous about any matters of fact he introduced into his stories, must have taken mischievous pleasure in composing this melange of misinformation paraded in the service of orthodox posture. At the same time he skilfully sustained a conversation which portrays character and evolves theme while keeping the story mainly within the comprehension of any relatively unlearned readers.

As to errors, chiefly advanced by the inflexibly positive Cunningham, they center around the so-called mottoes of the Popes and the proclamation of Papal infallibility. Concerning the "mottoes," R. M. Adams has pointed out that Popes do not take them, and that Joyce's characters have been made to allude, erroneously, to the "so-called *Prophecies of Malachias,* in which the Irish saint foretold, in a phrase apiece, the characters of the popes to come."[5] From this source, for instance, the "motto" of

Leo XIII would be neither Mr. Cunningham's intermittent Latin, *Lux upon Lux,* nor Mr. Fogarty's eager supplement, *Lux in Tenebris,* but *Lumen in Coelo.* Nor is Mr. Cunningham right in attributing *Crux upon Crux* to Pius IX; the twelfth century Irish saint's prophecy for this pope was *Crux de Cruce.* While Mr. Fogarty's dissent, though "positively" put down, may augment a reader's natural suspicion of anyone as dogmatic as Cunningham, his hearers allowed his "inference" that *Crux upon Crux* was "to show the difference between their two pontificates," and Cunningham continued freely, to the effect that Pope Leo was "a great scholar and a poet." Mr. Kernan (with that worldly taste for appearances which can account for some conversions) remarked that Leo "had a strong face." Mr. Cunningham specified that "he wrote Latin poetry." The remoteness of this lofty concept leads the men to muse on their humbler educations, which nevertheless Mr. Kernan compensatorily defends as plain and honest, with "none of your modern trumpery"; Mr. Power, with his usual discreet spareness of speech, says "Quite right," and Mr. Fogarty embellishes the judgment with the phrase, "No superfluities." With this flurry past, Mr. Cunningham continued implacably—he remembers "reading that one of Pope Leo's poems was on the invention of the photograph—in Latin, of course." The others worry this topic in their own ways; M'Coy considers "the photograph wonderful when you come to think of it," Power affirms that "great minds can see things," and then with a free associative grab Fogarty recalls that "the poet says: *Great minds are very near to madness.*"

It is Mr. Kernan who gives Mr. Cunningham the floor again by asking him whether "some of the Popes—of course, not our present man, or his predecessor, but some of the old Popes" were "not exactly . . . you know . . . up to the knocker?" (His question, with its businesslike phrase "our present man," places Kernan as one now reaffiliated and still a purveyor of scandal.) The precipitated silence makes way for Mr. Cunningham's most ponderous and preposterous display as supposedly well-informed layman. He agrees that the popes included "some bad lots," but goes on to "the astonishing thing" that among them all, even "the biggest drunkard" or "the most . . . out-and-out ruffian, not one of them ever preached *ex cathedra* a word of false doctrine." Mr. Kernan finds it possible to agree that this is indeed what Mr. Cunningham calls it, "an astonishing thing." Mr. Fogarty completes the circle for dogmatism chasing its own tail by explaining that "when the Pope speaks *ex cathedra* he is infallible." Mr. Kernan says he knows about that, and his recalling something about papal infallibility, though he "was younger then," is a reminder that these Dubliners at the turn of the century could look back to the Vatican Council of 1869–70 as within their lifetimes or at least of recent hearsay. Europe had so echoed with controversy, some of it published, before and during the Council that the matter would have seeped down to the level of common talk, and the Irish proclivity for discussion would have kept it in mind while working changes upon it. Mr. Kernan's recollections are vague, and after Mr. Fogarty interrupts to pour out more measures of the whisky, when M'Coy asks Kernan to go on, Mr. Cunningham feels called to break in and take over.

As if announcing a text from a pulpit he proclaimed: "Papal infallibility, that was the greatest scene in the whole history of the Church." When Power co-operatively asked how was that, Mr. Cunningham made an almost pontifical gesture; he "held up two thick fingers" as he spoke. What he pronounces is a tissue of misinformation, in some of Joyce's most esoterically ironic satire. After Joyce had visited the Biblioteca Vittorio Emanuele in Rome in November, 1906, to ascertain details about the Vatican Council as referred to in "Grace," he wrote a report to his brother Stanislaus. It was in a vein characteristic between them: "Before the final proclamation many of the clerics left Rome as a protest. At the proclamation when the dogma was read out the Pope said 'Is that all right, gents?' All the gents said 'Placet' but two said 'Non placet.' But the Pope 'You be damned! Kissmearse! I'm infallible!' "[6] Flippantly irreverent though he was, Joyce no doubt as usual had made sure of facts, to have his history straight in writing his parody of its distortion by his characters, especially that invincible ignoramus, the solidly pious Cunningham. However, Joyce was necessarily selective; he treated only the Council's last scene, and did not bring into the men's talk related preceding events, though John McHale, Archbishop of Tuam and the grand old hero of the Catholic Church in Ireland, was involved in them, in a way that both supports and contradicts Cunningham's notions, and that must have contributed to John of Tuam's legendary status among his countrymen.

It is credible too that a German's name should enter, though distorted, into this sickroom symposium a generation after the event. Dr. Johann Joseph Ignaz von Döllinger was a notable intellectual and man of public affairs, highly regarded in England as well as on the Continent; he was also a most prominent, energetic, and intransigent opponent of a declaration of papal infallibility. Not a cardinal, as Cunningham has it (nor even a bishop, as Marvin Magalaner ordains)[7] he was a priest, and a professor at Munich, first of theology and then of ecclesiastical history.[8] In his writings he had criticized Lutheranism as schismatic and had described the Pope as "supreme Teacher and Guardian of the Faith" and "the Visible Representative of Ecclesiastical Unity,"[9] while concerning St. Peter and the Papacy he had declared that "the continuance, increase, and growth of the Church rests on the office created in his person."[10] Nevertheless, Dr. Döllinger was a liberal Catholic, he had disapproved the promulgation in 1854 of the dogma of the Immaculate Conception, and for him papal primacy did not include infallibility.[11] Before the Council and during it he worked influentially and wrote extensively and sometimes pugnaciously against the proposal, and especially against the movement to have it declared by acclamation.[12] After the Council, called upon by the Archbishop of Munich to accept the Vatican decrees, Döllinger declared that "As a Christian, as a theologian, as an historian, as a citizen, I cannot accept this doctrine."[13] But he did not leave the Church, as Cunningham put it; he was excommunicated.[14] He lived on for twenty years, still regarding himself, he wrote, "comme membre de la grande Eglise Catholique,"[15] and he remained highly esteemed among more liberal European Catholics: he was accorded honorary doctorates by Oxford, Edinburgh, Marburg, and Vienna, and at Munich he was made rector-magnificus of the university by an almost unanimous election.[16]

Thus when Cunningham asserts that "John McHale" and "a German cardinal by the name of Dolling . . . or Dowling . . . or —" were the two *non placets* on the final ballot, he uncertainly names an eminent foreign figure as a steady intransigent in the dispute over infallibility, which Döllinger was, but also as a *non placet* in an election in which Döllinger, only a priest, had no vote. Nor is Cunningham correct about John of Tuam's *non placet* on the final ballot. Fogarty, though vague and though overruled, is nearly right in thinking "it was some Italian or American"—the two *non placets* were Fitzgerald of Little Rock, Arkansas, and Riccio of Cajazzo in the Kingdom of Naples. As soon as the Pope had confirmed the matter, Fitzgerald professed acceptance in the phrase *"Modo credo, sancte Pater"* and Riccio likewise knelt and said *"Credo."*[17] But Cunningham in his free arrangement of hearsay has concentrated all the paradoxical glory in those exemplary roles of defiance and submission on John of Tuam. As a formidable and beloved figure in Irish ecclesiastical and public life, McHale was well fitted to pass through history into folklore. And he had, in fact, uttered a *non placet,* but only in a preliminary, trial balloting, which could have been the source in truth of Cunningham's misconception.

In January of 1870 McHale, the oldest prelate as such in the Council,[18] was one of 140 who signed a petition against bringing up the matter of papal infallibility. On July 13 there was a trial ballot in which the vote was *placet,* 451; *non placet,* 88; *placet iuxta modum,* 62 (which latter were required to submit their amendments in writing), and in this test of the question Archbishop McHale, along with three other Irish bishops, was among the 88 *non placets.*[19] Joyce's statement to Stanislaus that before the final proclamation "many of the clerics left Rome as a protest" is half the story; though they could not with conviction vote *placet* they would not give scandal by voting *non placet,* and 55 of these bishops had written the Pope a dignified and high-minded letter expressing this position.[20] McHale, though he had spoken against the proposal, was not among those signers, nor did he like six others merely write "asking that they be taken as voting *non placet.*"[21] Evidently he was among those who before the final and official balloting "absented themselves without saying anything,"[22] for Dom Cuthbert Butler in his history of the Council records that Archbishop McHale and the Irish bishop Moriarty (presumably also an absenter) "seem to have been the only ones never called on to make a formal adhesion or to promulgate the decrees" and that "they made no move until 1875," when along with the other Irish bishops at the Synod of Maynooth "they signed a joint pastoral enforcing the definition of infallibility as of Catholic faith."[23]

Hot indeed it must have been for fatigued elderly clerics in Rome that July of 1870, and there were reasons besides the weather for some to withdraw, but Cunningham as popular historian apparently does not know much about that—how at the time of the trial ballot with a total of 601 (*placet,* 451; *non placet,* 88; *placet iuxta modum,* 62) there were still "about 76" others "actually in Rome who absented themselves from the Congregation."[24] Neither does Cunningham seem to know that by the time of the official balloting those present to vote had declined by 66 more, from 601 to 535 (*placet,* 533; *non placet,* 2). So nothing stands in Cunningham's own infallible way of promulgating a legend which gives its own kind of honor to the Church's most eminent and revered Irish dignitary. These Dubliners drinking Fogarty's half-pint at Kernan's bedside hear it from Cunningham that when "the Pope himself stood up and declared infallibility a dogma of the Church *ex cathedra,*" then that "very moment John McHale, who had been arguing and arguing against it, stood up and shouted out with the voice of a lion: 'Credo!' " "I believe!" Mr. Fogarty translates and affirms.

"Credo!" says Mr. Cunningham again, and adds that it "showed the faith he had."

This account, the story says, "had built up the vast image of the Church in the minds of his hearers" and his voice "thrilled them as it uttered the word of belief and submission," so that Mrs. Kernan, entering, finds "a solemn company," and when Mr. Power "with abrupt joviality" says they're "going to make your man here a good holy pious and God-fearing Roman Catholic," Kernan can only say, "I don't mind," meanwhile "smiling a little nervously." The scheme has carried through.

But so has Joyce's satire. Obviously few readers of "Grace," even those closest to the events of 1870, could be expected to detect Martin Cunningham's rearrangements of church history, though no doubt many of the faithful had absorbed equally garbled versions of the long struggle at the Council, together with legends of one intractable "Cardinal Dowling." Joyce would have been quite aware of all this; perhaps in his own apostasy and anticlericalism he took instead a malicious delight in supposing that many most knowingly able to correct Cunningham would be most irked at having the Council's troubled procedures thus slyly brought to mind. But this would have been only his incidental private fun, and in *Dubliners* (except for his sniping at Stanislaus in "A Painful Case") he did not lapse from his responsible role as artist. So Joyce kept "Grace" going on two levels, continuously, in this purgatorial bedroom scene. Though a knowledge of all that Joyce is manipulating may have its own considerable interest, the passage is telling without corrective annotation, since from the first and at successive instances readers can have caught its irony, most obvious in the diffuse, flabbily pretentious talk, but also apparent as Fogarty disagrees about details. Somebody is wrong, and even the readers who do not know that Fogarty is nearer right may sense in Cunningham's "Allow me" spoken so "positively" the overriding presence of the most suspect dogmatist in the lot, a man capable of being "encouraged by his own voice," and merely the biggest frog in a rather muddied little Dublin puddle. As the scene has proceeded, characterization and plot have intertwined; the satire is not static but evolves the consequences of the traits caricatured. By an appeal to a naïve conformity through a fragmented, inaccurate, and sentimental vision of the Church, and by the legendary glorification of a really notable Irish ecclesiastic, the scheme for Kernan's salvation works itself out, and he is dimly persuaded.

Characteristically, though, what seems to be weighing most at the moment with Kernan is the recollection of having once seen the old Archbishop John McHale in public, "a crabbed-looking old chap," with bushy eyebrows and "an eye like a hawk." The occasion was the unveiling (in 1879) of a statue to Sir John Gray, proprietor of the *Freeman's Journal* until his death in 1875, and a physician, a Protestant nationalist, and moderate advocate of Home Rule.[25] R. M. Adams reports that Kernan has some of his facts wrong,[26] and assuming Joyce knew what he was doing, as he generally did, here is a further picturing of an Irish tendency to rearrange details into a more inspiriting myth. So Kernan fancies he remembers John McHale at the ceremony bending his bushy eyebrows at the orator with a look that seemed to say, "*I have you properly taped, my lad.*" Kernan has it that the speaker was Edmund Dyer Gray, which leads Mr. Power to say "None of the Grays was any good." Through this little interlude the story has passed from the high thrilling moment of Cunningham's "Credo!" attributed to the great John McHale, and by way of Kernan's memory of "such an eye" in that old man, to Mr. Power's comprehensive sectarian derogation of "the Grays." Kernan having been lightly secured in the harbor of faith, the talk can turn to particulars and in an easier tone than with some of the matters they had skirted.

The little more than a page that closes the story's middle section and makes way for the men's presence at the retreat is a fine piece of Joycean dialogue, with five voices each heard characteristically (and one voice as characteristically silent) in a rapid exchange that cloaks purpose with banter. Mrs. Kernan, thinking it "wiser to conceal her satisfaction," and at the same time keeping her husband under pressure, said she pitied "the poor priest" who would have to listen to Kernan's confession, or "tale," as she called it. Kernan grew bluntly defiant at that, and claimed to be "not such a bad fellow." Cunningham "intervened promptly," to remind him, no doubt in his most orotund way, that they were all in it together in renouncing "the devil . . . his works and pomps." Mr. Fogarty laughed as he said, "Get behind me, Satan!"—looking at the others for agreement in the ambiguous mood they have come to. Though Mr. Power "said nothing," feeling "completely outgeneraled" amid so much caprice, nevertheless "a pleased expression flickered across his face"—his plan has worked, roughly speaking. Mr. Cunningham, still seriously concerned with means as well as ends, gets back to an instruction in fundamentals, but keeps it simple and easy—"All we have to do is to stand up with lighted candles in our hands and renew our baptismal vows." Mr. M'Coy, still at the edge of this circle, now tries again with something more than his repeated "Is that so?" and says, "O, don't forget the candle, Tom, whatever you do." That gives Kernan an opening for a little restorative self-assertion. He will "draw the line there," he will "do the retreat business and confession and . . . all that business" but, he repeats, "no candles! No, damn it all, I bar the candles!" and "conscious of having created an effect," he continues "to shake his head to and fro." The others play along with him in this game of ambiguities; they laugh "heartily" and his wife, who presumably understands him well, says, "Listen to that!" and when he calls candles "the magic-lantern business," she adds, "There's a nice Catholic for you!" Invigorated by his pretense of nonconformity, Kernan repeats, "No candles!" and "obdurately" declares "That's off!" On this caricature of the snatched but still smouldering brand, and this jangling of conventions and essentials in which Kernan is as muddled as anyone else, the purgatorical bedside conference ends.

The final episode, the following Thursday evening, has for its Paradise "the Jesuit Church in Gardiner Street." The focus broadens to the story's widest Dublin scene, then narrows again somewhat, but not to fall primarily upon Tom Kernan, though the part he will play is presumable from what is seen when he kneels, following "the general example." He is not to be glimpsed thereafter standing (surely with his candle) repeating his baptismal vows; much less will the story go with him into the confessional. This is not reticence on Joyce's part; he did not hesitate to set down young Stephen's exchange with his confessor. Instead, the story now is of that mass of men containing those five, quiescent this side of desperation, and then it turns full upon the preacher and his discourse, where it ends, though not necessarily on his concluding sentence, and certainly not on any last word in the established repetitious process he typifies. The implication here, as in other *Dubliner* stories, is of a closed circle, in a return to a familiar ceremony, presumably to be followed by lapse into the more ordinary life of Dublin's commoners, whom Joyce sees as not merely average sensual men but those especially beleaguered by confusions environmentally imposed and compounded.

The movement into this third scene by ellipsis is firmly made. With the church "almost full" of "gentlemen . . . well-dressed and orderly" and with others entering "at every moment," the five are already placed. In a bench near the pulpit sits Mr. Cunningham with Mr. Kernan, as if he has sought to bring him as close as possible to the persuasion that is to save him. Mr. M'Coy sits in the bench behind them, alone, and behind him in the next bench are Mr. Power and Mr. Fogarty. They have "settled down in the form of a quincunx," a figure corresponding to the position of Christ's five wounds on the cross, and corresponded to by the courageous in the fifth heaven of Dante's *Paradiso*. Such symbolism is not, of course, these Dubliners' design. Mr. M'Coy "had tried unsuccessfully" to find a seat with others of the party, and once they were settled down with himself in the center of the pattern, "he had tried unsuccessfully to make comic remarks," but gradually he adapts himself to the situation.

Mr. Cunningham finds it permissible, however, to whisper to

Kernan and draw his attention to others in the congregation; whether or not it is so intended, it expands what Cunningham had said in Kernan's bedroom about "a nice collection of scoundrels, one and all" who are "going to wash the pot together." So there too was "Mr. Harford, the money-lender," who had been with Kernan at the time of his fall and apparently had deserted him; Mr. Harford now sits "some distance off." There was also a character disparaged in "Ivy Day in the Committee Room"—"Mr. Fanning, the registration agent and mayor maker . . . sitting immediately under the pulpit," which may signalize something other than religiosity, for with Fanning is "one of the newly-elected councillors of the ward," and the sermon they are to hear would allow it is not incongruous if at this retreat for businessmen the men bring some business with them. All are seen more or less in that aspect: there "to the right" is old Michael Grimes, "owner of three pawnbroker's shops," and "Dan Hogan's nephew, who was up for the job in the Town Clerk's office," and "farther in front" is "the chief reporter of *The Freeman's Journal,*" the Mr. Hendrick who appears in "A Mother." There is also "poor O'Carroll, an old friend of Mr. Kernan's, who had been at one time a considerable commercial figure" and who thus might be thought to take on an admonitory aspect for Kernan. But the sight of all these men together has had the effect Cunningham probably intended in pointing them out; "Mr. Kernan began to feel more at home." There and in that state the story leaves him, with only a few more confirmatory glimpses—his kneeling as he "followed the general example" when Father Purdon mounted into the pulpit; and his settling back on the bench, holding on his knee the hat his wife had "rehabilitated," while he "presented an attentive face to the preacher." There is a touch of pathos in that pose of this flighty wayward man, and as the story proceeds its suggestion of a general obscure doom may also fall most closely on this particular figure, the hero of "Grace."

The red-faced Father Purdon, after "struggling up into the pulpit" and kneeling for a silent prayer, announces his text, chosen as "specially adapted for the guidance" of "business and professional men." It is this: "For the children of this world are wiser in their generation than the children of light. Wherefore make unto yourselves friends out of the mammon of iniquity so that when you die they may receive you into everlasting dwellings." What follows for almost two pages, concluding the story, is Father Purdon's sermon in essence, given mostly in indirect discourse, but phrased, presumably, in his renowned pulpit manner—like that in fact of the popular Father Bernard Vaughan.[27] Admitting that it was "one of the most difficult texts in all the Scriptures to interpret properly," the preacher nevertheless proposed to develop it for the edification of "those whose lot it was to lead the life of the world and who yet wished to lead that life not in the manner of worldlings." He proceeded "with resonant assurance," the more so because he could say "he was there that evening for no terrifying, no extravagant purpose; but as a man of the world speaking to his fellow-men." From his text he has found that Jesus Christ sets "worshippers of Mammon" before men as paradoxical "exemplars in the religious life"; what this comes to, it seems, for Father Purdon is a matter of accounting. (Kernan has naïvely spoken of "the retreat business and confession and . . . all that business," and now the preacher himself, as purveyor of the means of grace, chooses the language of trafficking; Joyce's preoccupation with simony, more precisely displayed here than in "The Sisters," lies barely beneath the surface of this episode.) Calling himself "their spiritual accountant," Father Purdon "wished each and every one of his hearers to open . . . the books of his spiritual life, and see if they tallied accurately with conscience." Then before the suggestion of an audit could disconcert his hearers, they were assured that "Jesus Christ was not a hard taskmaster," but "understood" what Father Purdon called "our little failings . . . the weakness of our poor fallen nature . . . the temptations of this life." With gradual approach and soothing insinuation he tells them "We might have had, we all had from time to time, our temptations: we might have, we all had, our failings." Having led them this far step by easy step, now "one thing only" he "would ask of his hearers . . . to be straight and manly with God" as to their spiritual bookkeeping. With seeming liberality Father Purdon suggests some audits might tally "in every point," and such men might say, "Well, I have verified my accounts. I find all well." Then tactfully the preacher moves on to the cases, "as might happen," of "some discrepancies." Here the remedy is easy—"to admit the truth, to be frank and say like a man: 'Well, I have looked into my accounts. I find this wrong and this wrong. But, with God's grace, I will rectify this and this. I will set right my accounts.' "

Which is where the story ends, if not the sermon.

The narrating of this homily in indirect discourse creates an almost cinematic effect of withdrawal and long perspective. The more direct wording which Father Purdon then offered as a handy formula for his hearers is the extent of Joyce's further allusion to that conclave of Dublin men, and those five in their midst, with Mr. Kernan in the others' well-meaning, fumbling charge. The story's ending as it began, existentially, in the midst of things, and Kernan rehabilitated, hat and all, sitting up attentively, but thus perfunctorily ministered to, projects only an endless round of compulsive intemperance and conventional penance in his gradual decline. This may be not much different from the fortuitous lives of many men, but that pathos is incidental to Joyce's satire of simony and all who traffic in its dubious benefits. Father Purdon is meeting his congregation more than half-way, expediently to maintain their formal allegiance, but in a mode that will merely confirm them in the ups and downs of their dreary lives. For Kernan, the addiction to strong drink has been temporarily set aside by another seduction, in a confined pattern of alternating but almost reciprocal bemusings. So it is, after their fashions, with others as Joyce sees them. The story's last scene implies the widest look at Dublin in all of *Dubliners*. Here is a large church, filled with men of several sorts and conditions, yet all similarly engaged, like those in the quincunx, in a process as inescapably cyclical as the periodic auditing of books for a business conducted in the customary way at the same old stand. Red-faced Father Purdon, "a powerful-looking figure" reverently "observed to be struggling up into the pulpit," arrived there to resort to metaphor (in the common way of preachers, politicians, admen, and other men) as quasi-explanation and pseudo-proof, but also, in the story's ultimate irony, to be heard proposing a more divulging analogy than such a practitioner and prisoner of simony would have dared let himself admit, even to himself.

THE DEAD

The final story in *Dubliners,* and the one most generally and greatly admired, was a late fruition, and in the planning of the book an afterthought. On February 28, 1906, when returning to Grant Richards the signed contract for a collection then comprising twelve stories, Joyce wrote, "I have sent you [six days earlier, it was] a story *Two Gallants* and propose adding one more story to the book."[1] Evidently this last was "A Little Cloud," for on March 13 Joyce wrote that he would forward "in a week or so the last story which is to be inserted between *The Boarding House* and *Counterparts,*" and that is where "A Little Cloud" stands.[2] With it so placed and with "Two Gallants" added to the twelve of the contract, the collection of fourteen would have had its finale in "Grace," with that diminished ironic ending so satirical of the Church and its flaccid adherents. But something further was forming in Joyce's mind, and of different complexion and import.

In September of that year he wrote his brother Stanislaus of qualms about his work. He felt occasionally that he had been "unnecessarily harsh," had "reproduced (in *Dubliners* at least) none of the attractions of the city," nor "its ingenuous insularity and its hospitality."[3] Since "The Dead" somewhat remedies this lack, that might be thought a main intention. What seems, however, more significant than Joyce's concern about Dublin ingenuousness and hospitality is that the story which had immediately preceded "The Dead" in the order of writing was "A Little Cloud." If the proposed collection of fourteen stories had been published, and promptly, this latest-written one still would not have supplanted "Grace" at the end, where Joyce had grouped what he called "stories of public life in Dublin";[4] by his fixed plan "A Little Cloud" would have stood eighth, where it remains, now exactly midway. There perhaps it is to be considered pivotal, for this story next-last written, like "The Dead," turns in its epiphanal climax upon a husband's increased awareness, melancholy but enlarging.

The concluding paragraph of "The Dead" is often admired for its lyricism.[5] What is more remarkable is the passage of ten pages preceding it, the episode of Gabriel and Gretta alone in their hotel room, and Gabriel in his final solitude as she sleeps. Nowhere has Joyce developed a scene more penetratingly, with economy yet with that minute relevant continuity which can give a page of fiction candid persuasiveness. Like any such vital passage, it does not stand alone, but draws upon what has more lengthily gone before, all the to-do of the holiday party and Gabriel's perturbations during it. A subtle but potent feature of "The Dead" is its pace, leisurely yet economically progressive; it is an adagio with no gesture either hurried or superfluous. The subject for the larger portion being an evening party with a miscellany of guests, the general structure is casual, incorporating by simple onward movements the diverse incidents that lightly sketch idiosyncrasies, and the story's texture is correspondingly variegated. The characters rise above apathy yet seldom to animation; there is banter and movement and amenity, but it takes all of Mary Jane's and her old aunts' efforts to keep the party going. These Dubliners' lives imply a sort of sluggish aimlessness which convention has largely imposed and now mitigates in small ways. There are meetings and greetings, musical performances by two of the three hostesses, dancing, and a supper, with a suggestion of dull surfeit in the monotonous style as "The raisins and almonds and figs and apples and oranges and chocolates and sweets were now passed about the table and Aunt Julia invited all the guests to have either port or sherry." There is an after-supper speech, with an extravagant toast to the hostesses, and a song to them as "jolly gay fellows"; there is as the party is breaking up a well-worn humorous family anecdote about Grandfather Morkin, and the departing guests hear from above-stairs an Irish folksong, the effect of which on Gretta is a bridge to the story's closing episode. All through the party minor characters move into narrative focus briefly and out again; the group is neither small nor homogeneous enough to support much extended conversation. There are some brief exchanges, a few spurts of curiosity, and even a bit of acrimony, but the most sustained positiveness, behind which a spontaneous vitality is felt, is from the lively nationalistic Miss Ivors. However, she will not remain for supper, giving no more reason than that she "did not feel in the least hungry" and "had already overstayed her time," and her independence and withdrawal from the party set up a contrast with it and the others there.

More particularly she has challenged Gabriel and moved him to hypersensitive self-defensive reaction. What the party is left with as their nearest approach to a common interest is not Irish nationalism but music, and more especially singers. Fond retrospective talk of those great ones dead and gone, the aunts' perceptible agedness, and discussion of monks' austerities "to remind them of their last end" all sound the recurrent note of mortality, and help make way for the epiphany which is to come to Gabriel through his wife's recollection of one who sang who had died young and obscure. For, crowded and faceted as it is, "The Dead" does have a protagonist in Gabriel, and his primacy is maintained. He has a part, sometimes prominent, in most of the action, much of its quality is transmitted through his feelings, and the story's climax is in his self-examination and access to further awareness. The narrative is not altogether in his point of view, it begins without him, and some of its incidents though in his presence are objectively self-sustaining, without coloration by his view of the matter. On the whole, however, "The Dead" is tinged by Gabriel's moods and shaped to his temperament—his sentience, his considerate affections, his apprehensiveness, ambivalence, and consequent liability to discomposure, his basic generosity and receptiveness to insight.

That which it tells of Gabriel "The Dead" also seems, in some ways, to tell of its author. Professor Harry Levin has written what has become a fixed point of reference: "Gabriel Conroy is what Joyce might have become, had he remained in Ireland."[6] The story's web of roots in Joyce's own life runs wide and sometimes very deep. These parabiographical elements are of two kinds, though, and their separateness should be seen in a critical view of the story. The plain factual connections, interesting as they may be, are merely adjunctive, as always with raw material given genuine artistic transmutation. Since fiction's main worth derives not from whatever facts the artist may have had to draw on but from what he was inclined to do with them, for the critic to reverse that order of values (as is done in much dead-end identification of sources) is not only to turn aside from the work of art in itself, but perhaps to be left with a now fictitiously tainted biography. It is well to remember, instead, that the more vitally creative an artist is, the more does he tend to render any sources only subordinately relevant. Used with discretion as well as enterprise, knowledge of sources can thus illuminate the work of art in detail and as an entity, and may allow a glimpse at the artist himself in a correspondingly revealing gesture, as with Joyce in "The Dead."

Richard Ellmann, in his constant diligence and with characteristic judiciousness, has assembled many facts related to "The Dead" yet without making their dimensions the measure of the story. The Morkan sisters, Gabriel's Aunt Kate and Aunt Julia, spinster music teachers, seem based on two of Joyce's maternal great-aunts, who did conduct the "Misses Flynn school," at 15 Usher's Island.[7] (This is not an island but a street, a quay, bordering the south bank of the Liffey, a short distance west of Adam and Eve's Church, where for years Miss Julia of the story had been leading soprano in the choir—"riverrun, past Eve and Adam's," *Finnegans Wake* has it to begin with.) Joyce's great-grandfather Flynn did own a starch mill in Back Lane, did have all his daughters trained in music; then at the "Misses Flynn school," which two of them conducted, their niece Mary Jane Murray, Joyce's mother, received lessons in piano and voice, dancing and "politeness."[8] To that same "dark, gaunt house" (and the houses on Usher's Island are still that) the Joyces would go each year for the party given by the Flynn aunts, now Mrs. Callanan and Mrs. Lyons, and Mrs. Callanan's daughter Mary Ellen, the niece of the story, and Joyce's father would carve the goose and of course make a fulsome speech.[9] Stanislaus Joyce tells in *My Brother's Keeper* how his parents would go up from Bray to Dublin for parties in the Christmas season, leaving the children at home and staying overnight at a hotel. If this is considered a source for a similar detail in "The Dead," a drastic adaptation must also be seen, for Stanislaus has it that their mother "would give the servants many anxious recommendations," whereas in the story Gabriel is the constantly anxious one about his family's welfare and Gretta is sure the children will be all right.[10]

According to Richard M. Kain, Kathleen Sheehy (of the family Joyce knew so well in his student days) "may have provided a model for Miss Ivors" as the "ardent nationalist,"[11] and Ellmann learned from Mrs. Mary Sheehy Kettle that her sister did wear an austere bodice and sported a patriotic pin as described in the story.[12] Joyce himself, like Gabriel Conroy, did write reviews for the *Daily Express,*[13] a moderate paper inclined toward toleration between Catholics and Protestants and a possible *modus operandi* between Irish nationalism and the Empire. (Lady Gregory had written a letter of introduction in Joyce's behalf to the paper's editor.)[14] As a far source for "The Dead," Gerhard Friedrich proposed that a Bret Harte novel, *Gabriel Conroy,* may have supplied not only the name but the snow imagery,[15] but Ellmann notes the presence on Howth of a publican named Gabriel Conroy and reasonably supposes that "probably" Joyce knew of him.[16] Ellmann suggests that the mention of Gabriel's mother's "sullen opposition" to his marrying Gretta stemmed from Joyce's paternal grandmother's life-long refusal to forgive her only son for marrying into a family, the Murrays, whom she considered beneath the Joyces.[17]

Most centrally related to the story and most directly translated into it are certain events in Nora's earlier life and some aspects of Joyce's attitude toward her. How deep this connection runs, even to the point of identification, is seen in his letter from Dublin to her in Trieste, on August 22, 1909—"Do you remember," he writes, "the three adjectives I have used in *The Dead* in speaking of your body. They are these: 'musical and strange and perfumed.' "[18] That letter comes at the conclusion of a series of violently emotional ones prompted by the false suggestion that a former associate, Vincent Cosgrove, had shared Nora's favors at the time Joyce first knew her in Dublin. That Joyce's involvement was at once ardent and disturbing, especially through its undeniable claim on a resolutely detached young man, is plain from a passage in an early letter (August 29, 1904) which repudiates "home, the recognized virtues, classes of life, and religious doctrines" but speaks his devotion with a troubled weighing that discloses ambivalence in him as well as the ambiguity of their relationship:

> I have noticed a certain shyness in your manner as if the recollection of that night [June 16—later to be Bloomsday] troubled you. I however consider it a kind of sacrament and the recollection of it fills me with amazed joy. You will perhaps not understand at once why it is that I honour you so much on account of it as you do not know much of my mind. But at the same time it was a sacrament which left in me a final sense of sorrow and degradation—sorrow because I saw in you an extraordinary, melancholy tenderness which had chosen that sacrament as a compromise, and degradation because I understood that in your eyes I was inferior to a convention of our present society.[19]

It had been indeed an odd wooing and winning; the precipitate rejection of conventions had already laid on its own burdens, and "much of" his "mind" may have remained less than candidly acknowledged by Joyce himself.

Still there was passion as well as melancholy, and as these had striven against each other in Joyce, so were they made to do in

Gabriel. Joyce attributed to Gabriel the ardor of himself on the verge of leaving Ireland with Nora; in that autumn of 1904 Joyce had written her: "Why should I not call you what in my heart I continually call you? What is it that prevents me unless it be that no word is tender enough to be your name?"[20] while Gabriel, as they are walking after the party to find a cab, remembers writing "years before" to his wife: "Why is it that words like these seem to me so dull and cold? Is it because there is no word tender enough to be your name?" And in this passage of the story there occurs a minute but interesting preponderance of the autobiographical. Gabriel is a settled teacher whose only writing told of is weekly reviews, whereas Joyce taught for a while but only of necessity, yet Gabriel is made to think that, along with their children and her household cares, "his writing . . . had not quenched all their souls' tender fire."

Gabriel in "The Dead" has no reason, as Joyce once mistakenly thought he himself had, to suspect the woman he loved of an earlier infidelity, and with a friend. Joyce did have what he made a cause for jealousy analogous to what Gabriel feels, and here the detailed connections are very close, although the fictional transmutation is both an enhancement and a masterful ordering. In her girlhood, in Galway, Nora Barnacle had known and "was very fond of" a handsome dark-haired young man named Michael Bodkin, a university student who was her "great admirer" and "died very young," according to an account dictated years later by Nora's girlhood friend Mary O'Holleran.[21] Bodkin became ill, and, according to Ellmann, when he knew Nora was to go to Dublin, he got up from his sickbed to sing a farewell to her outside her window, and in rainy weather, and then word came soon after to Nora in Dublin that he was dead.[22] In the story it is not told that the young lover sang at Gretta's window, but that he did come in the rain, though ill. Ellmann reports that Joyce had conducted "minute interrogations of Nora even before their departure from Dublin"; he "was disconcerted by the fact that young men before him had interested her," and "did not much like to know that her heart was still moved, even in pity, by the recollection of the boy who had loved her."[23] This Michael Bodkin who had died young but remained in Nora's memory was to haunt Joyce even more.

In 1912, five years after the writing of "The Dead," Joyce was again in Ireland, in Galway, and with Nora, with whom he went to the races; he also bicycled seventeen miles to Michael Bodkin's grave at Oughterard.[24] The next year he distilled from this a note to *Exiles,* suggesting Nora as the woman brought to Shelley's graveside, where she "weeps over Rahoon too, over him whom her love has killed, the dark boy . . . her buried life, her past."[25] Rahoon is the Galway cemetery, and conveniently a more musical name than Oughterard, and the passage furnished the title, "She weeps over Rahoon," for a typical Joyce lyric, simple, plainly but romantically imagistic, and metrically flexible and euphonious. There where the dark lover lies his sad voice still calls,

> Ever unanswered, and the dark rain falling,
> Then as now.

In the poem's last stanza, as at the conclusion of "The Dead," the theme is universalized; the lovers' deaths are prefigured in that earlier one of the dark lover. And as the snow was general over Ireland, so rain falls—"softly . . . dark . . . muttering"—throughout the poem's felt time-span. Here Joyce has reduced a range of experience to a single situation and mood, and has distilled the truth that no anonymous skull can be the *memento mori* which a personal recollection is, especially when it involves love as time's enduring opponent and pitiful victim. The stasis of the poem represented, however, no corresponding poise in its author. Joyce as lover was passionate, diffident, haughty, sentimental, extravagantly moody, and capable of a jealousy that seemed compulsive—as was his way in imagining other kinds of betrayal. At the conclusion of *Exiles* Richard says, "It is not in the darkness of belief that I desire you. But in restless living wounding doubt."[26] Seemingly Joyce decreed it so for himself with Nora, at least in their first years. And perhaps it was similarly so for him as to Ireland—"desire" but without "belief," and equated to "a wounding doubt" in a perpetuity of pros and cons.

While Gabriel Conroy is also an ambivalent man, and though like Joyce he is "sick" of his own country, in the first part of the story he seems not just the contented but enchanted husband, and on their way to the hotel and for the first moments alone with his wife he is alive with desire. At the same time he is a gently considerate man—as is seen in his other relationships too —and his approach to intimacy with Gretta is tentative, awaiting spontaneous response. Sometimes he seems timid, but timidity need not be seen when his behavior is simply tactfulness and refined feeling. The frustration of his desire this night of the story is by chance; only the song's awakening of an old memory has come between his wife and him. And to suppose that Gretta has been gnawed at by a lifelong secret grief which, discovered, will now forever inhibit their marriage would also be a morbid sentimentalizing of the story. Gretta is too real for that; she is also very Irish, delightfully so, and in a completely womanly way. She is both animated and self-possessed, capable of allowing her husband's uneasiness in his gruff resistance to what of Ireland is most native to her. Inclined to gaiety, she is capable of pity too, and is sensitive to the party's sad undertones, which come to a privately rooted crisis of feeling for her because of the song. Through her Joyce has revealed his own painful knowledge of melancholy recollection, as through Gabriel he may have implied regret for his aversion from Ireland.

The fullness of Gabriel's experience may even allow him to figure in that aspect as the man Joyce would have wished to become by remaining in Ireland. Gabriel's new knowledge of the devoted young lover long dead is initially a shock and a threat of reproach, but reverberations deepen as he ironically and then sympathetically leads Gretta to fill in the details, which under his enlarging mood elicit the vast configuration of his epiphany. The four-page passage in which the tearful Gretta gradually discloses the story of Michael Furey, while Gabriel's responses pass from surprise and condescension to dismay, sympathy, and humane insight, is a potent transmutation that gives objectivity, pattern, and elevation to some of Joyce's own scattered and restive experiences. "The Dead" may be judged a crowning accomplishment of the artist in search of epiphany as that self-knowledge which casts a larger shadow of representative truth. It stands apart from the other stories by the quantity and weight it carries of Joyce's subjectively colored Dublin memories and by a larger synthesis of acute private experiences and their wider import.

"The Dead" does not depart from the generally realistic intent of *Dubliners,* yet herein more than in any other of the stories a protagonist is constituted to be Joyce's undeclared but fully empowered surrogate. Gabriel too is reluctant to serve, withholding himself from the land, its language, and politics; and he is intent on at least temporary escapes to the Continent. His withdrawal goes far enough to make for uneasy ambivalence, and it reaches to the painful knowledge that separation has its price. In this "The Dead" does not contradict what has gone before, but expands themes latent in the earlier stories. In particular it shows Gabriel, though lacking distinction and force, to be a better man within Dublin's milieu than either Little Chandler or Mr. James Duffy, or than the benighted enmeshed fellows in "Grace"; and it not only comprises but advances beyond those themes of separatism, shamed disenchantment, or elementary response to human claims in the three boyhood stories. "The Dead" may be viewed as genuinely an epilogue to *Dubliners,* at basis most directly personal, but also bringing its local subject and general import into furthest perspective and fullest light.

In Joyce's picturing of the party at the Misses Morkans' house the considerable technical accomplishment itself merits attention, and this will more clearly disclose continuity and evolvement of theme underlying a seemingly casual structure and an opalescence of mood. Though "The Dead," running to about eighteen thousand words, might be called a novella, it is scarcely typical of this form. The distinctly separate scenes are not as numerous and the chronology is not as extended as for instance in James's "The Pupil" or "The Aspern Papers," or even in Katherine Anne Porter's "The Cracked Looking Glass" and "Hacienda." Joyce's story has only the two main sections; first and far larger is the party, with Gabriel recurrently a central figure, sometimes actor with others, sometimes subjectively reactive; the second section, after the brief interval of a cab ride, sees Gabriel and Gretta alone in the hotel. At the story's beginning the scene is set without them, but they are being awaited, and they appear soon. Gabriel disappears from the narrative, for several pages, to see to sobering up the probably "screwed" Freddy Malins; in the two pages of talk that follows Aunt Julia's singing, the narrative is not dependent on his consciousness of it, and at the table after carving "he took no part in the conversation" that went on during the meal. Nevertheless "The Dead" is his story in the main, and a superb narrative art keeps it so, in focus against a populated backdrop and amidst a variety of sufficient characterizations. As to this latter, units of dialogue and action are made to lead into each other with the air of a convivial but not especially sprightly party taking its natural course, drifting within the bounds of a conventional occasion in the lives of ordinary people. Still there is a remarkable, almost constant interplay between the commonplace and the revelatory, in the multiple minor events with their objectively sketched actors, and as sounded in the variable stream of Gabriel's restive, anxious, and sometimes resistant consciousness.

This annual affair—for "members of the family, old friends of the family, the members of Julia's choir, any of Kate's pupils that were grown up enough, and even some of Mary Jane's pupils too"—is large enough to keep Lily the caretaker's daughter busy answering the door and helping the gentlemen leave their overcoats on the ground floor while sending the ladies on up to their hostesses. It is a household of spinsters, the two old aunts and their niece who "had been through the Academy" and "had the organ in Haddington Row," and many of whose pupils "belonged to better-class families on the Kingstown and Dalkey line" and were presented each year in "a pupils' concert . . . in the upper room of the Antient Concert Rooms." Most notable among the guests is the tenor Mr. Bartell D'Arcy, whom "all Dublin is raving about," according to Mary Jane. It is not, however, a distinguished company, and Gabriel, seeing that the men's "grade of culture differed from his," rejects a plan to quote Browning in his speech, thinking it would appear he was "airing his superior education." Even with Browning eliminated there will be something wrong with his performance, and something other than just the retained reference to the Three Graces and Paris. The real source of Gabriel's doubts in advance he avoids defining; the constant uneasiness beneath the surface of his reflections and behavior is to rise up as sharp antithesis and deceptive exaggeration in his speech. Not that his audience, with Miss Ivors gone, will notice. They will complacently applaud the strained perfunctory discourse, and not altogether mistakenly, for like most common folk they will not be so put off by the vaguely sensed artifice of a gesture as to miss its basic kindliness.

After the dancing "the younger ones" had been sent in to supper first, and when Aunt Julia sings, their "loud applause was borne in from the invisible supper-table"—by such means does Joyce suggest a large party. Yet like the "two young men . . . drinking hop-bitters" who eye Mr. Browne respectfully as he copes with "a goodly measure of whisky," or like "the four young men" who made off to "the refreshment-room" when Mary Jane began playing her "Academy piece" but returned at the end to clap most vigorously, many of the number implied remain anonymous. A Mr. Bergin and Mr. Kerrigan are mentioned only as Mary Jane arranges partners for the dancing. Five young women are named but remain bit-players to fill out the scene. Three of them are served lemonade by Mr. Browne, and among these Miss Power, thus provided for and then given Mr. Kerrigan to dance with, is heard of no further. Miss Daly, more prominently, plays the piano for the dancing, is promised Mr. D'Arcy as a partner, and "will carve the ham." Miss Furlong, "one of Mary

Jane's pupils," having had Mr. Bergin as a partner, wants the name of the waltz Miss Daly played; at table she asks for a small slice of the breast and differs with Mr. D'Arcy's favorable opinion of the leading contralto of "the opera company which was then at the Theatre Royal." Then there is Miss Higgins, of whom it is to be known only that when Gabriel carving asked "what for you," she answered "O, anything at all, Mr. Conroy." Finally there is Miss O'Callaghan, not mentioned until the end of the party, when she stays behind with D'Arcy and plays his accompaniment and then comes down the stairs with him to say she has been "at him all the evening" to sing; she thinks "Christmas is never really Christmas unless we have the snow on the ground," and with Mr. D'Arcy and the Conroys in the cab which is to drop Gabriel and Gretta at the Gresham, Miss O'Callaghan declares "They say you never cross O'Connell Bridge without seeing a white horse."

These glimpses are scattered through the story; they extend the scale of the scene and also maintain the action's casual tone. Such appearances are epiphanal in Joyce's lesser way, the naturalistic glance, the fleeting instance epitomized. And these minor characters in their brief moments have some representativeness. The young men who retreat to the bar during the music and return to applaud most loudly are everywhere known, signatures without need of names; and the effaced Miss Higgins' willingness to have "anything at all" of the goose may echo with the question of how life itself will serve the likes of her. In any large social group there may be a Miss Higgins, and someone as positive as Miss Furlong, as vapid as Miss O'Callaghan; but such lesser persons in "The Dead" are not there to substantiate a slice of life so much as to help create the illusion of a party's variable inconsequential drift that may contain more persistent thematic trends, especially in the protagonist's consciousness, encompassed by all this overt action objectively represented, but in reacting to it also playing out, privately and at intervals, his own particular adventure. Thus at times, when the movement is almost altogether Gabriel's introspection, the party is only fluctuantly sensed at the margin of his awareness and the reader's. In more dramatized passages, where main figures converse and act, while there is this rich incidental realism there is also an accumulating potential of relevance to Gabriel's progress and impending access of vision. In these terms the detailed variegated narrative becomes not just a concourse of sounds but a tone poem. And in "The Dead" narrative art, as always at its best, has the power even beyond that in music of suspending matter in a felt deliberate prolonged approach to saturation, with the crystal yet to take completed form.

Such development depends in part on those major characters most closely surrounding and affecting Gabriel. There are the three hostesses, and especially the two old aunts, to whom he is most dutiful and whose pathos he senses. D'Arcy, as a well-known tenor, enhances the party's preoccupation with music and musicians; moreover, he implements the plot by singing the air that so affects Gretta as to condition the final scene evocative of Gabriel's epiphany. There is the volatile Miss Ivors, whose cordial jesting with Gabriel as "West Briton" for his reviewing in the *Daily Express* ruffles his practiced aloofness, and whose suggestion that the Conroys join her and other ardent nationalists on a visit to the Aran Islands exposes Gabriel's Continent-oriented escapism. There Gretta Conroy is glimpsed, as at various moments, as a spirited woman, clasping her hands and exclaiming delightedly at the thought of visiting Galway again, and especially drawn to the impulsive, independent Miss Ivors, whom she sums up as "you're the comical girl, Molly." These two women, similarly animated and spontaneous, are paired and yet opposite in impingement upon Gabriel. Miss Ivors' challenge was open and politically argumentative, and Gabriel resists and refuses it as such. Gretta's challenge is not a contention, and not even intended; it is on human terms and inheres in her selfhood as wife and as sentient mortal being, and Gabriel's increasing response is as husband and as member of the family of man. So Gretta is of most importance, constantly as wife and often in wifely role as agent of insight, but Miss Ivors has served conversely to set off something of the negativity Gabriel is to be brought out of.

Less important, but with his uses, there is Mr. Browne, the wizenfaced Protestant, who heartily exercises a laborious wit. His talkativeness does raise topics that lead into narrative themes, and at his departure there are implications that color the lightly defined but contributive image of Mary Jane. Then too there are the Malins—Freddy, the unattractive, ineffectual, alcoholic "young man of about forty," and his white-haired old mother, stout and feeble, on her annual visit from her place in Glasgow with her married daughter, and possibly personifying a maternal Dublin which has brought up the likes of Freddy, for she epitomizes a fixed dullness that must be listened to, with perfunctory respect, and at the door she must be shielded from the chill of outer weather. Finally among the characters closest to Gabriel there might be said to be one more, and as in *Ulysses*, the ghost of the mother. She enters, as such ghosts usually do, on the stream of meandering association. While Mary Jane is performing, Gabriel's eyes wander to the pictures above the piano, including one of "the two murdered princes in the Tower," done in "red, blue and brown wools" by Aunt Julia "when she was a girl," and Gabriel recalls similar handiwork, "a waistcoat . . . with little foxes' heads upon it" his mother had made him "as a birthday present." Joyce inherited such a waistcoat from his father,[27] and perhaps one of his aunts had worked such a sampler as a schoolgirl; out of such oddments a writer synthesizes the illusion of a character's mind drifting from incidental stimulus through random association to some telling preoccupation. Looking at his mother's photograph which the sisters have on display, Gabriel remembers her as without musical talent but admired as "the brains carrier of the Morkan family." The photograph images a dominant nurturing (like Ireland's?) in that the mother "held an open book . . . and was pointing out something" to the boy Constantine, Gabriel's brother, "who, dressed in a man-o'-war suit, lay at her feet"—and who is now a priest, "senior curate in Balbriggan." Gabriel resentfully recalls his mother's "sullen opposition" to Gretta, whose naturalness offended her pretensions to conventional dignity. Here may be discovered seeds of Gabriel's aloofness and hypersensitivity; it would seem also to adumbrate the influence of Ireland as source of Gabriel's conflicts, like Joyce's.

The Misses Morkan's annual party—"For years and years it had gone off in splendid style"—as a holiday custom and ceremony has the ambiguous tone of all anniversary occasions, in one further arrival and its recollections, a reassembling subtly not the same, the paradox of a containment of change, and the underlying melancholy of a ceremoniously festive looking before and after. The time is the year's beginning—Freddy Malins' unsteadiness is the more regrettable in that "his poor mother made him take the pledge on New Year's Eve," and when the Conroys get out at the hotel the cab driver salutes and says, "A prosperous New Year to you, sir." There has been anticipation; the old aunts eagerly have awaited Gabriel's arrival, the women hope to hear D'Arcy sing, and Gabriel looks desirously toward being alone with his wife. The Conroys do arrive, but late; D'Arcy does not sing until the party is dispersing, and then unsatisfyingly; and when finally Gabriel and Gretta are alone together, it is not as he had wanted.

Less specifically, and variously but with cumulative import, other incidents touch upon the theme of containment. The old aunts and their niece have lived in the "gaunt" old house "a good thirty years," ever since Mary Jane was "a little girl in short clothes," and the three of them represent Dublin musical culture at its semiprofessional, semisocial median, conventionalized and static, even as to the music they repeatedly perform. They also typify the aridities and seclusion of Dublin spinsterhood, and over the two aunts hangs the deepening shadow of mortality. The story is thus permeated by antitheses, the party's gaiety is of the resolutely arranged kind, and now at the turn of the year Janus obtrudes both his faces, as the concentric circles of time and Dublin and privately determining event variously hold all the characters, but ultimately to the fixed center. The familiar anecdote about Grandfather Morkan, with Gabriel as elaborately humorous raconteur, is laughed over once more at the party's end, but not for what it ironically mimes, an Ireland habituated to the repetitive and to sorts of servitude. The glimpses of Mary Jane throughout "The Dead," though only by simple objective mention of her efforts as hostess, coalesce unobtrusively into the outline of one who, despite some attainment and grace, is limited by circumstance to a meager personal life. Less extensive in the narration but more poignant is the incident of Miss Julia Morkan's performance of "an old song" of hers, "Arrayed for the Bridal." Here the specific pathos exceeds the diffused melancholy of Mary Jane's situation and the still more covert implication of long-dead Grandfather Morkan's legendary adventure.

This last is rehearsed by Gabriel, in mock-heroic fashion, as the three hostesses are at the door below, seeing off Mr. Browne, old Mrs. Malins, and Freddy, who is out searching for a cab. Gretta is still upstairs, "getting on her things," says Aunt Kate; and when the piano is heard, Mary Jane explains that "Bartell D'Arcy and Miss O'Callaghan aren't gone yet." In this pause Gabriel fills the time by elaborating the anecdote facetiously, in the form it has taken on over the years. Like many a more than twice-told tale, it is recurred to as sustenance for a flagging conversation. Mary Jane, shivering, she says, at the thought of the guests' journeying in the cold, elicits Mr. Browne's stout boast that he'd "like nothing better this minute than . . . a fast drive with a good spanking goer between the shafts," which leads Miss Julia to say "sadly" that the Morkan family "used to have a very good horse and trap," and when Mary Jane, laughing, adds "The never-to-be-forgotten Johnny," Mr. Browne the outsider wants to know "what was wonderful about Johnny" and Gabriel is off once more on the matter of "the late lamented Patrick Morkan, our grandfather," and his horse. Weekdays it was accustomed to "walking round and round to drive the [starch] mill," but "one fine day the old gentleman . . . harnessed Johnny" and dressed himself "to drive out with the quality" to the park. When Johnny "came in sight of King Billy's statue" he began to walk round it, and "round and round he went," with "the old gentleman . . . highly indignant," exclaiming "Can't understand the horse!" Gabriel offers a fanciful and a real explanation—"whether he fell in love with the horse King Billy sits on or whether he thought he was back again in the mill." There are "peals of laughter" following "Gabriel's imitation of the incident"; the hearers, bemused by repetition, are not conscious of analogy.

"King Billy" was of course King William III, the last of Ireland's military conquerors, establishing at the end of the seventeenth century the onerous and uneasy rule that was to rack Ireland and vex England for over two hundred years. An equestrian statue to this conqueror was installed in 1701 at College Green, the very heart of Dublin, before the gates of Trinity College and at the juncture where several streets feed westward into the main crossing of the Liffey. Whatever the imagined emotions of the horse Johnny, the patriotic Irish did not love the statue, and it remained an object of nationalistic protest. It was often defaced and smeared with filth, and in 1710 the figure's sword and truncheon were broken off. In 1715 it was put on a higher pedestal, for greater safety as well as eminence, and thereafter a watchman guarded it. It was decorated with orange flowers or colors every July 1 and November 5, in token of William's conquest of Ireland and of his birthday. At one time those passing by were required to doff their hats or pay a fine of £5 or go to prison. In 1805, on the night before November 4 a student pretending to the watchman that he had been sent to decorate the statue covered it with tar and grease. In 1822 there was particularly heavy street fighting over the customary November decoration; and on the night of April 7, 1836, an explosion blew the statue off its pedestal and dismembered it, but it was reassembled and reinstated, on a high heavy pedestal surrounded by railings with lampposts at the four corners. Forays against this symbol of English rule continued as the tides of resistance surged; the statue so often assailed and re-established was finally blown up in 1929.[28]

However, while King Billy's statue, at the time of Gabriel's story and Joyce's, had two centuries of exacerbating history for the Irish, it is not the political aspect or concomitant violence that is taken account of in Gabriel's comic recital of Grandfather Morkan's discomfiture and bewilderment by a horse habituated to a treadmill. The family joke, laughed at long after its novelty had dried up, and retold for souvenir's sake, is itself a habit, among those whose lives are closely contained. What old Patrick Morkan could not understand in his horse is transparent in Joyce's Dubliners; the stories' burden is of little people in a limited, subservient cycle, and not only thus caught but irreversibly conditioned. So Freddy Malins no doubt will again take the pledge and backslide once more, like his counterpart in "Grace." So Mary Jane presumably will move on in spinsterhood, more knowing and assertive than Maria of "Clay" but similar in a dutiful cheerfulness. Though Miss Ivors contends with Gabriel more forcibly than does Hynes with those deficient in patriotism in "Ivy Day," and more independently separates herself from the others, her liveliness is within nets, as Stephen called them, of nation and language. And old Aunt Kate's scandalous complaint that it was "not at all honourable for the pope to turn out the women out of the choirs . . . and put little whipper-snappers of boys over their heads" is a protest against change in her sister Julia's long time status as leading soprano at Adam and Eve's, though Miss Kate also believed Julia "was simply thrown away in that choir," and ambivalently declared too that she did not "question the pope's being right," which indeed brings her full circle.

Mary Jane is more frequently glimpsed and generally in her role as hostess (as helpful to the narrative as to the guests) but she too can be detected as one contained by Dublin, restricted to something less than her worth. Joyce does not press the point. It can be passed over without reduction of "The Dead" in its main import, but to note Mary Jane herself alone in the midst of things is to find one more shade in the story's refracted coloration. She is never the center of the others' sustained attention except when she performs "her Academy piece, full of runs and difficult passages," yet she is often quietly influential. Having come thirty years ago as a little girl to live in this house, she must be well on her way to forty. Church organist and piano teacher, she is "now the main prop of the household." Taking most active part as hostess, she not only arranges partners for the dancing but guides conversation at the supper table. She is not blasé, however, or even completely self-assured, and having performed to "great applause" for those who "had begged" her "to play something," she blushed and rolled up her music "nervously" and "escaped from the room." Still she is not too timid to speak out; she says sensible things, and sometimes tactfully eases the situation. To Aunt Kate's objecting that Julia's "slaving there in that choir, night and day" had been "all for what?" Mary Jane, turning and smiling, asked, "Well, isn't it for the honour of God?" As Kate continued her complaint and even turned it upon the pope, Mary Jane "intervened pacifically" and warned that such a remark was "giving scandal to Mr. Browne who is of the other persuasion." Then while Aunt Kate denied questioning the pope but still protested, Mary Jane interrupted soothingly and almost as if to a child—"when we are hungry we are all very quarrelsome"—and carried them in to supper. Beyond her range she is less assured, and when Miss Ivors would not stay, she said "hopelessly" she was "afraid" her guest hadn't enjoyed herself "at all," and gazed after this more dynamic, independent woman's laughing departure with "a moody puzzled expression." At supper Mary Jane "waited on her pupils and saw that they got the best slices" (of goose, ham, spiced beef) and then "settled down quietly" to her meal while the old aunts "were still toddling round the table . . . giving each other unheeded orders." The "hot floury potatoes" Lily brought had been "Mary Jane's idea" and "she had also suggested apple sauce for the goose" but this had been overruled by old Aunt Kate on typical grounds—"plain roast goose without any apple sauce had always been good enough for her and she hoped she might never eat worse."

As supper proceeds and the talk turns to the opera company

then in Dublin, when Freddy Malins speaks rather disputatiously about a "negro chieftain" singing in the Gaiety pantomime, Mary Jane "led the table back to the legitimate opera" with mention of *Mignon,* for which "one of her pupils had given her a pass," but "it made her think of poor Georgina Burns," and thus it is, on a melancholy cue from the almost middle-aged spinster, that the talk turns further and further back in reminiscences of great singers dead and gone. Later Mary Jane is again the pivot point, in time and beyond insularity, for when Mr. D'Arcy, speaking of "as good singers today as there were then," warmly tells the contradictory Mr. Browne that they are on the Continent and cites Caruso, Mary Jane says, "O, I'd give anything to hear Caruso sing," and this intervention having lessened the strain, Mr. D'Arcy then "politely" asks old Aunt Kate to tell them of the tenor Parkinson. Then as there is mention of Mount Melleray, where Freddy is going for a stay (presumably recuperative) with the monks, Mr. Browne declares he wishes his church had some such hospitable arrangement but asks with Protestant incredulity about the monks' practice of sleeping in their coffins. Aunt Kate says, and repeats, that it is "the rule of the order," and obviously this makes it as plain to her as the superfluousness of apple sauce with roast goose. Freddy (perhaps with some disclosure of his rueful state of mind) tries to explain that the austere practice is in expiation for "all the sinners in the outside world." Mary Jane says simply that "The coffin is to remind them of their last end." Here again she not only carries the conversation forward toward a central point, but in so doing she sounds the motif on which the story is to move toward its conclusion. Her sound remark, sensibly made but casting its long shadow, silences the table until old Mrs. Malins, ever ready with the trite, comes up with the pronouncement that "they are very good men, the monks, very pious men." As the wine is passed a further silence falls, in anticipation of Gabriel's speech and toast, and now in self-consciousness "The Misses Morkan, all three, looked down at the tablecloth." Gabriel's extravagant and ambivalent performance follows, and at the toast Mary Jane must explain to Aunt Julia, who has not heard, that "He says we are the Three Graces." Mary Jane has been casually lumped with her two aged aunts in the unrealistic wish that they "may long continue," and she remains seated with them as the others stand and, under Mr. Browne's lead, with Freddy Malins' pudding fork beating time, they sing "For they are jolly gay fellows."

Such is Mary Jane, incidentally glanced at, yet emergent under Joyce's deft narrative touches and quiet empathy as someone with a life, a story of her own though not told, but uniquely part of this eventful yet largely melancholy pageant of Dubliners. Then at the guests' departure there is a further glimpse of Mary Jane. In the hall, when Aunt Kate wants the door closed, lest Mrs. Malins "get her death of cold," Mary Jane says "Browne is out there," and Aunt Kate, lowering her voice, says he is "everywhere," which is true enough of this assertive fellow, but Mary Jane "laughed at her tone" and "archly" said, "Really, he is very attentive." Aunt Kate, in her former tone, perhaps severe, remarks that "He has been laid on here like the gas all during the Christmas," but then she laughs too, "this time good-humouredly." Browne comes in, laughing excessively and pointing down the snow-covered quay where Freddie is still whistling for a cab; Mary Jane, glancing at Gabriel already in his overcoat and Browne in his overcoat and fur cap, shivers and says, "It makes me feel cold to look at you two gentlemen muffled up like that. I wouldn't like to face your journey home at this hour." How much may be sensed in that shiver and the words themselves; what is the cold she feels; what may be the personal tinge under the appearance of speaking to Gabriel as well as Browne? Not a whole history should be read into this; "The Dead" is not this spinster's story, much less Mr. Browne's, and not Gretta's, either; it is Gabriel's, with all else shaped and subordinated to his progress this night. Nevertheless even the most briefly noted characters are for that time distinctly present, each in his or her own right as a being, and while the focus pauses upon any one of them, that figure asserts its idiosyncrasy and implies the continuum of its identity. Thereby it bespeaks empathy, with the peculiarly touching appeal of the minor and the obscure, whom fate itself seems never to have accorded full attention, so little is seen of the personal life. Yet it is known to be there, in the nature of things, and as with Mary Jane—the perpetual flame of consciousness, flickering in the shifts of circumstance, and, however modest its enterprise of selfhood, intent on its maintenance, and forward-looking with whatever fear it has been required to learn and whatever hope it can allow.

It is one of Joyce's achievements as fictionist that throughout *Dubliners* almost every figure, however slight the role, can loom as possible protagonist in another story. The potential becomes strong in an intermediate character such as Mary Jane, who not only transcends Gabriel's conventional description in his speech as "talented, cheerful, hard-working, and the best of nieces," but is also recognizable for much beyond what the story specifies. This kind of import marks a technical advance and artistic excellence typical of the Chekovian-Joycean short story, which is not definable merely as to its open structure but for what this supports, a texture of denotativeness that approaches the poetic mode. While the finest lyric poetry is more compact than any fiction, because more nearly focused on a moment rather than a continuity and allowed a more subjective language, it is not more scrupulous than these stories with their unostentatious deliberate movement over which hangs the shimmer of the implicative. From this there is derived the instantly perceptible vitality not only of protagonists but of minor characters casually and marginally engaged in the action. So with the fatalistic but enduring aunt in "Araby," and with those in the committee room given less scope than the opposed Henchy and Hynes, and Kathleen as that mother's daughter, and those others who gathered solicitously around Kernan's bed of pain and disgrace.

In this connection E. M. Forster's classic distinction between flat and round characters requires some further definition. In fiction of significance, this is not to be applied as either/or—fully rounded or utterly flat—and moreover, one measure of excellence in fiction is the enrichment and intensified realism provided through minor characters of sufficient contour to suggest the possibility of extension toward the round. Here, however, a quite obvious limitation enters; adjunctive figures must be kept both relevant and subordinate to the main characters as these carry the action onward and evolve theme. By such measures—the partial rounding out of lesser players while keeping them contributory to the narrative's main flow and import—Joyce shows his mastery in story after story, but never more so than in "The Dead," with its large and various cast, its close groupings and its action modulated between the objective and subjective, and yet with its commitment to a protagonist almost continuously involved, both in the events and in his complex responses. To keep Gabriel surrounded by the crowd and yet never quite to lose sight of him is only part of it; the rest, on which the story hangs in essence, is to show him confronting, with what face he can, the faces he must meet (not only Browne's and the Malins', but Miss Ivors' and a dead boy's, and Gretta's in a fuller light) while facing himself more and more directly and thereby looking out more widely than ever before.

The psychological reciprocity in this application of the golden rule is demonstrated in minor ways as stages on Gabriel's road to his all-embracing epiphany. By intuitive observation of others Gabriel comes to further self-knowledge. Correspondingly, "The Dead" illustrates the highest art of fiction in that the culminating realization, sustained by all that has gone before, also reflexively enhances this precedent detail as the now ripened fruit of experience, which the reader gathers into his possession of the story as a complete work. Gabriel's response to Aunt Julia's singing is one of the firmest steps in his progress, and in retrospect one of the most directly relevant. But there are others all along within the story's presentational continuity; and Gabriel's discomfitures, evasions, and recognitions constitute a sequence of emotions that continues most intensely in the final scene. It has begun almost at once for Gabriel, in his cordially intended conversation with Lily the caretaker's daughter, who took his overcoat when he arrived. She was friendly too, but when he suggested that "one of these fine days" they'll be going to her wedding she answered "with great bitterness" that "The men that is now is only all palaver and what they can get out of you," and Gabriel "coloured, as if he felt he had made a mistake," and did not look at her as he kicked off his snow-covered galoshes. The tone of present and past is sounded in her phrase "the men that is now," and under the added suggestion of some others' duplicity and evasiveness Gabriel, though a devoted husband and father, somehow feels reproved and hurries up the stairs to the party after making the amend of a coin for "Christmas-time." The suggestion that Lily may have been badly treated by a man is kept operative when Aunt Kate later tells the Conroys she's "not the girl she was at all" and wonders "what has come over her lately."

Not only does this support the theme of masculine irresponsibility which runs through *Dubliners,* but the charge is to be implied against Gabriel himself, by Miss Ivors, in terms of Ireland's claim upon him. While her twitting of Gabriel for writing reviews for a neutralist paper is in friendship, it is also made "abruptly . . . gravely . . . bluntly . . . frankly," but after calling him "West Briton" she says she was only joking about that. Her suggestion that the Conroys come on a month's summer excursion to the Aran Islands—Ireland at its most remote and unmodified—is made "eagerly" with obvious cordiality, but she presses the claim of the Irish language and of "your own people, and your own country," which, she tells him, "you know nothing of." Having thereby driven him to retort that he is "sick of" his own country, she demands reasons while at the moment he is too agitated to reply, and then having teased a smile from him, she teasingly repeats "West Briton," whispering it in his ear. This volatile yet firm-minded woman is too much for Gabriel; she makes him blush and blink and retort heatedly. Her manner with him is possible not only because they "were friends of many years," but because she is his equal in a way that no one else at the party can be, since she had been at the university in his time and had since, like him, been a teacher. Her challenge touches a raw spot, an aloofness that is not poised but uneasy, resting on divided allegiance.

Gabriel Conroy is no Stephen Dedalus, however. He is not to escape from Ireland, yet he is to read such a signature as Stephen never deciphered. He is not striving categorically and with equal force to surmount three nets, as was Stephen. Catholicism figures hardly at all in "The Dead" except as the unquestioned belief of those to whom Browne is uniquely "of the other persuasion," and religion does not seem to weigh upon Gabriel. Though with his brother a priest and he a teacher he would be conformist, and that could be part of a pressure that makes him "sick of" his country, the story does not elucidate such an element. The issue of nationalism comes a bit closer. Gabriel as a faithfully Catholic and educated son of Ireland might long for France and Germany "partly to keep in touch with the languages," but he admits it is also "partly for a change," which may be, in part, away from just such heckling recruitment as Miss Ivors subjects him to, as well as from the day-to-day isolation in that minority who, like the paper he writes for, would live and let live. What is most plainly indicated, however, by Gabriel's inability to rally firmly against Miss Ivors is an incertitude too deeply rooted to be entirely scrutible. He can produce two specific ordinary reasons for vacationing abroad, but he dare not probe the ambiguities of his attitude toward Ireland. So "he tried to cover his agitation" by dancing "with great energy," and then escaped from Miss Ivors along the easiest route at that large party, by going with conventional politeness to talk to the dullest woman there, Freddy Malins' mother. To her rambling inconsequentialities he half-listens while trying to pull himself together, only to have his wife come along with a repetition of Miss Ivors' invitation. Here the ultimate challenge to Gabriel is foreshadowed. His precarious equanimity is to be disturbed by issues not primarily political, theological, or even conventionally social but rather over the intimately personal, yet as it opens upon universals.

Such is Gabriel's response to Aunt Julia's singing, and it is of a kind to presage the ultimate step in his epiphany. While pondering with a sort of timid egotism the strategy of the speech he is to make at the supper, he is drawn out of himself by the murmur and "irregular musketry of applause" as Mr. Browne "gallantly" escorted the grey-haired singer into the room (perhaps in something of young Joyce's formal manner with his mother at the Sheehys' evening parties).[29] Aunt Julia was "smiling and hanging her head," but then the practiced singer emerged as, "no longer smiling," she "half turned so as to pitch her voice fairly into the room." She will be heard admiringly here, and Joyce was to allow something of her Dublin repute to come within Leopold Bloom's ken—"Kept her voice up to the very last. Pupil of Michael Balfe's, wasn't she?"[30] In "The Dead," though, it is altogether as Gabriel sees her, with appreciation for her sustained art itself and of herself grown old. Once more at this traditional party repetition enters; when Mary Jane plays the prelude Gabriel knows it is to be "an old song of Aunt Julia's—*Arrayed for the Bridal.*" Her voice, "strong and clear in tone, attacked with great spirit," and Gabriel listening could "feel and share the excitement of swift and secure flight," but only as he refrained from "looking at the singer's face." Here in this juncture of essence and mutability something is added to Gabriel's store of intimations that not only accumulate but finally coalesce, to produce the transcendent summary vision. Meanwhile, with the song ended the singer's face is to be seen again, with the applause bringing "a little colour" into it "as she bent to replace in the music-stand the old leather-bound songbook that had her initials on the cover"—the initials which have not changed any more than her "old" song, "Arrayed for the Bridal." Solitary at the story's end, in the full dawning of his epiphany, Gabriel is to remember having "caught that haggard look upon her face . . . when she was singing." Song and a singer's life are comprised at a point of supreme beauty and melancholy like that in Keats's odes, and for Gabriel love and human lives are to stand in a similar conjunction of ideality and mortality.

This, however, is yet to come in the story. Gabriel still has his speech to make; and by Gretta's revelations he is yet to be brought, beyond all that, to a fuller acknowledgment of self and the human condition. This which is to be his private epiphany is of universal import. It is also, for Gabriel, an excruciation. A hard time he has had of it, and is to have, on his way to ultimate vision but with elements yet so contradictorily mixed in him. Which is to be fully displayed in his after-dinner speech. His approach to that and the performance itself show him at his poorest. This low ebb offers structural, thematic antithesis to what he is to achieve in the large vision with which his story culminates. Gabriel thus outlined is Joyce's most complex Dubliner, because his contrarieties exist together with long-sustained engagement, professional and personal, and at the level of some cultivation. Only Stephen, with his wider range of mind and unique brilliance, as well as his more vigorous and sustained *non serviam,* is closer to the person Joyce was; but Gabriel, like some other *Dubliners* characters in lesser degree, may suggest aspects of Joyce not revealed through Stephen, to whom a more special role was delegated, and who died young, by his fond creator's favor—and perhaps before he could become not his race's but his author's conscience, as some of the *Dubliners* men had showed signs of doing. In the lengthier first portion of "The Dead" Gabriel, impinged upon by various persons and demands, reacts sometimes dutifully, sometimes evasively. Thus he is seen at extremes—a prudent, considerate man, and not without purpose, yet restive, withdrawn, tending toward artificiality in his self-defensiveness, and rebellious but secretly so except at the moment when Miss Ivors provokes his retort that he is sick of his own country.

Having escaped her by going to talk with old Mrs. Malins, when Freddy approached Gabriel took the occasion to leave them and "retired into the embrasure of the window." As his "warm trembling fingers tapped the cold pane" he meditated a further withdrawal:

> How cool it must be outside! How pleasant it would be to walk out alone, first along by the river and then through the park! The snow would be lying on the branches of the trees and forming a bright cap on the top of the Wellington Monument. How much more pleasant it would be there than at the supper-table!

This desire for coolness and solitude (casting its vision beyond any actual view from the gaunt house by the Liffey) is scarcely to be labeled a death-wish, but a stress of oppositions in Gabriel's life is suggested by such inclination toward escape. A particular stimulus which has brought it to the surface appears as he is running over the headings of his speech: the possible quotation from Browning reminds him of a phrase he had used in his review, and Miss Ivors' praise of that, and the matter of her sincerity, and another question both broader and nearer—"Had she really any life of her own behind all her propagandism?" He has felt her force, though, and is "unnerved" at the thought that he would be under her "critical quizzing eyes" as he spoke. He plans a crafty retaliation, an indicting of the "very serious and hypereducated generation" for lack of the old virtues, not only "hospitality" but "humour . . . humanity." That, Gabriel thinks, would be "one for Miss Ivors." Since she does not stay for supper he cannot have this sly petty triumph over her, but the concept does enter into his speech, and it not only underlies his contrasting of past and present but it may represent the ironic echoing back upon himself of his question about having "really any life" of one's own.

The antitheses Gabriel proposed in his speech exceed his control. He does not face them decisively but vacillates between yes and no, the only reconciliation a sentimental blurring of distinctions. Ambivalence appears throughout, first facetiously, in the strained manner of the perfunctory occasional orator, but seriously too, in concerns emergent as he proceeds. Beginning, he speaks of himself and the others as "the recipients—or perhaps, I had better say, the victims—of the hospitality of certain good ladies." Sincerely praising the Irish "tradition" of "hospitality," he admits some might call it a "failing" but granting that, he resolves it in rhetorical device, as "a princely failing." Proceeding with his elderly aunts chiefly in mind, but still irked by his encounter with Miss Ivors, he presents a formal bouquet of compliments that is laced with the nettles of his own unrest. The stresses in his speech are ostensibly between claims of past and future but primarily between realizations and an evasive wistfulness in himself. With Miss Ivors gone, he still relieves his resentment by suggesting that the "new generation," though "serious and enthusiastic," may "lack those qualities of humanity, of hospitality, of kindly humour which belonged to an older day." There is something of confession in his calling the present "a sceptical and . . . a thought-tormented age," especially since he carries over that phrase from his review; and there is illusion in his reference to the past's "spacious days," whose famous singers they have recalled. But were they, he says, "to brood upon" all such "thoughts of the past, of youth, of changes, of absent faces," they "could not find the heart to go on bravely" with their "work among the living," those "living duties and living affections which . . . rightly claim . . . strenuous endeavors."

In Gabriel's conditional positiveness there is a foreshadowing of a more comprehensive vision. The after-supper speaker has declared that to look back might inhibit present resoluteness and action, but Gabriel's full epiphany turns upon acknowledgment inclusive of all that has gone before, and the dead past will rise to instruct him in the way of life. That will come only through his deepened sense of "living affections," by way of some painful self-recognition and the empathy into which that admits him. Gabriel is never heroic, even at his most generous, but he becomes the more exemplary as an insecure, alienated being, tardily integrated, yet finally receptive to vision. Meanwhile in concluding his speech he was still skirting actualities and veiling them in perfunctory locutions. He toasts the Misses Morkan as "the Three Graces of the Dublin musical world," but with less hyperbole he credits old Aunt Kate for her "good heart," her "too good heart," and says of Aunt Julia, with justice to the singer at least, that she "seems to be gifted with perennial youth." This does not directly deny but minimizes the intimation of mortality he has glimpsed in her face, and his summary of Mary Jane as "talented, cheerful, hard-working and the best of nieces" scarcely recognizes this almost eclipsed but sturdy and sensitive personality. Consequently he can toast them all together in conventional terms, wishing them "health, wealth, long life, happiness and prosperity" and can extend the extravagant wish that they may "long continue to hold" their "proud and self-won position." As occasional after-dinner speeches go, there must be not a few poorer than Gabriel's and not many much better. It takes its place in "The Dead," however, as something more than detailed realism. The *Dubliners* stories do not tend to naturalism's oppressive surfeit of mere data. While Gabriel's speech is quoted in full and runs along continuously (except for Mr. Browne's hearty "Hear, hear!" and some glimpses of other listeners' reactions), this is not excessive, since its overtones echo Gabriel's moodiness, and its artificiality vibrates with his unrest. The reader has been prepared to hear between the lines, and that makes Gabriel's public discourse a further private psychological revelation, and a preparation for denouement.

A telling indicator of the elements so mixed in Gabriel is Gretta's understanding of the man as he contains them. On arrival at the party she jests freely about the "awful bother" he makes over his family's health, which Gabriel genially understands, looking at her with "admiring and happy eyes"; later, alone in the hotel room, when he speaks leniently of Freddy Malins, Gretta says, "You are a very generous person, Gabriel." The old aunts, too, have laughed at the "standing joke" of Gabriel's extreme "solicitude" about his wife and children, but he is "their favorite nephew"; they depend on him to look after Freddy Malins if he's been drinking, and to carve the goose and make the speech; and old Aunt Kate says, "I always feel easier in my mind when he's here." Miss Ivors, also, comprehended Gabriel's various qualities; she would have been glad of the Conroys' company on the visit to the Aran Islands, she argued the more strenuously within the freedom of a long-standing friendship that even permitted some playful mockery, she admired his review and respected him as an intellectual equal while deploring his indifference to nationalism, and her flexible manner suggests she discerned his hampering incertitude and made what allowance she could. Nor did Joyce in this story take the tangential view of pure satire. Gabriel's is the most rounded character delineation in *Dubliners,* and in psychological comprehensiveness surpasses anything else in Joyce's work except the portrait of Stephen, and its extension in the "Telemachia." Furthermore, the youthful Stephen is never known at Gabriel's stage of maturity, experience, and responsible involvement.

Gabriel's hesitancies and fluctuations of mood are to be seen growing out of good intentions complicated by multiple insights and contradictory circumstance. It is partly because Gabriel is intellectually alert as well as morally sensitive that he can be preyed upon by doubts and despair, in that weighting down and threat of inhibition to which open minds are susceptible. Nevertheless in relativism's changeable climate Gabriel will come to realize that a man must make do, and not by withdrawal but by whatever engagement is feasible, and of whatever degree and durability. Such a commitment must be more than resignation to impasse, however, and here what can tip the balance is something beyond surrender or even compromise—it is the added imperative from a further awareness. This, over and above its naturalistic miscellany, is what "The Dead" is about; this is what makes it Gabriel's story, as it moves toward his epiphany. And makes it, in its way, Joyce's high point.

Despite the scope of Gabriel's cumulative insights, here as in all the *Dubliners* stories Joyce's realism holds well this side of exaggeration. "The Dead" does not propose any ultimate, or indeed anything humanly unique. Though Gabriel's empathy at last identifies him with all mankind, and though it enlarges his love for his wife and stabilizes it still more deeply, this is not represented as arrival at a poise beyond doubt and restlessness. Such a possibility is not excluded, but all the story presents is a climactic spot of time. Vicissitudes with their extremes will continue to enforce relativism and may reinflict the paraplegia of ambivalence. This hour at the hotel may be Gabriel's supreme moment, and he may never again rise to such comprehensiveness; certainly if he progresses by its light it will be along the average human way of steps forward interspersed with loss of ground, and gain itself will be tentative. What is to come thereafter the story does not stipulate or even suggest. Thus it holds to the high level of fictional realism where there are no final arrivals this side of death and nothing irreversibly achieved, and no mortal life or even any dramatized sequence of it can take on the immutable fair attitude of statue or urn.

Joyce had hungered for permanence; the desire is detectable beneath records of his rebellious withdrawal and unrest. Religion had pressed upon him the concept of the changeless; insecurity in his youth had augmented his desire for poise. Yet peace was something the world did not give Joyce, and he soon decided it was not to be had from heaven, either. Then, like many others, Joyce sought it in art. He not only mulled over the aesthetics of stasis in his notebooks, he entrusted declamation of it to Stephen. Yet since his practice was not in painting or sculpture but in narrative continuities, this only reinforced his awareness of private variance amidst variables. Nevertheless in *Dubliners* he refined his primary concept of epiphany from static glimpse to dramatic disclosure, under the aspect of mutability but in the humane light of what he called and had ventured to conceive of as "moral history," even envisaging "spiritual liberation."[31] *Dubliners* closely read can be seen based on this humanistic premise even in delineating social obstacles, circumstantial hazards, and personal inadequacies. Throughout *Dubliners* and especially in "The Dead" what is represented is not finally contained, but is only a segment. Yet this can be a real continuum wherein uncertainty and inconclusiveness attest "the very world of all of us," with its actual private issues and determining personal choices, under the flow of time and within vicissitude, and to be reasserted or modified or surrendered, whether consciously or in forgetfulness. Representation of the human condition under this aspect is realism at its most scrupulous and profound.

What Joyce so well achieved intrinsically and with magnitude in "The Dead" and in lesser degrees and dimensions in all of *Dubliners* provides a point of critical reference. This, like other abstractions in aesthetics, is subordinate to an art's unique containments of matter and conveyance of qualities, but by its basic validity the principle indicates the *Dubliners* stories as major fictional work, of considerable artistic significance. What is shown is that the so-called open-ended story paradoxically exacts a further refinement of unity. This is achievable in an epiphany —whatever name is given any such subjective distillate and consolidation, and whether the increase in awareness is the reader's alone or his recognition of it as a consummate passage in a character's experience, yet within the story's means and its unconstrained province. Concerning this aspect of fictional technique Professor Kenneth Burke has defined narrative resolution as "a point where some notable latent motive becomes patent," something "ambiguously prepared for" and "implicitly there" in the "previous developments," whereby it "serves to cap or consolidate the story by letting us see the previous situation in a new light." In such a development, he says, a "sensory image" like the snow in "The Dead" becomes "mythic image . . . more than 'just snow.'" At this point, he concludes, the narrative must stop, since "if the implications of the new dimension were developed further, the unity of the story would be destroyed."[32] Some such qualification is recognizable in all sorts of literary works, from lyrics to tragedies, and embracing the whole range of fiction. In these compositions it may be seen that when, in Professor Burke's phrase, they "stop 'enigmatically' at the point where the unveiling of the new dimension (the 'epiphany') takes place," the "unity" thereby preserved is something more than rhetorical, and more too than a mere single effect, imagistic or thematic, secured by the ordering of logically related detail.

Unity in works of art which rise above formulae is essentially unlike the various arrangements produced by philosophy, science, or practical techniques. Philosophy, in diverse hands from the mischief-making Plato on, overweeningly yearned toward the Absolute, and later shunned it, but by steps purporting to be absolutely sure. Even now the most finicky philosopher must make definitions and set these into a system—and it is by excessive professionalism under this rule that many contemporary practitioners have painted themselves into several small corners of their spacious apartment. Conversely, science contents itself with areas physically bounded, wherein its works are made autonomous (in its closest but still distant likeness to art), and mans its multiplying compartments diligently, not straying from them into indulgence of the metaphysical, or even the humanistic. The literary artist, neither scientist nor philosopher, subsists in the open under heaven's eye, yet without presuming to stare into it, and looks to horizons which move at his every step. Obviously the unity in his works is radically different not only from that refinement to an explicit demonstrable proposition sought by science or philosophy, but from the formulations intentionally underlying (however insecurely) the rhetoric of theologian, publicist, or politician. This plain primary distinction may be neglected in any overt and extractive emphasis upon a literary work's logical and rhetorical elements. Isolating and defining of theme, analogy, source, or symbol may strip the creation down to its skeleton, provoking wonder whether these bones ever lived under a reading so indifferent to the animation they invisibly support. Unfortunately, though, the picked-bare structure may gain too exclusive repute as the tangible and complete artistic entity, the real thing in itself. But literature cannot suffer such specialization of outlook or rule of method, and indeed should not crave supposed privileges and immunities. Literature instead must respond to the contrarieties and mysteries of the human condition, with its general flux and personal vagaries, seeing each existence inconclusively suspended, perhaps subject to no final judgment, though it has been intently self-aware and at moments absorbed in vision and passionately assertive.

Hence some hazard may lurk in the concept of snow become "more than 'just snow,'" rising to "mythic image." To put it another way, more things than just snow have entered into Gabriel's evolving epiphany, for which snow becomes an effectual signature. To sense a story's culmination as such is to have absorbed all effects into one effect that nevertheless does not erase them. In a genuine aesthetic experience a song's final chord not only reasserts the key but can commemorate the work's elements and progress. The effect is not intrinsic in the chord; other songs may conclude with the same notes, yet they will resound uniquely of a source, a progress, and its elements. Presumably this is what Professor Burke means in speaking of a consolidation. When he puts it that as the "sensory image" becomes "mythic image" it "serves to cap and consolidate," it might be recalled that whatever caps a spire asserts the spire's substance, structure, and reach. Even a playing card, when it trumps, becomes more than just its face, because of a particular history in that hand. In "The Dead" what snow as "more than" snow seeks to evoke is actively imaginative response, spontaneous, personally conditioned, and inwardly felt, to include consciousness of Gabriel as a living being at an expansive moment in his enlarging existence.

Then, though, the hand is played out, the song ends, and within fictional entity existential reality lays its hold upon protagonist and reader, as it has on the artist. Yet just because of this the outcome may be also quite other than enigmatic. Indeed, in "epiphany" as aesthetic effect the momentary awareness can be fully illuminating, within its own terms, circumstantial, temporal, and personal. And this comes of a pure creativity. The fictionist has scrutinized behavior as conduct, in the socio-individual nexus, but always seen as the gesture of a unique being.

The artist's mode in its entirety, like his style, has been the man himself, in rational-compassionate response to men and women he writes of. Donne's passage holds here; it is the mark of the artist that his total way of being involved with mankind can make any man's death his concern. Conversely, while the census-taker and the actuary both have their data, neither of these statisticians as such counts the tolling bell; and while the philosopher may draw a self-conscious conclusion from the fact that all men are mortal, profession obliges him to keep an eye out for major premises. The fictional artist does not thus press on toward specialized certainty; his glimpses are casual, his scrutiny eclectic. *Dubliners* not only excludes some Dublin strata but treats a comparatively few types, nor do their stories comprise their lives entire—not even that of old Maria, who is not yet come to the way of her death and her meeting it. Yet "Clay" is superbly unified, with particular effect transcending not only its chronology but the sum of its data. The fictionist thus has his own dialectic, maximizing the individual, but with only tentative implication of representativeness and no presupposition of universals or of individual stability. Moreover, the work is validated only by readers' reciprocal intimations.

That stories can turn on fateful moments in more than the mere logic of an effect from a cause, through the poignancy of a being's progressive experience, sensed by writer and reader in its quiddity and existential actuality, is richly illustrated in "The Dead"; this is at the center of its potency, which so many have acknowledged. The snow, "general all over Ireland," and falling before the mind's eye, leaves the reader in Gabriel's mind with multiple precipitations there as phenomenal as the forms taken by water, and as transient. Not that artists have found it easy to moderate their share of that universal thirst for absolutes which shows at all times among all peoples, especially in mythic religion, the law, and custom, wherein modification always seeks new fixity. Not all men can face relativism as did Keats or Chekov, each in his own way, or Santayana in his; few can, like E. M. Forster, refuse to believe in belief while postulating the excellence of sensitivity, considerateness, and pluck.[33] Yet while seriously intended fictional and dramatic art, responsible to knowledge of human vicissitude, suggests no timeless felicities, it can thereby, paradoxically, become classic, in laying hold on certain completions of awareness.

Literature acknowledges that life, prodigal in its possibilities, offers no guarantees, and provides no finalities except in death, whether of body or heart, as Joyce's Gabriel Conroy discerns. Nature verifies the same story, variously. Men gape at fossils, for what these so obviously say of transitoriness; a more astounding thing about natural selection is its proof of what choice can come to, as in the sea's strangest species, extant but imprisoned in their excessive irreversible specializations. For them time as opportunity has ceased; they have had their day as surely as the extinct. So even before a man must take his place in some stratum of earth, he may come to the end of his rope, but if he does, his story as such is over, for literature is always "occasional" and turns on happenings—even if only the quick but summary glimpse in a brief lyric. As to man's external containment, time itself then, not space and matter, seems most decisive. Apparently one-directional in this universe, and certainly so in this planetary system with its dying sun, time the giver and destroyer is yet the continuum fully pervaded by transcendent consciousness, and would thus seem even more profoundly the frame of literature than of music—though here too not its substance. This Yeats acknowledges when paradoxically he fancies that once out of his material and temporal existence he still would "sing . . . of what is past, or passing, or to come," and not all in all, but at such points.

What literature can offer, then, is the great common truth of possibly climactic awareness, the human achievement of cumulative transcendent insights, but only as relative absolutes within time and changes. The unavoidable sense of this context, bringing in the recurrent note of melancholy in the one stasis of mortality, its intimations of infinitude, is what makes literature augustly inclusive of the human, beyond scientific and philosophical conclusions about man, (and above any total credulity in the name of the haphazard, the desultory, and the random.) A unique magnitude is achieved by individual assertion—the lyric poet's own, directly put, or the fictionist's and dramatist's as delegated to characters and modulated by compassionate observation, invoking consensus. Whether it be seen as of the artist himself or his fictitious proxy, the movement within time is under the exacting consciousness of discrepancy between the ideal and the actual, yet capable of further vision, looking before and after, and rising to magnanimity in its acknowledgments. Such was Joyce's concept of that human potentiality and dramatic possibility which he termed the epiphany. It is demonstrated throughout *Dubliners,* but never more powerfully than in "The Dead," and while it may remain an open question whether thereafter Joyce moved away from this concept of fiction and sought another kind of containment, nevertheless that should not overshadow the stories.

Criticism of such achievement dare not envy the definition possible under more objective disciplines lest it fall into identifying the literary work's entity as no more than formal rhetorical deployment of theme, or a certification of biographical cliché, or a structuring dependently analogical, or a mere vessel for containment of myth, archetype, or symbol. It may be possible to make such identifications, but most readily in a pretentious and labored work; and they do not disclose the essence of works of the first order, which are belittled by such assumptive and exclusive treatment. To contemplate subdued old Maria as archetypically related to the Blessed Virgin Mary is to pass by her story's delicate realities; to rest on generalizations about Joyce's successful flight out of Ireland may be to see Little Chandler so tangled in Dublin's nets that his "tears of remorse" are not sensed as perhaps a closer approach to grace than Father Purdon's auditors stood in the way of knowing. And to consider the stories' endings as compositionally loose taperings-off, in a loss of momentum and intensity, is to see enervation where the "enigmatic" was to be found, and to neglect an aesthetic summons to empathic intimations. To fault Joyce's stories for "inconclusiveness" is, besides a devaluation of them, a misapprehension of literature.

By its instances *Dubliners* projects the principle that the modern open-structured short story should be recognized as more than "just" narrative. It tends toward the condition of the lyrical in celebrating some moment of gathered and clarified awareness. It remains dramatic in that the perception is arrived at through an objectified progress, rather than being rendered in essence out of a poet's own experience. It moves closer also to lyric effect by its compression, ellipsis, and connotativeness that lay claim upon the reader's collaborative intuition, while retaining dramatic narrative's prolonged cumulative intensification that makes denouement so peculiarly powerful, especially when, as with some Joycean epiphanies, it is in the privacy of a character's dawning realization. Gabriel's evolving vision is the most comprehensive and profound human experience Joyce ever represented. If anything in his work deserves the often too easily bestowed term *universal,* this is it. "The Dead" goes even further than is defined by Hugh Kenner's statement that "The epical narrative has concluded by gathering up the quality of a whole civilization in the isolation of Gabriel Conroy."[34] True as this is, there is, besides his isolation, Gabriel's achievement of enhanced relation, with Gretta, and with mankind living and dead. It is not just of man and wife, though in that aspect the story reaches deep. It is not just of Gabriel in Ireland, or of Gabriel versus Ireland. It is of the individual and the human condition, and of the paradox that what is most personal fully realizes itself only in generous interpersonal references.

That vision may lapse does not detract from its reality in its time, or its validity in the process of experience, and in Joyce's picturing of such realizations a relative idealism is not precluded. Morality thus has a point of entry into literature, but it is on its own there, as in life; correspondingly, the significant yet tentative consistencies of art may be paralleled in conduct. It is in this that *Dubliners* transcends Dublin and its people sociologically defined, and takes a central position between a Zolaesque naturalism and all sentimentalisms, whether of Dickens' or of Hardy's stripe, perfectionist or fatalistic. What is central in the stories, beyond the ethical or sociological, is the high pathos of those moments when human beings, assailed on their unsteady way, grasp an approximation and achieve a wider view, the more affecting for its vulnerability to further change. It is as to the creation of this most inclusive effect, which encompasses inconclusiveness, that the story's basic unity is to be assessed. Herein is the real aesthetic necessity for the pause at the point of epiphany. That is not an empty narrative convention but a way for preservation of essence.

Moreover, such a comprehensive gathering up at the level of transcendent awareness, by being set in the context of mutability, can attain an ultimate realism. It is the function of literature to assent to and even assert this reality, with due reservation. Since life in its totality (and bearing thus upon the individual inescapably) has no discernible beginning or ending, no long-enduring rationale, and its only abiding fact is fluctuation, art would pause at strategic points, would conservatively isolate an insight and consolidate selectively whatever has contributed to its meaning and thus has illuminated a portion of the path of experience. Art arises from a human necessity to assimilate and dominate, conditionally, the fact that life in the large, on the whole, and under the aspect of infinitude is always miscellaneous and disorderly, often inconsequential, and at its boundaries inscrutable. Under such universal conditions, in order to compose himself and his creations the literary artist must stop short of outright claims, both in what he asserts and in his manner of propounding it. Basic to an honest realism is its sustained recognition that human consciousness does project values and is motivated by such concepts, but that these are of various kinds at various levels according to the individual and circumstance, and even at its most vigorous and loftiest such assertions are limited, fluctuant, and assailable.

The fate of *Dubliners* in its day and since—its comparative neglect by conventional readers and the critical overemphasis of its sociological aspect—illustrates how a genuine literary accomplishment is against the grain of modernity, where the sentimentalism of absolutes is endemic in various forms. Too largely left unoccupied (as with many such areas now) is the broad middle ground of a rational, value-oriented, empathic art, relativistic and humanistic. It was on this ground that the open-structured short story found a place, with Chekov its great pioneer and still unsurpassed exemplar to a significant movement of twentieth-century fiction in English. The trend has had numerous capable followers, and for them the intent relevance, the undemonstrative but genuine empathy, and the permissive relativism and confronted inconclusiveness which Joyce wrought into *Dubliners* has remained a model. Its benefit is more than a demonstration of possibilities in a localized naturalism or a delineation of human solitariness. It is chiefly the proving of open narrative structure as best presenting realities of crucial experience, transitory but illuminating. Such fictional method achieves the very thing that superficial reading says it lacks, unity. This is, however, of a high and special sort, not reposing on either formal intellection or rationalized cliché, but a dynamic containment fixing the pure sense of a value glimpsed in its real human context, circumstantial and psychological. While *epiphanies* was Joyce's specialized name for this effect, in itself it was not new when Wordsworth spoke of "spots of time" and narratively demonstrated it, for instance in "The Two April Mornings"; and before that, lyrically, the awareness precipitated as cumulative and consummate realization is what is unified in the typical "when . . . then" sequence within sonnets, contributing experientially, beyond rhetoric, to their organic form.

Since the essence of open-structured stories is in what they most revealingly turn upon in the continuing flow of experience, that disclosure (whether for protagonist or reader or both) has a peculiar power, as a center that holds all else in arcs about it, transcendently pervading what is past, or passing, or to come, but without describing any complete, precisely containing circumference. As represented by Joyce's stories the epiphanous experience, while subjective and transitional, is given the tone and enduring containment of a finished work of art. Its resonances are echoes, not prophecies or proclamations; its unities, though comprising less than eternal and universal truth or any pretense thereto, still conserve the essence of a meaningful event in a personal history and adumbrate thereby a humane signification; its enigmatic pauses admit intimation and enfranchise empathic imagination. The insight, truly received, is seen as circumstantial and only in a pause, but what is in reality arresting can be aesthetically arrested and "treasured up on purpose to a life beyond life." Such are the epiphanies in *Dubliners,* and the greatest of these, for protagonist, for the reader, and presumably for Joyce himself, is Gabriel's.

As in many of the *Dubliners* stories, but in "The Dead" most of all, the dawning of the protagonist's epiphany is a solitary, subjective experience, but with roots in immediate and precedent event and in associations casual yet intently personal. Here runs the central vein of Joyce's realism, between naturalism and surrealism, and not a compromise, rather a viewing of the human condition more truly than either extreme of fiction. The thread of Gabriel's troubled consciousness is woven in with the lives of others; it is conspicuous and unique, but it is bent and held within the socio-ethical fabric, and his deepest self-realizations are found through his essentially generous responsiveness. In broadest terms his epiphany is the subsidence of unsettled personal conflict into fuller knowledge of life's ineluctable paradoxes, as his ambivalence is contained and transmuted into comprehensive empathy.

The good fortune of this enlarging experience, like many such gifts, befalls seemingly by accident. Yet the event is implicit in Gabriel's situation. It is not a superficially contrived and spurious finality, but a profound resolution. It does not invalidate the precedent realities which it subordinates within a larger configuration. Gabriel's advance, though hesitant, is not in itself fortuitous. The invitation had come to him once before, not just from Miss Ivors, but more essentially when Gretta "clasped her hands excitedly and gave a little jump," and said, "O, do go, Gabriel. I'd love to see Galway again." Her "do go" acknowledges that he must make the decision, with all that implies, but were he to respond positively, she would be included, as she would love to be. The paradox of a mutuality dependent upon spontaneous individual assertion is summed up in that "do go." However, at this instant on the verge of a possible vision the beholder was found wanting, and thereafter he was to advance by slow steps only, and arduously.

The process was initiated by song, begun and broken off at the party's end after most had gone. The singer was D'Arcy, but not in the guise remembered by Molly Bloom, as "pretty hot for all his tinny voice" when he had kissed her on the choir stairs after she sang Gounod's "Ave Maria."[35] Here he is only a voice from the drawing room, heard by those gathered below in the hall and about to leave. When he comes down the staircase with his accompanist Miss O'Callaghan and is praised, but is reproached too by Mary Jane and Aunt Kate for breaking off, he complains "roughly" of being "hoarse as a crow"; then having buttoned himself up against the weather, he makes amends to his hostesses by recounting "in a repentant tone . . . the history of his cold," and the others console him with sympathetic advice "to be very careful of his throat." This is but a minor flurry, incidental to the story's naturalism; the song's deeper reverberations are in another quarter. Gretta, who had paused "near the top of the first flight" and stood fixedly attentive to the singing in the room above, has not joined in that casual talk, but now she asks the name of the song, and when he tells her it is "The Lass of Aughrim" but he "couldn't remember it properly," she repeats the title and adds merely that she "couldn't think of the name." Out of her previous knowledge of the song itself and from her mood about it this night is to come Gabriel's epiphany.

Arrested by the sight of her pausing listening, he has sentimentalized that image in terms conversely prefiguring realities he is to be confronted with. She was standing in a shadow and he "could not see her face," so that at first glance it seemed simply "A woman" and only by the cut of her skirt does he know "It was his wife." Later the movement will be reversed; in the range of a further knowledge he will see his wife as a woman. Now he merely fancies her as a painting, static, but the experience just beginning here is to be dramatic, an arrival at fuller awareness within eventful process. (Perhaps this first glimpsing of Gretta as told projects Joyce's concern with the aesthetic paradox of stasis—the fictional work of art arrested yet indebted derivatively to time and change and drawing its lively momentum from them.) Gazing up at his wife poised there in shadows, so attentive to a music he could scarcely hear, Gabriel found "grace and mystery in her attitude as if she were a symbol of something," though he must ask himself what. Of this he is to learn later, in terms both more personal and more general, according to the valid way of epiphanies. At the moment, though, he is fixed upon the image, her poise has held him, and here repetition, a common Joycean device, sustains the effect—"her attitude" . . . "in that attitude"—"a symbol of something" . . . "what . . . a symbol of"—"listening to distant music" . . . "*Distant Music* he would call the picture"—"If he were a painter" . . . "if he were a painter."

It is indeed a distant music, not only from that upper room there, but from Gretta's girlhood, and out of a separate part of her life, hitherto secret from him. The song, "in the old Irish tonality," is also on a folk theme and in the ballad mode; it concerns a lass seduced by a lord and now begging entry with her child into his house. What Gabriel overhears,

> "O, the rain falls on my heavy locks
> And the dew wets my skin,
> My babe lies cold . . ."

had been heard by Joyce, from Nora, and later from Nora's mother in Galway, the same stanza with only slight modification:

The rain falls on my yellow locks
And the dew it wets my skin,
My babe lies cold within my arms;
Lord Gregory, let me in.

As the ballad has it, when the lord demanded a token of identity, the lass asked him to remember "That night on yon lean hill/ When we both met together"; still he refused to admit her, and she drowned herself.[36] So it is a tale not just of death but of love denied. Aughrim, says Ellmann, is "a little village in the west not far from Galway,"[37] and this corresponds with Nora's girlhood knowledge of the song, and Gretta's too, since her people are from Connacht and in her girlhood she like Nora had lived in Galway with her grandmother. Another and more notable Aughrim may come to mind, the one south of Dublin, in County Wicklow, where in 1691 the Irish and their French allies suffered a final defeat that consolidated England's previous victories. Though certainly Joyce is using the ballad with its private matters, an historical association may deepen the melancholy. More importantly, by having D'Arcy break off and leaving the old tale uncompleted in "The Dead," Joyce properly subdues it to the larger theme: what the song arouses in Gretta and how her reaction affects Gabriel. Here fiction's textural complexity, as interactive subordination and emphasis, is well illustrated; and Joyce's control is the more admirable considering how much of Nora's biography he was transferring to Gretta and how surely he stopped short of an excessive use that would have intruded irrelevantly. Lengthy and substantial and variegated as "The Dead" is, and drifting as it does upon the meandering course of a crowded casual social affair, it is also masterfully economical—in fact, more remarkably so than some of the shorter and simpler stories.

Joyce's large economy gave about four-fifths of "The Dead" to the party and its breaking up; the Conroys' transition, walking and in a shared cab from Usher's Island to privacy in the Gresham Hotel, is accomplished briefly, though with some point;

the story's crown, its most extended, intense scene and Gabriel's epiphany, takes up less than a fifth of the pages. Yet the long approach has been winding in the one direction all the way. Though it is primarily through Gretta's remembered experience and the intermutations of their marriage that Gabriel's epiphany takes form, that is not all; the wider references and presagings deriving from the party and its people serve the story's private climax in its overtone of universality. In the great final episode Gabriel moves from increasingly revealing talk with Gretta to dialogue with himself that plumbs the pretenses and actualities of his being and carries him from frustrated sexual desire and irrational jealousy to shame for his egotistic insulation and thus to "a strange, friendly pity" and "generous tears," with a widening of empathy. This includes Michael Furey dead at seventeen and for love, and Gretta's girlhood sorrow still resurgent under the stimulus of an old song, and the haggard look of old Aunt Julia singing with undiminished art her ever more incongruous "old" song, "Arrayed for the Bridal." By such steps his vision grows to encompass mankind in the spirit of love under the bonds of mortality, for perhaps a greater identification and involvement with his fellow-beings than Gabriel had ever known till then.

After the practiced musical performances by Mary Jane and Aunt Kate and the supper-table talk about great singers, what halts Gretta on the stairs and holds Gabriel attentive to her is a simple ballad, archaic in tone and trite in substance. As with most old songs, its power is less in itself than in its ambience. Mary Jane's "Academy piece" had been a display of virtuosity, Aunt Julia's performance was more genuinely artistic, but "The Lass of Aughrim" sung hoarsely by the ungracious D'Arcy and left uncompleted has greatest potency, by private associations for Gretta, with transferred consequence for Gabriel. So it is from the outside world, and from the rejected unsophisticated west of Ireland and the pasts of other people, in a situation more foreign to him than the European continent as he knows it, that the distant music reaches Gabriel at last, to break over him in successive waves of feeling, and to carry him on in self-realization and in relation to the human community and condition. At the same time, since the challenge comes to Gabriel through his cherished wife, it not only touches him most closely but demands most candid response.

Gabriel's marriage involves love-making remembered and desire recurrent this night; he has been, also, a considerate and protective husband and father—and Gretta's easy way of jesting about his solicitude over their health suggests a secure marital companionability. Still Gabriel knows that his provident life as family man has been tinged with timidity, and his connubial sexuality has not had the stature of a grand passion. This man who has considered himself superior in culture, vocation, and cosmopolitan experience (to the extent of wondering whether a quotation from Browning would be above the heads of his hearers) is to feel himself inferior to a dead boy of seventeen, one who had put love above his own survival itself, and whose despairing eyes Gretta still can see "as well as well!" In the absoluteness of that unforgotten figure is an inescapable present reproach. It comes not from Gretta, who is merely for the while caught up in remembrance of an old sorrow; the challenge comes directly to Gabriel through a self-examination that must confess inconsistency and a consequent degree of ineffectuality. How has he faced the world and its most demanding realities, this man with "the face whose expression always puzzled him when he saw it in a mirror." The equivocations of his life come to mock him as "a nervous well-meaning sentimentalist," a "pitiable fatuous fellow." Though he is generous—and Gretta incidentally but fondly has told him so in their first moments together, while later Joyce allows himself so to describe Gabriel's tears—still in this passage with his wife he is a frustrated lover, then a disconcerted husband. The dead boy, at the moment more alive and compelling in Gretta's mind than he, is discovered as a formidable rival, remaining in her memory as other than anything Gabriel had ever been. How is he to rally to such rivalry, this less than whole-hearted man in whom conflicting divisions have reduced anything he could offer?

The question implicit in his situation is dramatically significant because, despite his idiosyncrasies as a restless but timid schoolteacher, minor reviewer, and anxious, diffident family man, he is broadly representative. This indubitable and partially fated Dubliner is also an average cultured Western man of his times, in sense and spirit. He provides an abstract of the fragmented and diminished existence which many in other places than Ireland are born to, under environment's erosions upon a personality of some earnestness but not unusually resourceful and vigorous. More especially Gabriel is civilized and decent, too, with the consequent restraints upon impulse and regard for mutuality, and though feverishly desiring his wife he feared "that diffidence was about to conquer him" as he waited for "some ardour in her eyes," without which "To take her as she was would be brutal." More broadly, as educated man he illustrates the paradox that to extend oneself is in some degree to lose what one has by natural right, as increased knowledge increasingly colors with a reductive relativism all that one has more surely credited before. In "The Dead" Joyce is suggesting how other men too may suffer the kind of loss he had known in the extreme degree commensurate with his genius and enterprise, and he is dramatizing the excruciation in the balancing of any such account.

Gabriel, in the presence of Gretta's past and of himself under this light, now stands at such a point, but that severe summing up is not to be the end of the matter. After his first jealous annoyance and growing humiliation he finds his way further with the objectivity and considerateness which make up magnanimity. Gradually transcending not only the egoism of his lust but other exclusive claims of an habitual tender relationship, he discovers new involvements of himself with others, under widened aspects. Joyce's concern with this theme is shown in the equal subtlety and firmness with which he treats the stages of the experience in that hotel room. Gabriel, though not unkindly, was almost condescending in wondering why the song remembered should now be moving Gretta to tears. Then at the glimpse of the lad in her girlhood he felt "dull anger" and questioned her "ironically." He even asked "coldly" whether she wanted to go to Galway perhaps to see this man; but told that the boy had died young and had been only someone "in the gasworks," (which Tindall somehow finds "moderately funny"),[38] Gabriel was now "humiliated by the failure of his irony." From that point he began to see himself critically, in "shameful consciousness" of having been "a ludicrous figure."

With this acknowledgment he can return toward essential relationship to his wife, though in another way than he had desired a short while earlier. It is no simple progression, however; vanity and sympathy were at odds in him. When he had first asked about the song, "A kinder note than he had intended went into his voice," and later, inquiring whether she had been "in love with this Michael Furey," he had "tried to keep up his tone of cold interrogation, but his voice when he spoke was humble and indifferent." The sadness veiling Gretta's voice as she told she "was great with" Michael Furey "at that time" then entered Gabriel's as he "caressed one of her hands" and asked "what did he die of so young?" At her saying "I think the boy died for me," Gabriel was "seized" by a "vague terror," but "shook himself free of it with an effort of reason," and asking no more probing questions, he "continued to caress her hand" as he listened, only prompting her gently to continue. So he learns of the lad Michael Furey, ill, but coming shivering in the rain to see the girl Gretta the night before she left Galway for the convent school in Dublin, and hears how he flung gravel against her window to bring her out to the end of the garden, and said he did not want to live without her, and then her hearing he had died a week later. Therefore when Gretta, having finished, "flung herself face downward on the bed, sobbing," Gabriel was tactfully "shy of intruding on her grief," and having let her hand "fall gently," he "walked quietly to the window."

These are not gestures of withdrawal but of considerateness, and of approach to a larger outlook. Between this woman asleep after her grief and the hotel window looking out on the falling snow Gabriel completed his journey toward epiphany. Realization grows as he "unresentfully" contemplates Gretta herself in further perspective, uniquely, "as though he and she had never lived together as man and wife." With his new knowledge that "she had had that romance in her life; a man had died for her sake," he muses on "what she must have been then, in that time of her first girlish beauty," and though like any lover he is unwilling to say she is "no longer beautiful," he knows hers is "no longer the face for which Michael Furey had braved death." This progressive vision of her is comparable to the matured humane recognition of his wife which Wordsworth arrived at: "A being breathing thoughtful breath,/ A traveler between life and death." Joyce has showed Gabriel closely aware of process in his experience—from what, he wonders, had his "riot of emotions . . . proceeded?" He enumerates events—"his aunts' supper . . . his own foolish speech . . . the wine and dancing, the merry-making [about Grandfather Morkan's horse] when saying good-night . . . the pleasure of the walk along the river in the snow" —and this last not the mere imagined pleasantness of going there "alone" and on into the park, as he had wished he could do after Miss Ivors' disconcerting challenges, but his actual "tender joy" as he had followed his wife through the slush while "Moments of their secret life together burst like stars upon his memory." Then into those recollections of vital happiness breaks the image of Aunt Julia's "haggard look," and he senses she "would soon be a shade with the shade of Patrick Morkan" and imagines himself seeking "some words that might console" Aunt Kate but finding "only lame and useless ones." The review-writer and speech-maker has passed beyond verbalizing to a closer encounter with ultimate realities.

Lying down beside his sleeping wife, and thinking of how there had been "locked in her heart for so many years that image of her lover's eyes when he had told her that he did not wish to live," Gabriel is moved to "generous tears," which gather "more thickly" as he imagines the "young man standing under a dripping tree"—that tree Gretta had mentioned as a detail of her indelible recollection. Thus closely does he enter into his wife's emotion, and having also included Michael Furey in his compassion, Gabriel felt that "Other forms were near," his "soul" having "approached that region where dwell the vast hosts of the dead." It is another crucial step in Gabriel's experience, as Joyce here sounds the phrase that is to entitle his story. Gabriel "was conscious of, but could not apprehend" the "wayward and flickering existence" of the dead. This has to do not with concepts of an after-life but with memories transcendent in present consciousness; neither is it a false melancholy, affected or morbid. Instead Gabriel is "conscious" that "these dead had one time reared and lived in" a "solid world" (presumably not just the habitations of men but the world of human acts and relationships) which becomes "grey" and "impalpable" as his "own identity" fades with it. "The Dead" is not primarily about death but about a living person's enlarging identification with the whole mortal life of man, a life which has some endurance as works and records, and may engender more of life through transitory remembrance by those who follow after, while thereby reminding them of mortality.

Empathy had brought Gabriel to a realization of the human condition as Conrad described it—"the sense of mystery surrounding our lives . . . our sense of pity, and beauty, and pain . . . the latent feeling of fellowship with all creation . . . the subtle but invincible conviction of solidarity . . . which binds men to each other, which binds together all humanity—the dead to the living and the living to the unborn." Conrad, speaking here of that to which the artist appeals, is claiming a universality and primacy for it under a natural human "capacity for delight and wonder."[39] In his phrasing of it as man's "sense of pity, and beauty, and pain" is suggested an organismic function, its factors coexistent and interactive. Thus the pathos of Michael Furey's fate and of Gretta's revived sorrow for him, and Gabriel's humility before passions more imperious than his own divided life has been capable of, are all expressed in his "generous tears." He is seen passing from an inhibiting uncertainty to the acceptance which must comprise opposites shading into each other in a complex that is reality. Thus from passion frustrated he has come to compassion realized, and from a half-alienated intellectual's unsteady, uneasy stance he has arrived at a committed, humane poise. The impalpable dead have commanded the attention of the living, at the party and thereafter, in such various aspects as Gabriel's mother projecting from a photograph her formidable qualities, Grandfather Morkan still involuntarily circling King Billy's statue, Parkinson's "beautiful pure sweet mellow English tenor" voice still resounding for Aunt Kate in the mind's ear, and Michael Furey's unforgettable eyes wide open upon Gretta with love and despair. And the living, remembering, have acknowledged not just death but life. Those monks sleeping in their coffins were looking toward an immeasurable existence; and at the supper table reminiscent talk of singers dead and gone vivified a present enduring sense of greatness in art. "Natural supernaturalism" permeates this story and suffuses it with significance; the multiple miscellaneous detail is at every point transcended by idea, in the characters' presently engaged but memory-haunted consciousness, and implicitly in the whole fictional effect.

All the incidental substance of "The Dead," however, and all its minor reverberations intensify the thematic focus on Gabriel. Having seen Gretta on the stairs as a picture and a symbol as yet unidentified, he had learned to see her more closely than ever as a person in her own absolute status, vividly alive and mortal, with a unique secret history that nevertheless corresponds to universally recurrent human ecstasy and grief. What Gabriel's progress signifies is the resolution of uneasy ambivalence into accepted paradox. Here nature makes widest way for art and puts greatest demand upon it. Inclusive contemplation of the antithetical and acceptance of the enigmatic can give a literary work not only magnitude but an enveloping unity, as Shakespeare understood and Keats recognized. A common but still august phrase for what Gabriel attained to is "the tragic sense of life." It is a phrase to be taken whole, however; this sense is tragic because life-oriented. The statement will be empty only to the nihilist who, if not denying the tragic, would at most equate it with the totally negative and meaningless. Those who wrench Hobbes's statement beyond its "natural man" context give themselves away in calling life nasty, brutish, and short; were it entirely nasty and brutish it would be insufferably long, the brute world does not know that it is brutish, and nastiness is determined by a human aversion, counterpart to a conceived and sometimes achieved decorum. Life is tragic not in that it is completely worthless or even predominantly evil; life is tragic because its largest human achievements are relative, its joys are vulnerable, and its infinite longings are in bondage to mortality. It is in awareness of this that a being's consciousness may be drawn along, further weighted yet the more propelled, as it descends, augmented, to its cessation in the sea of death.

It was thus with Gabriel. Lying awake beside his sleeping wife, turning to the window and watching the snowflakes falling "silver and dark . . . obliquely against the lamplight," he knew that "The time had come for him to set out on his journey westward." This is indeed what Professor Ellmann calls it, a "strange sentence." It may be taken, as he proposes, to imply that Gabriel is accepting, "half-consciously . . . the possibility of an actual trip to Connaught"—Gretta's home region in the west of Ireland. Ellmann further remarks, helpfully, that the sentence "suggests a concession, a relinquishment," in a turning toward "the primitive, untutored, impulsive country from which Gabriel had felt himself alienated."[40] Possibly one may note also that though Gabriel's mood is melancholy, the turn he is making is not altogether in surrender but is toward an implied value, for himself and as a general human possibility. This journey westward which it is now time for Gabriel to set out on may indeed be to Galway and scenes of Gretta's girlhood and perhaps even to the Aran Islands with Miss Ivors' party, but something more is involved. It is not to be imagined that Joyce elaborated this complex story merely to show a person's meekly changing his vacation plans, even if in deference to a good friend's invitation and his dear wife's wish. Such an absurd reduction of the story is not generally voiced, but it may seem suggested by formula readings which see Gabriel as a man totally defeated because of his failure to escape from Ireland. Nor need the story be taken to mean that Gabriel will turn his back on the Continent and its culture, and thereby sacrifice in some part his way of being.

It is in fact the opposite. "The Dead" is a story of growth, enlargement of outlook, increase in knowledge, access to vision. Though Anthony Burgess sees little in "The Sisters" but "the image of a paralyzed priest and a broken chalice," and does not note the ambivalence in Little Chandler nor the dramatic tension in "Ivy Day in the Committee Room," he discovers in "The Dead" that "the living and the dead coexist; they have strange traffic with each other," and as for its being time for Gabriel "to set out on his journey westward," Burgess explains that "The west is where passion takes place and boys die for love; the graveyard where Michael Furey lies buried is, in a sense, a place of life."[41] To which it might be added that Gabriel too has felt passion, and some terror, and pity; and a certain private self-defensive vanity has died in him for Gretta's sake. Thus do the dead reconcile the living to each other, and to life itself, of which mortality is the enhancing frame. The contemplated journey westward, while actually into the provincial, is also symbolically toward the primary and the essential. For the restless and somewhat rebellious man Ireland with its uttermost Aran Islands or the Continent and its languages may seem to pose not only opposite values but mutually exclusive choices, yet could not one steadied mind learn to embrace both? Conversely, what doctrinaire expatriate, either Irish or American, has understood the Continent, or really tried to, or has become acclimated to anything but a like coterie there? Certainly not Joyce, who lived a more insulated life abroad than he had in Dublin, and retained as a most vital impulse his backward regard for Ireland and the

Irish. So reading yet once more that often quoted proposition—"Gabriel Conroy is what Joyce might have become, had he remained in Ireland"—one might find an overtone suggesting there could have been, after all, that second volume of short stories. On the other hand, it may be supposed that with Gabriel's epiphany Joyce had gone as far as he could, and far enough for a conciliation which rounded out this phase of his work. Such amelioration of a fluctuant, inwardly contending ambivalence did not require a denial that opposites exist, but merely their acceptance, and not just in theory but as entering into one's portion of life. Toward such equilibrium Gabriel has yearned and tended; essentially he has already set out on his "journey westward," by the slow advances of his increasing comprehension. That Joyce stood with him at the window can be said without implying that either Gabriel or he went the rest of the projected way.

Its stages should be taken account of in summing up the story. From the beginning Gabriel is seen perturbed by uncertainties and self-doubts, and the contrarieties in his after-dinner speech are only partially obscured by its hazy rhetoric. Confronted by the ghost of the absolutely ardent young Michael Furey, he had confessed himself a "pitiable fatuous fellow," but this extreme humility, a candid acknowledgment of self in a certain context, has been led up to by his earlier considerateness, however inadequately defined, for those about him, as with Lily or Aunt Julia singing or his wife listening on the stairs. Arrived at the hotel and at all he learned there, his sentimentalized concept of Gretta as model for a painting, "Distant Music," has been changed to "a strange friendly pity" as he looked on her asleep and imagined her "in that time of her first girlish beauty." While distances have increased, resonances have become clearer. The snow that tapped lightly upon the windowpane "was general all over Ireland." This implication of a common condition is extended by Gabriel's hearing, on the swoonlike verge of sleep, "the snow falling faintly through the universe." This abstraction has emerged, however, out of particular realities. The snow falls, he muses, "on every part" of central Ireland, "upon every part of the lonely churchyard" containing Michael Furey's grave. By its "falling into the dark mutinous Shannon waves" and thus disappearing it is not only multitudinous and widespread as Homer saw it,[42] and subject to solution in another form of itself, but, as Burns found it, an image of transience. Yet in its return to water the snow is also part of nature's cycle, less accidental and more self-sustained and sustaining than man's cyclical history as Joyce later fancied and illustrated it. And Gabriel's imaging the waves as "mutinous" may be thought to have arisen from a penitent sense of his rebelliousness, upon which a steadier milder influence has descended, yet not foreign to his nature, but its own element in rarefied modality, returned into it.

Thus in the concluding passage of "The Dead" the snow as symbol is put to widest use. If, as some may professionally insist, its drifting on the crooked churchyard crosses, the spears of the little gate, and the barren thorns is Christian symbolism, the concept of crucifixion still would involve, as with Michael Furey himself, not just suffering and death but life and love. It is in the august dimensions of the universal that Gabriel is conscious of the snow falling "upon all the living and the dead." This, the story's final phrase, is the summing up of Gabriel's epiphany. One movement from the particular to the general has been in the repeated phrase "their last end"—Mary Jane had used it to explain what certain monks are reminding themselves of by sleeping in their coffins, and it is as "like the descent of their last end" that Gabriel hears the faint fall of snow "through the universe." As he heard this, Gabriel's "soul swooned slowly," wrote Joyce. This unusual phrase should not carry either of two common literary associations, whether of fainting in the manner of delicate maidens or of deepest sleep. Gabriel's swoon is neither inanimate repose nor collapse, but trancelike arrestment by an absorbing vision, in which the immediate and personal are diffused into the universal.

It is in this sense that Gabriel has felt his "own identity . . . fading out"—that self he was all too conscious of, earlier in the story, as the prim, timorous, egoistic sentimentalist. Conversely, in his humbling self-examination and his increasing extensions of empathy his naturally generous spirit has attained to a magnanimous involvement with "all the living." It is in awareness of their company as well as of the dead that he has come to feel he must "set out on his journey westward." His climactic experience parabolizes the psychological-ethical process of finding one's life by losing it, of proving genuine identity by identification with the inclusive reality of the humane, and of realizing love most fully through its reciprocal beneficences. Beyond this is the fullness of the knowledge that ardor, the condition of insight, though subject to time and change, can also transcend them, as does this work of art which is its celebration, in Joyce's largest shadowing forth of an epiphanal experience.

Notes

INTRODUCTION

1. "The Other Side of James Joyce," *Arizona Quarterly,* IX (Spring, 1953), 10.

2. *Accent,* Winter, 1944. Reprinted (pp. 47–94) in *James Joyce: Two Decades of Criticism,* ed. Seon Givens (New York: Vanguard Press, 1948). Hereinafter mentioned as *Two Decades.*

3. "The Moral Vision in *Dubliners,*" *Western Speech,* XX (Fall, 1956), 196.

4. Marvin Magalaner and Richard M. Kain, *Joyce: The Man, the Work, the Reputation* (New York: New York University Press, 1956), pp. 99–100. Hereinafter referred to by title.

5. *James Joyce* (New York: Scribner's, 1950), p. 102.

6. *Letters of James Joyce,* ed. Stuart Gilbert (New York: Viking Press, 1957), p. 60. Hereinafter referred to as *Letters.*

7. *Letters of James Joyce, Volume II,* ed. Richard Ellmann (New York: Viking Press, 1966), p. 99. Hereinafter referred to as *Letters, II.*

8. *Letters, II,* p. 134.

9. Richard Ellmann, *James Joyce* (New York: Oxford University Press, 1959), p. 543. Hereinafter referred to as Ellmann.

10. *Letters, II,* p. 137.

11. Ellmann, p. 216.

12. *Two Decades,* p. 66.

13. *Ibid.,* p. 67.

14. *Ibid.,* p. 58.

15. *Ibid.,* pp. 84, 85.

16. *Ibid.,* pp. 76, 77.

17. *Ibid.,* p. 87.

18. *Ibid.,* p. 49.

19. *Ibid.,* p. 72.

20. *Ibid.,* p. 54, p. 56.

21. *Letters, II,* p. 134.

22. *Ibid.,* pp. 122, 123.

23. *Letters,* p. 64.

24. *Ibid.,* p. 60.

25. *Axel's Castle* (New York: Scribner's, 1931), p. 191.

26. *Two Decades,* p. 457. Reprinted from *Writers Today,* ed. Denys Val Baker (London: Sedgwick and Jackson, 1946).

27. *Books Today* (*Chicago Tribune*), Sept. 20, 1964, p. 5.

28. *Joyce: The Man, the Work, the Reputation,* p. 60.

29. Ellmann, p. 171 n.

30. *Letters, II,* p. 106.

31. *The Letters of W. B. Yeats,* ed. Allan Wade (London: Rupert Hart-Davis, 1954), p. 597.

32. "Ulysses, Order, and Myth," *Two Decades,* p. 201. (Reprinted from *The Dial,* Nov., 1923.)

33. "Dubliners and Mr. James Joyce," *The Literary Essays of Ezra Pound* (Norfolk, Conn.: New Directions, n.d.), pp. 399–401.

34. From Lady Morgan's *Journals,* according to W. Y. Tindall, in *A Reader's Guide to James Joyce* (New York: Noonday Press, 1959), p. 6.

35. *My Brother's Keeper* (New York: Viking Press, 1958), p. 90.

36. "A Study of James Joyce's *Ulysses,*" in *Two Decades,* p. 251. (Reprinted from *Polemic,* 7 and 8, 1947, and supplemented.)

37. Ellmann, pp. 14–20, *passim.*

38. *James Joyce and the Making of Ulysses* (Bloomington: Indiana University Press, 1960), p. 57.

39. *Ibid.,* p. 19.

40. *My Brother's Keeper,* pp. 61, 62.

41. *Ibid.,* p. 62.

42. *The Portable James Joyce* (New York: Viking Press, 1947), p. 18.

43. *A Reader's Guide to James Joyce,* p. 6.

44. *The Novel and the Modern World* (Chicago: University of Chicago Press, 1939, rev. ed., 1960), p. 63. (References are to the revised edition, but the passages quoted were left almost unchanged from the first edition.)

45. Ellmann, p. 285.

46. *The Novel and the Modern World,* p. 64.

47. *Ibid.,* p. 65.

48. *Ibid.,* p. 63.

49. *The Lonely Voice* (Cleveland: World Publishing Co., 1963), p. 113.

50. *Ibid.,* p. 114.

51. Ellmann, p. 238. Also Herbert Gorman, *James Joyce* (New York: Farrar and Rinehart, 1939), p. 176.

52. *The Lonely Voice,* p. 125.

53. *Ibid.*, p. 127.
54. Mary and Padraic Colum, *Our Friend James Joyce* (London: Gollancz, 1959), p. 86.
55. *That Summer in Paris* (New York: Coward-McCann, 1964), p. 229.
56. Ellmann, p. 238. ("Interview with S. Joyce, 1954.")
57. *Letters*, p. 64.
58. *Ulysses* (New York: Modern Library, 1934), p. 8.
59. *James Joyce: A Critical Introduction* (Norfolk, Conn.: New Directions, 1941), p. 32.
60. *Western Speech*, XX (Fall, 1956), p. 208.
61. *Ibid.*, p. 199.
62. *Stephen Hero* (New York: New Directions, 1944), p. 213.
63. *Letters*, p. 55.
64. *My Brother's Keeper*, p. 104.
65. "Joyce and the Epiphany," *Sewanee Review*, LXXII (Winter, 1964).
66. *Epiphanies* (Buffalo: University of Buffalo Lockwood Memorial Library, 1956).
67. Robert Scholes and Richard M. Kain, *The Workshop of Daedalus* (Evanston: Northwestern University Press), pp. 11–51.
68. *The Classical Temper* (London: Chatto and Windus, 1961), p. 214.
69. *Our Friend James Joyce*, p. 104.
70. *Letters*, p. 70.
71. *Letters*, pp. 62, 63.
72. "Editor's Preface" to *Dubliners*, in *The Portable James Joyce* (New York: Viking Press, 1947), p. 18.

THE SISTERS

1. *Dublin's Joyce* (Bloomington: Indiana University Press, 1966), pp. 50–53. More fully, *Time of Apprenticeship: The Fiction of Young James Joyce* (London: Abelard-Schuman, 1959), pp. 72–96.
2. *The Lonely Voice* (Cleveland: World Publishing Co., 1963), p. 114.
3. Richard Ellmann, *James Joyce* (New York: Oxford University Press, 1959), p. 88.
4. Magalaner, *Time of Apprenticeship*, p. 84.
5. *Dublin's Joyce*, p. 50.

6. *Letters of Henry James,* ed. Percy Lubbock (New York: Scribner's 1920), II, 181.

7. L. A. G. Strong, *The Sacred River* (New York: Pellagrini and Cudahy, 1951), p. 17; W. Y. Tindall, *A Reader's Guide to James Joyce* (New York: Noonday Press, 1959), p. 16. (Other Joyce critics have made the same assumption.)

8. Ellmann, p. 40, and see illustration opposite p. 80.

9. See *The Workshop of Daedalus,* ed. Robert Scholes and Richard M. Kain (Evanston: Northwestern University Press, 1965), p. 17.

10. *Ulysses* (New York: Modern Library, 1934), p. 216.

11. Marvin Magalaner and Richard M. Kain; *James Joyce: The Man, the Work, the Reputation* (New York: New York University Press, 1956), pp. 73, 74.

12. "Joyce and the Modern Novel," *A James Joyce Miscellany* (New York: The James Joyce Society, 1957), p. 12.

13. *James Joyce: The Man, the Work, the Reputation,* p. 74.

14. Ellmann, p. 170.

15. *Ibid.*, p. 171.

16. "Simony, the Three Simons, and Joycean Myth," *A James Joyce Miscellany* (New York: The James Joyce Society, 1957), p. 23.

17. "The Gnomonic Clue to James Joyce's *Dubliners,*" *Modern Language Notes,* LXII (June, 1957), 421–424.

18. *A Portrait of the Artist as a Young Man,* ed. Chester G. Anderson (New York: Viking Press, 1968), p. 159.

19. *Stephen Hero* (Norfolk, Conn.: New Directions, 1944, 1955), pp. 198, 200, 201, 202, 203.

20. *Ibid.*, p. 201.

21. *The Catholic Encyclopedia,* ed. C. G. Herberman *et al.* (New York: Robert Appleton, 1912), XIV, 1.

22. *Schaff-Herzog Encyclopedia of Religious Knowledge,* ed. E. M. Jackson (Grand Rapids: Baker Book House), X, 429.

23. *Encyclopedia of Religion and Ethics,* ed. James Hastings (New York: Scribner's, 1921), XI, 526.

24. *Ibid.*, p. 526.

25. *The Catholic Encyclopedia,* XIV, 1.

26. Acts 8: 9–24.

27. *Encyclopedia of Religion and Ethics,* XI, 514.

28. Herbert Gorman, *James Joyce* (New York: Rinehart, 1948), p. 208.

29. *Dublin's Joyce,* p. 53.

30. *Letters of James Joyce, Volume II,* ed. Richard Ellmann (New York: Viking Press, 1966), p. 111.
31. *A Portrait of the Artist as a Young Man,* p. 98.
32. *Ibid.,* p. 159.
33. *Ibid.,* p. 158.
34. *Ibid.,* p. 162 (italics added).
35. Ellmann, p. 19.
36. *Ibid.,* p. 170.
37. See *A Portrait of the Artist as a Young Man,* p. 244.
38. See Brewster Ghiselin, "The Unity of Joyce's 'Dubliners,'" *Accent,* XVI (Spring and Summer, 1956), pp. 75–88, 196–213.

AN ENCOUNTER

1. Magalaner, in Marvin Magalaner and Richard M. Kain, *Joyce: The Man, the Work, the Reputation,* (New York: New York University Press, 1956) p. 76.
2. *Ibid.,* p. 77.
3. *A Portrait of the Artist as a Young Man,* ed. Chester G. Anderson (New York: Viking Press, 1968), p. 66.
4. W. F. Wakeman, *Evening Telegraph Reprints,* No. II; *Old Dublin, First Series* (Dublin, 1887), p. 24.
5. *Ibid.,* p. 24.
6. *Letters of James Joyce, Volume II,* ed. Richard Ellmann (New York: Viking Press, 1957), p. 137. (In the text the word is "minutes," not "moments.")
7. Magalaner, *op. cit.,* p. 76.
8. *Ibid.,* p. 75.
9. *Ibid.,* p. 76.
10. *Letters, II,* pp. 309–10.
11. Robert Scholes, "Grant Richards to James Joyce," *Studies in Bibliography,* XVI (1963), 147, 148.
12. Richard Ellmann, *James Joyce* (New York: Oxford University Press, 1959), p. 340.
13. *Ibid.,* p. 361.
14. *Ibid.,* p. 395.
15. John J. Slocum and Herbert Cahoon, *A Bibliography of James Joyce* (New Haven: Yale University Press, 1953), p. 96.
16. Ellmann, p. 340.
17. Stanislaus Joyce, *My Brother's Keeper* (New York: Viking Press, 1958), p. 63.
18. *Letters, II,* p. 309.

ARABY

1. "Dubliners and Mr. James Joyce," *The Egoist*, I (July 15, 1914), 14; *The Literary Essays of Ezra Pound* (Norfolk, Conn.: New Directions, n.d.), p. 400.

2. *A Portrait of the Artist as a Young Man*, ed. Chester G. Anderson (New York: Viking Press, 1968), p. 67.

3. *Letters of James Joyce*, ed. Stuart Gilbert (New York: Viking Press, 1957), pp. 63–64.

4. Richard Ellmann, *James Joyce* (New York: Oxford University Press, 1959), p. 40 n., and see illustration opposite p. 80.

5. *A Portrait of the Artist as a Young Man*, p. 184.

6. Magalaner, in Marvin Magalaner and Richard M. Kain, *Joyce: The Man, the Work, the Reputation* (New York: New York University Press, 1956), p. 78.

7. *A Portrait of the Artist as a Young Man*, p. 65.

8. *Letters of James Joyce, Volume II*, ed. Richard Ellmann (New York: Viking Press, 1957), p. 111.

9. Ellmann, pp. 42, 43.

10. *Ibid.*, pp. 34, 35.

11. *Ibid.*, p. 43.

12. *James Joyce and the Making of Ulysses* (Bloomington: Indiana University Press, 1960), p. 57. (First edition simultaneously published in England by Grayson and Grayson and in the United States by Harrison Smith and Haas, in 1934.)

13. Ellmann, p. 36.

14. *Ibid.*, p. 43.

15. *The Critical Writings of James Joyce*, ed. Ellsworth Mason and Richard Ellmann (New York: Viking Press, 1959), pp. 175–186.

16. *Ibid.*, pp. 73–83.

17. *Ibid.*, pp. 76–77.

18. *Ibid.*, p. 78.

19. *Ibid.*, p. 78.

20. *A Portrait of the Artist as a Young Man*, p. 65.

EVELINE

1. John Kelleher, when a colleague at the Bread Loaf School of English, Middlebury College.

2. At the National Library in Dublin Patrick Henchy obligingly wrote these down as conjectures.

3. *A Reader's Guide to James Joyce* (New York: Noonday Press, 1959), p. 22.
4. *Time of Apprenticeship* (London: Abelard-Schuman, 1959), p. 153.
5. Tindall, *A Reader's Guide*, p. 21.
6. Richard Ellmann, *James Joyce* (New York: Oxford University Press, 1959), p. 43.
7. *A Reader's Guide*, p. 21.
8. *Dublin's Joyce* (Bloomington: Indiana University Press, 1966), p. 55.
9. John J. Slocum and Herbert Cahoon, *A Bibliography of James Joyce* (New Haven: Yale University Press, 1953), p. 94.
10. Herbert Gorman, *James Joyce* (New York: Rinehart, 1939), p. 127.

AFTER THE RACE

1. John J. Slocum and Herbert Cahoon, *A Bibliography of James Joyce* (New Haven: Yale University Press, 1953), p. 94.
2. Richard Ellmann, *James Joyce* (New York: Oxford University Press, 1959), p. 169.
3. Slocum and Cahoon, *op. cit.*, pp. 93, 94.
4. Ellmann, p. 171.
5. *Ibid.*, p. 196.
6. *Ibid.*, p. 171.
7. *The Critical Writings of James Joyce*, ed. Ellsworth Mason and Richard Ellmann (New York: Viking Press, 1959), pp. 106–108.
8. *Ibid.*, p. 106. See also Stanislaus Joyce, *My Brother's Keeper* (New York: Viking Press, 1958), p. 199.

TWO GALLANTS

1. Richard Ellmann, *James Joyce* (New York: Oxford University Press, 1959), p. 222.
2. *Ibid.*, p. 215.
3. *Letters of James Joyce, Volume II*, ed. Richard Ellmann (New York: Viking Press, 1966), p. 92.
4. *Ibid.*, p. 129.
5. Robert Scholes, "Grant Richards to James Joyce," *Studies in Bibliography*, XVI (1963), p. 143.
6. *Letters of James Joyce*, ed. Stuart Gilbert (New York: Viking Press, 1957), p. 60.

7. Ellmann, p. 228.
8. Scholes, p. 144.
9. *Ibid.*, p. 145.
10. *Letters*, p. 62.
11. *Letters, II*, pp. 184–185.
12. *Letters, II*, p. 137.
13. Ellmann, p. 238.
14. Mary and Padraic Colum, *Our Friend James Joyce* (London: Gollancz, 1959), pp. 46–48.
15. "The Unity of Joyce's *Dubliners*," *Accent*, XVI (Spring-Summer, 1956), pp. 75–88, 196–213.
16. Information from Mrs. Nora Duff, the genial proprietress of Buswell's Hotel, Molesworth Street, Dublin.
17. *Picturesque Dublin, Old and New* (London: Hutchinson, 1898).
18. *Time*, July 12, 1963, p. 40.

THE BOARDING HOUSE

1. *Surface and Symbol* (New York: Oxford Press, 1962), p. 199.
2. *Ulysses* (New York: Random House, 1934), pp. 297, 308.
3. *Ibid.*, p. 309.
4. *Dublin's Joyce* (Bloomington: Indiana University Press, 1966), pp. 49–50.
5. *Letters of James Joyce*, ed. Stuart Gilbert (New York: Viking Press, 1957), p. 60.

A LITTLE CLOUD

1. "Pound on Joyce," *Shenandoah*, Vol. III, No. 3 (Autumn, 1952), 7.
2. Ludwig, "James Joyce's *Dubliners*," *Stories: British and American*, ed. Jack Berry Ludwig and W. Richard Porier (Boston: Houghton Mifflin, 1953), p. 387.
3. William York Tindall, *A Reader's Guide to James Joyce* (New York: Noonday Press, 1959), p. 28.
4. *Letters of James Joyce, Volume II*, ed. Richard Ellmann (New York: Viking Press, 1966), p. 182.
5. John J. Slocum and Herbert Cahoon, *A Bibliography of James Joyce (1882–1941)* (New Haven, Conn.: Yale University Press, 1953), p. 96.
6. "First Flight to Ithaca," in *James Joyce: Two Decades of Criti-*

cism, ed. Seon Givens (New York: Vanguard Press, 1948), p. 72. (Reprinted from *Accent,* Winter, 1944.)

7. *Dublin Old and New* (London: George G. Harrop and Co., Ltd., n.d.).

8. *Ibid., passim.*

9. *Picturesque Dublin Old and New* (London: Hutchinson, 1898).

10. "First Flight to Ithaca," *James Joyce: Two Decades of Criticism,* p. 72.

11. *James Joyce's Scribbledehobble: The Ur-Workbook for Finnegans Wake* (Evanston: Northwestern University Press, 1961), p. xv.

12. *A Portrait of the Artist as a Young Man,* ed. Chester G. Anderson (New York: Viking Press, 1968), pp. 81, 82.

13. Stanislaus Joyce, *My Brother's Keeper* (New York: Viking Press, 1958), p. 55.

14. *Letters of James Joyce,* ed. Stuart Gilbert (New York: Viking Press, 1957), p. 297.

15. Richard Ellmann, *James Joyce* (New York: Oxford University Press, 1959), p. 143.

16. *Letters,* p. 295.

17. *Finnegans Wake* (New York: Viking Press, 1944), p. 231.

18. Ellmann, p. 20 n.

19. *Letters,* p. 61.

COUNTERPARTS

1. Richard Ellmann, *James Joyce* (New York: Oxford University Press, 1959), p. 247.

2. *Ibid.,* pp. 18, 19.

CLAY

1. Magalaner, in Marvin Magalaner and Richard M. Kain, *Joyce: The Man, the Work, the Reputation* (New York: New York University Press, 1956), p. 85.

2. See Marvin Magalaner, "The Other Side of James Joyce," *Arizona Quarterly,* IX (Spring, 1953), pp. 5–16; and also William T. Noon, S.J., "Joyce's 'Clay': An Interpretation," *College English,* XVII (Nov., 1955). Some of Magalaner's *Arizona Quarterly* piece is reproduced or paraphrased in *Joyce: The Man, the Work, the Reputation,* pp. 84–90.

3. *A Reader's Guide to James Joyce* (New York: Noonday Press, 1959), p. 29.

4. Richard Ellmann, *James Joyce* (New York: Oxford University Press, 1959), p. 18.

5. Richard B. Hudson, "Joyce's 'Clay,'" *The Explicator,* VI (March, 1948), item 30.

6. Ellmann, pp. 19, 196.

7. Part III, pp. 1–2. (Ed. Rosa M. Barrett; no publisher indicated.)

8. *Ibid.*

9. Misprinted as "tracts on the *walks*" in *Modern Library* edition and in *The Portable Joyce;* corrected in the Penguin Books edition and in the definitive text (Viking Press, 1967).

10. As explained by Mrs. Nora Duff, proprietress of Buswell's Hotel, Molesworth Street, Dublin.

11. *Joyce: The Man, the Work, the Reputation,* p. 85.

12. *The Nigger of the Narcissus* (Garden City, N.Y.: Doubleday Page, 1925), p. xii.

13. Mary and Padraic Colum, *Our Friend James Joyce* (London: Gollancz, 1959), p. 17.

14. *A Reader's Guide to James Joyce,* p. 30. (And commissioned or not, the "gentleman" obviously is not in uniform, for he "raised his hat" to Maria. All this is no mere quibble; "colonel-looking" is one of Joyce's nicest stylistic touches in establishing a special tone, upon the sensing of which depends characterization and the story's full effect.)

15. Noon, "Joyce's 'Clay': An Intrepretation."

16. "Maria's Song in Joyce's 'Clay,'" *Studies in Short Fiction,* I:2, (Winter, 1964), 153, 154.

17. Noon, "Joyce's 'Clay': An Intrepretation."

18. *The Bohemian Girl* (Boston: C. C. Birchard, n.d.), p. 72.

19. Hudson, "Joyce's 'Clay.'"

A PAINFUL CASE

1. Richard Ellmann, *James Joyce* (New York: Oxford University Press, 1959), p. 238; see also p. 215.

2. Stanislaus Joyce, *My Brother's Keeper: James Joyce's Early Years,* edited with "Introduction" by Richard Ellmann (New York: Viking Press, 1958), p. 159.

3. *Ibid.*, pp. 159–160.

4. *Ibid.*, p. xxii.

5. Ellmann, p. 91.
6. *The Critical Writings of James Joyce,* ed. Ellsworth Mason and Richard Ellmann (New York: Viking Press, 1959), p. 72.
7. *My Brother's Keeper,* p. 160.
8. *Ibid.,* p. 106.
9. *Ibid.,* p. 160.
10. Ellmann, p. 39.
11. *My Brother's Keeper,* pp. 169–170.
12. *Ibid.,* p. 170.
13. *Ibid.,* pp. xvii, xix.
14. *Ibid.,* p. 160.
15. Ellmann, p. 147.

IVY DAY IN THE COMMITTEE ROOM

1. *Letters of James Joyce,* ed. Stuart Gilbert (New York: Viking Press, 1957), p. 62.
2. "Grant Richards to James Joyce," *Studies in Bibliography,* XVI (1963), 151, 152.
3. Richard Ellmann, *James Joyce* (New York: Oxford University Press, 1959), p. 231.
4. *My Brother's Keeper* (New York: Viking Press, 1958), p. 206.
5. *Ibid.,* p. 206.
6. Sir Sidney Lee, *Edward VII* (New York: Macmillan, 1927), pp. 166, 167, 172.
7. *A Reader's Guide to James Joyce* (New York, Noonday Press, 1959), p. 36.
8. *My Brother's Keeper,* p. 206.
9. *The Mirror in the Roadway* (New York: Knopf, 1956), p. 296.
10. *Letters of James Joyce, Volume II,* ed. Richard Ellmann (New York: Viking Press, 1966), p. 109.
11. Stephen Gwynn, *Doublin Old and New* (London: Harrop, n.d.) p. 7.
12. *Ulysses* (New York: Modern Library, Random House, 1934), p. 111.
13. *Ibid.,* p. 109.
14. Ellmann, p. 33.
15. *My Brother's Keeper,* p. 9.
16. Ellmann, p. 33; Stanislaus Joyce, p. 46.
17. Mary and Padraic Colum, *Our Friend James Joyce,* (London: Gollancz, 1959), p. 167.
18. *My Brother's Keeper,* p. 168.

19. Magalaner in Marvin Magalaner and Richard M. Kain, *Joyce: The Man, the Work, the Reputation* (New York: New York University Press, 1956), pp. 81, 82.

20. *The Mirror in the Roadway*, p. 298.

21. *The Lonely Voice* (Cleveland: World Publishing Co., 1963), p. 120.

22. Magalaner, p. 81.

23. *Ibid.*, p. 62.

24. *Dubliners* (New York: Modern Library, n.d.), pp. x, xi.

25. *Surface and Symbol* (New York: Oxford University Press, 1962), p. 5.

26. *Dubliners*, p. x.

A MOTHER

1. *My Brother's Keeper* (New York: Viking Press, 1958), p. 6.

2. Richard Ellmann, *James Joyce* (New York: Oxford University Press, 1959), opposite p. 80.

3. *Letters of James Joyce, Volume II*, ed. Richard Ellmann (New York: Viking Press, 1966), p. 174.

4. *Ibid.*, p. 174 n.

5. *May It Please the Court* (Dublin: C. J. Fallon, Ltd., n.d.), p. 25.

6. *Ulysses* (New York: Modern Library, Random House, 1934), p. 747.

7. *A Reader's Guide to James Joyce* (New York: Noonday Press, 1959), p. 37.

8. *Ulysses* (New York: Modern Library, 1934), p. 258.

9. Misprinted as *men* in Modern Library edition.

10. Ellmann, p. 305.

GRACE

1. *The Listener*, LI (March, 1954), 526.

2. Richard Ellmann, *James Joyce* (New York: Oxford University Press, 1959), p. 369.

3. *Surface and Symbol* (New York: Oxford University Press, 1962), p. 178.

4. *My Brother's Keeper* (New York: Viking Press, 1958), pp. 227–228. Stanislaus Joyce identifies Father Purdon with the Father Bernard Vaughan mentioned by name in *Ulysses* (Modern Library ed., p. 216) and describes Vaughan, an English Jesuit who had

preached in Dublin, as "a vulgarian priest in search of publicity," one who "used to deliver short breezy talks from inappropriate places, such as the boxing ring before a championship match."

5. *Surface and Symbol*, p. 178.

6. *The Letters of James Joyce, Volume II*, ed. Richard Ellmann (New York: Viking Press, 1966), p. 192.

7. *Time of Apprenticeship: The Fiction of Young James Joyce* (London: Abelard-Schuman, 1959), p. 167.

8. *Encyclopaedia Britannica* Fourteenth Edition, VII, 508.

9. Dom Cuthbert Butler, *The Vatican Council: 1869–70*, ed. Christopher Butler (Westminster, Md.; Newman Press, 1962), pp. 85–86.

10. *Ibid.*, p. 86.

11. *Encyclopaedia Britannica*, VII, 508.

12. *Ibid.*, p. 508; also Butler, pp. 87–88.

13. Butler, pp. 432–433.

14. *Ibid.*, p. 434.

15. *Ibid.*, p. 438.

16. *Encyclopaedia Britannica*, VII, 508.

17. Butler, p. 414.

18. *Ibid.*, pp. 174, 176.

19. *Ibid.*, pp. 400, 402.

20. *Ibid.*, pp. 408–409.

21. *Ibid.*, pp. 307, 357.

22. *Ibid.*, p. 409; and see *Letters, II*, p. 193, line 3. (Final clause in note 1 is imprecise.)

23. Butler, p. 425.

24. *Ibid.*, p. 400.

25. *Dictionary of National Biography*, VII, 452.

26. *Surface and Symbol*, p. 181.

27. See note 4.

THE DEAD

1. *The Letters of James Joyce, Volume II*, ed. Richard Ellmann (New York: Viking Press, 1966), p. 131.

2. *Ibid.*, p. 131.

3. *Ibid.*, p. 166.

4. *Ibid.*, p. 111.

5. For instance, Harry Levin, *James Joyce* (Norfolk, Conn.: New Directions Press, 1941), p. 36, and W. Y. Tindall, *A Reader's Guide to James Joyce* (New York: Noonday Press, 1959), p. 47.

6. "Editor's Preface" to *Dubliners,* in *The Portable James Joyce* (New York: Viking Press, 1957), p. 18.

7. Richard Ellmann, *James Joyce* (New York: Oxford University Press, 1959), p. 254.

8. *Ibid.,* p. 17.

9. *Ibid.,* p. 255.

10. *My Brother's Keeper* (New York: Viking Press, 1958), p. 38.

11. *Dublin in the Age of William Butler Yeats and James Joyce* (Norman: University of Oklahoma Press, 1962), p. 89.

12. Ellmann, p. 256.

13. *The Critical Writings of James Joyce,* ed. Ellsworth Mason and Richard Ellmann (New York: Viking Press, 1959), contains twenty-one Joyce reviews published in Dublin's *Daily Express,* between December 11, 1902, and November 19, 1903.

14. Ellmann, p. 112.

15. "Bret Harte as a Source for James Joyce's 'The Dead,'" *Philological Quarterly,* XXXIII (Oct., 1954), pp. 442–444.

16. Ellmann, p. 256.

17. *Ibid.,* p. 17.

18. *Letters, II,* p. 239.

19. *Ibid.,* pp. 48, 49.

20. *Ibid.,* p. 56.

21. Ellmann, p. 164.

22. *Ibid.,* p. 252.

23. *Ibid.,* p. 252.

24. *Ibid.,* p. 335.

25. *Exiles* (New York: Viking Press, 1951), p. 118.

26. *Ibid.,* p. 112.

27. See Padraic Colum, *Our Friend James Joyce* (London: Gollancz, 1959), pp. 180–181; Herbert Gorman, *James Joyce* (New York: Rinehart, 1939; rev. ed., 1948), p. 348; *Letters,* p. 312. This waistcoat is now one of the items exhibited at the Martello Tower at Sandycove, Dublin.

28. Stephen Gwynn, *Dublin Old and New* (London: George G. Harrop & Co., Ltd., n.d.), *passim.* See also *Dublin in the Age of William Butler Yeats and James Joyce,* pp. 16–17.

29. Eugene Sheehy, *May It Please the Court* (Dublin: J. C. Fallon, Ltd., 1951), p. 22.

30. *Ulysses* (New York: Random House, 1934), p. 160.

31. *Letters of James Joyce,* ed. Stuart Gilbert (New York: Viking Press, 1957), pp. 62–63.

32. "On Catharsis, or Resolution," *Kenyon Review,* XXI (Summer 1959), 363.
33. "What I Believe," in *Two Cheers for Democracy* (New York: Harcourt, Brace, 1951), pp. 67, 73.
34. *Dublin's Joyce* (London: Chatto and Windus, 1955), p. 68.
35. *Ulysses,* p. 730.
36. Ellmann, p. 295.
37. *Ibid.,* p. 257.
38. *A Reader's Guide to James Joyce,* p. 48.
39. "Preface," *The Nigger of the Narcissus* (New York: Doubleday, Page and Co., 1925), p. xii.
40. Ellmann, p. 258.
41. *Re Joyce* (New York: Norton, 1965), p. 44.
42. Ellmann, p. 260, quotes Thoreau's translation of this passage from the twelfth book of the *Iliad.*